INTO THE WHIRLWIND

Books by
Elizabeth Camden

The Lady of Bolton Hill
The Rose of Winslow Street
Against the Tide
Into the Whirlwind
With Every Breath
Beyond All Dreams
Toward the Sunrise: An Until the Dawn Novella
Until the Dawn
From This Moment

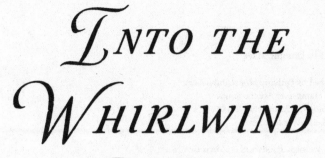

INTO THE WHIRLWIND

A NOVEL BY

ELIZABETH CAMDEN

BETHANYHOUSE

a division of Baker Publishing Group
Minneapolis, Minnesota

© 2013 by Dorothy Mays

Published by Bethany House Publishers
11400 Hampshire Avenue South
Bloomington, Minnesota 55438
www.bethanyhouse.com

Bethany House Publishers is a division of
Baker Publishing Group, Grand Rapids, Michigan

Printed in the United States of America

Library of Congress Cataloging-in-Publication Data
Camden, Elizabeth.
    Into the whirlwind / Elizabeth Camden.
        pages cm
    Summary: "After a fire destroys Chicago, Mollie is desperate to save her
business. With everything at risk—including her heart—can she rise from the
rubble?"—Provided by publisher.
    ISBN 978-0-7642-1024-2 (pbk.)
    1. Women-owned business enterprises—Fiction. 2. Clock and watch
industry—Fiction. 3. Great Fire, Chicago, Ill., 1871—Fiction. I. Title.
PS3553.A429I57 2013
813'.54—dc23   2013010864

Cover design by Jennifer Parker
Cover photography by Mike Habermann Photography, LLC
Cover background photo © Chicago History Museum

CHICAGO
OCTOBER 8, 1871

A wall of fire towered over Mollie. The city of Chicago had been burning for hours, the scorching wind stirring up firestorms that barreled down the narrow streets and illuminated the night sky. It was getting hard to breathe. Smoke and ash hung in the air, coating Mollie's throat until her thirst grew more painful than the blistering heat. The crush of people jostling to flee northward made it hard to even keep standing.

The city Mollie loved so well was being destroyed as flames engulfed buildings, weakening them until they collapsed into piles of rubble, blocking escape routes and sending throngs of people into greater panic. By tomorrow, Chicago would be nothing more than a smoldering ruin.

"Mollie, watch out!" Zack shouted. She followed his line of sight. A riderless horse careened straight at her, cutting through the people packed on the street. A woman screamed and dove for cover, but Mollie was trapped by the wagon beside her. She flinched away from the stallion's flailing hooves just as Zack's hands closed around her waist, hauling her out of harm's way a second before the horse barreled past.

"Thank you," she gasped before her throat seized in a fit of coughing.

"Come on," he commanded, grabbing her hand and pulling her forward. "We've got to get across the river before the bridge burns. We can make it, Mollie." He grinned down at her, his teeth flashing white against his soot-stained face.

Zack Kazmarek was a savior in the chaos, his powerful build shouldering through the crowd and helping them both get farther north. A layer of ash covered his coat, but it couldn't disguise the jacket's fine cut or his confident manner as he pushed onward. Zack had accompanied her into a literal inferno, but never once had he complained.

Why would a man who disliked her be so generous? For three years, Zack had been icily aloof toward her, so why should he risk his life to help her?

The crowd thickened near the Rush Street Bridge. Ahead of them, people yelled and started pushing the crowd back. It was impossible to hear what they were saying over the roar of wind and the clamoring bells, but as she got closer, Mollie saw the problem.

The bridge was on fire.

"We can still make a run for it," Mollie said, and she pushed forward.

The bridge was a hundred yards long, and orange flames were licking at the wooden railings. The planking smoldered where cinders ignited the wood, but most of the bridge looked sound. A few people made a dash for it, and with the wall of fire behind them, Mollie intended to get across that bridge.

Zack's hand was like iron as he hauled her back and whirled her to face him. His eyes glittered in a face streaked with soot and sweat as he stepped closer, shouting over the roar of wind and fire.

"That bridge isn't going to hold!" he shouted. "I won't watch you kill yourself. We can make it to the bridge on Clark Street."

In all the years she had known the impeccable Zack Kazmarek, there had never been a hint of a pulse beneath his tailored suits and starched collars, but now he looked at her with desperation in his eyes. He grasped her arms as though he couldn't bear to let her go and it made her think . . . well, it looked as if he actually cared about her. Which was impossible . . . they barely knew each other.

Until six days ago, they had never even had a real conversation. Until six days ago, Zack was merely the lawyer who signed her paychecks and intimidated the stuffing out of her.

Six days ago was another lifetime. . . .

SIX DAYS EARLIER

The paper was thick and creamy, embossed with a gold letterhead and engraved ink. Mollie read the note for a second time.

Miss Knox,
I would like to meet with you to discuss a potential business venture. I will call at the 57th Illinois Watch Company at 2 p.m. this afternoon.

Zachariasz Kazmarek,
Attorney for Hartman's, Inc.

Despite the note's formal tone, Mollie was smart enough to be scared stiff.

Zack Kazmarek was the legal mastermind behind the city's most elite mercantile empire. Half of Chicago was in his back pocket, and the other half was afraid of him. Mollie fell into both categories. He had always been coolly polite to her, but Mollie knew better than to let that lull her into a false sense of security. After all, the rumors about Mr. Kazmarek were legendary.

The workshop was filled with the sounds of whirring lathes as workers constructed the tiny watch components, but the distinctive tapping of Frank Spencer's cane cut through the noise.

"Good news?" he asked.

"I don't know," Mollie said. She leaned closer so her voice would not be heard over the steady grind of the workshop and read the note to Frank in a low voice. Frank's sightless eyes stared straight ahead as he absorbed the words, memorizing them with his impressive mind. Not many people would have hired a blind man for their attorney, but Mollie was eternally grateful to Frank for saving her father's life at the Battle of Winston Cliff, and he would always have a home at the 57th Illinois Watch Company. Frank was like a second father to her, and she trusted him implicitly.

Frank rubbed his lean jaw as he considered the message. "In all the years we've been dealing with Hartman's, they have never come in person to the workshop. This is odd." Concern was plain in his tone. Frank was the only other person in the company who understood how precarious their financial situation was.

The 57th Illinois Watch Company made the most beautiful watches in America. With enameled dials and hand-engraved gold cases, each watch was a marvel of engineering combined with spectacular artistry. They were also outrageously expensive, which meant Hartman's was the only store in Chicago that could afford to carry them. With its marble floors and crystal chandeliers, Hartman's supplied the millionaires of Chicago with sapphires from India, perfume from France, and Italian suede leather so soft it draped over the hand like silk. They also sold the jewel-encrusted timepieces from the workshop of the 57th Illinois Watch Company.

When she inherited the company three years ago, Mollie realized their glaring vulnerability. They sold *all* their watches to Louis Hartman's grand store, and having only one client meant they could be wiped out the moment the mercantile king decided to use another company to supply watches for his store. Her company was at the mercy of Hartman's, which was why a sudden visit from the store's lawyer was so worrisome.

Mr. Kazmarek intimidated Mollie down to her fingertips, and she twisted the note between her hands. "I was about to settle down to lunch, but now I'm too nervous to eat anything," she confessed.

Frank looked anxious too, rubbing his hands against his vest, his eyes darting around the workshop as though he could still see. "Is everything presentable? If the lawyer is coming, he may want to inspect the property."

Mollie surveyed the workshop. She loved every square inch of this old building, with its exposed brick walls and high windows. The cavernous room was dominated by twenty worktables set at shoulder height so the technicians could work without stooping. Each technician had a jeweler's loupe over one eye and used pins and tweezers to fit delicate components together. On the other side of the room, the artisans engraved the gold watch covers. Her most valuable assets were Ulysses and Alice Adair, a married couple whose artistic creations fashioned from gold, enamel, and gemstones were soaring hymns to beauty.

Mollie's earliest memories were of playing among these tables, watching in awe as her father created the most beautiful watches in the world. When she was younger, Mollie was convinced her father was as clever as Leonardo da Vinci as he assembled whirring, ticking pieces of metal into tiny machines that kept perfect time. Unlike the ordinary watchmakers on the East Coast, Silas Knox's watches were masterpieces of artistry, and the elite of Chicago gladly paid staggering sums for them.

Mollie had the artistic skill of a small head of cabbage, but she excelled at business and knew every facet of watchmaking from the ground up. She learned to make mainsprings when she was only ten years old. By age twelve, she could attach winding screws to the internal mechanisms and eventually mastered every phase of the watchmaking process. Now that she was in charge of the company, she balanced the accounts and managed the business operations, but she still loved donning her jeweler's loupe and assembling the delicate gaskets, springs, and rotating wheels as she indulged in the sheer joy of making a pocket watch. And the best part was that tomorrow morning she got to wake up and do it all again.

But only if she could keep the business afloat. "Alice, can you help me straighten up the office before Mr. Kazmarek gets here? I need this place to look spotless."

Alice set down her engraving tool. "An important meeting, is it?" she asked, her voice still carrying a trace of an Irish lilt. Alice's artistic skill had brought her a long way from the girl who fled the Irish potato famine two decades earlier.

There was no need to spread anxiety around the workshop before she even understood why Mr. Kazmarek was coming. "Just a meeting with one of Hartman's men," Mollie said casually.

Alice pushed herself to her feet. "Come on, let's fix you up, then. With that hair and outfit, you look like the prison warden getting ready to lock up the inmates for the night."

Mollie glanced down at her starchy white shirt and plain skirt. "What's wrong with how I look?"

"Braids don't belong on any woman over the age of twelve unless she intends to frighten the children."

With her mass of spiraling dark curls, braids were the only way Mollie could beat her hair into submission. "This is a business meeting, not a social call."

Alice grasped Mollie's shoulders and guided her toward the washroom, where an old mirror hung on the outside of the door. "And if the business is with Hartman's, you need to look the part. Stylish, elegant, and rich." Alice shrugged out of her silk Japanese shawl and draped it around Mollie's shoulders.

Mollie traced a finger along the hand-printed silk. "This looks like it belongs in the Louvre."

"It belongs around your shoulders," Alice asserted. She liberated Mollie's inky black hair and fluffed the strands until they hung down her back in a wanton display of poor taste. With her pale skin and sky blue eyes, Mollie knew she was pretty enough, but her hair was a nightmare, always spilling out of whatever bun or braid she tried to force it into.

"Alice, I've met with Mr. Kazmarek dozens of times with my hair in braids. He hasn't turned to stone yet."

Frank pulled up a chair and took a seat. "What is he like, this Mr. Kazmarek?"

Mollie studied her thumbnail while Alice kept working at her hair. In truth, Mollie had always been overwhelmed whenever she met with Hartman's attorney. "I don't know much about him. I negotiate the quarterly payments, deliver the designs for the coming season's watches, and leave."

"But what is he *like*?" Frank pressed. "Does he have a sense of humor? Does he meet your eyes when you speak with him? Or is he always glancing about as you negotiate?"

"I don't really know," she confessed. "I try to finish business as quickly as possible and get out. He has a little blue finch in his office named Lizzie. That bird never stops flitting about the cage, and sometimes she even breaks into song."

Frank sighed in frustration. "Mollie, you have been meeting with this man for three years, and all you know about him is that he has a pet finch?"

Putting it that way, she did feel a little foolish. It was a lot easier to watch the bird than to meet the eyes of the man who held the future of her company in his hands. There were glaciers in the North Sea that shed more warmth than Mr. Kazmarek. He was a handsome man, towering well over six feet, with dark eyes and black hair. Or was it brown? She didn't really know . . . it made her too nervous to look directly at him.

"Well, the rumors about how he conducts business are pretty shocking," she confessed, leaning forward to relay a few of the choicest rumors about Mr. Kazmarek's strong-arm tactics for dealing with the seamier side of Chicago's mercantile world.

Alice finished arranging her hair. "There," she said with satisfaction. "You look like a Botticelli masterpiece."

Mollie stared at the results in amazement. She supposed her hair did look rather fetching the way Alice had it tumbling down like the women in one of the great romantic paintings so popular in Europe now. Two delicate gold combs anchored her hair at the crown of her head, leaving the rest free to spill down her back, but it was completely impractical. "This hairstyle will last for about five minutes," Mollie said. Even now a few strands were falling forward and she reached to smooth them back into place.

"Leave them! The goal isn't order," Alice said. "I know that must seem strange to that accountant's brain of yours, but trust me, you look fabulous."

"Stunning," Frank agreed.

Mollie shot an amused glance at her blind attorney. "How would you know?"

"I know Alice Adair, and her artistic judgment is flawless. Leave your hair alone. You need to impress Hartman's man."

There was a crash from the other side of the room. A metal bowl clanged to the floor and sprayed a fine layer of dust at the feet of Declan McNabb. The diamond powder! Declan, their metal polisher, used a paste of diamond powder and almond oil to buff their metal into a mirrorlike shine. He had just spilled a hundred dollars' worth of diamond powder on the floor, and Mollie was not sure it could be salvaged.

But that wasn't her concern. It was the panic in Declan's eyes that was the problem.

"Wh . . . wh . . . why . . . why . . ."

Mollie knelt beside Declan and placed a hand on his knee. How awful to see a grown man become unglued this way. Declan was a strong, handsome man, but when the tremors hit, he was as fragile as an eggshell. "Calm down, Declan. Write the words if you can't speak them."

Declan reached for the pad of paper on his table, his trembling hands scribbling the words. *Why is a lawyer coming? Are we in trouble?*

His questions were a stab in Mollie's heart. They weren't in trouble *today*, but they would be if they lost their contract with Hartman's, and then people like Frank and Declan would be out of a job. Declan could never find another job. He suffered from the nameless affliction that tormented so many veterans of the Civil War—the trembling and panic that came from nowhere and descended like a suffocating cloud, making it impossible to see daylight.

During the war, Mollie's father had been a member of the 57th Illinois Infantry, a regiment that met its end backed against a cliff and was decimated in a three-day shootout that killed, crippled, or maimed the majority of the soldiers. The survivors of that battle were like brothers to her father, and he sent out word that any wounded veteran of the 57th could find employment at his watchmaking factory in Chicago. He renamed the company in honor of his old battalion, and fifteen of the forty employees were veterans with various afflictions. Alice's husband had lost his right leg, but was still one of the world's best gold engravers. Gunner Wilson, or Old Gunner, as they sometimes called him, had lost an arm, but kept the workshop as clean as a surgical operating room. Frank had been blinded by flying shrapnel, and when there wasn't enough legal work to keep him occupied, he was able to polish metal. Declan was a healthy, able-bodied man, but his shattered mind left him with soul-destroying attacks of anxiety.

Mollie found the dustpan and nudged the top layer of the precious diamond powder into the pan, but most of it was ruined. "I don't want you to worry about this," she said to Declan. "I am always in talks with the buyers at Hartman's, making sure we are delivering what their customers want. This is no different."

Not quite true, but Declan was getting worse, a layer of perspiration soaking his skin and the muscles in his face twitching. What must it be like to be trapped inside a shattered mind? Declan was only thirty-two years old, a handsome man who had been in college when he volunteered for the Union Army. It was hard to look past his infirmity to see the courageous man her father once knew. As badly as she ached for Declan, Mollie feared the impression he would make on Mr. Kazmarek.

Mollie swept the last of the ruined diamond powder into the dustpan. It wasn't the first time Declan's trembling hands had spilled the diamond powder or broken a tool, and it wouldn't be the last. Declan was a liability to the company, and the prudent thing would be to ask him to leave for the rest of the day.

What sort of impression would a twitchy, mentally unstable metal polisher make on Mr. Kazmarek? Every instinct urged her to get Declan out of sight. How else could she present a lean, competent organization to their only client?

But she couldn't send Declan home. He was an intelligent man who would know exactly why he had been asked to leave, and she could not do that to him. She would not deny the human dignity of the men who made this company great.

Let Zack Kazmarek see the 57th in all its magnificent, imperfect glory. Mollie would ensure these people would have employment for as long as they kept turning out the world's most beautiful timepieces.

Given Frank's gentle scolding for her ignorance about Hartman's attorney, Mollie took care to scrutinize Zack Kazmarek as he paid his first visit to the workshop. He was a tall man with a powerful build, dark hair, and fierce black eyes that scanned the workshop like a hawk searching for prey. He looked flawless and intimidating in his tailored jacket, vest, and stiff white collar. Even the wind blowing from the open door behind him did not ruffle his carefully groomed hair.

Mollie hurried forward to meet him, scurrying up the half flight of stairs to join him on the landing. "Mr. Kazmarek, welcome to the 57th Illinois Watch Company. We are honored to have you here."

He took her hand but said nothing as he scrutinized her. That piercing gaze had been known to quell union leaders and businessmen all across the city, and she bobbed her head in an anxious greeting. Another gust of wind blew in behind him, and Alice's artfully placed combs began to slip from their mooring. Why had she let Alice talk her into this ridiculous hairstyle?

"You look different," Mr. Kazmarek said with an impassive face.

In the three years they had known each other, it was the first personal comment he had ever made to her. "Won't you come inside? I'd be pleased to show you our workroom. We have a total of forty employees, divided into eighteen distinct specializations." She took a few steps down the stairs as she gestured toward the tables. "Everything from the cutting of metal to the engraving of the gold covers is done right here in the workshop."

He made no move to follow her or to close the door, and the gusting wind was a problem. She darted back up the stairs and pulled the heavy door shut. "We can't allow unsavory debris in the workroom," she said apologetically. "The mechanisms inside the watches are very delicate."

A hint of a smile hovered on his face. "Did you really just say *unsavory debris*?" It was the first time he had ever smiled at her, and she noticed the corner of his front tooth was chipped. Just a tiny flaw in his otherwise impeccable appearance. How was it she had never noticed it before?

If she wasn't so nervous, she might have shared in his amusement. "Each watch consists of 115 separate pieces, most smaller than a grain of rice," she said. "Once they are assembled, any dust or, yes, *unsavory debris*, can add friction and throw off the pivoting and rotating parts. We must keep the workshop in pristine condition."

As she stepped down the half flight of stairs, the weight of her hair slid further down the side of her head, the combs barely holding as she began showing Mr. Kazmarek the shop. "We make all the screws, gaskets, and springs right here in the shop. You will notice that we have a set of brand-new lathes for polishing the metalwork."

Mr. Kazmarek seemed disinterested. "Is there someplace we

can go to speak in private? As my note indicated, I have a business proposition I'd like to discuss."

A business proposition didn't sound like he was getting ready to cancel their contract, but she couldn't be sure, and her heart thudded like it was about to leap from her chest. She forced her voice to be calm. "I have an office at the back of the shop. I'd like to ask our attorney to join us. I never make any decisions without Frank Spencer's advice."

"Naturally," Mr. Kazmarek said. As they walked toward the office, Mollie noticed he was not entirely disinterested in the 57th. His dark eyes scanned everything, taking in the arrangement of the worktables, the tidy bins of supplies, even noting Ulysses Adair's crutch propped against his worktable. As they passed Ulysses, she asked him to send Frank to her office.

It was going to be a tight fit inside. She had no desk, just a large table filling most of the space where Mollie conducted the business operations of the company. Stacks of accounting books and technical manuals usually cluttered the table, but in preparation for the meeting, she had stashed them in the storage room.

"Please have a seat," she said as she led him into the office. "Can I get you something to drink? We always have a kettle of tea warming."

Was he even listening to her? He wasn't looking her in the eyes, but there was a half smile on his face. "I can't tell you how tempted I am to pull that comb out."

Her eyes widened. His voice was smooth and low, like warm chocolate with a dash of cream. It was entirely inappropriate for a business meeting. Even as he spoke, the comb slid lower and more tendrils of hair broke free. This was ridiculous. It was going to be impossible to concentrate when her hair was about to come tumbling down.

"Would you excuse me for a moment? I'll go find what is keeping Mr. Spencer."

The moment the office door closed she ripped both combs from her hair. It streamed behind her as she scurried to Alice's worktable. "Quick! I am about to go into the most important business meeting of my life and I look like the harlot of Babylon."

Alice smothered her laughter as she twisted Mollie's hair back atop her head. "I'll use a few pins this time," she said.

How could her sensible attorney take a disliking to a man so quickly? By the time Mollie returned to her office, Frank and Mr. Kazmarek were trading swipes at each other.

"So you never actually attended law school," Mr. Kazmarek stated bluntly.

Frank sat a little straighter in his chair. "I obtained my license by clerking for two judges from the Illinois Supreme Court," he said stiffly. "It is an entirely acceptable way to attain a legal education. It was how Abraham Lincoln became qualified to practice law."

One of Mr. Kazmarek's dark brows flew upward. "So you are comparing yourself to *Abraham Lincoln?*"

"It is a much better way to learn the law than sitting in a classroom at Yale." The way Frank said *Yale* made the school sound like a pair of unwashed socks.

Mollie's eyes widened. Hadn't she just told Frank of Mr. Kazmarek's infamous reputation? Or the rumors about the fish? "My goodness," she said pleasantly. "I leave for two minutes, and I find the Goths assaulting the Visigoths."

Mr. Kazmarek shot to his feet. Was he flushing? It was impossible for her to tell as he cleared his throat, adjusted his collar, and assumed the formal demeanor she was so accustomed to seeing from him. He held out a chair for her, and she clenched the rim of the seat so her hands wouldn't tremble.

"I'll get right down to business," Mr. Kazmarek said as he sat once again. All trace of his earlier humor vanished, and he projected the air of brisk professionalism Mollie was accustomed to. "A few years ago, Hartman's made the strategic decision to begin acquiring our best suppliers. It makes sense for us to own the major artisans who supply our goods. We have been consistently impressed with your watches and would like to buy the 57th Illinois Watch Company."

Mollie couldn't speak. She thought they might have a complaint with her watches, or she feared they might want to terminate their contract, but never had she imagined they might want to buy her out. While she sat in dumbfounded amazement, Mr. Kazmarek continued to outline the deal.

"We want the entire company. That means all the equipment and inventory in stock. The deal would need to include all the property, technology, and artistic designs of the past and present."

While he talked, Mollie's brain snapped out of paralysis and began calculating numbers. She had fifteen thousand dollars' worth of unsold inventory, but the real value of the company was in their equipment and designs. The reputation of the 57th was also worth something. She couldn't consider selling for anything less than forty thousand. Maybe even forty-five if she wanted to push her luck.

When Mr. Kazmarek got around to talking figures, her heart almost stopped. "Given the value of current inventory and your reputation for quality, we are prepared to offer sixty thousand dollars. Payable in cash. Immediately."

Mollie was stunned, especially as Mr. Kazmarek continued talking and the deal got even sweeter. "We want Miss Knox to be in charge of ongoing operations and are prepared to pay a three percent royalty on all future business. We want to move quickly on this deal, so the offer is good only until next Monday morning, a week from today."

Just as hope began to unfurl in Mollie's heart, a cloud descended. There was something in this workshop more valuable than beautiful watch designs or enameled dials. "And my employees? What will happen to them?" She held her breath as she waited for his answer.

"Keep them," he said. "We don't want to interfere with anything that has gone into the artistry of the watches we see on display at Hartman's."

What a relief it would be to have the burden of ownership lifted so she could devote herself to watchmaking once again. No more snapping awake in the middle of the night worrying about invoices and payments. She smiled so wide it made her face hurt. "What do you think, Frank?"

"Why do you need an answer so quickly?" Frank asked. "This company has been in the Knox family for thirty years. Selling it is not something that should be rushed."

He was right. It was easy to set a valuation for the inventory and equipment, but what about the worth of her father's internal watch mechanism? Their reputation for beauty and quality had taken decades to establish, and it would take them a while to assess its proper value.

"How about until the end of the month?" she countered. "That will give me time to do a suitable accounting. I'd like to do long-term projections on the value of our designs. And compounded interest on our current equipment, of course."

It was impossible to read Mr. Kazmarek. How could a man appear so cordial, even as his message was so ruthless? "Monday morning. Nine o'clock. If we don't have an answer by then, we will make an offer to acquire another watch company."

The words caused her stomach to sink like a stone. She couldn't afford to lose Hartman's business, but it would be suicide to let him know how rattled she was by the prospect. If he knew he had her over a barrel, he might tighten his deadline even more. "I appreciate your offer and will give it proper consideration."

A bit of humor lightened his gaze. "Why do you say 'proper consideration' with the same tone you say 'unsavory debris'? This is a smashing offer, and you know it."

She did not flinch. "I like the offer. I don't like the deadline."

"It is unconscionable," Frank added. "Maybe that's how they teach lawyers from Yale to operate. Not here."

Mr. Kazmarek's demeanor did not falter as he kept his gaze locked on her. "Don't let Mr. Sunshine over there distract you. I am offering you a once-in-a-lifetime opportunity to merge your company with the most prestigious store west of New York. There are people who would sell their firstborn for such an opportunity."

Mollie had a respectable bank account, but sixty thousand dollars was a fortune. And she could keep working here, earning a salary, and enjoying a portion of the profits through the royalty split. The only thing she would lose by accepting the offer was control. For the past three years, at the dawn of every day, she'd worried about how to protect her employees. Her father was a disaster as a businessman, and this company would have run aground had she not been there to rein in his wilder impulses. The long-term survival of the company rested entirely on her shoulders, and Mr. Kazmarek was watching her as if she were a ripe pear about to drop from the tree.

She couldn't think with him in this tiny office. He was too overwhelming, sucking up all the oxygen. He would keep talking, distracting her from the deluge of thoughts that were fighting for space in her mind.

"I will calculate the numbers and be in contact with you soon," she said, proud of the professional tone she managed to project.

Mr. Kazmarek stared at her. It was odd how quickly he could slip back into the hard-nosed persona that always intimidated her. "I have been doing business with you for three years," he said in a formal tone. "In all that time, you have consistently impressed me as a businesswoman of faultless logic. Don't let me down now."

He stood and took his leave.

2

Zachariasz Kazmarek surveyed the garden behind the Hartman mansion, sheltered by a screen of poplar trees and wisteria vines. It was hard to believe he was in the middle of Chicago. There were at least forty people gathered for Josephine Hartman's evening soiree on the flagstone terrace of her garden, soft music coming from the open doors leading into the opulent home. Lanterns flickering beneath the leafy trees illuminated the evening.

"Try this," Louis Hartman said as he pressed a snifter into Zack's hand. "It is fifty-year-old cognac imported from the misty hills of southern France. My wife thinks there will be a market for it here."

Zack took a sip of the cognac. Such a drink wasn't normally to his taste, but working at Hartman's meant that certain foibles had to be observed. Josephine's annual trips through Europe were a whirlwind tour to acquire new offerings for the store, and everything was first sampled here in their palatial home. This evening, she was serving caviar from Copenhagen and cognac in glasses from the renowned Venetian glassworks. The linens covering the garden tables came from Ireland, and the candles flickering in the lanterns were made at a monastery in Spain.

Last year, Zack had accompanied the Hartmans on their trip to Europe, visiting Harrods and learning as much as he could about the luxury retail business.

Zack swirled the cognac in his glass. "Your wife said it is the best?"

Louis shrugged his shoulders. "Given what she paid for it, it ought to be."

"If it has Mrs. Hartman's approval, it will sell." Just like those outrageous watches he had been researching all week. Ever since he became the lead attorney for Hartman's, it never ceased to amaze Zack what rich people would pay for an ounce of perfume or a yard of silk, but those pocket watches were like something a Medici prince would own. Zack didn't judge how rich people spent their money; he was simply glad they did and that he had finally earned enough to join their ranks. Not that he squandered his money frivolously. In the years since he began earning his appallingly generous salary, there was only one luxury he had purchased for himself. It was a shocking extravagance, but something he enjoyed looking at every day.

Louis leaned in a little closer. "Have you issued the offer to Mollie Knox?" he asked in a low voice.

Just the mention of that woman's name made Zack stiffen, but he disguised the emotion. "I met with her this afternoon," he said casually. "She has the offer."

"Strange bird, that one."

Zack merely nodded. "I think she will see the wisdom behind the deal. I don't anticipate any trouble from her."

He needed to tread carefully here. Louis Hartman had a bizarre mistrust of any close affiliation between his suppliers and employees. Zack's predecessor had been caught taking bribes from suppliers who were anxious to have their goods sold at Chicago's premier store. Hartman was a millionaire many times over, but like most men who had clawed their way to the top, he was obsessed with the bottom line and loathed the prospect of being cheated. Zack knew better than to indulge his irrational yearning for Mollie Knox. Yielding to that weakness could get him fired.

"Get her on board quickly," Louis said. "I had a good relationship with that woman's father, so I want this deal locked down tight. Immediately. Don't let her get sentimental and try to wiggle off the hook."

Which showed that Louis didn't know much about Mollie Knox. That woman was the most efficient, practical person he had ever met. She was going to analyze the deal six different ways before signing on the dotted line. She might sell the world's most gloriously impractical watches, but her brain was as logical as an accounts chart.

"I gave her one week to consider the deal," Zack said.

"A week? I would have offered her a day."

Zack shook his head. "That sort of speed will make her suspicious. Trust me, she won't do anything that might endanger that ragtag gang of people she has working for her. She will be looking for safety and security in this deal. If we push too hard, she'll balk, and there is no comparable watchmaker in the entire country."

A waiter stepped onto the terrace, but he carried no champagne or imported delicacies. A troubled look on the man's face roused Zack's interest as the waiter headed straight toward him, then leaned over to whisper discreetly.

"Sir, a woman claiming to be your mother is here to see you."

Zack didn't let his expression change. "Is she alone?"

"Yes, sir."

There could be a million reasons for his mother's unexpected arrival, none of them good. He turned toward Louis, forcing a pleasant smile to his mouth. "If you'll excuse me. A bit of family business," he said, then followed the waiter into the house, down a hallway lit with crystal sconces, and toward the servants' entrance. Had there been an accident down at the docks? He'd been begging his father to quit his job for years. No sixty-year-old man should still be loading grain elevators, but Zack had failed at pounding that fact into Jozef Kazmarek's thick skull.

His mother was fidgeting in the room near the servants' entrance, her colorful but threadbare shawl in stark contrast to the fine black broadcloth the Hartman servants wore.

"Is Papa all right?" Zack asked, holding his breath.

His mother's smile set him at ease. "Oh yes," she said as she reached up to hug him. "Well, he has been arrested, but he is perfectly fine aside from that."

His shoulders sagged. "What has he done this time?"

One might think his mother ought to be upset at a time like this, but she appeared oddly excited. Proud, even. Her eyes sparkled, and she clasped her hands together. "Well, you know there is a Russian delegation in town. . . ."

"A Russian *trade* delegation," Zack clarified.

His mother waved her hands dismissively. "All the same thing. There is a Russian delegation in town, and your father could not pass up an opportunity like this. He marched right down to City Hall to confront them. . . ."

His mother rambled on, but Zack stopped listening. Last night, he had explained to his parents that the men from Russia were in Chicago only to discuss shipments of dried beef. The Russian delegation had no influence with the czar, nor were they responsible for the massacre following the January Uprising eight years ago in Poland.

Neither of his parents had ever set foot in Poland, but memories among Chicago's Polish community were long. All four of

Zack's grandparents were Polish refugees who were driven from their land as Russia whittled away at the dwindling autonomy of their homeland. His grandparents' devotion to Poland had taken root in both of Zack's parents. When the last vestiges of Polish autonomy were wiped away in 1864, his parents responded by doubling their efforts to save Poland.

He turned his attention back to his mother, who was rambling on about how brave his father had been when he'd forced his way inside the room where the Russian delegates were meeting with Chicago's mayor.

Almost as if she had been there to witness it. "Mother, please tell me you didn't go with him to City Hall."

"Of course I did! We needed as many people as possible so we could make an impression on those Russians. There were nine of us from the Polish Society. I was the only woman, and they left me alone, but they arrested all the men. I told everyone you would come and get them out of jail. *'My son is a famous lawyer for Hartman's,'* I told them. They already knew that, since we brag about you all the time." She pinched his cheek. "We are all so proud of you."

He pressed his mouth into a hard line. This wasn't the first time he had bailed members of the Polish community out of jail, nor would it be the last. Did they truly believe their saber-rattling could be heard by the czar? Or that he would care? At least his mother had not been hauled away to face the indignity of sitting in a jail cell. He squeezed her in a big hug and pressed a kiss to her forehead. His soul ached to see her tireless efforts for a cause she could never win. She had been at it all sixty years of her life and would probably be carrying the battle flag until her dying day.

"Is something amiss?" Louis Hartman stood in the doorway, his glittering wife beside him. Zack could feel his mother cringe, embarrassed by her homespun clothing in light of Josephine's elegance. There was no need for her embarrassment. The Hartmans were fully aware of Zack's gritty roots.

Zack straightened. "My father has need of me back home," he hedged.

Mr. Hartman drew on his cigar, the tip glowing in the gathering darkness. "Not trouble on the docks, is it? Is he still working after all these years?"

Zack nodded. "Still working. I can clear this up in short order."

He didn't have any secrets from Louis Hartman, but he didn't want his mother exposed to any more embarrassment in front of Josephine Hartman. He would never forget the day both Hartmans had paid a call to their grubby tenement overlooking the docks sixteen years earlier. In those days, Zack had been working as a longshoreman, hauling huge crates of imported merchandise out of ships and into the warehouses owned by Louis Hartman. It was Zack's suggestions for streamlining the operations that first brought him praise, but it wasn't until the incident with the fish that Louis Hartman decided to pay him a visit.

In addition to the department store, Hartman's operated the best restaurants in Chicago. Zack had gotten wind that one of Hartman's merchants was substituting cheap trout for genuine white perch, and Zack was incensed. Zack barged into the merchant's genteel office, grimy and sweaty from the docks, hauling a huge basket of trout over one shoulder. Dumping a hundred pounds of dead fish onto the merchant's hand-carved desk, he made his position clear.

"That's what cheap trout looks like. Don't mistake it again." He dropped the dripping basket on the silk rug and returned to the docks.

Zack was only a twenty-year-old longshoreman, but a clever one who had already saved Hartman considerable sums by negotiating deals with the Irish labor unions who shipped their goods. Hartman prized loyalty above all else, and when word of the fish incident reached him, he saw long-term potential in the brash longshoreman. Louis Hartman offered to sponsor Zack to attend college, then bring him into management of the Hartman empire. He needed a lawyer whose allegiance was unquestioned but had the raw, aggressive spirit to tackle the burgeoning industrial world of Chicago.

Growing up, Zack lived with two other Polish families in a tenement apartment amidst the network of warehouses and stockyards that lined the docks. Louis came to the tenement to meet Zack's parents and assure them he would not only pay Zack's expenses at Yale, but also would provide a small stipend to the Kazmareks to compensate for the loss of Zack's wages. His parents had been too proud to accept the stipend, but Zack pounced on the chance to attend college. After college, it was understood Zack would return to Chicago and work for Hartman.

With his new wealth, Zack was able to buy a fine townhouse where he invited his parents to live with him. They accepted his offer, even though his father refused to quit working on the docks.

"Can I loan you a carriage?" Louis asked. "It might be difficult to get a streetcar this late in the evening."

It was true. They could probably still catch the last of the streetcars to the jail, but by the time Zack had secured his father's release, they would be facing a long walk home. "I would appreciate that," Zack said.

3

M ollie lived in a three-room apartment above a green-grocer. It was a cozy home with two bedrooms, a parlor, and a sticky alcove window overlooking the city she loved. There was a pump in the main room to bring up fresh water, but no kitchen. Who needed a kitchen in a city where every street corner had vendors selling piping hot sausage rolls, fresh pretzels, and sauerkraut just as good as that made in Berlin? Anytime Mollie was hungry for fresh food, she could sprint downstairs and buy something from the greengrocer on the first floor.

It had been three years since her father had passed away, and his bedroom remained untouched. All his clothing, his papers, everything was exactly as it had been on that terrible morning she discovered him dead in his bed. Her valiant, brave father who'd founded a company, employed hundreds of men over the decades, and fought in the Civil War had died quietly in his sleep.

On the evening of Mr. Kazmarek's stunning offer, Mollie entered her father's untouched bedroom and began hauling out boxes of old papers, receipts, and records from over thirty years of the watch business. Frank lived in an apartment across the hall, but he joined her at the small parlor table while Mollie sorted through the paper work, reading aloud the first few sentences of each document. Frank set up a system for organizing the papers into financial accounts, records of sale, and original cost basis.

"Do you think we can trust them?" Mollie asked. For a blind man, Frank had an astounding knack for reading people. Maybe it was his ability to sense tension in a voice, or maybe, as a man in his sixties, he had simply been on the planet long enough to understand the ways of the world better than she. Frank was a father, an advisor, and a friend all in one man.

"I don't know them well enough to answer that," he said. "You have a valuable company, and their price indicates they recognize that."

"Do you think I should sell?"

Frank's smile was sad. "I can't tell you what to do, Mollie. This is your company, and you have a head for business as good as any man I have ever met. I think the price is fair, if that is what you are asking." He shifted in his seat. "I am exhausted. What time is it?"

Mollie lifted the heavy gold watch from her skirt pocket. "Almost eight o'clock." Mollie's thumb caressed the dent in the watch's cover before closing it. It had been her father's watch; now it was her most precious keepsake. The dent in the cover was from flying shrapnel during those terrible days her father had been pinned against the side of that cliff with the rest of the 57th. Despite its dented cover and battered appearance, it still kept perfect time.

"I know that selling is the financially responsible thing to do," she said, her thumb pressing into the dent in the watch cover. "But I worry about losing control. I worry they'll tell me how to make my watches. Or make them cheaper. But my worst fear is they won't like a one-armed enameler. Or a metal polisher with shaky hands."

"Or a blind attorney." Frank said the words without flinching, his head held high.

"Yes," she admitted. "I worry about that most of all."

Frank drew a heavy breath. "Mollie, the day I was blinded, I laid in the dirt not knowing if I was going to survive another hour. Once I knew I would make it, my greatest fear was that I would no longer have a purpose in this world. It is the fear of all crippled men, but your father did a great thing by making room for us at his company. He never pitied us, never lowered the bar. He expected an honest day of work from every man, and we gave it to him." Frank leaned forward, his sightless eyes staring her straight in the face.

"Mollie! Don't lower the bar for us. If you coddle us, we lose our manhood. We lose our pride, and that is the most precious thing any man can have. Pride is the builder of bridges. It is the architect of dreams and the tamer of storms. It makes us want to rise out of bed so we can find dragons to slay and damsels to rescue. As long as we have pride, we have the spark that will illuminate our lives for a thousand days."

Mollie crossed to the window, gazing down at the streetlamps casting a warm glow through the avenue. Such brave words, but Frank was a strong man who could always rise to the challenges thrown in his path. Others weren't as courageous, and it was her job to protect them. If she sold the company, Mr. Kazmarek might show up in his faultlessly tailored suit one morning and fire every veteran of the 57th, and she would be helpless to stop him. But if she didn't sell, she would lose the Hartman contract and the entire company might go under.

Why couldn't she keep operating the company as she always had? Right now, everything was perfect. They made spectacular watches, and their profits were healthy. If she had a magic wand, she would freeze the world exactly as it was at this very moment.

She had a home she loved and a company she adored. She lived in the most vibrant city in America, burgeoning with wealth, ambition, and the best of cultures from all over the world. This offer from Mr. Kazmarek threatened everything she held dear.

For above all else, Mollie feared anything that would bring change into her carefully crafted, perfect life.

Planning for the next season's watches was one of Mollie's favorite activities. On Thursday evening, when Alice and Ulysses suggested a visit to the Krause Biergarten to talk about upcoming designs, Mollie quickly agreed.

The workers of the 57th had been coming to the famous outdoor gathering spot ever since Mollie had been a child riding on her father's shoulders. With dozens of long tables beneath the spreading branches of chestnut trees, throngs of working-class people gathered to listen to music, play chess, and savor the freshly made German sauerkraut and bratwurst. From the neighboring tables, Mollie heard people speaking German, Polish, and Italian, with plenty of Irish accents in the mix. Chicago was a melting pot with fresh waves of immigrants flooding in daily, and none more plentiful than the Germans who had brought the tradition of the outdoor Bavarian biergarten to America.

"The four hundredth birthday of Nicolaus Copernicus is coming up," Ulysses said. "What do you say we design a commemorative watch celebrating the solar system, with a ruby in the middle of the watch cover to represent the sun, and gemstones surrounding it to represent the planets?"

Mollie's brow wrinkled. For the most part, their commemorative watches sold well, but if gemstones were involved, the price soared, and they needed to be careful. "It sounds odd to me, but what do you think?" she asked Alice.

"I can make it beautiful," she said, "although do you really think people care about Nicolaus Copernicus?"

Frank leaned forward. "Shh!" he said with a grin. "I hear a bunch of Poles at the table behind us. They are liable to go on a rampage if you insult their patron saint."

Ulysses glanced over his shoulder at the group of Polish immigrants who were paying them no mind as they moved checkers across a game board, but Ulysses was never one to miss an opportunity. "Nicolaus Copernicus was a lion of a man," he proclaimed in a full voice. "A Polish warrior who conquered the night sky armed with nothing but a telescope and the awesome power of his mind." Bracing his crutch beneath his shoulder, Ulysses raised himself up on his one leg and raised his voice to echo over the crowd. "Like Prometheus stealing fire from the gods, Copernicus captured knowledge of the heavenly bodies and brought it down to mankind. The Copernican revolution will echo through the ages. He deserves to be commemorated in ruby, sapphire, and diamond."

By now he had attracted the attention of the Polish men at the neighboring table, who raised their glasses and stamped their feet in praise. One of the Poles summoned a serving woman and whispered a few words. Moments later, the waitress wended her way through the tables to deliver pints of cider.

"From the gentlemen playing checkers," the woman said as she set a mug before Ulysses, who grinned as he raised the pint to the group of Poles before taking a deep draught.

Mollie looked at Alice. "Draw up some designs, and I'll do the cost estimates," she said. "I'll need a 30 percent return on investment to even consider it. I dread a repetition of my father's disaster with the Queen Victoria watch." No one needed a reminder of Silas Knox's reckless venture to make a watch surrounded with twenty-five diamonds to celebrate the Queen's twenty-fifth jubilee. Mollie tried to stop him, saying no one in America would buy such an extravagant watch for a foreign monarch, and she had been correct. They had had to disassemble those watches and sell the diamonds back to the jeweler at a loss.

Her father was an atrocious businessman, but Mollie could usually rein in his more extravagant impulses. While other girls her age were being courted and finding husbands, Mollie trained wounded veterans in the art of watchmaking and devised ways to keep the company afloat. Not that she resented the work—she loved making watches and felt called to help these brave men find a new purpose in life. The entire company now rested on her shoulders. It was a precarious balancing act, and she dreaded any change or surprise that would jolt her out of the well-worn path she had created.

A gust of wind rustled through the trees, sending a cascade of autumn leaves swirling through the air. Normally it was chilly by October, but it had been unusually hot and dry all summer, which had extended into autumn. She was glad for the warm weather, which meant she could linger in the torch-lit garden with her friends. The only thing waiting for Mollie at home was isolation, worry, and doubt.

She couldn't keep news of Hartman's offer a secret from the Adairs. And once Ulysses and Alice had learned of the proposed sale, it had only taken a few hours before everyone knew of the offer from Hartman's to buy the company.

Ulysses took a deep draught of cool cider and then wiped the foam from his lips with his sleeve. "If you don't sign those papers, is Hartman going to take delivery of the quarterly shipment on Monday?"

It was a question that had been plaguing Mollie for days. She had a huge stock of watches in preparation for the Christmas season in her storage room. If Mr. Kazmarek made good on his threat to cut them loose on Monday morning, she would be left with a fortune in unsold inventory. "He did not say."

Frank's face was grim. "And I suppose his deadline on the same day as our quarterly delivery of watches was just a happy coincidence."

Alice put a warm arm around Mollie's waist. "I don't believe they would cut you loose if you don't sell. Your father was friends with Louis Hartman. Back since before you were born, right, Mollie?"

Not quite. Mollie had been ten years old when Louis Hartman had visited her father's tiny watch shop on Columbus Avenue. In those years, Hartman was buying property all up and down Columbus Avenue in preparation for his six-story palace of marble and crystal. Mollie's father had been one of the many merchants who had had to move when Louis Hartman built his colossal department store, but it was a blessing in disguise. Louis Hartman was so impressed with the whimsical quality of Papa's watches that he had begun carrying them at the store. Without the expense of maintaining a retail shop, Papa earned more money and had never been happier. The cozy relationship with Hartman's allowed Silas Knox to let many of the business aspects slide as he developed ever more spectacular watches.

Frank looked pensive as he rolled his tankard between his hands. "This company has been in the Knox family for thirty years," he said gravely. "Something doesn't seem right in demanding an answer so quickly."

Frank was right. She didn't need to accept Mr. Kazmarek's edict without question. There were four more days before she needed to make a decision, and she would not do so without demanding more information from Hartman's intimidating attorney.

ElizabethCamden

ElizabethCamden

From his office on the sixth story of Hartman's Emporium, Zack Kazmarek sat behind his grand desk of polished walnut and fought to keep his temper.

"Let me get this straight," he said as he wrestled with impatience. "We've got fifty thousand dollars' worth of chinchilla furs sitting at a port in New York because the tariff has not been paid."

Anthony Willis, his clerk, cleared his throat. "Yes, sir."

"And the furs have been there for a week."

"Yes, sir."

The furs should have been loaded onto a train and speeding toward Chicago. Hartman's sold most of their furs in the months leading up to Christmas, and any delay meant a loss of revenue. Nevertheless, his contract had been explicitly clear. The tariffs were to be paid by the Brazilian exporters, which had been figured into the negotiated price. Zack could send a wire to Hartman's New York bank and pay the tariffs within the hour, but that wasn't how he did business.

"Wire New York and refuse shipment of the furs," he instructed the clerk. "Give the ship's captain twenty-four hours to pay the tariff, or he can take the furs back to Brazil." Zack would not submit to corporate blackmail, which sometimes happened when people underestimated him. Zack wanted those furs, but he didn't *need* them.

"A few years ago we did business with a fox fur trader from Quebec named Babineaux," Zack said. "Get the merchandising department to see if Babineaux can deal in time for the Christmas rush." Fox fur wasn't as desirable as chinchilla, but he needed an alternate plan in case the furs from Brazil failed to come through.

As anticipated, this sent the merchandising department into a fury. Within twenty minutes a red-faced Mario Girard was in his office, waving last year's Christmas receipts inches beneath Zack's nose. "Fox fur! Fox fur at Christmas?" The man sounded as outraged as if Zack had suggested they serve cold gruel at a banquet for the Queen. "Look at these records! Last year we sold every chinchilla fur within three weeks of delivery. We need those furs!"

Zack plucked the papers from Mr. Girard's hands. "First, I am not using Hartman money to pay off a corrupt ship captain from Rio de Janeiro. Second, if you ever shove papers in my face like that again, I'm using them to line Lizzie's cage." He tossed the pages back at Mr. Girard, who snatched them against his chest before they fluttered to the ground. Making matters worse, Zack had just learned that the Brazilian ship captain also had three hundred pairs of hand-tooled leather boots that had been destined for Hartman's. The boots were in the same legal quagmire due to the tariff issue.

"How am I to convince the ladies of Chicago that fox fur is as luxurious as chinchilla?" Mr. Girard demanded. "What kind of woman would settle for fox fur when she had her heart set on chinchilla?"

Zack's smile was tight. "You'll reach deep inside that clever brain of yours and conjure up a reason. Don't make me do your job for you." Growing up, his mother had been lucky to have a coat at all, let alone quibble over the fabric. To this day his mother refused to let him buy her decent clothing, insisting on wearing the same kinds of clothes she had been able to afford when she was a laundress. His thoughts were interrupted by a knock at his door, and his clerk entered.

"Yes?" Zack asked.

"There is a woman here to see you. Miss Knox, from the 57th Illinois Watch Company."

Zack blinked. "Does she have an appointment?"

He knew she didn't. An appointment with Mollie Knox was not something he would have forgotten, but he needed a moment to gather his thoughts. There were only two words in the English language that could knock him off-kilter. Mollie and Knox.

"No, sir. She wishes to discuss terms for the offer of sale."

Zack hoped the flush wasn't showing on his face. What sort of sap was he that his heart sped up just knowing that woman was standing on the other side of the office wall? This unwelcome attraction to Mollie Knox was liable to get him fired if he couldn't rein it in. He walked to Lizzie's cage and slipped in a wedge of apple, which delighted the finch. She flitted about the cage, chirping and whistling, then rushing back for another piece of apple.

Actually, he was surprised it had taken Miss Knox this long to demand to see him. There were aspects of the contract that were a little odd, but the terms were nonnegotiable, and he would tell her that in no uncertain terms.

"Tell her I am unavailable," Zack said.

The clerk cleared his throat. "I already did that, sir. She is adamant."

Zack paused, which was enough to send Mario Girard into a renewed tizzy. "We are about to lose our Christmas supply of fur, and now you are feeding that silly bird and wasting time over some woman. I want to know when I'm getting my chinchilla furs."

Zack slipped another wedge of apple into the cage and stared as Lizzie pecked at it. He was double-booked for most of the day, and this disaster with the Brazilian shipment was another headache to complicate matters. The last thing he needed was Mollie Knox flinging a healthy dose of chaos into his day.

Why was he so irrational about her? Rigid, repressed women were not his preferred choice, but there was something about her, always so starchy, so uptight, that first caught his attention. And she was passionate about her watches, no doubt about that. Anyone who heard her rhapsodize about the perfection of spring-loaded mechanisms could not doubt her love for her craft. Zack knew all about hopeless romantics; he had been raised by a pair of them. To this day he was bailing his parents out of one ill-advised scheme after another as they pursued their hopeless quest. Mollie was different. She was half passionate artisan, half cold-blooded businesswoman, and the combination enthralled him.

"Kazmarek!" Mr. Girard barked. "When am I getting my chinchillas? And my leather boots?"

Zack walked back to his desk. "When a Brazilian ship captain pays the tariffs. Not before. Get some alternative sources of fur lined up in case he refuses." Although Zack was certain the captain would ultimately pay the tariff, sometimes business required a little bare-knuckle boxing, and it was a game Zack enjoyed. He came of age sweating alongside the roughest thugs in the city and never backed down from a fight. That poor deluded captain had no clue whom he was dealing with.

The clerk watched from the doorway, exquisitely uncomfortable with the raised voices. "What shall I tell Miss Knox?"

"Tell her to come back this afternoon. I'll see her at two o'clock." He only wished he was as comfortable doing battle with Mollie Knox as he was with a Brazilian ship captain.

The hand-carved mahogany doors of Hartman's Emporium looked heavy, but Mollie never knew for certain because a sharply dressed doorman always opened them as patrons entered. She loved the scent of lemon polish and freshly cut roses that always graced the entrance. The crystal chandelier suspended over the entryway and new gaslight fixtures cast a magical glow throughout the interior. The first floor of the two-acre building was filled with a staggering array of goods. Women could buy hand-woven rugs from Persia or perfume from France. She could never resist trailing her fingers over the plush suede boots and silky scarves in the Women's Department. Other departments stocked a sumptuous display of jewelry, china, leather goods, even food and wine.

Showing up on bended knee before Zack Kazmarek held as much appeal as a case of chicken pox, but it had to be done. Mollie wore her favorite outfit—a smartly tailored amethyst purple suit made of moiré fabric, with a tightly cinched jacket and frothy lace kerchief at her throat—to lend her confidence.

She was breathless after climbing five flights of stairs. The top floor of the building was entirely offices—some belonging to Hartman's, some leased by other businesses. The hallway was spacious and well lit, but had nothing like the opulent splendor of the first floor open to the public. Her nerves stretched tighter as she walked to the final office at the end of a long corridor.

She was shown inside, where Zack Kazmarek sat behind his desk like a king. He did not rise as she entered the office. "Miss Knox. Braids again. Pity."

She touched the back of her hair. She had artfully coiled the heavy braids into a compact bun at the nape of her neck. She thought it fetching but remembered what Alice had said about braids. She raised her chin a notch. "I hear braids are all the rage among the female prison wardens. It makes them look powerful."

"That's one word for it." He gestured for Mollie to sit.

She arranged her skirts to release a little nervous energy. "I came to discuss finalizing the contract," she said. With the expansive view of Chicago behind him and the massive desk before him, Zack looked like some sort of emperor ready to broker deals for world domination. Or smash a small watch company beneath the heel of his boot. She swallowed hard. "I need more time before I can make a decision."

"And why is that?" His face remained impassive, his voice chilly.

She glanced out the window behind him, looking at the sprawling city of Chicago. The downtown area was bisected by a river in the shape of a Y, with the business district hugging the shores of Lake Michigan. Mollie pointed to an area clustered by the railway station just south of the river. "Do you see where East Street abuts the railroad tracks?"

There was a rasp of expensive fabric as Mr. Kazmarek turned to glance out the window. "I see it."

"Those railroad tracks are new, and they are only three blocks from my workshop," she said. "After they were laid down, the value of my building has soared. I need more time for a building appraisal. I also need to evaluate the potential new revenue streams coming in from the East Coast. All this takes time."

His face remained unmoved as he twirled a pencil between his fingers. "Miss Knox, although I may be fascinated by new revenue streams coming in from the East Coast—and trust me, *I am*—it is not possible to extend the deadline. Monday morning. Nine o'clock. If you don't agree to sell, I will make an offer to another watch company by ten o'clock."

Her eyes narrowed. "The financial well-being of forty employees rests on this decision. Those people are like my family."

"Those people are your employees, not family. Never confuse the two."

"Then I want to negotiate for control over the personnel working at the company."

He shook his head. "No deal. We want all assets of the 57th Illinois Watch Company. Every scrap of equipment, every piece of unsold inventory, every unused matchstick in the drawers. I don't want to muddy the contract with exceptions. The offer is for the sale of the entire company. Take it or leave it."

"Why are you being so hard-nosed about that deadline? Another week will not hurt."

His reply was nonchalant. "If you are concerned about your employees, take the deal. It is a good offer, and you know it. And I doubt you will feel any less conflicted about your decision a week from now. True?"

He was right, but she didn't want to admit it. She vaulted out of her chair and stormed over to the window. She wanted to break something. She wanted to pretend this past week had never happened and she could happily go about making her watches and providing a decent livelihood for people who depended on her. She stared moodily out the window. "I am due to send another quarterly shipment of watches to you on Monday. If I don't sign the contract, will you still accept delivery?"

"No," he said bluntly. From behind her, his voice was soft and tempting. "Of course, you could avoid all this stress and simply sell us the company."

She swallowed hard, twisting her gloves between her hands. "Why do I feel like Eve being offered the apple?"

If he was insulted by her reference, he gave no appearance as he leaned back in his chair and watched her through those laughing dark eyes. At first she had thought he had black eyes, but on closer inspection they had flecks of amber in them. Like obsidian. "Miss Knox, you are a bottomless well of grim anxiety. A fortune is about to be dumped into your lap. A normal person would be dreaming about opening a bottle of champagne or planning a trip to the south of France, but not Miss Knox. Oh no. She is all about calculating revenue streams while she leaches all the joy out of life."

She tightened her mouth. "I am fighting for the livelihood of my employees, and you interpret that as leaching *all the joy* out of life."

"Every drop. And I don't even think you enjoy it all that much. Instead of spending your weekend with your accounting books, why don't you go watch the sunset this evening? Better yet, there is a White Stockings baseball game tomorrow. Do *something* besides indulging that grim streak of anxiety you have been feeding all week."

"I hold the fate of forty employees and their families in my hands, and you think I should go to a baseball game?"

He swiveled back in his chair. "What if a comet hits the earth tomorrow and we are all dead? Wouldn't you be glad you spent your final few hours outdoors with friends, enjoying a cold drink and a warm pretzel, watching the finest baseball team this side of the Mississippi take on the Philadelphia Athletics? Or would you prefer staring at columns of financial equations? Judging by those lines on your face, it looks like you spend far too much time curled up with those accounting ledgers."

If she hadn't been feeling so brittle, the words would not have hurt, but did he know what it felt like to have responsibility for so many people? Maybe she didn't have time for baseball or watching sunsets, but that didn't mean she leached all the joy out of life.

Mollie stood and needlessly adjusted a bit of the lace at her throat. "You can search for the next decade, but you will never find a better watch company on the continent. I will let you know when I've made my decision."

4

It was Sunday before Mollie figured out why Hartman was so desperate to buy her out.

On Sunday evening, her mind was too numb to process any more equations, and she allowed herself the temporary diversion of flipping through old product designs buried in her father's trunk. That was when she saw the deed stuck in the pages of an old product manual.

Her fingers trembled as she lifted the certificate from the pages. On thick paper, embossed with a stamp from the state of Illinois and signed by the county clerk, was a deed of ownership to half an acre on Columbus Street. It was where her father's first shop, one of six properties that were torn down to make way for Hartman's grand store, had been located.

The deed described her father's lot as half an acre in size. The footprint of Hartman's Emporium was two acres.

Snatching up the deed, she dashed out of her apartment to Frank's place across the hall and pounded on his door. The scales were falling from her eyes. Zack Kazmarek's offer demanded "all unsold inventory, equipment, designs, and all other property belonging to the 57th Illinois Watch Company." It was a quick and sneaky way for them to get ownership of that half acre.

As soon as Frank answered the door, she got right down to business. "Frank," she said in a trembling voice, "when you sell a piece of property, don't you have to surrender the deed?"

"Yes. You sign over ownership, and the deed passes to the buyer."

Her fingers began to tremble. "I don't think that land deal for my father's property was finalized," she said in a shaky voice. "I am holding the deed to that piece of land here in my hands."

Frank straightened. "Then the deal was never legally closed," he said bluntly.

"If we still own that piece of land, what happens to the building sitting on it?"

Frank's voice was firm. "It makes you part owner."

The breath left her body. If Frank was right, it meant she owned twenty-five percent of that palatial six-story building of marble and crystal. No wonder Mr. Kazmarek had been so insistent on speed!

She had never seen Frank Spencer angry, but as the implications sank in, he was furious. "They *knew* about this. It explains their ridiculous need for haste. They waited until your quarterly delivery of watches was due before springing it on you. They were trying to paint you into a corner so you'd jump at the offer."

A rush of heat prickled her skin, and she fanned herself with the deed. Her father loathed the bookkeeping aspects of business. He wrote receipts on napkins and took payment in promissory notes, then never bothered to cash them. But this deed took the prize. "My father thought he sold it, but he was always so scatterbrained when it came to business. Why would he still have this deed?"

"Who knows?" Frank said. "Hartman would have bought half a dozen other small businesses in order to clear the space for that monster of a store. Somewhere along the way, a bookkeeper got sloppy. Even if your father received money for the sale, the property was never officially transferred unless the deed was signed and recorded at the courthouse. *You own that land.* Kazmarek knows it, and that is why he is bullying you into a sale."

Mollie didn't feel entitled to that building. She didn't want any part of it, but what Mr. Kazmarek had done was nasty and mean and underhanded. While her mind was still reeling, Frank kept rattling off more information. They could not be completely sure of ownership until they went to the courthouse tomorrow morning to confirm there was no subsequent deed. The courthouse would not open until nine o'clock on Monday morning. Mr. Kazmarek had threatened that if she had not delivered her affirmative reply, he would be canceling their contracts and making an offer to another watch company by ten o'clock.

Frank's expression was grim. "Don't trust them, Mollie. Any company that would use underhanded tactics like this is not someone you want to be working for. If you sell the 57th to them, we will be under their heel. Walk away. Fast."

How could she walk away when she was contracted to deliver three dozen watches to them tomorrow morning? She needed the revenue from that shipment to continue operating. It would take time for her to find other merchants on the East Coast who could afford to sell her watches, and Hartman's was going to give that time to her because she had something they wanted.

She had a deed to the land where their store sat.

By the time Mollie rode the streetcar and crossed the bridge into the neighborhood where Zack Kazmarek lived, she had worked herself into a fine rage. It wasn't about the money. Truly, she didn't feel entitled to any piece of that opulent palace on

Columbus Street; it was his strong-armed manipulation that infuriated her.

The air was hot and smoky tonight. It smelled like there was a fire somewhere in the city, which was not unusual for Chicago. Either that or someone was burning leaves, which was a foolish thing to do when the city had been parched by the drought all year.

What a fine townhome Mr. Kazmarek lived in. Built of pale limestone, the attached townhouses all loomed three stories high with mansard roofs and charming flower boxes in the windows. The brass mailboxes conveniently had the owners' names engraved on the front, making it easy for her to find the Kazmarek residence. She rapped on the brass knocker, feeling her resentment simmer higher. The veterans who worked at the 57th had all suffered on behalf of a country, while men of privilege like Zack Kazmarek curled up in their cozy townhouses and counted their money.

When the door opened she was ready to tear into him, but bit her tongue when she saw a tiny old woman smiling up at her.

"Can I help you, miss?"

Mollie glanced at the woman's curious dress. Couldn't Mr. Kazmarek pay his servants enough for decent clothing? The woman's shawl looked like it had come from another century, and her skirt was a wild conglomeration of pink, violet, and indigo-blue floral prints. Mollie cleared her throat. "I'd like to see Mr. Kazmarek, please. I know it is late, but I have business with him."

"Are you the watchmaker?" The old woman's eyes sparkled and without waiting for an answer, she turned and spoke in a rapid stream of foreign language. An older man with the same laughing eyes as the housekeeper stepped up to the door.

"Miss Mollie Knox?" he asked.

Had they been expecting her? "Yes. I am here to see Mr. Kazmarek. Is he at home?"

"Come in, come in," the older man said. "I am Jozef Kazmarek, but everyone calls me Jozef. This is my wife, Joanna." Jozef wrapped a big callused hand around Mollie's elbow and pulled her inside. Like his wife, he wore working-class clothing.

"Your name is Kazmarek as well?" Mollie asked curiously. "You must be related to Mr. Kazmarek?"

"Zack is our boy," the older man said proudly.

"Our son," Joanna added. "Isn't he handsome? Of course he knows it, and—"

"And it goes straight to his head," the elder Mr. Kazmarek said. "He went out to listen to a polka band at the biergarten, where the girls always throw themselves at him."

Mollie looked at the both of them. Mrs. Kazmarek had rough, callused hands, much like her husband's, as if she had spent her life hanging laundry or hauling water. As the older pair continued to rattle on about various neighborhood girls who were trying to land their handsome son, Mollie glanced around the interior of the curious home. Despite the grand entryway, the parlor to her right was chaotic, as if the contents of a warehouse had been dumped inside. There was almost no furniture, but towers of papers, wooden crates, and books crammed every square foot. Not even nice books either. They were ratty books that looked like they'd been salvaged from a tinker's wagon. Bundles of newspapers were stacked so high they seemed ready to topple over. Mrs. Kazmarek saw where she was looking and scurried to pull the pocket doors closed, cutting off her view of the strange room.

The dining room, mercifully clear of the clutter that choked the other room, was on the opposite side of the hallway. Over the table was a large oil painting. The painting was . . . well, it was simply breathtaking.

In shades of green and amber, a girl stood in a summer garden, gazing at a watch in her palm. Dappled sunlight filtered through the leaves, illuminating the girl's white dress so she looked lit from within. The brushstrokes were too choppy to reveal many details of the girl's appearance, but she looked soft and lovely standing in the patches of light. Peaceful. Luminous.

"What a lovely painting," she said softly.

"It is a Monet," Mrs. Kazmarek said. "He is all the rage in Paris. Zack was in Europe last year, and he insisted on buying it. I am glad you like it." Mrs. Kazmarek elbowed her husband, some unspoken communication flying between the two. Before Mollie could interpret the strange gesture, Mrs. Kazmarek nudged her back toward the kitchen.

"Come down to the kitchen where we can get better acquainted," she said. "Zack has told us so much about you."

"He has?" Why would any man talk to his parents about a person he was trying to swindle?

"Oh yes. He told us what pretty hair you have, but—" Mrs. Kazmarek winced a bit when she glanced at Mollie's braids. "Oh, yes. I see what he means. Come, you must let me fix your hair sometime. I would so enjoy that. I always wanted—"

"She always wanted a daughter," Jozef said.

"You hush! This is between girls."

Mollie wanted to leave. If she couldn't talk to Mr. Kazmarek, she needed to get back home to Frank, but the sound of a bird chirping came from down the hall. Peeking down the hallway, she saw a little blue bird flitting about a cage. "Is that the finch from Mr. Kazmarek's office?"

Something about this eager little bird had always appealed to Mollie. She drew closer and admired the peacock-blue plumage of the finch.

"That's Lizzie," Mrs. Kazmarek said. "Zachariasz fusses

over that bird like it is a princess. He can't stand the thought of her alone in that dark office all weekend, so he brings her home every Friday."

Maggie poked a finger through the iron bars and let the bird peck at the fleshy tip. It was hard for her to imagine that intimidating man fussing over anyone, let alone a little bird. From down the hall Mollie heard the front door open, then a heavy tread and the rich timbre of Zack Kazmarek's voice from the front of the house.

"There is a fire on the south side of the city," she heard him say. "You can smell the smoke on the wind. It looks like a bad one."

Mollie stepped into the hallway to see him kiss his mother on both cheeks. The affection he had for the older woman was evident as he gave her a reassuring hug. "Don't worry, Mama," he soothed. "I went up to the top of the bell tower on St. Mark's to get a good look. It's on the other side of the river and won't get anywhere near us." When he released his mother and saw Mollie, there was a stiffening of the muscles in his face. His humor vanished, replaced by the formality she was accustomed to.

"Miss Knox," he said cautiously. "What brings you to this part of town so late on a Sunday evening?"

It was awkward to have a blunt conversation in front of the man's beaming parents, but there was no help for it. "I came to discuss business."

He disengaged his arm from Mrs. Kazmarek's shoulders. "Mother, will you get us something to drink? I'm parched."

As Mr. and Mrs. Kazmarek went to the kitchen, he shrugged out of his overcoat. "Please don't take this amiss," he said with his back to her as he hung the coat, "but in the future, I would prefer that you didn't call at my home. It looks bad."

"Such a concern for propriety," she said. "The irony."

He turned at her sarcastic tone. "What is that supposed to mean?" he demanded.

Mollie stepped a little closer and lowered her voice so his mother would not overhear. "I found out *exactly* why you people are so adamant I sell out by Monday morning. It won't work. At nine o'clock tomorrow morning I will be at the courthouse so I can prove you tried to lie and swindle us out of a fortune."

He stiffened. His polite demeanor evaporated and his eyes narrowed. "I don't take words like that lightly."

"I don't use them lightly," she said in a harsh whisper. "We found the deed."

"What deed?" he snapped.

"The deed to half an acre on Columbus Street. At nine o'clock tomorrow morning, I will be at the courthouse with my attorney to verify my ownership of half an acre sitting beneath Hartman's store. And if you dare cancel the contract on our quarterly shipment of watches, I'll assert ownership to a portion of the building as well."

"Don't threaten me." If his tone were any colder there would be ice crystals in the air.

She raised her chin a notch. "You've been threatening *me* all week."

Mr. Kazmarek glanced down the hallway at his parents, but they were still preoccupied in the kitchen and paying them no mind. That didn't stop Mr. Kazmarek from clenching his jaw and leaning down to speak to her in a menacing whisper. "Miss Knox, here is a piece of free legal advice. Don't ever show up at my house and call me a liar in front of my parents."

"I don't know a prettier word for it," Mollie said. "Why else would you leave us so little time to make a decision? And right before you were to pay us for the quarterly shipment."

Mr. Kazmarek turned away from her as though he couldn't

bear to meet her eyes. With an angry jerk he shrugged out of his suit jacket so quickly a gold cuff link went flying. He tossed his jacket onto the table and scooped up the cuff link. He glared at her as he refastened it.

"Miss Knox, you are a beautiful woman, and I have always admired your commitment to your business, but you know nothing of judgment or of human behavior. If you did, you would never have come into my home and used words like *swindle* and *liar*."

His tone was scathing, and the heat simmering in his eyes made her pause. She drew her breath to suggest they step outside where they could speak openly when a boom shattered the night.

Mollie flinched and covered her ears. The windowpanes rattled and a vase slipped off a table, smashing on the floor. Mrs. Kazmarek's screech came from the kitchen. "What happened?" she hollered.

Zack raced to a window, and even from a distance Mollie could see an orange fireball in the sky, pillars of flames shooting straight upward. His face went white. "The gasworks have exploded."

"No!" Mollie's eyes widened with horror. The gasworks were at least five miles away, but such an explosion would be a catastrophe. Chicago was accustomed to dealing with fires. All through the hot, dry autumn it seemed as if there had been an outbreak almost daily, but nothing ever lit up the sky like this. The gas would fuel a roaring blaze for hours.

Mrs. Kazmarek moaned and twisted her hands. "What about our work? All our work?" she said weakly.

"Come, let's go up on the roof so we can see better," her son said in a grim tone. Mollie followed the family as they climbed up two flights of stairs. The stench of acrid smoke filled her nose the moment she stepped onto the roof. On the other side of the river, an angry orange blaze illuminated the night sky, chunks of burning debris flying on the wind.

Mrs. Kazmarek clasped her hands and moaned, but her son tried to console her. "It is on the other side of the river, Mama. We will be safe here. *Your work* will be safe."

From here, it was easy to see how the Chicago River divided the city into three distinct sections. A huge swath of the south side was ablaze, but the river would keep the north and west sides safe. Her apartment was north of the river, but with the way the wind was blowing and the size of that blaze, everything south of the river was at risk.

Her gaze followed the rapidly blowing smoke, watching in horror as it tracked straight toward her factory. "I've got to get out of here," she said as she whirled around and scurried down the stairs. Heavy footsteps pounded behind her.

"Tell me you aren't headed where I think you are," Zack said.

"I've got inventory at the factory. And equipment. I've still got plenty of time to get it out."

They reached the ground floor, but he blocked her exit. Firm hands clamped around her shoulders and gave her a brisk shake. "Don't be an idiot," he growled. "You don't have a prayer of getting all that equipment out of the building. Stay here where it is safe."

"Mr. Kazmarek," she said through clenched teeth, "I've got fifteen thousand dollars' worth of watches sitting in that building. The train depot is only three blocks from my factory door. I expect that every factory on East Street is now loading their inventory into boxcars and sending it out of the city. I intend to do the same. Get out of my way."

The older Kazmareks came barreling down the staircase and raced to fling open the doors leading to the parlor. They threw traveling cases on the floor and began plowing through the stacks of papers, throwing some stacks to the side and stuffing others into the traveling bags. Zack did not release her shoulders, but threw a frustrated glance at his parents.

"Mama, I told you. Our house is safe."

The charming, tiny Mrs. Kazmarek reared up with fury in her eyes. She held a fistful of papers aloft. "This is my life's work!" she roared. "Our people depend on these papers. Our hope. Our dreams!"

The elder Mr. Kazmarek stepped away from a tower of papers. The whites of his eyes were wide with panic, but he latched on to Mollie's arm. "A train?" he asked her. "You know of a train leaving the city?"

Mollie nodded. "I expect every factory south of the river is stuffing them now as we speak. I need to get south so I can get my inventory aboard."

Mrs. Kazmarek stumbled forward. "Can you take our bags? Zack! You must take our bags and get them on that train. You must!"

Zack's mouth thinned to a hard line. He glared at the half-stuffed traveling bags, then down at Mollie. "Miss Knox, I would be happy to go with you to the factory and help load your equipment, provided you can get my parents' bags on that train."

It would be a blessing to have a strong man to help her get space on that train. Mollie tried to hold down her panic as she took in the chaos of the parlor. "Hurry. I can try to get your bags out, but you have to hurry."

A quiet rage simmered through Zack as he marched alongside Mollie. At least there was no need to speak to her. The clang of church and school bells pealed nonstop in an effort to rouse the city. It was nearing midnight and some of the people straggling onto the street were still wearing nightclothes.

They made good time until they crossed the river, where people fleeing the fire clogged the streets. He and Mollie were like fish battling upstream, as they seemed to be the only two people heading toward the fire. Everyone else was fleeing to the safe side of the river, carrying packs over their shoulders, hauling trunks, navigating around wagons and carts piled high with furniture, bags, even mattresses. With a huge satchel hoisted over his shoulder and a smaller one tucked beneath his arm, Zack plowed forward, Mollie trailing in his wake.

He didn't even want to look at her. All he wanted to do was get to her factory, load those watches onto a train, and then see the last of her. The deal to buy the company was over. After this evening, she probably would no longer have a factory to continue making those ridiculous overpriced watches.

"Could you move a little faster?" she said from behind him.

It was the third time she had ordered him to speed up. He was plowing forward through a sea of humanity, making good progress clearing a path for her, and she had the nerve to complain. A glance at the skyline showed that the fire was less than a mile from her factory.

Zack took a shove against his ribs as a man carrying a cage full of chickens toppled against him. He glared back at Mollie. "Would you like to take the lead?" He didn't expect an answer, and he didn't get one.

It was a good thing he couldn't see her. If she had been a man, he would have tossed her out of his house the moment she had called him a liar. As it was, he had stood there in stunned disbelief as a woman he'd idolized for the better part of three years flung vile accusations at him.

"Mr. Kazmarek, could you please move a little faster? I've got fifteen thousand dollars' worth of watches in that warehouse. I've already accepted that I'm going to lose my equipment, but if we hurry I can save the watches."

He stopped in his tracks. He dropped the satchel under his arm and then bent to let the huge bag on his shoulder roll to the ground with a heavy thump. He dragged in a lungful of air. "I'm carrying two hundred pounds. Do you want to help by taking one of them?"

Before he even finished his sentence, she grabbed the smaller bag and lugged it forward. He wouldn't have thought it possible, but she made good progress as she pushed her way through the crowd. "What is in this thing?" she gasped.

"Papers."

She struggled to haul the bag but did not slow her pace. "I know it is papers, I saw your parents stuff them inside. What on earth are they? The key to finding the Holy Grail?"

They were to his parents. "Never mind what they are. Just keep moving." He didn't expect Mollie's no-nonsense brain to be able to appreciate his glorious, foolhardy parents. Zack had been bailing them out of one disaster after another for years, but the one thing they had done right in their life was in these two bags. And littering the floor of his parlor. Filling his attic. Stuffed beneath beds and in closets. This was not the first time they had been terrified by the threat of a fire, and each time they had packed up their most valuable pages and begged Zack to get them to safety.

He would do so, even if that meant he had to spend an hour in the company of Mollie Knox. His mother really owed him for this one.

A gust of wind sent a wave of heat toward him. The fire was moving fast, and a glance at Mollie's face showed him the terror reflected in her blue eyes. She heaved the bag forward and quickened her pace. No complaints, no whining. She was scared out of her wits but kept moving forward. Against his better judgment, a twinge of pity took root.

"Give me the blasted bag," he growled. He tucked it under his arm and strode forward.

"Are you sure?" She was breathless as she struggled to keep up with him. "You've been carrying it forever and must be exhausted."

"Miss Knox, I worked for seven years as a longshoreman hauling two-hundred-pound crates off the wharves of Chicago. A few satchels of paper aren't a problem."

"You did?" She sounded as shocked as if he'd suggested he had built the Pyramids. "I never thought of you as anything but a lawyer."

He tightened his mouth. He'd been thinking of her as a woman whose hair he wanted to run his hands through. A woman holding a watch in a summer garden. "I've never thought of you as someone who could tear herself away from her accounting ledgers." Not really true. He thought of her sitting beside him on a blanket beneath the stars. Or at a baseball game. Holding a baby. He'd long ago accepted that he was a hopeless sap over this woman, but he would get over it.

The night sky was illuminated only by the eerie orange glow of the fire. As they rounded the corner onto East Street, the crowds thinned. Most people were long gone, and it was easy for Mollie and Zack to jog toward the factory. The sparse traffic on the streets seemed more ominous than the surging crowds. Without the noise and bustle of the foot traffic, it was easier to hear the snapping timber and the menacing roar of the fire now only a few blocks away. The endless clanging of church bells merely added to the sense of urgency.

The moment her factory came into view, Mollie raced ahead

of him toward the metal door, but as she fumbled for the key, the door opened from within.

"I figured you'd be by soon," a man said as he pushed himself forward on a crutch.

"Ulysses!" Mollie embraced the man and Zack noticed the empty space where there should have been a leg. "We've come to get the inventory out," Mollie said.

"We're one step ahead of you, Mollie-girl. I boxed up the watches and the lathes and they are on the train. Declan crated up the equipment, but we could use some help getting it to the train depot."

The transformation on Mollie's face was amazing. A smile lit her eyes as if the sun were bursting behind them. "God bless you, Ulysses!"

It was dark inside the factory, but enough of the orange-tinged light filtered through the high windows to illuminate the dark silhouettes of people inside. Zack didn't know who these people were, but their loyalty to the 57th was strong enough for them to leave their own households vulnerable while they rushed to the aid of the company.

A balding man reached out to shake his hand and introduced himself as Oliver Wilkes. "I've worked at this company since I was fifteen," he said. "This equipment won't go up in flames while I've got a heart still beating in my body."

Equipment for making watches was mostly small, and they packed up the tools quickly. Five minutes later, Zack and Oliver Wilkes carried the crated equipment to the depot. A single train remained at the station, the doors of the boxcars wide open as workers from the nearby factories stuffed the interiors with bolts of fabric, half-made furniture, and pieces of machinery. Mollie's stash of watches and her few crates of equipment were an easy fit. It was dark inside the musty interior of the boxcar, but Zack loaded the crates into a corner and secured them with bands. He stacked the two satchels from his parents on top.

"Do you know where this train is headed?" he asked Mollie.

She glanced over her shoulder. "Someone from the piano factory said it is going to Evanston to wait out the fire. If the tracks aren't damaged, it should be back in a day or two. I'm not sure what I'll do then."

Her lip wobbled as her gaze tracked back to the empty factory. In all likelihood, there would be nothing left of her building when the train returned. Earlier this evening, he had wanted to shake her until her teeth rattled and those ridiculous braids came tumbling down, but it was hard to resent a woman who held up so valiantly as her world burned to ashes around her.

"Could someone help us?" a voice shouted. Zack sprang down from the boxcar. At the neighboring car, two men were struggling to lift a piano. Zack vaulted over to prop his shoulder beneath the heavy back end of the piano. Two mighty heaves and they hoisted the piano into place. Behind him, three more upright pianos waited to be lifted aboard. It took less than five minutes to load all three inside.

The railroad yardmaster walked along the lines, sliding the heavy doors closed with a loud, clattering rasp. "That's it, then," he called out.

A man came running down the platform, waving his hat. "Have you got any more space?" He was breathing so hard he doubled over, but managed to keep speaking. "I've got two dozen oriental rugs less than a mile away. I can get them here in ten minutes. Please. *Please*."

The worker shook his head. "Can't wait any longer. We just heard that Michigan Avenue is on fire. I've got to get this train out before the fire hits the tracks. Maybe you can catch a train on the north side of the city."

The man shook his head. "No good. The State Street Bridge is on fire. No way out." Zack didn't think the news could get worse, but it did. The rug merchant breathlessly recounted how a paint factory had caught fire, spilling barrels of oily waste into the river. "It is a complete disaster," the rug merchant said. "The river is on fire and the bridge is about to go under. The fire has jumped the river to the north side."

Zack looked down at Mollie, her face blanched with shock. "Then it is headed for my home," she whispered.

His heart lurched as he watched the color drain from her face. His west side townhouse was still safe, but Mollie's north side home was not going to be spared. "Come back home with me," he said. "It is the only place that will be safe for you."

She swallowed hard and straightened. "I'm going north." Picking up her skirts, she started dashing up the street before he could stop her.

"Miss Knox!" Such formalities sounded ridiculous. "Mollie! Mollie, don't be a fool!" he yelled after her, but if she heard him, she made no indication as she ran faster. Her skirts were hiked around her knees as she bolted forward, and he watched until she was swallowed by the crowd heading north.

A group of men clustered around the rug merchant, who had a better idea of where the fire was going. The heat and wind were whipping up firestorms that careered down narrow alleys, creating columns of fire that looked like tornados, picking up burning timbers and hurling them through the air. The timbers landed on wooden roofs, igniting building after building. The fire had already leapt north of the river in two places, where the roof of a turpentine plant had caught fire. If the roof caved in, there would be another huge explosion.

And Mollie was headed straight into the center of it. Did she even realize how bad it was on the other side of the river?

He didn't stop to think, he just ran after her.

The farther north he traveled, the worse the congestion. The street was littered with sofas, highboys, and abandoned stoves. The owners put them outside and fled, assuming things left in the middle of the street would be safer than in the wood-framed buildings. The abandoned property slowed the crowds and added to the panic. His foot caught on a bedframe, but he regained his balance and kept pushing farther north.

"Mollie!" he shouted, looking in vain. Cinders flying on the wind felt like burning pinpricks on his face. He swiped his face and squinted to see through the smoke, looking for a brave, foolhardy young woman wearing a light blue dress. He shouldered forward, past a woman lugging an iron kettle and a horse that had collapsed from exhaustion.

He saw her angling through the crowd. "Mollie!" Unencumbered by the bags and cases that most people carried, she was making quick progress.

He bolted after her. "Are you insane?" he said as he drew alongside her. "The bridge is on fire and it's dangerous out here. Come back home with me."

She barely spared him a glance. "I'm heading for the Rush Street Bridge. I heard it's still open."

He grabbed her arm, and she skidded to a stop. "Mollie, it's not safe. The roof of the turpentine plant is on fire. It is only a matter of time before it blows, and you are heading straight into the worst of it. You can't save your home. You need to accept that."

"Don't you understand?" She was practically screaming. "Frank Spencer is at my apartment. He is *blind*. I can't leave him there."

Understanding hit him like a kick in the gut. There was total anarchy in the streets, and it was hard to stand upright in the crush of surging bodies. Children were crying, a horse that had thrown its rider galloped in a panic. And every few minutes a downburst of wind brought a shower of sparks and ash down from the sky. No blind man, no matter how capable, could navigate this chaos.

Rather than come with him to safety, Mollie was heading into the path of the fire. He didn't know if he should hug her or strangle her. "Then I am going with you."

Mollie didn't trust Zack Kazmarek any further than she could throw him, but at this moment, he was a good man to have at her side. He looked angry enough to spit, but he said nothing as he grabbed her hand, took the lead, and began clearing a path for her. He was at least a foot taller than she and made better progress barreling through the dense traffic and abandoned wagons. A sharp pain in her shin from hitting a potbellied stove almost sent her to her knees, but Zack hauled her upright. Why had people been so foolish as to dump their belongings in the middle of the streets?

Every bell in the city must have been ringing. From the courthouse, the schools, and even the churches, every bell was clanging. Could anyone possibly still be asleep? Mollie reached for her father's watch. It was an hour past midnight, but it seemed every person in the city had flooded into the streets.

If she was this frightened, how terrified must Frank be? Would he even still be in his apartment? The southern skyline was ablaze with an unholy red glow, but the fire still seemed to be about a mile from her apartment. At the end of the street, a handful of firefighters battled the blaze, grasping hoses as jets of water arched toward the flames.

A bearded man carrying a typewriter jostled her forward,

driving her to her knees and causing her to scrape the palms of her hands on the gravel. Zack's strong hands encircled her arms and hauled her upright. "Take it easy," Zack bellowed at the man.

The street was chaos. A young boy clutched a struggling puppy, while his father balanced an oversized family portrait on his shoulder, unaware a spark had landed on the canvas and it was burning. Wagons piled with belongings snarled the forward momentum. Mollie clutched Zack's hand, terrified of getting separated from him.

It was getting hard to breathe, every lungful hot with smoke. Two men loitering outside by the broken window of a tavern took swigs from a bottle of whiskey. One man tossed the half-full bottle into the air, and the other took out a pistol and shot it, shooting a spray of whiskey over the crowd. "Whoo-hoo!" the shooter howled in delight. A drenched bystander lunged at the drunken shooter, landing a fist in his face and knocking him out cold.

These people were turning into animals. Mollie stared in horror. Was this what became of people confronted with losing everything?

Zack tugged her forward. "He did us all a favor," he said. "Drunken idiots firing into a crowd will make this stampede even worse, and we've got to hurry. The turpentine plant is about to blow."

He was right—it made no sense to get distracted by the drunken fools. She needed to rescue Frank, but traffic had slowed to a crawl. The intersection of the street was blocked by a fire engine angled at the base of a grand church. A crew of firefighters manned the engine, cranking the pistons and holding the canvas hoses to shoot streams of water in high arcs over the fire.

Lines of fatigue were carved onto the firemen's faces. These brave men were manning their engine while their own homes were probably burning, but here they stood, laboring in the scorching heat to save the city. "God bless you, sir," she said to the exhausted fireman holding a hose as the crowd pushed her forward.

For every drunken idiot, there were a dozen people who lifted a fallen woman to her feet or carried a child to safety. Men who sacrificed their own homes to keep the fire hoses functioning. She glanced up at Zack. There was a man who helped a woman reach the other side of town to rescue a blind attorney he barely knew. Had she been wrong about Zack?

The ground shook and a deafening boom sounded from behind. She fell to the ground, clasping her hands over her ears. The weight of Zack's body covered her back, protecting her from the catastrophe behind them.

Heaven help them all, the turpentine plant had just exploded. *Please, God, I'm sorry. I wish I had been a better person.*

Screams and shrieks filled the air, and a wave of blistering heat scorched her skin. The stench of burning chemicals seared her throat, and a wind so fierce it whipped her hair from its moorings pummeled them.

Please, God, don't let me to burn to death. She turned in Zack's arms, clasping him around his back and pressing her face against his chest. She didn't want to die alone.

Sparks showered down. Was a wall of fire coming next? She squeezed her eyes shut. If the flames were next, she didn't want to know.

She clung to Zack tighter. Was this man going to die because he'd tried to help her? "I'm sorry," she whispered against his neck.

"I'm sorry, too." His arms tightened as another massive roar filled the night air, a different noise than before. She glanced across the street just in time to witness the bell tower of the church collapse, the massive stones tumbling down, bringing the rest of the building down. Within seconds the grand church was a pile of bricks and shattered glass.

An eruption of limestone dust burst from the rubble of the church. Mollie buried her face in Zack's jacket to protect against the onslaught of chalky powder. It was hard to draw a proper breath. Zack hauled her upright and propelled her forward.

"Mollie, watch out!" he shouted. She followed his line of sight. A riderless horse was careening straight at her, cutting through the crowd of people packing the street. With people crowding her on all sides, there was nowhere to run. The whites of the horse's eyes rolled as he thrashed through the crowd. Mollie flinched away from its flailing hooves just as Zack's hands closed around her waist, hauling her out of the way a second before the horse barreled past.

"Thank you," she managed to gasp before her throat seized up in a fit of coughing.

"Come on," Zack commanded, grabbing her hand and pulling her forward. "We've got to get across the river before the bridge burns. We can make it, Mollie." He grinned down at her, his teeth flashing white against his soot-stained face.

The crowd grew even thicker near the Rush Street Bridge. Ahead of them, people yelled and started pushing the crowd back. It was impossible to hear what they were saying over the roar of wind and the clamoring bells, but as she got closer, Mollie saw the problem.

The bridge was on fire.

She pushed through the crowd. "We can still make a run for it."

The bridge was a hundred yards long, and orange flames licked at the wooden railings. Bits of the planking smoldered where cinders ignited the wood, but most of the bridge looked sound. A few people made a dash for it, and with the wall of fire behind them, Mollie intended to get across that bridge.

Zack's hand was like iron as he hauled her back. "That bridge isn't going to hold! I won't watch you kill yourself. We can make it to the bridge on Clark Street."

For the first time tonight, there was anger in his face. In all the years she had known the impeccable Zack Kazmarek, there had never been a hint of a pulse beneath his tailored suits and starched collar, but the way he was looking at her now, with desperation in his eyes, and grasping her arms as though he couldn't bear to let her go made her think . . .

She shoved the thought away. He looked mad enough to fling her into the river. "Why are you so angry at me?" she asked.

The question ratcheted him even closer to the boiling point. "Because for some insane reason, I adore you. For three solid years I have thought you were the closest thing to perfection on this earth, and I can't watch you risk your life crossing that bridge!"

Had she understood correctly? After all these years of cold decorum, Zack's eyes glittered in a face streaked with soot and sweat as he stepped closer, shouting over the roar of wind and fire. "I've been insane about you since the moment you waltzed into my office three years ago in that ridiculous suit and your hair as prim as a schoolmarm," he shouted. "Don't you *dare* get yourself killed on me now!"

Mollie was struck speechless. Heat blistered her skin and every breath of hot air scorched the inside of her lungs, but Zack Kazmarek *adored* her?

"I'm not going to get myself killed," she said, "but I am getting across that bridge." It was easier to run rather than continue this mortifying conversation. She turned and ran. Her boots clattered on the wooden planking, and she darted to avoid the spots where cinders ignited the parched wood. Zack's tread was heavy as he came bounding up behind her. The moment she reached the other side and her feet touched land, she sucked in a huge breath of air. She hadn't even realized she'd been holding her breath.

She doubled over, feeling lightheaded. Zack was by her side in an instant. "Can you get enough air?" he asked. He knelt down beside her, grasping both her hands in his. "Mollie, can you get air?"

She nodded, finally able to catch her breath again. She pushed herself upright, and Zack rose to his feet but didn't release her hands. He kept looking down at her with a combination of relief, hope, and something else she couldn't quite place.

"Why did you say you were sorry?" he asked. "Right after the turpentine plant blew and you grabbed on to me. You said you were sorry. What did you mean?"

She pulled her hands away. There was no point in denying the truth. Besides, it was easier to answer that question than to respond to his stunning declaration. "I said it because I'm sorry I dragged you into this mess! You would be safe at home with your parents if it weren't for me. I'm sorry for practically getting you killed."

His shoulders drooped a little, and there was no mistaking the wounded look on his face. It was almost as if she had struck him, but he masked it quickly by nodding and taking a fortifying breath. "All right, then," he muttered. "Let's keep moving."

5

The sun had risen by the time Mollie reached her apartment, only a tiny bit of daylight able to cut through the dense wall of smoke from the still-roaring fire. Mollie clambered up the staircase and ran down the hall.

Frank opened the door before she could even knock. She flung herself into his arms. "Thank God! I was afraid you wouldn't be here anymore."

He gave her a reassuring squeeze. "I was just about to head out on my own," he said. "From the sounds I heard outside the window all night, I knew I didn't have much chance in that stampede." He cocked his head. "Who is with you?"

Zack stepped forward into the apartment. "Zack Kazmarek. Mollie was at my townhouse when we learned of the fire."

Frank tipped his head back. If it was possible for a blind man to look down his nose at a person, Frank was doing it. "Ah. The college boy."

Zack held up his hands. "Please, don't rush to thank me. The building is about to burn down around you, so there's no time for gratitude."

"You can battle it out later," Mollie said as she fumbled with the lock of her apartment. If she hurried, there might be time to stuff a few belongings into a pillow sack.

"I've been listening at the window all night," Frank said as he followed her into her apartment. "About twenty minutes ago, I heard someone say the roof at the Waterworks has collapsed and the pumps have failed. There is no water left to battle the blaze. The firefighters have abandoned their engines and are evacuating the city."

Her last ray of hope died. The city had an inexhaustible supply of water from the lake, but if the pumps failed, there was no way to use it. Chicago was going to be destroyed.

She snapped into action. "I need to grab a few things before we leave," she said, rushing to her bedroom. With a tug she jerked her pillow from its case. What to take? Clothing. Shoes. Her hands shook as she stuffed blouses and undergarments into the bag. She snatched a green paisley scarf to protect her hair from falling cinders.

Nothing was more important than her father's photograph of the 57th. She raced into the main room, snatching the framed picture from the wall.

"You can't take that," Zack said. "It's too big."

By the flickering light of the fire, Mollie looked at the photograph. Taken the month before the final battle at Winston Cliff, the men looked stoic as they stared straight ahead at the camera. It showed Frank before he was blinded and Ulysses with both legs. In the front row was the famous Colonel Richard Lowe, one of the youngest colonels to ever serve in the army. Behind Colonel Lowe stood her father, the only man grinning in the portrait. This was how she would always remember Papa, trying to see the best in every hour of each day.

"I'm taking it," Mollie said. It fit awkwardly into the pillowcase. She had to yank out a skirt and a pair of boots, but they could be replaced. The large photograph made the pillowcase splay out. As she rearranged the fabric, Frank knelt down beside her.

"I've got the deed to the property on Columbus Street in my coat pocket," he whispered.

She turned to look at him. It would probably be worthless after tonight, but Frank was right. That piece of paper was the most valuable thing she owned. "Thanks, Frank," she whispered before pushing to her feet, awkwardly balancing the pillowcase on her shoulder.

"Ready?" Zack asked impatiently.

She nodded and reached out for Frank. She paused in the doorway, tempted to turn around for a final look at her apartment, but she couldn't do it. Her books . . . the sticky window with its charming view . . . She'd break down and bawl like a baby if she had to look at the home she was leaving for the final time.

"Let's go," she said.

The blaze was getting worse. Clinging to Frank, Mollie guided him as they navigated streets clogged with people hauling their belongings in carriages, wagons, and buggies. The thought of getting separated from Zack was terrifying. He carried her pillowcase while she clung to the hem of his coat as he pushed forward. Twice they had gotten separated, but the moment his coattails slipped free of her clutch, she shouted and he stopped for her.

Bits of flaming tar paper whirled through the air. One landed on the back of Zack's shoulder and the fabric started to smolder before Mollie swatted it away.

The two-mile diversion to rescue Frank had been costly. The

fire was gaining on them, and it was getting harder to breathe the hot, acrid air. Still pealing their warnings, church bells mingled with the sounds of people shouting and wagon drivers whipping panicked horses to push forward through the crowds.

Mollie spotted a little girl wearing a nightdress sobbing her heart out atop a half flight of stairs leading to a boardinghouse.

"Zack, wait!" Mollie shouted. He turned around and followed her gaze. He paused while Mollie darted up the flight of stairs to the blond girl. "Where are your parents, honey?"

"They're gone!" she sobbed. "I fell down, and by the time I got up I couldn't see them anymore!" Mollie could only imagine the terror the girl must be feeling. She couldn't be more than nine or ten years old. No wonder she had climbed up here to get out of the chaos on the street.

"How long ago did you get separated from them?"

"It seems like forever," she sobbed. "I've been looking for hours and now my feet hurt and I can't walk anymore, so I came up here."

Mollie's heart sank. If the girl had stayed in one spot, perhaps her parents might have found her, although, considering the crush of humanity packed onto the street, maybe not. Everyone was pushing north, and it would be hard to travel back the other way.

Zack guided Frank to the stone balustrade, then sprinted up the steps. "We need to move," he said in a low, urgent voice.

"This girl has lost her parents." Mollie had no idea what they were going to do. They couldn't abandon her, but they couldn't take her with them either. It was difficult enough guiding Frank.

Zack swatted away an ember that landed on his cheek. "I can carry her," he said. "We'll have to leave your pillowcase. I can't carry it and the girl."

Mollie's eyes drifted closed. Without that pillowcase, she'd lose the only photograph of her father. She'd have nothing but the clothes on her back, but she knew what she had to do. The lump in her throat made it too hard to speak, so she just nodded permission.

Zack tossed the pillowcase on the landing and knelt down for the girl to scramble onto his back. She still looked angry and frightened, but at least she was no longer sobbing. Zack scanned the scene before them and the ominous glow of fire to their left. So many of the alleys they had traveled down led to dead ends or were blocked by the rubble of collapsed buildings.

"I think our best chance is to head for the lake," Zack said. "Even if the whole city burns, we can wait it out in the water."

Mollie was so exhausted she didn't know what else to do. "All right," she said.

The girl's name was Sophie, and she was ten years old. When Zack was too tired to keep carrying her, Sophie wanted Frank to take over.

"I don't see why not," Frank said as he squatted down and Sophie scrambled onto his back. It took them all another half hour to navigate the streets cluttered with abandoned wagons and furniture before they reached the lake, arriving late in the afternoon.

Thousands of people were crowding the shore, some huddled in groups and others sitting or lying on the ground in exhaustion. Zack led them through the throngs of people until they made it to the edge of the lake. When Mollie turned around to see the city, she stared in slack-jawed amazement. The sky blazed in shades of red and orange with huge columns of black smoke billowing across it. Mollie repeatedly swiped at her clothing as

73

the hot embers settled on her dress and in her hair. And always, the fire kept creeping closer.

No one wanted to go into the lake. The fire heated the air, but it was October and the water was chilly. Mollie sank to the soft earth, the grass cool beneath her fingers and her muscles trembling with fatigue. What a motley collection they were. The fire was a great leveler. A woman in a silk gown with a triple strand of pearls around her neck sat beside a family of gypsies. Unlike on the street, where people had been trading rumors, everyone on the lakeshore was exhausted, watching the horizon in grim silence as eerie orange light flickered in their eyes.

One after another, the bells ceased ringing. The bell towers had either collapsed or the men ringing the bells could no longer afford to linger. In the absence of those clarion bells, all that could be heard was the deafening roar of the flames. If Mollie lived to be a hundred, she knew she'd never hear a more fearsome sound than that incessant roar.

Frank sat down beside her. "Are we going to need to go in the lake?" he whispered.

Mollie glanced around. The fire was now on three sides of them, the closest of which was about a half mile away. "I don't know."

"Then we've got a problem," he said quietly. "That deed won't survive a dunking. We've got to find a place to hide it. Somewhere the lawyer won't see."

It was hard to worry about the deed when all Mollie really cared about was getting a decent lungful of air. In weary exhaustion, she rested her forehead on her bent knees, beaten and spent. "I am not entitled to that store. I doubt it even exists anymore. I think most of the city is gone."

Frank reached out, fumbling until he grabbed her hand. "Those men tried to cheat you," he said in an angry whisper. "I owe your father more than I could ever repay, but the best I can do for him now is to make sure his daughter is taken care of. I won't stand by while someone swindles her. Mollie, we need to hide this deed somewhere safe. Now. Before that snake of a lawyer realizes we still have it."

Mollie looked around her. Burying the deed was impossible. Water would begin pooling after they scratched only a few feet into the sand.

"How long is your hair?" Frank whispered.

She grinned. When her hair was liberated from the twist coiled atop her head, it fell to her waist. Surely, even if they needed to escape the flames in the lake, she would not need to submerge her head.

"Pass me the deed," Mollie whispered. She would need to get away from Zack to unwind her hair and roll the deed inside. "Come along, Sophie. Let's go for a stroll. Maybe you'll see a familiar face in the crowd."

Zack turned to look at her in disbelief. "You can't be serious."

"We will just walk along the shore," she told Sophie, then tugged the girl to her feet.

Zack rolled his eyes but still didn't move. "Suit yourself," he mumbled, turning his attention to the ominous line of fire coming closer.

"Come along quickly," she urged Sophie. She ought to feel horrible about instilling hope in this child, but she needed an excuse to get away from Zack.

They hadn't even traveled a hundred feet when Sophie turned sullen. "I'm tired. I want something to eat."

So did Mollie. She didn't know what time it was, but they had walked through the night, all morning, and well into the afternoon. It had been a full day since she had had anything to eat, but she ignored the pangs of hunger as she knelt in the sand. Yanking the scarf from her head, she unwound her long swath of hair. With half a dozen hairpins held in her mouth, she rolled the deed into her hair and pinned it into place.

Sophie got in front of her face and stamped her foot. "I said I want something to eat. Now!"

Mollie had never been spoken to in that tone of voice in her entire life, and now this ungrateful little child was glaring at her like a miniature queen from a dark fairy tale. Mollie shoved the remaining pin into her hair, rose to her feet, and pointed to the lake. "Then dive in and catch us a fish. Otherwise, follow me back to Frank and Zack."

Sophie plopped to the ground like a rag doll, her heavy boots sticking out from beneath her lacy white nightgown. "This place is good enough. I'm tired of walking and won't do it anymore."

Mollie draped the scarf around her head and turned to walk away.

"Where are you going?" Sophie shot to her feet. "Don't you dare leave me here!"

"Sophie, you can follow me back to the others or you can wait it out here on your own. I will not argue with you."

She hadn't even finished speaking before Sophie scooted forward. "I don't like you people very much," she said as she came alongside Mollie.

Mollie swiped a tendril of hair out of her eyes. The deed was safe, and she was determined to live another day, if for nothing else than to beat the Hartmans in court. "And here I think of you as an endless fount of delight and good cheer," she said amiably.

"Huh?"

Mollie reached out for Sophie's hand. "Never mind. Let's go find the others."

~

It was dark by the time she arrived back at the lake, where Frank and Zack had once again reverted to bickering with each other. This time they were arguing about the tides on Lake Michigan.

"We need to pull back from the bank," Frank said. "High tide will be setting in soon, and that water is bound to be ice cold."

"Are you telling me you think there are tides on Lake Michigan? *Lake Michigan?*" Zack's voice dripped with incredulity, and given his background as a longshoreman, Mollie was inclined to side with Zack on a matter of lake tides.

"Tides are caused by the moon's pull on a large body of water," Frank said. "I'm surprised they didn't teach you that in college."

"Your scarf is burning!" Sophie said.

A cinder had landed on the trailing edge of Mollie's scarf, a rim of orange beginning to spread. Mollie whipped the scarf off and rolled it against the ground until the flame was snuffed out. Then she replaced the scarf. Better for the scarf to catch fire than her hair.

She met Zack's gaze. The cinders were floating through the air like large flakes of snow, impossible to avoid. The heat blowing from the south was scorching, and the fire had reached the stretch of trees bordering the lake. No one wanted to go into the water, but it was time.

Suction pulled at her boots as she plodded into the mud along the bank. It took a moment for the frigid water to penetrate her boots, and she tried not to wince. She pushed forward, water weighing down the hem of her skirts, chilling her ankles, her calves, then rushing around her thighs. It was freezing!

The next hours would always be a blur in Mollie's memory. The water was too cold to stand in for any length of time. Teeth chattering, standing in the water up to her waist, she watched her city burn. A solid wall of angry red flame towering into the night sky. By this time tomorrow, the prettiest waterfront in America would be a burned-over wasteland. When the cold became intolerable, she trudged back onto the banks, her sodden clothing keeping her safe from the falling embers for a short while.

As the hours passed, the fire continued its journey north. Weary and exhausted, Mollie pulled herself up to the bank a final time. She was filthy, bruised, and exhausted. Lying down on the ashy dirt, she slept.

6

Someone was shaking her shoulder. "Mollie, it is raining."
There was so much grit under her lids it was hard to open
her eyes. What had happened to her? Every muscle screamed
with pain as she rolled over. "Frank?"

He looked awful, with a soot-stained face and bloodshot
eyes, but he was smiling. "Mollie, it is raining," he repeated.

She looked up, cool water spattering her face. She blinked,
not sure if it was tears or rainwater that filled her eyes. Both,
probably. All around the shore, people were rousing from their
stupor, and Zack came to stand beside her. "It will all be over
soon," he said quietly.

Mollie nodded. She ought to feel relief that it was raining,
but it had come too late for her. She had nothing left and nowhere to go.

As if sensing her despair, Frank draped an arm around her
shoulder and gave her a little squeeze. "We will remember this
moment for the rest of our lives," he said. "What time is it?"

Mollie reached through the sodden fabric of her skirts to
fumble for her father's watch. As always, she pressed her thumb
into the dent on its cover before flipping it open.

It had stopped ticking. She had forgotten the watch was in

her pocket when she went into the lake, and it could not survive the dunking. At 8:24 on the evening of Monday, October 9, 1871, her father's magnificent watch had finally stopped working. This time when Mollie's eyes filled, there was no doubt it was tears blurring her vision. This watch that had saved her father's life kept ticking through three years of war, but could not survive being submerged in the lake during the great, terrible Chicago fire.

"What time is it?" Frank asked again.

She closed the cover, clutching the cool metal disk in her hand and instinctively pressing her thumb into the dent. "I don't know."

"It is a little after midnight on Tuesday morning," Zack said. "We need to find shelter."

Mollie nodded, but where could they go? Thousands of people were huddled on the shore, all stranded in the rain, all homeless. The fire was now far to the north, and it was cold. There would be no intact roof for miles, but even a wall would be good for taking shelter against this wind.

"We should head back into the city," Zack said. "Some buildings may still be standing. In any event, the shore is going to be pure mud soon."

They roused Sophie, who had managed to remain in a deep slumber despite the steady rain. She pushed Zack away. "Don't want to go," she mumbled.

Zack hauled her upright. "I'm willing to carry you piggyback or you can walk. But I'm not leaving you here in the mud. Now, which is it to be?"

Sitting in the muck and covered in a layer of ashen filth, Sophie's mutinous glare was imperious. "You can carry me," she said.

Zack squatted down. "And won't that be a treat for me."

Mollie clutched Frank's arm as they began heading back into town. Unlike the stampede earlier, the streets were nearly deserted as they left the lake. The farther they moved into the downtown area, the harder it was to endure. Her breath was shaky with sobs that would not come.

"Don't cry," Frank said.

If Frank could see what was all around them, he would be weeping too. Was it possible this was Chicago? There was nothing left. Nothing. Just heaps of smoldering rubble and tumbled-down walls. Not a single building remained standing as far as she could see. Not a tree or a blade of grass. The city she loved was gone. Miles and miles had been reduced to worthless wreckage.

Zack pointed farther west. "The damage doesn't look so bad over there."

Mollie squinted to peer through the darkness. In the diminishing light of the fire, she could barely see some crumbling walls in the distance. Her boots were wet, and each footstep brought shafts of pain from raw blisters. Zack didn't complain, but given the way he was limping, he was suffering as well. That horrible little girl still clung to his back, and she must weigh plenty.

They kept walking toward the structures ahead of them. Mollie wasn't certain how far they'd walked, but it was at least a couple of miles. "I think that is the Livingston Street Church," she said.

The windows had been blown out, but the walls were still standing. The roof was gone, so the church was open to the elements, but something about the building called to her. The openings of the Gothic windows still maintained their shape, and it reminded her of the drawings she had seen of the ruined cathedrals of Europe. As they drew closer to Livingston Street, other structures appeared to have survived as well. None of them had roofs or window glass, but at least the walls would provide some protection against the rain that was now falling sideways.

She blinked rainwater from her eyelashes as she glanced up at Zack. "I don't think we can go much farther," she said. "If it is safe inside the church, we should rest there."

Zack nodded. Noises from inside the church told Mollie that others had also fled there for shelter. It was too dim to see much as she guided Frank inside. People were huddled along the interior walls, trying to keep clear of the rain. Zack groaned as he knelt down and peeled Sophie from his back. He collapsed onto the ground and leaned back, his lungs still breathing heavily. There were snores coming from others in the church, and someone with an Irish accent was murmuring the rosary. In a corner, a woman was weeping inconsolably.

Using her foot, Mollie pushed some of the fallen timbers aside. "Here is a spot for you to lie down," she whispered to Sophie. The little girl looked dubiously at the spot, but must have been too tired to complain as she grimaced and cautiously lay down on the ground. Mollie was about to clear a spot for Frank when Sophie found her voice.

"It's always clean where I sleep at home," the little girl whispered.

Mollie decided not to comment, but kept pushing fragments of boards and glass aside. It was always clean where she slept too, but that was in the past. It was hard to believe anything would ever be clean again.

She guided Frank to the cleared space. "If you lie straight back, it is clear of rubble," she whispered.

"Thank you, Mollie-girl," he said as he lay down. "Thank you for everything. Your dad would be proud of you, lass."

Her lip started to tremble, and she turned away. If her breathing became ragged again, Frank would hear and know she was crying.

Despite her exhaustion, Mollie was too tense to lie down to sleep. Her business was gone. Her home was lost. She had nothing but a scorched dress and a pocket watch that didn't work.

And a deed.

Mollie reached up to unwind the heavy coil anchored to the back of her head, letting the scrap of paper fall out. It was a little rumpled, but the deed was in perfect shape. Aching with weariness, she tucked it inside her bodice.

She wished that sniveling woman in the corner would quit crying. Weren't they all miserable enough without having to listen to that? Normally at a time like this she would pray, but the spirit was not with her. Why would God rob her of everything? Mollie closed her eyes and turned away, tears trickling down her face. Now she was no better than the woman in the corner.

A noise outside caught her attention. Was someone shouting out there? The voice came from far away, but it was definitely the sound of a man shouting in the distance.

If there was some new calamity on the horizon, Mollie didn't want to know. But . . . was the man laughing?

She pushed herself to her feet and walked to the opening of a window. Bracing her hands on the grainy ledge, she cocked an ear to hear.

"Don't despair!" the distant voice called out. "The sun is going to rise tomorrow and shine on this city." The wind carried his voice away, and Mollie could only hear fragments of what he was calling out with such vigor. Rain spattered her face as she leaned out the opening of the window, desperate to hear more.

"We will rebuild! A new start!"

Mollie sucked in a breath of air. Was it possible someone could have such energy on a night like tonight? The man was getting closer and easier to hear. Zack came to stand behind her, and the reassuring weight of his hands settled on her shoulders. Frank sat up to listen as well.

"I've got nothing left," the strange man yelled into the wind. "I have lost everything but my wife and my two hands and my hope," he shouted. "God gives every one of us hope, brothers. Tonight we sleep, tomorrow we rebuild. This is Chicago! Do you hear me, brothers? *This is Chicago!*"

"Amen!" a woman called from somewhere across the street.

"Amen to *you*, sister," the man responded as he kept walking down the street, getting closer to the church. "We are a city of broad shoulders and strong backs. We are alive, and God is good. Mark my words—in one year this city will be bigger and stronger than before. Don't despair!"

Mollie squinted as she tried to see the man as he strode past the church. The light of the fire was fading and he was just a shadowy, faceless figure striding through the street, like a town crier from days of old. He brought a beam of light slicing through the darkness. Others in the church stood to listen as well.

"God has given the soul of man wings," the town crier said. "We will use those wings to carry us into daylight. The clouds are lifting. *The clouds are lifting*, brother, and tomorrow sunlight will break through."

The man walked farther down the street, calling out words of comfort to the thousands of people huddled behind walls and beneath blankets. Mollie clutched at the opening of the window, wishing he would return. "Keep talking, brother," a man called out from somewhere across the street. Mollie strained to hear the town crier as he continued calling out into the ruined landscape.

"Our city will rise again!" he shouted. "Out of tragedy we will build something great. Don't despair, Chicago. Don't despair!"

The woman in the corner had stopped weeping. Zack leaned

over to whisper in her ear. "It's true, Mollie," he said. "Everything that man said is true. Tomorrow we begin rebuilding. Playing music. Dancing. I promise you."

She leaned against him, drawing on his strength and thanking God for sending that strange messenger out onto the streets. She had been wrong to despair, and already her strength was beginning to rally. She wanted to say something, but her throat was too clogged with emotion to speak. She didn't know if she was about to laugh or cry, but she knew one thing to the marrow of her bones.

This fire would not be the end of her.

7

Zack dreaded waking Mollie up. Morning light illuminated the filthy, dilapidated chaos inside the church. None of the pews or stained glass windows had survived. Mounds of slate and rock from the collapsed roof were strewn across the ground. Exhausted refugees slept propped against the walls of the church, their soot-stained faces slack with exhaustion. Everyone here was homeless. Mollie didn't even have the paltry belongings she'd stuffed into the pillowcase, only the clothes on her back and a scorched green scarf balled up beneath her sleeping head. He hoped her dreams were peaceful, for in a few moments she would awaken to the catastrophe that had befallen her.

Could he persuade her to return home with him? Rumor had it that everything west of the river was untouched by the fire, which meant his townhouse had survived. He wanted to extend the protection of his home to Mollie. Never had he seen a woman as brave as she had been for the last thirty-six hours, and it confirmed what he had believed about her all along. She was worth fighting for, and he wanted her to be a part of his life.

With each step, gravel and cinders crunched beneath his boots as he moved to Mollie's side and hunkered down beside her. He gently shook her shoulder. "Mollie, it is morning," he whispered. He braced himself to see her peaceful face cloud over with despair, but she surprised him. Pushing herself up on an elbow, Mollie winced through aching muscles and scanned the wreckage in the church.

"What a mess," she said. "Such a lot of unsavory debris."

Relief trickled through him. She couldn't be too devastated if she had the strength to summon up a sense of humor. "I need to get home and check on my parents. They are probably tearing their hair out by now."

"I understand." She rolled into a sitting position and moaned. The lawyer, Frank, had awoken and was gingerly moving to sit up.

"Take it easy, Frank," Mollie warned. "It's a mess in here, so don't try to move around until I can clear some space."

Others were rousing in the church as well, and it would only be a matter of time before Princess Sophie would awaken and start issuing orders. Zack needed to talk to Mollie, and he didn't want an audience.

"Let's go outside," he said, grasping her elbow and helping her rise. "We've got a few things to discuss before I leave."

It was tricky navigating toward the street. Each footstep brought a smoky stench from the rubble crunching beneath his feet. The uneven ground made him balance each step, but at last they made it to the street. *Can this really be Chicago?* By daylight, the city looked even worse than the previous night. A few skeletal walls of buildings dotted the destroyed landscape. The rubble was covered in a layer of ash and soot, casting the world into ghostly shades of gray. Even the sky was a dull, leaden gray.

"Listen, Mollie, I need to get home and let my parents know I'm alive. Then I am coming back for you. If my home is still standing, I'll provide a place for you and Frank as long as you need."

"Why would you do that?" She looked a little taken aback, which surprised him.

Because he loved her. Because they had just experienced the worst two days imaginable, and the bond that had been forged between them was not something to be tossed away. If Louis Hartman didn't like it, he would quit. The fire had just taught Zack what was most important in this world, and she was looking straight at him.

"Look around you," he said. "Half the city is homeless, and you will need a place to stay."

She pulled a few inches away, drawing her green scarf tighter around her shoulders. "The other night," she began hesitantly.

"Yes?" he said softly. The other night he had flung caution to the wind and shouted his true feelings for her. He ought to be embarrassed, but he wasn't. In those few moments after the turpentine plant had blown, she had clung to him when they thought they were about to die. They had established their first tentative steps toward building a foundation for their future. The breeze coming in from the east ruffled her hair, and he had to restrain himself from stroking it away from her face.

"The other night I went to your house about a deed to a piece of land on Columbus Street."

His face hardened. "Not that again."

"Yes, that again."

Frustration rippled through him. He dragged a hand through his rumpled hair and scanned the horizon. "I don't want to talk about this. We've both got more important things to worry about."

"I know what I saw," she insisted. "I read the document word for word to Frank, and he says it is a legitimate deed. He said a properly executed deed would have been filed at the courthouse the moment the deal had closed, not sitting in a trunk at the foot of my father's bed."

Zack took a moment to choose his words. He needed to handle this carefully. "Mollie, we both saw the courthouse burn to the ground, and there are no more city records to prove who owns what. Your apartment is gone. There is no way we can ever prove what you had because every record of the transaction no longer exists."

"I still have it."

His eyes widened, and he paused. "What?"

"I still have the deed. It was rolled into my hair when we went into the lake last night. I've still got it."

That certainly changed things. He didn't move a muscle and kept the expression on his face carefully neutral. "Can I see it?"

Mollie angled her body away from his view as she dug inside her bodice. After tugging the document free, she held it before her, the early morning light illuminating the engraved blue ink and embossed stamps. Her father's signature was clearly on the bottom line. Zack reached out to take it.

"No!" She yanked it away, curling protectively around it.

He felt like she had slapped him. "What do you think I am going to do, snatch it and throw it in the lake?" he demanded in an angry voice. She took a step back, and he followed. "Do you?"

"Shhhh!" she said in a fierce whisper. "People are still sleeping!"

He stepped closer, his face inches from hers. "And I am dying here because a woman I have hankered after for years just kicked me in the teeth. *Again.*"

Mollie blanched. "Why do you keep talking like that? We barely know each other!"

He was mad enough to spit fire. "I couldn't court a woman who did business with Hartman's," he ground out. "That was the quickest route for me to get canned, but after the fire, I don't care anymore about rules. You are a woman I want in my life, but my hand to God, if you keep accusing me of trying to swindle you, I am liable to combust."

Her eyes narrowed in distrust, and he was smart enough to know that blasted scrap of paper was going to be a wedge between them forever unless he could figure a way to dispose of it.

He settled his hands on her shoulders. "Mollie, you have a piece of paper. In the coming years, the court system in this city is going to be swamped with a legal quagmire the likes of which this country has never seen before. With the archives of the courthouse in ashes, there is no way to prove the legitimacy of that deed."

"No way to *disprove* it either."

"Exactly." He turned her around and cupped the side of her face. He tried using a gentle pressure to nudge her face up to look at him, but she resisted. "Mollie, I have cared about you for years. I have made a great study of Mollie Knox and the way she runs her business, but you know nothing about me. I suppose it is not fair for me to expect you to trust me when I've never been more than the man signing off on your quarterly revenue statements. Come live at my house. Bring Frank. Heaven help me, you can even bring Sophie, but come. I can't stand the thought of you shivering in that church. No matter what it takes, I intend to earn your trust, and after that, you'd better put an armed guard around your heart, because I plan on winning you and folding you into my life. Fair warning, woman."

Mollie squinted at something over his shoulder, and Zack

realized she had not been paying attention to a single word he'd said. "I wonder what that boy is doing," she said.

A block away, a boy with a stack of papers was walking down the street, handing out a piece of paper to the few people who were picking through the rubble. A newsboy? Mollie was already heading toward him, and Zack had no choice but to follow.

The newsboy saw Mollie and met her halfway. "Fresh news, no charge," he said, as he pressed a single sheet of paper into Mollie's hands. The *Chicago Tribune* banner graced the top of the single sheet of paper.

Mollie looked at the boy in amazement. "I saw your building go up in flames with my own eyes," she said. "How can you be back in business so quickly?"

The boy grinned. "We found a building on Canal Street with a printing press ready for use. It will be a while before we can get a full issue out, but our equipment can produce newssheets. If you have anything that needs reporting, we are at Number 15 Canal Street."

"Do you know if the fire jumped to the west of the river?" Zack asked, holding his breath.

"It did not," he said. "We've got people out mapping the damage and will make a better report in tomorrow's paper." Then the boy's good humor sank. "The fire got the Union Baseball Grounds. No more White Stockings for a while."

Zack winced. Somehow losing the baseball stadium added insult to profound injury. The White Stockings meant a lot to this city. Last night as he was trying to sleep, he had toyed with the idea of sponsoring free baseball games to bring a tiny glimmer of enjoyment to the people. It couldn't happen without a stadium.

The newsboy strode on, and Mollie scrutinized the paper. "Look here," she said excitedly. "They have a column announcing the names of people who have been reported lost. I wonder if Sophie's name is here."

Zack scanned the page. Sure enough, two columns of names had been printed: one of people who were missing, and the other of children who had been found and where they could be located. Sophie's name was not on the list, but doubtless that list was going to swell into the hundreds, perhaps thousands, within the next day or two.

"I'll need to report Sophie," Mollie said, "but Canal Street is so far, and I need to find food and water first."

"Mollie, come home with me now," he said. "The fire didn't jump the river, and that means I've got a home with plenty of food and fresh water. Come home with me."

But Mollie still stared at the newssheet as though it were Scripture handed down from on high. "Look at this! It says here that the Judson Furniture Factory has been burned out, but they are setting up at a warehouse on Wentworth Avenue, and employees may report to work on Wednesday morning, 9 a.m." She clasped the sheet of paper to her chest and looked out at the distance, the weak light of the morning shining in her face. "Just think!" she said on a trembling breath. "If the train with my equipment made it out of the city on time, there is no reason I can't swing right back into action, too. The Judson family will be making furniture again at this time tomorrow morning. *This time tomorrow morning* that company is going to be making furniture! Can you believe it?"

Zack didn't know if she was the bravest or most foolish woman in all of Chicago. In the wake of the fire, demand for furniture would be fierce, but for pricey diamond-encrusted pocket watches? Still, he would be a monster if he said anything to dim the hope blooming on Mollie's face. Her smile was a gleaming flash of white in her soot-stained face. She had just been clobbered with a cataclysmic tragedy, and rather than whining about what she had lost, her practical little brain was already working double time to repair the damage.

She was magnificent. She could literally walk through fire and emerge stronger than before. He cupped Mollie's face between his palms and tilted it to look up at him. Her face was dirty and her eyes red from grit—and Zack knew he looked no better—but she was precious to him and he wanted her to know that.

"Mollie, I'm coming back for you. Don't leave the church. I need to be able to find you again."

She dropped her gaze but made no move to shrug away from his hands as he held her face. "The satchels with your parents' papers," she said. "Don't worry. I'll be sure they get them back."

"That's not what I'm talking about, and you know it," he said. "I'll be coming back because I meant what I said last night. About my . . . inconvenient feelings for you. They haven't gone away." Such familiarity on a public street in the middle of the morning was shocking, but none of the rules applied anymore. He leaned over and kissed her mouth, holding her face between his palms. She made no move to push him away, and he kissed each of her cheeks, then pressed a kiss to her forehead. "You taste like soot, woman."

She laughed, and he impulsively swept her up into a bear hug. To his amazement, she returned his embrace, wrapping her arms around the top of his back. She felt custom-made to fit perfectly against him. They were alive, and they were going to survive, and someday soon they would thrive again. With Hartman's a smoking rubble, Zack was probably out of a job, but he still had his brain and a strong back. If nothing else, there would be plenty of manual labor needing to be done in the coming months.

"We're going to be okay, Mollie," he whispered in her ear.

Her arms tightened around him, and he didn't want this moment to end. "I'm coming back for you."

And within his embrace, he felt her nod in agreement. They had just been through the worst two days imaginable, but Zack's heart soared.

8

The next few days would be etched in Mollie's memory as a curious blend of exhaustion and euphoria. Upon returning to the church, she met Sandra Rutter, the woman who had been crying in the darkness the previous evening. Waddling through the rubble with her hand protecting her protruding belly, it was obvious Sandra had good cause to be terrified. "I am about a week overdue," she told Mollie. "This is my first baby, and I've been a little tense, even before the fire."

At least Sandra had somewhere to go. Her husband had already set off to see if he could find a way to get to Lexington, where Sandra had family.

The city distributed a few supplies for clearing rubble, and Mollie used a shovel to clear away broken glass and the charred remnants of the church pews, shoveling until blisters were worn into the palms of her hands. Clearing the church had been an instinctive reaction. All signs indicated that she was going to be homeless for a good long while, and the church was as good a place as any to seek shelter. When Mollie was too exhausted to heft another load, she sat beside Frank and read him every line of the newssheet. Sophie leaned against her, disappointed her name was not among the children listed as missing. "Perhaps your parents didn't know newspapers were publishing the names of lost children," Mollie said. "We'll keep checking every issue."

One of the other refugees in the church was Andrew Buchanan, a dentist with the widest handlebar mustache Mollie had ever seen. The dentist found a broom and swept a portion of the nave clear before setting out his dental equipment. He propped a sign outside the church offering dental services. "People still need work on a bad tooth, even after a fire," he said.

When no one showed up for Dr. Buchanan's dental services, he cheerfully joined them in lugging boulders into the piles that were forming on the street. As the afternoon wore on, the fifteen people working inside the church had cleared the worst of the rubble away. They divided the area up into living spaces, with Dr. Buchanan taking the east side of the nave and Sandra Rutter asking for a spot beside Mollie and Frank. "Just until my husband returns with train tickets to Lexington," she said as she gingerly lowered herself to the ground.

Ralph Coulter was a lumber dealer who'd managed to watch his only ship sail safely out of port while the fire raged, although he had been unable to rescue his storage facility. He asked for a spot near the front of the church. "I can put a sign out and take orders from there. People will be in need of lumber," he said.

Throughout the work, a curious sense of exhilaration filled Mollie. Never had she made friends as quickly as she did with the other refugees while they cleared the church. Her back ached, the blisters on her feet were getting worse, and it was hard to ignore the hunger pangs, but everyone was determined to get this church cleared and remain in good spirits while they did it. Perhaps tomorrow they would start enumerating their losses, but for today, it felt right to laugh as they made the open-air church into a makeshift home.

Sometime during the afternoon, a wagon laden with bread

and apples lumbered down the street. Mollie set the shovel down and gestured to Sophie. "Come on. Let's get in line for something to eat. You can help me carry things back."

"You go get it," Sophie said. "I'm too tired to go." The little girl remained perched atop a mound of rocks that had been piled against the wall of the church.

"Then I'm sure you'll be too tired to eat what I bring back," Mollie snapped. She had no experience with children, but surely this child was extraordinary in her insolence.

The dentist was far more even-tempered. He twisted the curl of his handlebar mustache with a broad smile on his face. "Not to worry, little Miss Sophie," he said amiably. "We'll turn your portion over to Mrs. Rutter for the baby to eat."

The outrage clouding Sophie's face was comical. "That baby can't eat yet! It's still in Mrs. Rutter's tummy and doesn't deserve to eat anything." Her tirade bounced off the walls of the church, causing everyone's head to swivel in her direction. Mollie took a step toward the girl.

"Everyone in this church has been working for hours except you," she said. "Even Frank has helped, and he is blind. The men have all been doing hard manual labor while you've braided your hair a dozen times. Now, hop down and help me carry the food back to the church."

Sophie's lower lip jutted in mutiny as she scrambled down to follow Mollie. There was a huge cluster of people gathering around the wagon, but it was amazing how orderly people were as they awaited their turn.

A big, brassy red-headed woman in the bed of the wagon handed out the food. She had a hearty smile and radiated energy as she handed over sack after sack of apples and bread to the weary, soot-stained refugees.

"You look too clean to have been in the fire," Sophie told her.

The woman smiled. "Clever girl," she said. "I am from Milwaukee." Mollie's brows shot up in amazement, but the woman had not quit speaking. "I came with my husband, who is a Milwaukee firefighter. On Sunday night, the mayor of Chicago sent telegrams to all the surrounding cities, asking for help. We loaded our fire engines on a train and got here Monday night. The fire was still burning, but there was nothing we could do without the water pumps working. At least we can help pass out food today."

A lump filled Mollie's throat as she accepted a bag of apples. "Thank you for coming from so far away. It means a lot to us."

"Fire crews came from Indianapolis and St. Louis too," the redheaded woman said. "People from all over the country are sending help. Don't you fret, ma'am. This city will be back up on her feet in no time."

Returning to the church, Mollie sat with Frank and Sophie on the front steps to devour the apples and some of the bread. From here she could see dozens of people scrambling through the streets. Already piles of tumbled-down bricks and granite block were being mounded up in order to clear the streets. Rumor had it the city was going to send in wagons to collect the rubble and dump it into Lake Michigan. For years there had been talk of filling in a portion of the harbor, and it looked like that rubble would be put to good use.

"It makes sense," Frank said. "I only wish I could do more to help."

Mollie swallowed. For a man of Frank's pride, the previous day of being led about by the hand had been a bitter pill. Even now, there was little Frank could do other than try to stay out of the way as the debris was cleared. No matter how brilliant his mind, the only skill that was desperately needed right now was a strong back and a pair of hands that could hoist away rubble.

"I expect there will be plenty of legal work soon," Mollie said. "Everyone in the city will need to file insurance claims, but how can they even prove that they had a policy? Or document what they have lost?"

Frank straightened a bit. Even though his pale gray eyes were useless, Mollie could see every flicker of emotion as he weighed the problem. "Good point, Mollie-girl. I expect a bunch of insurance companies will go under because of this. And lining up to make a claim against a bankrupt insurance company is something that will require the expertise of an attorney."

Mollie's mouth went dry. Her building and equipment were fully insured with the Old Chicago Insurance Company, but that company did business with hundreds of companies in Chicago. If everyone filed a claim at once, it would bankrupt her insurance company. She tried to keep the despair from her voice. "Yes, I expect there will be plenty of legal work soon."

"What did I hear about that dentist putting a sign outside the church advertising his services? Perhaps I should do the same."

"I can find out where he got the paint and make a sign for you."

When Frank smiled, it transformed his entire face. "Free legal advice," he said. "It is important that everyone knows it is free. I wouldn't feel right taking money when I'll be living off charity for the next few weeks." He took a large bite of his apple and had a hard time chewing because he was smiling so broadly. Within the space of sixty seconds, the prospect of having something useful to do had transformed Frank from a broken cripple into a man with a mission.

There was a commotion from behind them as Andrew Buchanan came bursting out of the church, his face pale beneath the soot. "Come quickly, Mollie! Mrs. Rutter's water has broken."

The dentist looked terrified as he wrung his hands, and

Mollie realized with sickening clarity that she was the only other adult woman taking shelter in the church. She swallowed hard and shot to her feet. "Sophie, help Frank get back inside," she said as she hurried to follow Dr. Buchanan. The light was starting to dwindle inside the walls of the church, but Sandra Rutter was sitting on the steps of the chancel, her face white with fear.

Mollie rushed to her side, placing her arm around Sandra's back. The woman was trembling like a frightened mouse. "Is it true?" Mollie whispered. "Your water has broken?"

Sandra was so tense she was barely able to nod. Her husband had not yet returned from his quest to find train tickets out of town. Not that Mrs. Rutter could travel at this point. This baby was going to be delivered in a burned-out church, and there was no help for it. The dentist hovered nearby, and Mollie glanced over to where he had laid his dental equipment on a clean towel. "I think you probably have the most medical training of anyone here," she said.

"I've never delivered a baby! Until eighteen months ago, I made pillows for a living!"

"Where did you get your dental degree?" Mollie asked.

"The Ohio College of Dental Surgery," he said weakly.

Mollie walked over to the area where the dentist had laid out his equipment in preparation for his nonexistent customers. She picked up a towel and a bar of soap and slapped them into his hand.

"Make them proud," she said firmly.

Word spread quickly to the people in nearby buildings about Mrs. Rutter's condition. They brought over pots of water, clean toweling, and a kerosene lantern. Mollie had been praying for the emergence of a physician, but Andrew Buchanan, dentist and pillow maker, was the best they could do.

And Mrs. Rutter was terrified. "I can't believe this is happening," she wept. "I'm going to die in the dirt with my baby." Nothing Mollie said consoled the woman, but this sort of fear was dangerous. Mrs. Rutter was surrendering to the waves of despair that engulfed her and the pain that was tearing her in two.

Her husband appeared just as the sun was going down, proudly holding aloft two tickets to Lexington. "We can leave first thing in the morning!" he proclaimed as he burst into the church. Sandra, her face bathed with perspiration in the cool autumn evening, turned her head toward her husband with all the anguish in the world in her eyes. "Too late, my darling man," she said before dissolving into tears.

Mr. Rutter's face went white. "I see," he said softly.

He knelt beside his wife, taking the cloth from Mollie's hand. "We can do this," he murmured softly. "I don't know why these tragedies have befallen us so quickly, but the Lord has not abandoned us, and He will see us through this night." As he stroked his wife's brow with the damp cloth, the tension eased from her face.

Everyone in the church stayed awake as Mrs. Rutter labored through the night. She lay propped against her husband's chest as he rocked her gently, hour after hour. "The Lord is beside us tonight," he said. He pressed his cheek against his wife's hair and murmured the words softly. "Can you feel him, Sandra? He is walking alongside you and bathing you and our baby with the light of His love. Undying, unending love. "

Within the circle of the kerosene lantern, it seemed such an intimate thing to witness, but there was no room for privacy or embarrassment. Mollie was mesmerized. Such an abundance of loving care Mr. Rutter showered onto his wife.

It made her wish Zack were there. How strange that ever since his bold declaration of his feelings, she could not stop thinking about him. The crisis of the fire had forged them together in a common mission, but the longing she felt for him was based on more than that. For the first time she was able to see him as a man. A bold, confident man who was protective of those within his care. He was loving toward his parents and had accompanied her into a literal firestorm. He had been very decent to Sophie, even though the girl was a holy terror. The fire burned away the trappings and revealed the true character of a man, and her instincts told her that Zack Kazmarek was a good one. In proper time, they would untangle the mess the deed had caused, but for now she desperately craved his comfort. His humor and his strength. Watching the way Mr. Rutter tended his wife made her miss Zack even more.

Poor Andrew Buchanan looked as white and limp as a sheet of wet paper, but he stood bravely ready to assist as Mrs. Rutter's time drew near. Three hours past midnight, the squalling cries of a baby boy broke the stillness of the night.

"Hello, baby Joshua," Sandra said on a shaky breath as the dentist placed the infant in her arms. In the coming hours, everyone in the church stepped forward to admire the red-faced baby. People taking shelter in nearby buildings had been listening as well and came to offer their best wishes upon hearing the cries of the infant.

Mollie rejoined Frank where he leaned against the side of the wall. A wistful smile hovered on his face. "That was the most amazing thing I have ever witnessed," he said simply.

Mollie nodded. "Me too."

9

Mollie would never forget the joy that surged through her when Zack Kazmarek came striding through the ruined streets toward the church. He had come back!

It had been three days since he had left on that cold morning outside the church, and she wondered if his impassioned words were motivated only by the overheated emotions the crisis had aroused. But here he was, carrying a sack of food and wearing a grin that made her weak in the knees. With his rugged work clothes and chipped-tooth grin, he was the handsomest man in the world. His enthusiastic bear hug ought to have cracked her ribs but only made her laugh instead.

Within an hour they were arguing like two cats in a gunnysack.

"I can't believe you are trying to get that watch company back in operation before you have a decent place to sleep," he growled as he helped her set up a tent inside the nave of the church.

The city had distributed the army surplus tents to the homeless, and they were springing up like mushrooms throughout the burned district. Five tents had been allotted to the refugees taking shelter in the church. They were setting them up within the church walls to take advantage of the protection from the wind.

Mollie unfolded the scratchy wool fabric to assess its size. "I can't rest easy until I find a space to lease for my company," she said. "I can practically *hear* the spaces for lease getting snapped up, like locusts pouncing on the few scraps of grain left in the fields."

After reading the newssheets, the magnitude of her problem had become starkly clear. The fire had burned a four-mile path along Lake Michigan that was almost a mile wide. More than a hundred thousand people had been left homeless, and half the businesses in the city had been burned out. People lucky enough to have survived the flames were leasing whatever available space they owned. Basements, attic space, spare bedrooms, even hallways were being offered to those looking for shelter or to reopen a business.

Zack squatted down to stretch the fabric tight. "You won't even know if you have the materials to go back into business until you go to Evanston to see if the train made it out of the city in time."

It was true. All of her watchmaking equipment had been loaded onto the train that night. Either it had survived or it hadn't, but she couldn't afford the time to travel to Evanston to find out. Her time was best spent finding a clean, well-lit place where she could swing back into business, and desperate people were snapping up those few remaining spaces with each passing hour. How many times had she explained that to Zack? Of course, he had an ulterior motive for wanting her to track down that train.

"If you are so desperate to secure your parents' belongings, feel free to go hunt them down yourself."

Zack dropped the tent pole, although it looked as if he'd rather snap it in half over his knee. "I *can't* leave Chicago now," he said. "Hartman's store burned to the ground and is teetering on the edge of financial disaster unless I can figure out a way to force the insurance companies to make good on our claims."

She straightened, rubbing her aching back. "We are in perfect agreement," she said. "Absolute, blinding, perfect agreement. I'm staying here to find rental space, and you can go file your insurance claims." Although she would prefer he stayed and helped her find rental space. It would be nice to have a man she could lean on, if only for a few hours. Hartman's might be teetering on the edge, but the 57th had already plunged over, and she needed to climb out of the hole they'd fallen into.

Besides, she rather liked being with Zack. Just knowing this strong, courageous man cared for her was wildly flattering, and he was becoming more attractive to her by the moment. He wasn't a lawyer anymore. He was a man who had risked his life to save her and walked across three miles of burned-out wasteland to see her.

Two hands settled on her shoulders, and Zack tugged her toward him. He placed a kiss on her forehead before whispering into her ear. "I wish we were in blinding agreement about where you should live. You should be under my roof, woman."

A shiver raced down her arms, and she hid her smile against the clean white cotton of his shirt. When he was near, the air felt charged with contagious energy, making her feel more alive.

"I don't like it when grown-ups hug each other," Sophie said from the corner of the church. "It's icky."

Mollie stepped back a pace. As disagreeable as Sophie's tone was, the girl was correct. This church sheltered a dozen people, and she should not subject them to the sight of her snuggling up to Zack. The Rutters and their new baby would be leaving on tomorrow's train, but the rest of them would be living in these humble tents for weeks, maybe months.

"Let's go outside so I can say good-bye properly," Zack said.

There was no privacy on the street either. With most of the buildings collapsed into mounds of rubble, there was no shadowy corner to withdraw to, so Zack stood with her on the crumbling steps of the church, cradling her face in his big, strong palms. "I don't know when I can come back," he said. "The second you get tired of living in a smelly old surplus tent, I want you to come across town to my house."

Mollie nodded and stepped closer. How safe she felt standing within the circle of his arms and laying her head against his chest, where she could hear the strong beating of his heart. "I heard it the first time you offered," she said with a smile in her voice. "And the fifth, and the tenth."

He pinched her cheek. "Such a clever lass. I knew there was a reason I liked you."

Why didn't she just leave with him? When she glanced over at the church, she saw Sophie reading the daily newssheet to Frank while Dr. Buchanan played a game of dice with the lumber merchant. "I'm not sure I can explain it," Mollie said, "but I feel bonded to these people. I can't leave to go live in the lap of luxury while they are all stranded here."

"You can sleep in my root cellar if it would make you feel better."

A burst of laughter escaped her lips, and she clapped her hand over her mouth. She was falling for this man with each passing minute. "Zack," she said firmly. "I am staying here. Go file your insurance claims."

Was it her imagination, or did the landscape seem bleaker after Zack left? After fetching a bucket of water for Mrs. Rutter, Mollie was about to set off on her quest to find rental space when a familiar voice echoed down the street.

"Alas, fair Mollie!" Ulysses called out. "Through fire and rain, through the storms of despair, we have at last come full circle!"

Mollie's head shot up. The world's two best gold engravers were walking toward her. "Ulysses!"

Hobbling on a crutch, Ulysses headed toward her with his wife, Alice, and Declan McNabb walking alongside him. Frank recognized the voice too and rose to greet the trio.

A grin split Ulysses's face as he increased his pace. He clapped Frank on the back, then embraced Mollie. "I feel like Theseus wading through streets of the devastated labyrinth to find the solace of friends in the wilderness."

"How did you know we were here?" Mollie asked in amazement.

Alice held up a newssheet. "We saw an advertisement you placed about a lost girl living with you. We've been taking shelter in the cellar of our house, but it's hard for a one-legged man to get in and out of a cellar. We figured it would be better to come join you folks at the church, if there is room."

Mollie glanced at the pair. Alice's silk Japanese scarf was draped around her shoulders, but it was filthy and dotted with scorch marks. They were both carrying bulging pillowcases. Mollie's heart sank. "You lost everything, then?"

A sheen of tears pooled in Alice's eyes, but she blinked them back. "Everything. But we escaped with our lives, and we found Declan the next morning."

Mollie glanced over at Declan, whose eyes were haunted while the side of his face kept twitching. The war had destroyed this man's nerves, and the trauma of the fire must have awakened all the old terrors. Thank goodness Alice had found him.

Alice had not stopped speaking. "We told Gunner about you, and he'll probably be coming too."

"Come inside and let me show you around our castle," Mollie joked, placing an arm around Alice to lead her inside.

Mollie's quick glance around the church confirmed there

would be enough tent space for the newcomers, but her heart was sinking. Even as she was barely keeping her body and spirit together, remnants of the 57th were beginning to gather around her. She would need to find a way to get this company back in action, and soon.

Too many people depended upon her to fail.

Before the fire, Zack's office had boasted an oriental rug and a hand-carved antique desk of black walnut. Today, he worked on a pine door stretched on top of two sawhorses in the corner of a Chinese laundry. Amidst the kettles of steaming water, indoor drying racks, and the caustic scent of lye, the laundry was an unconventional place to do business, but nothing was ordinary about life in Chicago after the fire.

The door banged open, and Louis Hartman strode in. "Status update," he barked before coughing from the lungful of detergent and steam. He covered his mouth with a handkerchief. "Of all the places . . . couldn't you have found one that didn't reek of lye?"

Zack smiled and rose from the overturned apple crate he'd been using as a seat. "It beats the smell of soot."

Lines of exhaustion were carved onto Hartman's unshaven face. Like the homes of many of Chicago's millionaires, Hartman's mansion had been reduced to a pile of smoldering ash. Today, it was easy to see Louis's working-class roots as he wore scuffed boots and a simple cotton shirt with the sleeves rolled up instead of a starched collar and a gold watch chain.

"I spent the morning with Josephine, trying to reconstruct the crystal and china inventory." He set a sheaf of papers on Zack's makeshift desk. "We think it was worth around forty thousand dollars, but how we can prove that is anyone's guess."

Zack's shoulders sagged. "I can send to Paris to see if they have records of our recent purchases." The merchandise destroyed in the store was worth close to half a million dollars. Every record, file, and bill of sale had been lost in the flames, and they were going to have to battle with the insurance companies to prove what had been lost.

But that was a challenge for another day. Today they needed to get the reconstruction project underway. Louis wanted his glittering store to reopen on the same plot of land on Columbus Street on the six-month anniversary of the fire, but there was a matter that needed to be set to rest before they could proceed with rebuilding.

Zack cleared his throat. "The land on Columbus Street," he said. "We may have a bit of trouble from Mollie Knox about that."

Louis stopped pacing to pin him with a suspicious stare. "Knox? The watchmaker's daughter?"

"Yes. She claims her father never properly sold a piece of the land on Columbus Street. And surprise, surprise . . . she still has the deed."

Zack watched Hartman carefully. There was no sign of concern as he stared directly at Zack. "Did she show it to you? The actual *deed* to a piece of land I own free and clear?"

"I saw it. It looks authentic, although she didn't actually let me get my hands on it."

The fact that Mollie still did not trust him after what they endured together smarted, but why should she? After all, she had a legitimate case, and both he and Louis knew it. The shoddy work of Zack's predecessor accounted for the loophole that meant Silas Knox had never formally surrendered the original deed. If they had succeeded in buying her company, all this would have been water under the bridge. As it was, her ownership of that plot of land presented a problem. A big one that was half an acre wide.

Hartman's eyes turned to steel. "Look, I paid for that land ten years ago. I built on it, paid taxes on it, and operated a business on it for more than a decade. I won't let that woman waltz in and demand payment when her father already profited plenty from that plot of land."

"It might be worth it to buy the deed from her," Zack pressed. "If we rebuild without clearing this up, it will come back to haunt us."

Louis slapped his gloves on his thigh. "I'm not paying twice for something I rightly own," he snapped. "I worked hard for every dollar to my name, and I won't be pressured into paying twice by that woman. The county courthouse and every record inside is now a smoldering ruin. If Miss Knox wishes to try to prove her claim, good luck to her."

It was true that this city was about to descend into a legal quagmire of contested deeds, lawsuits, and insurance claims. With so much of the city's legal and banking records destroyed, litigants in court cases were unlikely to receive any form of justice.

Zack shot to his feet. "What am I supposed to do, Louis, lie to her? It was one thing to pressure her to sell us her company, but I'm not going to lie to her about the deed."

Louis clapped him on the shoulder. "You don't have to. The failure of my previous lawyer to finalize the paper work for that sale is *confidential information.* If she asks you questions, evade her. Anything else is a breach of the confidentiality a lawyer owes his client."

He didn't like it, but everything Louis said was true. Under no circumstances was Zack at liberty to tell Mollie what he knew about their shaky legal claim to that piece of land. He owed Louis Hartman more than he could ever repay, and cleaning up the disaster left by his predecessor was a small enough burden to bear.

Zack returned the shoulder clap. "I'll see what kind of deal I can work out with her," he said.

Zack was going to have to race to catch the last streetcar across town. With the flood of insurance work and rebuilding tasks, his days always ran late, but tonight he had planned a special treat for Mollie and he was not going to miss it.

A grin of anticipation lit his face as he dashed toward his house. He could smell the pierogis even before he opened the door. Nobody made the classic Polish dumplings better than his mother, and she had been cooking all day to supply his request. He'd seen the inadequate food the relief wagons were distributing, but today Mollie and the others at the church would dine on the world's best pierogis. His mother's dumplings, filled with simmered beef, potatoes, and cheese, would be a welcome change from bread and apples.

He threw his leather case down and raced toward the kitchen. "The pierogis are ready?" An oversized basket was filled to the top with the warm delicacy, and another towering platter steamed on the countertop.

"Get something to eat, Zachariasz," his mother said. "You left while it was still dark this morning, and I know you haven't eaten a single thing all day."

Zack was already wolfing a pierogi down. "Had to meet the five a.m. train," he said. "It had a delivery of construction supplies for the new store, and someone needed to sign for it."

Joanna poured him a glass of milk and pushed it across the counter. "You'll be no good to that pretty watchmaker if you are dead on your feet. That shirt smells. Go change while I pack this last batch up."

Zack wolfed down another dumpling, drained the glass of milk in one draw, then wiped his mouth with the back of his hand. "I am already late, and I'm not changing my shirt." He grinned as he imagined the expression on Mollie's face when she tasted her first homemade pierogi. Someday he wanted to drape her in pearls and fill her evenings with music and dancing, but for now, the best thing was to fill her with a decent meal.

"Zachariasz, I am not having that girl think I raised a son who does not put on a starched shirt to court a woman. Go change, and I will pack this up."

"Mama, the people in that church live in squalor and sleep on the ground. They don't care if my shirt isn't starched."

It was the wrong thing to say to a woman who carried the fate of Polish cultural identity on her shoulders. "*I care*," she said. She hustled up the staircase to his bedroom, muttering over her shoulder. "My son went to Yale and works for the finest merchant in the city. He won't call on a girl stinking like a laborer."

There was no help for it. Zack vaulted up the stairs, tearing his shirt open and shrugging out of it as he went. He tossed it on the bed and grabbed a gleaming white shirt from his mother's outstretched hands. She beamed with pride as she handed him a pair of cuff links.

"I swear, old woman, you would try a saint's patience," he muttered as he fastened the onyx cuff link. "This shirt is going to be covered with a layer of soot by the time I get back."

"Bring the watchmaker back with you. We have plenty of room, and it is foolish for her to be sleeping with all those strangers in the church."

Zack didn't need any prompting from his mother on that score. Looting was getting to be a problem. Not that people in the burned district had anything worth stealing, but drunken idiots were merely out to cause trouble, and they were the most dangerous kind.

It was almost dark by the time he got to the burned district. Braziers were flickering in the darkness, and clusters of homeless people were warming their hands before the flames. In front of the church, a half dozen people were stooped over to collect bricks. The sight made him feel like he had just stepped back five hundred years into some medieval wasteland where peasants toiled in the dirt. The city had asked people to sort bricks into two piles: those that could be reused for building and those too badly damaged for reuse. Builders were paying five dollars for every wagonload of usable bricks.

A figure separated from the group, and the little ash-covered urchin came bounding toward him. "Did you bring us something to eat?" Sophie eyed the basket like a jackal as he reached in and handed her a pierogi.

"Hello, princess. I am surprised you are still here."

"My parents probably don't get the newspaper," she said through a full mouth. "Otherwise they would have come here right away and I wouldn't be stuck in this nasty church. These are really good. Can I have another one?"

Zack scanned the group sorting bricks, looking for Mollie among the ragtag group of people. "Yes, you can have another, but they are for everybody, so I want to offer them around first. Deal?"

He didn't wait for an answer. He had just spotted Mollie bending over a mound of rocks, a pair of sturdy work gloves covering her hands. Even dirty and tattered, Mollie looked glorious. Her face was flushed with good health, and that amazing hair spiraled out of its bun, tendrils floating around her face as artfully as if they had been painted by da Vinci.

"Come get something to eat, Mollie."

At the sound of his voice, she reared upward, tossing a brick to the ground. In the dwindling light of dusk, the joy on her face made her seem lit from within. He didn't break eye contact as he walked toward her, gawking at her like a complete milksop, loving every second of it.

"You came back," she said simply.

He couldn't even think straight with the way she set her delicate little hand on his arm and gazed up at him like he was prince of the universe. "Did you think I wouldn't?"

She stood on tiptoes and kissed his cheek. "Just happy you did," she whispered in his ear.

Sophie tugged on the corner of his jacket. "Can I have another one?" she asked, her cheeks still bulging with a homemade pierogi.

Zack set the huge basket down on the steps. "Not until Mollie has had one."

He pulled the gloves from Mollie's hands and watched carefully as she took her first bite of a beef and cheese pierogi. Her eyes drifted shut as a look of bliss settled onto her features. She chewed slowly and with relish. "I may die from pleasure," she finally said, "but I want the world to know I died a happy woman."

Zack's chest expanded. He would cross the city to feed her every evening for the rest of his life if he could just watch that expression of sweet delight on her face. The woman he'd idolized for three years looked ready to faint over a gift he had brought her. He might be a sweaty Pole from the docks, but he had just made the most beautiful woman in Chicago sigh with pleasure.

The gathering darkness made it impossible to keep collecting bricks, and the people from the church gathered on the front steps before the brazier to devour the pierogis. Tired, dirty, and blistered, none of these people knew what the next few months would hold, but there was no despair here, only camaraderie forged by the harrowing experience of the fire. As much as he feared for Mollie living in these terrible conditions, the people who had banded together in this ruined church were creating a workable system there.

But not one that afforded much privacy. After they'd eaten and the veterans started recounting old war stories, Zack leaned down toward the woman he loved.

"Let's go for a walk, Mollie."

Frank Spencer stiffened, but Mollie's annoying lawyer spoke in a calm voice. "They say that when a wolf wants to lead a sheep to slaughter, he'll try to cut her off from the herd where he can do his worst in private."

There was snickering around the firelight as the entire herd moved in to protect the object of his affections. With the grinning faces of several men gloating at him, it would be impossible to sneak Mollie away. Zack turned to her with a pleasant smile on his face. "You know how in mythology the blind man is always the source of great wisdom and insight? Why couldn't you find one of *those* blind guys to be friends with?"

Frank appeared flattered by the statement. He grinned as he warmed his hands before the brazier. "Those blind guys also warned against Greeks bearing gifts. Probably because they never met a Pole."

Zack let the arrow glance off his skin. If he rose to the bait at every Polish joke, he'd still be nursing the bruises. Besides, there was music. In the burned-out post office across the street, someone had produced a harmonica, and they were clapping and singing from behind the crumbling walls of their shelter. That group of German immigrants played music almost every night— sometimes hymns, sometimes lively folk tunes like tonight.

Zack stepped toward Mollie, and without asking permission, tugged her into his arms. "Let's dance," he said impulsively.

Her eyes widened in alarm. "Don't be ridiculous."

Mollie was not the sort to be drawn out of her comfort zone without a little prodding. She tried to skitter out of his arms, but he hauled her back. "Let me do all the work, Mollie. I know what I'm doing."

Like any good Pole in Chicago, Zack had been dancing since childhood and confidently led Mollie in a rousing jig. She was clumsy at first, but all she had to do was follow his lead. The tension in her back relaxed, and she learned the steps. Her smile started out hesitant, then bloomed wider. With her face illuminated by firelight and laughter, she was perfect in his arms.

Within moments, Declan and Sophie joined the dance as well. Ulysses could not dance, but clapped his hands as Alice danced first with Dr. Buchanan and then the redheaded lumber dealer.

It was an evening unlike any he'd ever known before. With Mollie in his arms and the laughter of her friends around him, he was exactly where he wanted to be.

10

Waiting in line at the relief wagons became a daily ritual for Mollie. Each day, wagons loaded with food and fuel wheeled into designated locations throughout the burned district. Normally the refugees were orderly and patient as they endured the long lines, but Sophie had proven to be a trial.

One morning, Sophie sneered at the corn bread being distributed and demanded fried chicken instead. When the kind lady working the relief wagon apologized to Sophie for the poor selection of food, Sophie threw a tantrum, kicking the wagon and accusing the lady of being fat and lazy.

Mollie was stunned into mute stupor by the child's belligerence, but not so Ralph Coulter, the lumber merchant who was accustomed to dealing with brawny laborers. He marched Sophie back to the church and ordered her to sort an entire mound of bricks before she would be allowed to have a slice of corn bread. Sophie refused to work and approached each person in the church for a share of food. Having heard of her behavior, no one gave her anything until she finished sorting the mound of bricks.

Mollie had been mortified by Sophie's tantrum, but Dr. Buchanan was more sympathetic. "That girl is a brat and a half," he said to Mollie, "but some of her behavior may be simple fear over what has become of her family. I lost my own parents around her age, and that sort of fear isn't something you forget."

After the incident, Sophie had been banished from the relief wagon, which was a shame because this morning the wagons brought a welcome blessing. Mollie's heart kicked up a pace as she eyed the piles of clean clothing, pairs of donated shoes knotted together by their laces, and amazingly, bars of soap. After wearing the same filthy dress for over a week, Mollie was anxious for something that did not reek of smoke. It felt like Christmas morning as she and Alice riffled through the mound of clothing on the street corner, holding skirts up to the early morning light and eying them for size. Most were patched and threadbare, but they were *clean*. Mollie grabbed a couple of items that looked like they might be small enough for Sophie.

They carried their treasures back to the church, where the rumble of snores from the nave indicated others were still sleeping. Mollie and Alice tiptoed to the rear corner, where two blankets had been strung up for privacy. It would be wrong to step into clean clothes when she was so grubby, meaning a frigid sponge bath was necessary. Mollie fetched a bucket of water from the barrel outside the church, but she dreaded taking her clothes off in the chilly October air.

Huddling with Alice behind the screen of blankets, her numb fingers unlaced her bodice and peeled out of her clothes. The stone floor was cold and grainy beneath her feet, but prancing helped minimize the contact. Alice's teeth chattered as she held the cake of soap in her hand. "My husband had his leg taken off without anesthesia," she whispered. "You'd think I could face an icy sponge bath without complaint."

Mollie grinned and snatched the soap. "One would think, you awful chit!" She tried to be quiet in deference to the sleepers on the other side of the blanket, but it was impossible once the chilly rag trailed across her skin. Both of them giggled and whimpered like children, and a sponge bath had never been accomplished with such speed.

Alice usually wore a pre-Raphaelite artist's smock from London or a Japanese kimono or some other wildly impractical garb. Today, though, she put on a brown muslin dress that looked perfect for milking a cow. Mollie's gray plaid skirt clashed with the black blouse dotted with little pink flowers, but neither of them cared. The garments were clean and warm.

Unfortunately, Mollie had found no suitable shoes among the mounds of donated items. Over the past few days, the soles of her boots had split as she'd walked mile after mile, looking at the dwindling supply of spaces for lease. She didn't need a lot of space to make watches, only someplace that was spotlessly clean and well lit. She'd looked at the basement of an orphanage and the storage shed of a hardware store. Both were too grubby to be turned into the pristine condition necessary for the assembly of precision watches, and she was growing disheartened as fewer spaces remained available.

But today she would venture forth and try again. She'd be lucky if her split boots could withstand the walk, but what other choice did she have?

"Let's gather up those nasty clothes and burn them," Alice said of the discarded pile of filthy clothing. Every item of their clothing was scorched with holes from falling cinders and reeked of smoke.

"Good plan," Mollie said, scooping them up and piling them into Alice's outstretched arms. Then she saw her green paisley scarf. That scarf had been draped over her head and shoulders as they fled through the burning streets. It had protected her from the sheets of rain. Later, she had wadded it up and used it for a pillow. It was so filthy and marred with cinder holes, it was hard to even see much of the original paisley pattern.

Mollie lifted the shawl, letting it drop into a large square, dots of light shining through the dozens of tiny holes. A wave of pressure swelled in her chest, and she began carefully folding the shawl. It was dirty and smelly, but she would find a place to keep it safe until she could wash it properly. She would never wear it again, but she never wanted to forget it either.

After Sophie awoke, Mollie helped the girl change into the clothes that had been donated by strangers. The muslin skirt fit well enough, but the green flannel shirt was far too big. "This will have to do for now," Mollie said as she folded the cuffs up Sophie's arms, so small they looked like toothpicks emerging from the sleeves.

Mollie glanced at the dirty white nightdress at Sophie's feet. "Would you like to keep your nightgown?" she asked the girl. "Someday you might want to show it to your children so they will believe you survived the great Chicago fire. It will help you remember these days."

Sophie's lip curled. "I don't need to remember anything. I hate these clothes and I hate living in this smelly church. At my house, I get to eat whenever I want and I never have to do chores."

Mollie no longer got annoyed when Sophie mouthed off like a brat. Besides, Sophie was more tolerable when she was fully occupied. "Well, we have plenty of chores for you today. I will be hunting for space to lease, so that means you will need to fetch the coals to heat water. You remember where they are distributing coal?"

Sophie nodded.

"And you can read to Frank when today's newssheet comes out. And if he has any errands for you to run, I want you to do them without complaint, is that clear?"

ELIZABETH CAMDEN

Sophie had developed a curious fascination with Frank Spencer. Each time a newsboy brought a fresh sheet of news, Sophie scrambled to snatch a sheet and rushed to Frank's side to read it to him.

Within the past few days, word of Frank's free legal advice had circulated among the homeless, and people had begun visiting the church to speak with him. Frank's memory was an amazing thing, and he was able to cite the legal code that people would need to file their insurance claims. Many of the visitors were illiterate or had broken English, so Sophie carefully wrote out Frank's instructions on scraps of paper that had been brought by the relief workers. Dr. Buchanan had offered to help, but Sophie seemed strangely determined to be the only one to help Frank. Mollie figured it was because writing notes was easier than sorting bricks, but so long as Sophie was contributing, she would not quibble.

With only a handful of spaces left in the city to lease, she had bigger problems to worry about.

After four days of failing to find a space to lease, Mollie could delay her trip to retrieve her belongings no longer. Besides, if her watchmaking equipment had not survived, the desperate quest for rental space was pointless.

Ulysses accompanied her on the train to Evanston. With each mile, her nerves twisted a little tighter as she worried that her watches might not have survived, but upon arriving at the appointed depot, that fear dissolved.

A clerk was eager to tell her of the heroism of the railway operators on the night of the fire. The train carrying her watches and equipment had been the last one to make it out of Chicago. It was a 120-ton force of iron and steel that barreled through the flames to safety, and now Mollie clutched a precious bag of watches in her lap on her return journey.

She had her watches, all six crates of watchmaking tools, and a large bag belonging to Mr. and Mrs. Kazmarek. The only thing they hadn't been able to find stacked in the cavernous warehouse was the couple's smaller bag. Mollie and Ulysses had prowled the warehouse for almost an hour, looking beneath bolts of fabric, piles of furniture, and crates that had been whisked out during those final desperate hours. If the bag was there, they couldn't find it.

She was still thinking about that lost bag on the journey home, but the visual splendor outside the train window was spectacular. The autumn countryside was painted in vivid shades of orange, yellow, and scarlet. Looking at the riot of color, it was hard to believe she was only a few miles away from the barren wasteland of Chicago. After a week of seeing only shades of ash gray, the rich autumn colors were a balm to Mollie's spirit.

Ulysses's words broke her calm. "Alice tells me she thinks you're being led astray by Zack Kazmarek."

At Mollie's indrawn breath, Ulysses continued. "She says the man looks at you like he wants to lay the world at your feet, and that you are just as smitten. I've never known you to show that sort of interest in a man before."

Mollie shifted in discomfort. No man had ever sheltered her body as buildings exploded behind them. No man had ever looked at her with his heart in his eyes or kissed her soot-stained face while he smiled in joy. Zack had been coming to the church every day to see her. Some days he teased her, others he flirted, and others he worked alongside the laborers to help clear the street of rubble.

"He has been kind to me, that's all."

"I don't want to throw a cold rag on your enthusiasm, but Frank doesn't trust him."

Mollie tensed. "Frank doesn't know him as well as I do."

"Frank Spencer is one of the wisest men I've ever known," Ulysses cautioned. "Last night, as we were heating coals in the brazier, he told me that there are precious few advantages that come from being blind, but one is that you are never swayed by a pretty face. 'I'll bet my last dollar Kazmarek is a looker,' he said."

The jostling of the train made the deed tucked inside Mollie's bodice chafe against her skin. She rested her forehead in her hand, the weariness of the last week catching up with her. "I wish I could forget about this deed. It would be so much easier to pretend I never saw it and continue business as usual. Zack has been nothing but kind and helpful to me. I don't believe he knew anything about this deed."

Ulysses smiled sadly. "Sun Tzu warned, 'Keep your friends close, but your enemies closer.' Sounds to me that may be what Mr. Kazmarek is trying to do by being so nice to you all of a sudden." Ulysses shifted in his seat, twirling his crutch like he always did when he was pensive. "Look, I don't know Mr. Kazmarek or Louis Hartman, but these are desperate times. Men do strange things when their livelihood is on the line. Don't let any smooth-talking attorney convince you otherwise until you have proof. Frank has concerns, and you need to pay them heed before you let yourself fall into Kazmarek's hands like a ripe plum." Ulysses sat back and set his crutch to the side. "Then again, Frank could just be a worrisome old woman."

Mollie let her gaze trail outside. Frank and Ulysses were her father's oldest friends, and she would trust them with her life, but they hadn't seen Zack that night. They hadn't been clasped in his arms for a few moments when they thought they were about to die. The morning after the fire, as she stood outside the church, filthy and soot stained, Zack's exhausted face had such a mingling of hope and affection on it. Frank and Ulysses knew nothing of *that* Zack Kazmarek.

She was twenty-six years old, and it was time to trust her own instincts without being discouraged by the well-meaning concerns of her father's old friends.

⁓

In the coming days, Mollie looked forward to Zack's visits each evening. It was often after dark when he arrived, but he always brought some sort of Polish delicacy cooked by his mother. He didn't make any more attempts to separate her from the others, and it felt nice getting to know him in the presence of the other refugees. As they gathered around the brazier each evening, Zack told her about his days as a longshoreman. They listened to Ralph Coulter talk with pride about buying his first lumber schooner two years ago. Inevitably, the veterans drifted into talking about the war, but Mollie never minded. As old Gunner chewed on the butt of an unlit cigar, Mollie was eager to hear stories about her father, or of the valiant Colonel Lowe who became a national hero after saving the regiment at the battle of Winston Cliff.

Sitting on the steps of the church within the warm circle provided by the brazier reminded Mollie of how her father used to describe life during the war. Sometimes he and the other soldiers camped in barns, sometimes under the stars. They were usually either too hot or too cold. Hungry or wet or blistered. They were exhausted from not knowing what would happen the next day or terrified because they did. Throughout it all, there was a camaraderie that was forged by the harrowing experience of war that would blaze for the rest of their lives.

And in a strange way, Mollie knew these days would be the same for her. The fire had been the worst experience of her life, but it had brought out the best in the people around her.

She knew this magical spirit could not last forever. She had no home and no place of business, and the odds of her collecting on her insurance were slim. Sophie was probably an orphan, and the prospect of raising her was as appealing as hauling a millstone around her neck for the next ten years. The fire was forcing her to live in a world she had never prepared for, but as her gaze trailed to Zack, an irrational sense of well-being settled over her. Somehow, no matter what whirlwind would scoop her up next, she knew she could survive if Zack Kazmarek would ride it with her.

11

M ollie's insurance company was going out of business.
     She'd been standing in line with Frank for the past six
hours, getting sick to her stomach as the rumors raced down the
line that stretched three city blocks long. Hundreds of policyholders were lined up outside the shack where her insurance
company had set up shop. After years of faithfully paying that
policy, Mollie was going to collect only three cents on the dollar.
The shoemaker standing in front of her was weeping, blowing
his nose into a huge handkerchief as his wife stared straight
ahead with a face of stone. The air was thick with dreams that
were collapsing. It was so hard to stand still in this infernal line
as anger twisted her emotions tighter.

     When it was her turn, Mollie saw the owner of her insur-
ance company for the first time. Sitting behind a makeshift desk
made of a door balanced atop two barrels, the old man wore a
soot-stained suit and haunted eyes. Using the stub of a pencil,
he wrote a promissory note to Mollie with shaking hands. This
man had lost everything as well, and three cents on the dollar
was likely better than some people would receive. She tried to
be kind as she signed the papers, but exhaustion was settling in,
and it was hard to even move the pencil across the page.

All Mollie wanted to do was sink into the barren wasteland that was Livingston Street and weep, but she needed to be alert as she guided Frank home. "What kind of business can I run for eight hundred dollars?" she asked weakly. It wouldn't even pay rent and salary for a month.

"Don't worry, Mollie-girl, we'll figure something out," Frank said. "Bankers are going to need to loosen up their credit, and the 57th has a strong reputation. We might qualify for a loan."

But Frank couldn't see what was in front of them. Miles of wasteland with mountains of rubble growing so massive the wreckage was beginning to tumble into the newly cleared streets. With a hundred thousand people burned out of their homes and businesses, the lines for bank credit would make the Great Wall of China look stubby in comparison.

She was tired as they neared the church when a well-dressed man approached her. "Excuse me, ma'am. Could I trouble you for directions?"

The gentleman was clearly a stranger to this neighborhood. Dressed in a fine black jacket with a peach satin waistcoat, he looked as dapper as if he were about to visit the queen.

"What are you looking for?" Mollie asked.

"I need to find the Livingston Street Church. I've business there."

Mollie noticed the rolls of oversized drafting paper the stranger carried beneath his arm. She brightened. "Are you an architect coming to look at the roof?"

Confusion tinged the man's face. "I am an architect, but haven't been commissioned by the church. I am afraid I am booked solid with building engagements for the next two years, but I'll be happy to have a quick look and lend my professional opinion."

"I see," Mollie said. She gestured down the street. "The church is a few blocks that way. You can follow us, as we are headed to the same place. May I ask what your business is?"

The man fell into step alongside them. "My daughter is staying there. We were separated the night of the fire."

"Are you Sophie's father? Mr. Durant?" Mollie asked, a surge of hope blooming inside.

"Why, yes. Are you Miss Knox?"

Mollie didn't reply, she just flung her arms around the stranger and hugged him with all her strength. Thank God Sophie was not going to be an orphan!

The gentleman seemed a bit taken aback by her exuberance, but Mollie's sense of decorum had loosened its grip in recent days. The architect set his hands on her shoulders and patted her awkwardly. "Yes, well. I must thank you for looking out for my daughter. It seems she has been in good hands."

Mollie introduced Frank and explained how they had found Sophie atop a flight of stairs during the fire. As they set off for the church, Mr. Durant explained what had happened that night.

"My wife and I have two-year-old twin boys. We had our hands full, and Sophie was clinging to my jacket as we made our way north. We got separated, but by the time I noticed, there was no sign of her. Just the crowds and the heat and the avalanche of noise."

Mollie nodded. As long as she lived, the bellowing roar of the fire and incessant clanging of the bells would haunt her memory. It was easy to see how Sophie's cry for help would have been lost in that chaos.

"I'm glad you finally saw our newspaper announcement," Mollie said. "And you have a safe place to take Sophie? The church is not the best environment for a young girl."

Mr. Durant affirmed that he did. "We've lost our home, but my brother has a fine mansion on Prairie Avenue where we have been staying. My wife is finally beginning to recover and should be ready to take Sophie on."

Mollie glanced up at the man. "Sophie is fine, but your wife was injured?"

Mr. Durant waffled a moment before answering. "Charlotte has a delicate constitution," he finally said. "The fire rattled her senses, and the boys are a challenge. As is Sophie, of course. When we saw your advertisement in the paper, you can't imagine how we rejoiced, but Charlotte nearly had a nervous breakdown at the thought of dealing with the girl on top of everything else. And as we are guests in my brother's home, we needed to be sure Charlotte was capable of dealing with Sophie before we brought her aboard. Poor Charlotte got rattled at the very thought of Sophie underfoot."

Mollie was stunned, and when she looked over at Frank, she saw his mouth open in disbelief. "More rattled then a ten-year-old girl who had been burned out of her home and lost everyone in the world?" he demanded.

A flush darkened Mr. Durant's face. "You have my gratitude for looking after Sophie," he said stiffly. "I am thankful she was in the care of a man with perfect judgment, for I surely am not. And while I enjoy a good intellectual debate about which child a man should focus on in a life-or-death situation, I believe I have been separated from my daughter long enough."

Mr. Durant's rebuke did not sit well with Frank, whose eyes turned hard as they walked back to the church in silence. Animosity crackled in the air between the two men, but all that was swept away the moment they drew near the church and Sophie looked up from where she was sorting bricks in the yard.

"Daddy!" she screamed. The girl was a streak of green flannel as she dashed across the yard. Mr. Durant squatted down to catch Sophie as she flew into his outstretched arms. Mollie's mistrust of the man dissolved as his hearty laughter filled the air and he rocked Sophie in his arms.

Sophie's joy did not last. "Where did you go?" she demanded. "I looked for your name in the newspaper every day, and it was never there." Mollie gasped as Sophie hit her father on the shoulder, pounding him with all the strength her spindly arm could deliver. "I couldn't find you, and I've had to live in this smelly old church for days and days."

Mr. Durant tried to hold her swinging fists. "There, there, my dumpling. My little princess. Daddy is here now. He'll buy you a pretty doll on the way home. Would you like that, princess?"

She smacked him again. "I don't want a doll, I want new clothes. And a puppy. And I want fried chicken and strawberry shortcake and hot chocolate."

People on the street stopped sorting bricks, waiting to see how the fastidious gentleman would handle such demands. Mr. Durant stood and grasped Sophie's hand. "We will stop at the sweet shop on the way home."

Mr. Durant looked about until he spotted Mollie. "My thanks again for looking out for Sophie. I am indebted to you, Miss Knox. I am staying at Prairie Avenue with my brother. If ever you have need of anything . . . *anything*, I want you to remember the name Raymond Durant." He pulled a square of paper from his pocket. "Here is my brother's address."

Mollie nodded. In all honesty, she was not sorry to see the last of Sophie, but in a strange way it was a bittersweet moment. Sophie's departure was the beginning of the end of a chapter. Others would be leaving the church in the coming days, and this terrible but oddly wonderful time of her life would come to an end.

~

Later that day, an unexpected arrival came in the form of Mrs. Kazmarek's second satchel. A burly train station employee unloaded it onto the church floor, a cloud of dust kicking up as it landed with a thump. "It got buried beneath a dozen barrels of pickles."

Mollie needed a strong man to help her lug the bag to the Kazmareks' townhouse across the river, which ruled out both Frank and Ulysses. Declan was nowhere to be found, which meant that Andrew Buchanan, dentist, pillow maker, and baby deliverer, had volunteered to help her.

"The dental business isn't going quite as smashingly as anticipated," he said as they set off on the two-mile walk. Dr. Buchanan's sign had been posted outside the church for twelve days, but no customers had surfaced. Frank joked they should have billed Sophie's parents for metaphorically kicking them all in the teeth for a solid week.

Dr. Buchanan twisted the curl of his mustache as he walked beside Mollie. "I could use the income," he admitted. "It looks like my insurance will be no good, and I still have debts from getting started in the business."

Dr. Buchanan had shared his life story while everyone was gathered around the braziers one evening. He'd been orphaned at age ten and had no relatives, but a sympathetic woman down the street took pity on him and let him sleep beneath her stairs. He made pillows by day and studied hard by candlelight, always dreaming of someday becoming a dentist. By age thirty, he had finally had the funds to go to dental college. After years of struggle, his fledging practice had been wiped out in the fire. He now had little besides the clothes on his back and a case of dental equipment.

As they drew closer to Zack's neighborhood, excitement began to pulse through Mollie. "A moment, please," Mollie said as she adjusted the collar of her shirt and finger-combed her hair. Knowing Zack hated the braids, she had left her hair trailing down her back, secured only by a clip at her nape. During the walk, it had taken on a life of its own, curling out at all angles.

Mrs. Kazmarek was delighted to see her. "How pretty you look," she said, nodding approvingly at Mollie's fall of hair. Then Mrs. Kazmarek caught sight of the battered leather satchel in Dr. Buchanan's hand.

"My work!" she said as she clasped her hands together. Tears filled the old woman's eyes as she knelt down on the front stoop of the townhouse to touch the bag.

All Mollie wanted to ask was if Zack was home. As if reading her mind, Mrs. Kazmarek stood and patted her on the shoulder. "Poor Zachariasz is going to be spitting nails that he has missed you."

Mollie felt like the sun had just fallen from the sky. "He isn't here?" For pity's sake, it was Saturday. Shouldn't he have been there?

Mrs. Kazmarek prodded them inside and back to the dining room, the only room that was not crammed with towers of boxes and books and papers. She pulled out a chair and bade Mollie and Dr. Buchanan to sit. "He needs to move quickly with those New York insurance companies. He is afraid they may try to declare bankruptcy before he can file his claims, so he has been working seven days a week."

"I see," Mollie said softly. Mrs. Kazmarek opened the battered satchel at her feet and hauled out stacks of the papers, inspecting each batch before setting them on the dining table. There was a curious mingling of relief, delight, and pride on Mrs. Kazmarek's face as she kissed each batch of papers.

"If you don't mind my asking," Mollie said, "what precisely are those papers?"

Mrs. Kazmarek laid a hand gently across the top of the pages, and a hint of sadness tinged her face. "These bags contain our history. The history of the Polish people."

Mollie's brows lifted in surprise. Mrs. Kazmarek pushed herself to her feet and retrieved a framed photograph from the hall table. "This is a picture of my parents," she said. "You see how thin my father looks? How poor his clothing? That's because he was conscripted into the Russian army for two years before he could escape. For centuries, the people of Poland have been mistreated. Their land stampeded, their treasures plundered. The Russians and the Germans have partitioned our land so that Poland is no longer on the maps of Europe."

Mollie knew plenty about Poland. It was impossible to live in Chicago and not be aware of the waves of Polish immigrants who'd settled in the city.

"Even here in America, we struggle," Mrs. Kazmarek said. "People laugh at our accents and make jokes about our culture, but they cannot stamp out the Polish people. We refuse to disappear. So I will preserve the memory of our grand and glorious history." The sorrow faded from Joanna Kazmarek, and her face became one of strength and beauty. "There was a golden age of Poland," she said, her voice vibrating with pride. "A time when people from all over Europe came to study at our universities, benefit from the wealth of our land. As we spread out across the world, it is important we *remember*."

Her lips compressed. "Zachariasz has no patience for all this. No interest in Poland. We could not even get him to learn to speak Polish! But whenever Jozef and I meet someone from Poland, we listen to their stories and record their memories."

Through the arched doorway, Mollie could see down the hall to a room piled with towers of papers, books, and photographs. "That is what is in the front room?"

Joanna nodded. "Those are the memories. And this is the

book," she said, laying her hand on the stacks of paper before her. "I read everything sent to me by the Polish immigrants, and when I find something truly unique, I make a copy here on these pages. Someday I will publish these pieces for all the world to see. What good is our work if all it does is fill this fine home to the rafters? I will write a book and make sure it is in every library of this country. The memories of our people must never be forgotten. I will protect and shine them until they gleam like diamonds in the darkness."

Mollie found the woman's passion touching, but Dr. Buchanan's response amazed her. He was on the verge of tears. "I wish I had someone like you in my life," he said. "I don't know the first thing about who I am or where I came from. My parents died before I thought to ask them about such things. What kind of name is Buchanan? German? Irish? I don't even know. All I know is that I was born and raised on Union Avenue, but that's all burned down now. No past, no future."

Mrs. Kazmarek leaned across the table and cuffed him on the arm. "You can be Polish," she said. "Come. I am feeding you a bowl of good hot *flaki*. Your first step to becoming an honorary Pole."

Five minutes later, Mollie and Dr. Buchanan had piping hot bowls of thick stew before them. Mollie recognized the slices of carrots and celery floating in the broth but wasn't certain about the meat that made the stew so hearty. She devoured the stew even though it wasn't the sort of dish she would appreciate under normal circumstances.

In contrast, Dr. Buchanan savored every drop. "You must show me how to make this flaki," he said. "Now that I've had it, I'll crave it for the rest of my life. What is in it?"

"You don't want to know," Mrs. Kazmarek said.

"Yes I do. It's delicious." Dr. Buchanan tilted his bowl to eke out the last drop.

Mrs. Kazmarek folded her arms across her chest and fixed the dentist with a sad smile. "Dr. Buchanan, I am older and wiser than the two of you put together, and sometimes you need to trust your elders. *You don't want to know!*"

Dr. Buchanan shrugged his shoulders but gratefully accepted Mrs. Kazmarek's offer for a second bowl of stew. While the older woman stepped into the kitchen for more flaki, Mollie glanced about the home that Zack lived in. Normally, a home was a reflection of the owner, but it was hard to tell much of anything about Zack from this townhouse. The front rooms were crammed with Mrs. Kazmarek's history project, but the dining room was clear of papers. It contained nothing but the table, four chairs, and the rather fetching painting of a girl in a garden Mollie had admired the first time she was here.

Mrs. Kazmarek slid the bowl of stew before Dr. Buchanan, then glanced up at Mollie. "You have noticed the Monet again," she said approvingly. "Zachariasz overpaid horribly for that painting, but he was determined to have it."

Dr. Buchanan swiveled in his chair to look at the painting. "Hey, she looks like you, Mollie."

Mollie looked closer at the picture. It showed a young woman with a cascade of black curls spilling down her back, but that was the only resemblance Mollie could see. The woman stood in a green meadow dappled with sunlight, holding something protectively in her hand. Mollie leaned forward to get a better look.

"She is holding a watch," Mrs. Kazmarek said. "A gold watch."

"Oh" was the only thing Mollie could think to say. Dr. Buchanan turned his attention back to his bowl of Polish stew, but Mrs. Kazmarek watched Mollie with the strangest look of expectation on her face. The woman didn't really think the picture looked like her, did she?

There were so many things about Zack she didn't know. In the past, he had been just an intimidating man in a starched collar with a list of rules she must follow. Now he was a man who had raced through a fire to save her. Who brought his pet bird home every weekend. And, for some reason, had horribly overpaid for a portrait of a girl holding a watch.

"Zack doesn't seem like the kind of person to get sentimental over artwork," she said.

Mrs. Kazmarek's smile was a curious mingling of love and pain. "He is very protective of the women in his life," she said. "Do you know how he got that chip in his front tooth?"

As Mrs. Kazmarek recounted the story, it made Mollie's heart ache. When Zack was a boy, his mother had been a laundress for a boardinghouse near the docks. Six days a week she hauled water and did heavy labor before walking two miles back to her neighborhood. A gang of young Irish troublemakers had taken to following her home. They trailed behind her, sneering out polka tunes with dirty lyrics and hoping to get a rise out of her. Sometimes it was only hurtful words, but other times they threw bits of rubbish at her or yanked on the back of her skirt. She always ignored them, but when Zack heard about it, he rounded up two other Polish boys and confronted the Irish gang. It was three against five, and the Irish boys were older than Zack and his friends. Zack was only fourteen years old, and it did not go well. Mrs. Kazmarek nearly fainted when Zack was carried home with two broken ribs and a chipped tooth . . . but the Irish gang left her alone after that.

It confirmed what Mollie was beginning to understand about Zack. Beneath his polished veneer of corporate success and finely tailored jackets, he was a rugged, aggressive man who would bluntly reach out and correct a wrong. Or defend a woman. Hadn't he stood by her side through the fire, hauling her to safety even when it meant he was thrust into danger?

Frank's warnings about Zack were wrong. It was understandable that her father's oldest friend would have the protective instincts of a lion, but Mollie was coming to know and trust a side of Zack that Frank would never be able to see.

~

Thank goodness for the pierogis Zack brings, Mollie thought as she pulled on her shoes.

In the past week, she had started feeling guilty about eating so well when others in the neighborhood subsisted on bread and apples. Three days ago, she had impulsively brought some of Zack's pierogis over to the German immigrants who lived in the burned-out post office across the street.

This morning, her generosity paid off when Mrs. Schneider came to tell her of a space in the Pilsen neighborhood that had just become available for lease. Some people renting an attic above a brewery had decided to move to St. Louis and walked out on their lease. That space would last only a matter of hours.

As Mollie dragged on her shoes, Declan insisted on accompanying her. "It isn't safe on the streets," he said.

Crime was becoming a problem as the surge of goodwill in the days following the fire began to evaporate. Hunger and desperation were powerful forces, and gangs of ruffians had taken to roaming the streets. The mayor had turned to one of the city's most illustrious residents, General Philip Sheridan, for help in restoring order in the city. Chicago was placed under martial law, and teams of soldiers patrolled the streets to keep looters at bay, but the city was still on edge.

Declan's nerves roared to life whenever he felt threatened,

and she doubted he had it in him to put up any sort of defense on her behalf, but she nodded solemnly. "I'd appreciate that," she said simply as they set off with a brisk pace.

Her tension ratcheted higher as they rode the streetcar to the brewery. With each stop of the car, Mollie gritted her teeth as passengers dawdled in their boarding and disembarking. She pinched the skin on the bridge of her nose as a man carried six small cages of chickens aboard. She was terrified the streetcar would not deliver them to the brewery fast enough to secure the space.

Declan sensed her anxiety. "What will we do if the space is already taken?"

"I don't know," she said quietly.

Declan grimaced and folded his arms across his chest. His hands were trembling, and he didn't want her to see. "I wish I could snap my fingers and fix this problem for you," he said. "Instead I'm just another burden. Like always."

"Nonsense."

"During the war, Colonel Lowe always knew the right thing to do. When we were moving through Virginia, the civilians despised us and wanted to see us dead, but Colonel Lowe would sweet-talk the mayor's wife or offer to harvest crops in the field. He always knew how to buy goodwill. He got us out of one scrape after another."

Mollie sighed. "Declan, you mustn't compare yourself to Colonel Lowe." Over the years she had heard plenty about the famous commander of the 57th Illinois Infantry, especially from Declan, who idolized the man. She had never met Colonel Lowe, but he must have walked on water given the way Declan, Ulysses, and even her father always praised his name.

"I can't help it," he said. "When my nerves get the better of me, I ask myself what Colonel Lowe would do. He was always so confident, even when we were pinned against that cliff and were looking at certain death. And I was such a coward," he whispered. "Even today, I fall to pieces when a door slams." He turned to look at her with pain-filled eyes. "I *know* there are no snipers lying in wait or cannons exploding, but they are with me every day, hovering just beyond my line of sight."

She laid a hand on his arm. "It is normal to be afraid of death," she said. "Perhaps if you came to church services with us, you would not fear it so badly."

The streetcar stopped at the 18th Street intersection, where the brewery was located, and Declan vaulted from the bench. He hopped out of the streetcar, and Mollie had to hurry to catch up with him. "Declan . . . I didn't mean to offend you. I just want to help. Perhaps a minister—"

He stopped to face her. "Don't you think I've tried that, Mollie? Sitting in a church makes me feel like a bigger failure because all those people crammed in so tight make me nervous and I just want to get away. It's hard for me to be alone but harder to be in a crowd." He turned and kept trekking forward. "There is no fixing me, Mollie," he said darkly. "I have a cracked soul."

Mollie trailed along beside him, scurrying to keep apace. "Your soul is *not* cracked. Perhaps you are not a hero like Colonel Lowe, but not many people are. If you compare yourself to Colonel Lowe, you will continue to berate and belittle yourself, and that is not fair."

They reached the end of the block. The brewery was a squat brick building of four stories, two smokestacks, and a short flight of stairs leading to the front door. "I think this is the brewery we are looking for," Declan muttered.

It was, but she felt like she was on the verge of something very important. Declan had been wrestling with these demons for years, and this was the closest he had ever come to opening his mind to her.

"Declan, you are precisely as God intended you to be, nothing more and nothing less. If you wish, we can find someplace quiet and you can tell me what is going on. *I want to help.*"

He squeezed his eyes closed. "Mollie, would you please just stop? Please."

His hands were shaking again, and Mollie felt like her heart was splitting in two. Ignoring Declan's pain had never helped in the past, but it seemed discussing it only made things worse.

A barrel-chested man shuffled up the steps, pulling an equally large woman beside him. He banged on the door, which was promptly opened by a laborer wearing a stained apron.

"I hear there is an attic for lease here," the barrel-chested man said. In his hand, he held a roll of bills. "I've got a leather-tanning business, and I've got cash if I can take possession today."

Mollie's heart lurched. While she and Declan had bickered on the sidewalk, that couple had slid in front of them and may have just snatched the last suitable space for lease in the city. And, given the size of that wad of bills, Mollie couldn't compete with him in a price war.

The brewer nodded. "If you have cash, I've got space."

Declan vaulted up the stairs, pushing in front of the leather tanner. "We've got cash," Declan asserted. "And I can do better than he can."

Mollie's palms started to sweat. This wasn't going to be good. The leather tanner puffed up his already overinflated chest and took a step toward Declan, almost knocking him off the small landing. "Move on," he growled. "We were here first."

Declan stood his ground, refusing to look away from the brewer. "We can pay your price," he said. "And I can fix the rust you've got on those pipes leading down the west side of the building." Stepping out to the sidewalk, Declan pointed to the rust corroding the drainage pipes on the roof. "If you don't fix that rust, your gutters and drainage system will be ruined by the next hard ice storm."

The brewer looked surprised. "You know pipes?"

"We are watchmakers and know metalwork," Declan said. "You won't find better tenants." Declan's face hardened with determination. "And watchmaking doesn't stink like a leather tannery would."

"Hey!" the tanner shouted.

It did not take the brewer long to make his decision. Mollie held her breath as the brewer led her up a narrow staircase and into a spacious attic, swept clean and well lit by a row of narrow windows. After the brewer named a price, Mollie quickly agreed and signed a contract for the space.

She'd be back in business soon! Excitement surged through her as she and Declan strode back to the streetcar stop. She glanced up at him. "What made you think to offer to repair the pipes?"

Declan looked a little sheepish. "I thought about what Colonel Lowe would have done in such a situation. It worked."

Mollie laughed. "Then tonight we will raise a glass to Colonel Lowe!"

12

"You agreed to pay us six dollars for the bricks, not five."
Mollie fought to block frustration from bleeding into her voice, but it was hard. Foraging through mounds of useless rubble in search of a few useable bricks had cost Mollie a sore back, scuffed knuckles, and two days toiling in air thick with ash.

"Lady, times are tight and I've got a business to run. Take it or leave it." The brick man's voice was small, hard, and rude. Tempers were growing short all over the city as the goodwill that had energized people in the early days after the fire evaporated. Crime was getting worse, with looters beginning to prey upon shops under the cover of darkness.

For the first time in her life, Mollie was beginning to understand the desperation in fighting for every spare dime. The brewer who leased his attic to her expected a four hundred dollar payment within a week, and she had no idea how she was going to pay it. With every beat of her heart, she was working toward hauling the 57th out of the slag heap and back into business. The idea of letting someone cheat her, even out of a dollar, was maddening.

She could refuse to sell the bricks to this man, hoping for a better offer, but she'd also run the risk of hoodlums showing up in the middle of the night and carting away all her hard-earned bricks while she slept . . . and sleep was a precious commodity. Nightmares about the fire jerked her awake almost every night, and she couldn't afford to lose any more sleep over an extra dollar. "Very well," she said, holding out her hand for payment.

Besides, she had something far more valuable in her bodice. Bringing up the subject of the deed to Zack was like playing with a lit fuse, but that deed was worth something, and she'd be a fool to overlook it. Everyone knew Hartman intended to rebuild his store on the same plot of land, and he didn't have clear title to do so until she surrendered this deed. Now that she knew there'd be precious little coming in from insurance, the deed was her last remaining asset to get the 57th back in operation.

It was time to find Zack and negotiate a settlement over the deed. He was the last person in the city of Chicago with whom she wanted to haggle. His reputation as a negotiator was legendary, and confronting him without Frank would feel like going into battle without a weapon, but Frank was likely to antagonize Zack. The two of them seemed biologically incapable of sharing the same air space without needling each other, so she'd be better off on her own.

Mollie sat on the church steps and finger-combed her hair. Despite her nerves, a part of her looked forward to seeing Zack again, and the man adored the sight of her hair. She took a little foolish pride in it as she let it stream down her back.

She used the long walk to his office at the Chinese laundry to run through her arguments. If she walked into this meeting unprepared, he'd have her hogtied and helpless within two minutes.

It took her over an hour to cross through the burned district as she navigated around piles of debris that swelled to monumental proportions. With the footprint of the ruined buildings erased from the landscape, the only indication of where the streets had once been were the weird twisted shapes of the lampposts. As the iron posts melted during the fire, the weight of the lamps caused them to bow to the earth. Hundreds of contorted lampposts, bent over like hairpins, were haunting reminders of the ferocious heat of the fire.

The Chinese laundry had escaped the blaze by only two blocks. As she stepped inside, the warmth of the kettles enveloped her, and she sighed in pleasure as the heat penetrated her numb limbs. She rubbed her hands as she glanced around the space. Two Chinese ladies used huge paddles to nudge clothing in the oversized kettles. In the back of the room, Zack sat behind a makeshift desk.

He shot to his feet. "Mollie!"

By heaven, he was attractive. In the heat of the laundry, he had removed his jacket and collar, leaving his white shirt open at the throat and showing a wide swath of his warm, tanned neck. But most disconcerting was his expression. With a smile so bright it lit his eyes and transformed his entire face, she knew her next words would erase that look of delight and throw a healthy dose of chaos back into both their lives.

"Hello, Zack. I've come to discuss a little business."

Even from across the room, she could sense the ripple of tension that gripped his frame. The light in his eyes faded, but his voice was carefully neutral. "Ah."

She held up both hands. "Now, don't get defensive. I want to discuss the deed like a rational person. I know I haven't always done that in the past."

Without a word, Zack pulled a chair from the corner of the room and placed it beside his makeshift desk. He nodded and gestured for her to sit. Even in his casual clothing, he instantly reverted to the Zack Kazmarek she had known for these past three years. Formal, stiff, and intimidating.

"What would you like to discuss, Mollie?"

There was nothing hostile or aggressive in his tone. He was flawlessly polite and rational, but she was quaking in her battered, insubstantial boots. She didn't want to risk their friendship over that deed, but if she didn't, where would Frank and Declan and all the others find employment?

She cleared her throat and began with the first of her carefully planned arguments. "I don't know why my father still had the deed to that piece of land in his trunk. You say Louis Hartman paid for it, but if that's true, the deed should have been surrendered. I don't suppose we will ever know the truth of the matter, but I am willing to compromise on a negotiated settlement. It seems like the quickest way for both sides to reach a resolution."

"I agree."

"Secondly . . ." She drew up short. "You do?" She searched his face to see if he was joking, but he looked impassive and businesslike.

"I am not at liberty to offer you a settlement without Mr. Hartman's agreement, but I'm working on that."

"You are?"

His black brows lowered. "Of course I am! What kind of idiot do you take me for?"

He went on to explain that he'd already been trying to soften Louis up to the idea. There was likely to be a backlog in the courts for years, but parties that had a mutual agreement might be able to shortcut that line.

"Don't get too excited," Zack said. "Louis is willing to spend a hundred dollars on a bottle of champagne, but he will also go to court if he thinks he is being cheated of a single dollar. It may take a while."

Zack's gaze flicked down to her mismatched plaid skirt and

flowered blouse. "While you are in this part of town, let's swing by my townhouse. You can pick out a bedroom for yourself and borrow some decent clothing from Mother. I'm tired of the thought of you shivering in that church. Not when I can provide you with a decent roof over your head."

"I'm fine at the church."

Zack would have none of it. "Mollie, that burned-out ruin isn't safe. Packs of vagabonds are roaming the streets, causing trouble. For pity's sake, that church doesn't even have a front door."

"Zack, it wouldn't be proper to move in with you."

"Don't be a stubborn idiot. You're wearing rags, and it looks like you haven't had a decent night's sleep in weeks!"

He was shouting at her now. Mollie glanced nervously at the two ladies hoisting dripping mounds of sodden cloth from the kettles, listening to every word.

"Could we please step outside? It's getting overheated in here."

He threw down a pencil and followed her out into the bustle of the midday street. "Mollie, you *can't* go on staying at the church. Winter is coming on."

She walked along the wooden plank sidewalk, drawing her cloak tight against the chill. How could she tell him the real reason she was afraid to move into his house? Frank and Ulysses's warnings echoed in her mind. Frank Spencer was possibly the wisest man she had ever met, and he had been sounding the alarm bells about Zack from the moment the man had offered to buy the 57th.

But even more disconcerting was that portrait of the girl in the garden in Zack's house. If what she suspected was true, how could she move into his home? She paused so she could look him in the face. "Zack, there is a painting in your dining room."

He stiffened. It was barely perceptible, but it was as if a wire had just pulled taut every muscle in his body. "What about it?"

She tried to think of a graceful way to ask her question. "Dr. Buchanan said it looks like me," she blurted out.

"I agree."

She waited for him to elaborate. He didn't. "That's it? You agree?" Pedestrians walking in the midday traffic jostled her, and a boy hawking eggs made it hard to hear. Zack pulled her into the courtyard of a boardinghouse where they were out of the line of traffic. He braced his boot along a low brick planter and stared at the hazelnut shrubs growing within.

"That painting shows a pretty girl holding a watch," he said softly. "There is no more practical, functional piece of equipment than a watch, and I admire watchmakers. The skill and the patience it takes to assemble hundreds of tiny components into something that functions in perfect, flawless harmony. If one tiny part breaks, the whole thing collapses."

It surprised her that he had paid such attention to the details of her business. He had seemed indifferent the day he'd visited the workshop, but as she was coming to learn, Zack was a master at disguising his interest. He had not stopped speaking, and she had to lean forward as his voice lowered, became sadder.

"I grew up watching the two people I love most in the world fling themselves against a brick wall year after year in a hopeless quest," he said. "My parents will be fighting to restore the Polish nation until their dying day, and they will lose. My father once saved six hundred dollars from backbreaking work hauling concrete off the docks. It took him a decade to save that money, but he gave every dime of it to a Polish lawyer who said he could block Russia from conscripting Polish men into the army. The lawyer took the money and was never seen again. My parents will never stop pouring whatever resources they have into their ridiculous, foolish quest. I can't stop them. I've tried."

Pain shadowed his black eyes, but there was hope too as he stared into the distance. "There is a beautiful insanity in their dreams," he said. "They flounder with no plan or wisdom to guide their passion. They will never be more than dreamers who shake their fists at the wind." He turned his shoulders, and Mollie could see his face plainly. "I see the same beautiful insanity in you, but it is different. You produce the most gloriously impractical watches on the face of the planet, but in doing so, you've got a business that feeds forty families. You've found room in your workshop to support a man whose hands tremble, for a lawyer who can't see. It isn't the world of watchmaking that spurs you forward, it is a commitment to those veterans."

Her heart expanded in her chest in a curious mix of pain and pleasure. How perfectly he understood her! No one had ever connected with her on such a level, and it was like stepping into a warm bath, surrounding her with comfort and security.

A curious light illuminated Zack's face. "My parents are driven by their hearts, and so are you. But, Mollie, you've got the brains and the patience and logic to make your dreams soar. Do you know how attractive that is to me? Even the way you dress is so prim and controlled, but you've got the instinct and heart of an artist bottled up inside." His gaze trailed to the waist of her skirt. Watching her with caution, he reached out to caress her hip, landing on the small hard disk of her father's watch in her skirt pocket. His voice was as warm as velvet. "You create spectacular watches, and yet your own pocket watch is a plain, sensible piece used simply for keeping time."

He was overwhelming. She ought to take a step back and brush his hand away, but she remained in place, so close she felt the heat radiating from his body. "It doesn't even keep time anymore," she whispered.

A hint of sympathy shadowed his eyes. "I expect you will fix that in short order."

It would be her first task the moment she had a functioning workshop. She looked down, staring at the open collar of his shirt. She must not let him sidetrack her. This was exactly what Frank had warned her about.

"I am not moving in with you," she said. "The city is building relief barracks that will be open in another week. The church is fine until then." She hugged her cloak tighter and took a step back from him.

"Think of the advantages," Zack pressed. "My mother will cook a hot meal three times a day. Anything you want. Pot roast. Mashed potatoes and gravy. Pierogis by the dozen."

Now he wasn't fighting fair. No matter how much bread or how many apples she ate, her stomach always felt empty. Mrs. Kazmarek's meals were magnificently filling, and she could not stop dreaming about them. She turned to look up at him. "What is flaki?" she asked.

"Flaki? Why do you ask?"

"When we took your mother's satchel to your townhouse the other day, she fed us flaki stew."

Zack blanched. "She didn't. She wouldn't dare."

Mollie almost laughed at his mortified expression. "She did. Since you are bragging about how wonderful it would be to have your mother cook for us, I am curious. What exactly is in flaki?"

"You don't want to know."

"That's what she said. Oddly, I find myself intensely curious."

Zack shifted and looked like he hoped the ground would open up and swallow him. "Did you know that flaki is the Polish word for *guts*?"

The mortified expression on his face made her want to double over with laughter, but she maintained a serene expression on her face. "Suddenly, the meager offerings from the relief wagon seem extra tempting today."

Before heading back to the church, she let Zack buy her a round of cheese and a cranberry pie to take back to the others. The food was welcome, but best of all was knowing that Zack was now on her side. He would reason with Louis Hartman about the deed, and this disagreeable business could be put behind them once and for all.

Zack's days were filled with insurance work and trying to contract with scarce workers to get the land on Columbus Street cleared and ready for building, but nothing would stop him from being beside Mollie as she got her workshop underway for the first time.

The attic smelled of the yeasty scent of beer and fresh pine resin. For the past two days, workers from the 57th had been building shoulder-high tables, and the salvaged watchmaking equipment had been installed that morning.

Pride mingled with concern as Zack watched Mollie prepare for her first task. He hovered nearby, fists clenched, as she set her father's watch on the table and put a jeweler's loupe to her eye. There was no way that waterlogged watch could be salvaged, and he ached at the thought of Mollie getting clobbered with yet another blow. She seemed undeterred. Using the tiniest pair of pliers Zack had ever seen, she opened the back cover, lifted away a metal frame, and then poked at a series of screws, gaskets, and springs. She had the concentration of a surgeon on her face. One miniature piece after another was removed, cleaned, polished, and oiled; then it was all reassembled into the tiny compartment the size of a nickel.

Everyone in the attic stopped work and gathered around her table as she neared completion. She held her breath as she fitted the back casing into place and turned the winding stem. In the silence of the workshop, a distinctive *tick-tick-tick* filled the air. Mollie's smile was so wide Zack thought her face would split in two. She took care to set the watch on the worktable before flinging her arms around his neck. He picked her up. The space was too confined to whirl her in circles as he wanted, so he buried his face in her neck.

"I'm so proud of you," he whispered in her ear.

After that day, he came to the workshop each evening to walk Mollie and the others home. With Ulysses hobbling on a crutch and Frank being led by the hand, the group would be an easy target for the bands of troublemakers that still roamed the city. Not that Zack minded walking the group home each evening. He always mounted the brewery steps as quietly as possible so he could watch Mollie for a few moments. She was so passionate about whatever she was doing, whether it was assembling a watch or reviewing new designs with Alice. But his favorite part was when Mollie finally noticed him standing in the doorway. Her eyes lit up, and her hand inevitably flew to her hair. She had taken to wearing it down, which made her as beautiful as one of the pre-Raphaelite portraits that were all the rage in Europe.

The only cloud darkening his horizon was the deed to a half acre on Columbus Street. Zack knew Mollie still carried it tucked into her bodice, and sometimes he saw a hint of caution lurking in her eyes when she looked at him.

As well she ought. That scrap of paper was worth something, and he was letting the woman he loved work herself to the bone collecting scrap metal and bricks in order to earn a few dollars.

Convincing Louis to settle out of court was going to be a battle. The day after Mollie got the attic workshop in operation, he confronted Louis on the newly cleared plot of land on Columbus Street. The air was thick with dust and ash as hundreds of workers scrambled to load debris into wagons heading to the lake. Survey stakes had already plotted out the boundaries of their property, and an engineer was preparing to backfill the land to raise the elevation. Louis himself was helping to measure out the stakes, ensuring the foundation would be precisely as he wished it.

"Mollie's deed can stir up a mountain of trouble if not properly settled," Zack warned him. "The moment we start building, power begins shifting to Mollie. As the value of the land rises, so does her motivation to dig in her heels."

Louis leaned over and jabbed a stake into the dirt. "I already paid for this land," he snapped. "Every square inch of it. Make this problem go away, Kazmarek. I don't care how you do it, but make it go away."

"Two thousand dollars should do it," Zack said.

"Make it go away without my having to *pay* for it."

One of the land surveyors heard the simmering anger and stopped to stare. This was not the sort of conversation that should be overheard. Zack leaned forward and lowered his voice. "The longer we wait, the more likely her blind lawyer will figure out the real value of this land. Then you'll be *begging* her to accept two thousand dollars."

Zack could practically see the steam heating up inside Louis. "Fine," he finally said through clenched teeth. "Tell her I'll pay her once the New York bank releases a new set of funds to me. I'm up to my eyeballs in debt after paying to get the land cleared, so she'll have to wait a few weeks for the money."

A surge of relief shot through Zack like a bolt of lightning.

The faster he could get that deed away from Mollie, the closer he'd be to clearing the last remaining impediment between them.

～

The familiar grinding, clicking, and hum of watchmaking surrounded Mollie. The brewery attic was cramped, smelled like burned hops, and was a little too dim, but she was in *full production*! The technicians had jeweler's loupes pressed to their eyes and tweezers in their hands as they assembled the delicate internal mechanisms. A steady punch and grind sounded from the corner where highly polished sheet metal was being stamped out to make new springs and screws.

But instead of making watches, Mollie pored over the latest newssheet from the *Chicago Tribune*. It was hard to believe, but Queen Victoria had heard of the devastation in Chicago and was shipping a thousand books from London in order to create a library for Chicago. Each day, the newspapers carried stories of people from far and wide who were sending help to perfect strangers. A town in Bavaria had raised two thousand dollars for their German brethren who immigrated to Chicago. New York, Boston, and Washington, D.C. had all sent funds. President Grant donated a thousand dollars of his own money.

Mollie was grateful for the swell of goodwill flowing into their city that made it possible to keep body and soul together, but they could not subsist on charity forever. With Hartman's wiped out, she needed to find other rich people who could afford to buy her watches. And quickly, before next month's rent came due.

She picked up a watch that had been rescued from the fire. The watches were too valuable to be left unattended in the church, so she carried the sack of watches with her to the workshop each day and home at night, where someone slept curled around them. Mollie ran her thumb around the intricate vines of wild roses engraved in the gold watch cover. Her business would go under unless she could convince one of the wealthy East Coast stores to carry these watches.

What about a watch commemorating the Chicago fire? If wealthy people were willing to write checks, would they be willing to purchase something from a Chicago company? Something that memorialized the fire? It was the sort of bold, audacious design that made many of their watches collectors' items.

Alice pounced on Mollie's idea. It would be an easy task to remove the current watch covers of rose vines, melt the gold, and etch a new design. Alice sketched some rudimentary designs within an hour. Mollie and Alice thought it was a grand idea, but Frank was skeptical.

"Why would anyone want a watch engraved with scenes of the fire?" he asked. "It sounds morbid to me."

Mollie did her best to describe Alice's sketch to Frank. "It is an oddly beautiful design," she said. "The tongues of flames curl around the perimeter of the watch, and in the middle is the silhouette of the Chicago skyline. I suppose it might seem morbid to someone who lives here, but what about the people on the East Coast? I think they might buy a watch they knew was made by the people of Chicago and sketched by an artist who actually saw those buildings go down."

"It is a risky move, but a good one," Ulysses said as he rubbed his jaw. "We've got a ton of inventory and no one to buy it unless we can think of something to compete with the jewelers back East. No one has ever done anything like this. I say we go. Fast, while sympathy is still riding high."

Alice estimated it would take a week to finalize designs and create a template. After that, they would disassemble the watches, melt down the covers, and commence engraving the new design. In the meantime, the watch technicians would continue working at full steam on building new watch mechanisms.

Her decision made, Mollie donned a jeweler's loupe and began the meticulous work of assembling the mainspring of a watch. She smiled in satisfaction as she fitted the narrow strip of metal into its case.

"Mollie?"

She let the loupe drop from her eye. "Yes, Declan?"

"We are out of diamond powder. I checked the inventory, and there is none left."

Mollie remembered the day when Declan had spilled most of the diamond powder on the floor. Had it only been three weeks since that day? It seemed another lifetime ago.

"We always bought it from Hewitt's Mill, but I hear they got burned out in the fire," Declan said.

Mollie bit her lip as she considered the problem. Without diamond powder, they couldn't get their metalwork polished as smoothly as necessary. It was the very first step in the watch-making process, just before they began stamping out screws, springs, and gaskets.

Before she could respond to Declan, the door flung open, and Mollie was surprised to see Zack, breathless and flushed from a dash up the staircase. "Mollie, love!" he said with a reckless grin. "Let's take a walk."

A thrill raced down to her toes when he tossed out casual endearments. She glanced at the others all working at their benches. "It is the middle of the day, Zack."

A grin tugged at the corner of his mouth. "And we all know Miss Knox would never slack off in the middle of the day." He strolled forward, his chip-toothed smile making her heart surge. "Well then, how about we go for a walk while we talk business? I've got important news." His gaze dropped to her bodice. "About a piece of paper you've been carrying about."

She caught her breath. If there was a settlement in the wind, she needed to know immediately. Without a second thought, she hopped off the stool and snatched her cloak. "I'll be back soon," she called to the others over her shoulder.

"What kind of business?" she asked the moment she stepped into the chilly autumn air.

Zack tucked her hand into the crook of his elbow and tugged her alongside him as he strode down the street. "My, my, aren't we single-minded," he said with a grin.

The street was dense with wagons hauling building supplies and workmen lugging sacks of barley into the brewery. Chicago had been a boomtown as far back as she could remember, but as the frenzy of reconstruction was added to regular business, it was hard to find space on the streets.

"You seem remarkably jolly this afternoon," she said, breathless from keeping up with his strides. He flashed her a heart-stopping smile as he pulled her behind an ornate iron lamppost. Big arms clamped around her, he whispered in her ear, "I am jolly because I've convinced Hartman to buy that piece of paper you've got tucked into your bodice. No court case, no waiting for your money. Two thousand dollars, payable in cash."

Her gaze flew to his. "Are you joking?" she asked. Her back ached from days of sorting bricks in order to collect five dollars per wagonload. *Two thousand dollars*. Two thousand dollars would buy materials for a year. It would pay her workers until she could ship her watches to the East Coast. Two thousand dollars meant work and hope and dignity.

"I wouldn't joke about something like that, Mollie. Hartman is flat broke until the bank releases an insurance payment at the beginning of November, but then we will pay you." He touched a finger to the collar of her blouse, sending shivers racing through her. "All you have to do is sign the back of that piece of paper. We leave it at the bank and close the deal as soon as the money comes through. It will all be written up in perfect detail. You can take it to Frank for review."

The weight of anxiety she didn't even know she had been carrying lifted away as she smiled up into his flashing dark eyes. Zack wasn't trying to cheat her, he was smoothing the way.

Everything was falling into place exactly as it should.

It took less than an hour to go to the bank and draw up the paper work for the proposed deal. Could it really be this easy? Zack and the banker lined all the documents up and assured her she'd have plenty of time to review them with Frank before closing the deal.

Afterward, Zack found a quiet courtyard to escape the bustle of the street. Surrounded by an ivy-covered stone wall and sheltered by the spreading branches of a hawthorn tree, it seemed they had just stepped into a refuge from the commotion of the city. Zack lowered his forehead to hers, and she savored his strength as she settled against him. "I need to go to New York and Philadelphia to wrangle with the insurance companies," he said. "I'll be gone at least two weeks, maybe three. We will close the deal when I return."

She nodded, already missing his warm, irreverent presence.

"You are *it*, Mollie," he whispered. "You are exactly the sort of woman I have always wanted to find. The city can burn to the ground, but you don't lose your head. You are passion and intelligence and beauty, and I love you to the bottom of my soul."

Mollie's breath froze in her lungs. She wasn't ready for this. Zack was a wild, unpredictable force of nature, while she lived

in an orderly world of ticking watches and production schedules. She wasn't ready for this, but there was no stopping Zack.

"I want you out of that church and into someplace safe," he
said. "I want to *marry you*, Mollie. Say yes."

She couldn't even draw a breath. Her life had been swept up
into a whirlwind, smashed into pieces, and then reassembled
into a wild and exciting world with which she had no experience.

She risked a glance at his face. "You know this terrifies me,
right?"

His gaze did not waver; it only became more tender as he
caressed the side of her face. "I'm betting you'll brave it out."

She wanted to, but this wild, impulsive urge was frightening.
She needed time to process the disordered jumble of feelings that
were so unfamiliar to her. "I need to get back to the workshop
and see about getting diamond powder."

He cocked a brow at her. "I lay my soul at your feet and you
want to talk about buying supplies?" He smiled as he leaned
down to touch his forehead to hers again. "I want to marry you,
Mollie. Say yes. Say yes, and we'll be one for the ages."

"I can't. Not yet."

"When I get back from New York."

"Not then either. Zack, I'm not impulsive. You can't rush me
into something like this."

Zack winked down at her. "How about I rush you into lunch,
then?" If he took offense at her refusal to budge on the proposal,
he gave no sign of it as he strode down the street, whistling in
good humor. Mollie had no desire to be trapped inside a fancy
hotel dining room, so Zack bought zesty German sausages from
a street vendor. She was amazed at the amount of spicy mustard
Zack slathered on the bratwurst wrapped in freshly baked bread,
but it was delicious. They found a place to eat away from the
crush of pedestrians on the street. She held their food as Zack

wrapped both hands around her middle and lifted her onto the ledge of a brick wall. Then he hopped up beside her.

"There is something I've been meaning to ask you," she said as she handed Zack a bratwurst. It was a little awkward, but if Zack was the man she was going to marry, she needed to know what she was getting into.

"Yes?"

"That story about the fish. Is it true?"

Zack's grin was roguish. "I don't know. What have you heard?"

"Something about a hundred pounds of fish dumped on a merchant's fancy desk. Is it true?"

Zack took a large bite of his sausage and watched her through laughing eyes as he chewed. How could she consort with a man with such a shocking reputation? She was a safety-and-security girl, and Zack was an untamed force of nature. He finished chewing and sent her a wicked grin. "It was trout," he said proudly. "And we've never had substandard fish palmed off on us since."

"If someone sold me shoddy merchandise, I would have filed a complaint at the Cook County Courthouse."

"I wanted the problem solved by lunchtime, not the next decade."

And that was the difference between her and Zack. She played by the rules, and he looked for any way to avoid them. He didn't actually break them, but he knew where he could bend, skirt, and twist them to his advantage. While she obediently filled out her insurance claim and collected three cents on the dollar, Zack went dashing off to New York to press his case.

Zack dragged her out of her comfortable world, but hadn't the fire already done that? In this new world, perhaps it made sense to ally herself with someone who was comfortable riding the whirlwind. Her heart had already been won; it was only her logical and cautious brain that resisted.

Looking at Zack's handsome face as he grinned down at her, she hoped her brain would be ready to follow orders when he returned from New York.

13

A little of the excitement faded from Mollie's life when Zack left town, although she was so busy at the workshop she was lucky to find time for lunch each day. There was a Polish grocery across the street from the brewery, and they sold prepared food to the hundreds of workers in the brewery district. Mollie sat at one of the tiny tables in the corner to enjoy a bowl of *borscht* with Dr. Buchanan, who was helping them with odd jobs at the workshop.

Actually, Mollie was certain that Dr. Buchanan suffered from terrible loneliness. "I like being with the people of the 57th," he admitted. "I've never really had a family like that. Dentistry is a solitary profession. I didn't think about that when I chose it."

He had developed a fondness for Polish cooking, and when he didn't take his meals at the Polish grocer, he hiked across town to share a meal with Zack's parents. Mrs. Kazmarek had adopted Dr. Buchanan as an "honorary Pole" and was happy to keep filling him with flaki, pierogi, and kielbasa. He had been wandering the city for a week, looking for a suitable room to lease where he might be able to restart his dental practice, but it seemed every available attic, shed, lean-to, or basement had already been snapped up.

Mollie considered her suggestion carefully before mentioning it to him. Self-sufficiency was important to a man's pride, and she didn't want to offend Dr. Buchanan, but perhaps there was a mutually beneficial arrangement they could make.

"I will be rebuilding my workshop on my land on East Street," Mollie said one afternoon as they took lunch. "I don't need a lot of room for watchmaking, and perhaps I could reserve a corner of the building for a dental shop. I could use a little income from a rental space," she added.

Dr. Buchanan immediately straightened, hope lighting his eyes. "When do you think you can have the building ready?"

That was the rub. Bricklayers and carpenters were more highly prized than diamonds. "All the builders I've spoken to are booked through spring," she said. "With luck, perhaps I can start building next summer."

The light faded from Dr. Buchanan. "I can't afford to wait that long." He finished his soup, then walked her back to the brewery. "I'll be back this evening to walk you and the others home," he said.

"Did Zack ask you to do that?"

Dr. Buchanan twisted the corner of his mustache. "He might have mentioned it in passing. That stash you folks cart back and forth every night is worth guarding, and there are still some rowdy elements on the streets." He winked down at her. "And it is not like I have been deluged with customers."

That night, as she fell asleep in the church, she added Dr. Buchanan to the list of people she prayed for.

~

Mollie emerged from a deep sleep as Alice shook her. "Someone is in the church," she said in a harsh whisper.

Mollie was still bleary as she pushed up onto an elbow, listening to footsteps shuffle outside her tent. With the flaps closed, no light penetrated the thick woolen fabric, and Mollie was blind to who was outside. People sometimes moved around at night to use the privy, but never did they stumble about this badly. And it sounded like more than one person.

"Who's out there?" a loud voice demanded from the opposite side of the church. It was Dr. Buchanan.

The glow of a lantern illuminated the space outside the tent, and Mollie peeked outside the flaps, squinting at the sudden light.

Her heart almost stopped. There were at least six strange men in the church! A redheaded man with a droopy mustache raised a rifle to his shoulder and swung it like a baseball bat at the tent where Ulysses and Declan slept. The tent collapsed and the men inside scrambled beneath the fabric.

"Where are the watches?" the redheaded man demanded. He yanked the tent to the side, wooden posts clattering across the floor. Ulysses searched madly through the blankets for his crutch, but Declan stared at the men, frozen in panic. Mollie felt just as helpless, crouched in the opening of her tent.

The redheaded man spotted her. As he drew the rifle back to strike, Mollie jerked the tent post, collapsing heavy folds of the tent on top of her, but at least she wasn't paralyzed anymore.

She pushed through the cloth, grasping the tentpole before her. "Get out of here."

"Where are the watches?" A brutal hand shoved her to the ground. The stranger jerked the tent from where it lay, exposing Alice, who clutched her blankets to her chest, her face white with fear. The man jerked the blanket away and began riffling through their clothes and blankets.

Ulysses hadn't found his crutch, but he dragged himself across the floor on his strong forearms. "Leave my wife alone," he growled. All around the church, people were emerging from their tents.

"Jesse, don't be an idiot!"

Was that Ralph Coulter's voice? Another tent collapsed as the strangers swiped at it with their rifles. Declan lunged at one of the intruders but fell when a bull of a man smacked him on the head with the butt of a rifle.

There was worse to come. They found Frank's tent, jerking it aside as Frank clutched the muslin bundle of watches to his chest, his sightless eyes wide with panic. One of the thugs riffled through his blankets. "Where's the stash?" the stranger demanded.

"Get out of here," Frank warned.

"Or what, old man?" The stranger punched Frank in the face. Even as he fell to his side, Frank maintained his grasp on the bag.

"Leave him alone," Mollie shouted. "He's blind!"

Pandemonium continued around them as the intruders ransacked tent after tent. Declan tried to get to Frank's side, but another man hit him from behind, driving him to the floor. Two of the men noticed how protective Frank was of the bag and honed in, circling like wolves. When they tried to pry the bag away, Frank rolled over onto it.

One of the men lifted his rifle and clobbered Frank in the side of his head. Two more brutal blows landed on Frank's head before Mollie could get to his side, swinging the tentpole like a baseball bat at the stranger's head. The thin pole didn't carry much weight. One of the other thugs pried it from her hands and shoved Mollie aside.

"Got it!" The man had wrestled the bag from Frank's arms and was poking through it. "Lookie here," he gloated. "We struck gold!"

The men lost interest in Frank, who lay motionless on the ground. Mollie stumbled to his side. "Frank? Frank!"

Having gotten what they came for, the strangers ran from the church, taking their lantern with them. The weak moonlight showed trails of blood streaming down Frank's face. His face was ashen, but his lips twitched as he tried to say something.

The others gathered around. Dr. Buchanan brought a towel and pressed it against the wound pulsing on Frank's forehead. "Hold on there, old soldier," the dentist said in a shaky breath.

Frank opened his eyes. "Mollie?"

She grasped his hand. "I'm right here, Frank. Gunner has run for a doctor. Just hang on."

Frank's mouth struggled to form words. There was enough light for Mollie to see something was badly wrong. One of Frank's pupils was huge, the other a tiny pinprick.

"Mollie," he gasped. "Your dad—greatest man I ever knew. Gave us dignity." His breath was jerky, and his voice was as pale as a wisp of smoke. "Thankful. I'm thankful."

Her vision blurred through the tears. "I know that, Frank. I need you to save your breath." But Frank stared straight ahead, his face blank in the moonlight. His lips stopped moving.

This couldn't be happening. Frank could conquer anything, rise to any challenge. He was a mighty oak tree that could withstand any storm and shelter her from whatever fears plagued her. He couldn't be this broken man sprawled on the church floor. Alice brought a bowl of water and squeezed out a rag, but Dr. Buchanan leaned down, his ear close to Frank's face, then laid a hand on Frank's chest. Mollie held her breath and waited.

"He's gone, Mollie."

She doubled over, clasping Frank's still-warm hand, still soft and pliable, but lifeless. Everyone from the church clustered around Frank's broken body, staring in disbelief. She looked to the sky, spattered with stars a million miles overhead. Somewhere out there, Frank's soul was speeding toward heaven. She knew that angels were waiting to receive him, and Frank would be able to see again through eyes that could behold the beauty of creation.

Frank's suffering was over.

"We should pray," she said weakly. But her mind was blank. How could she pray when her heart was splitting apart in grief? Frank had been taken in such a brutal manner, but he was now looking down on them. She was weeping for herself, not Frank. But as tears fell and prayers were said, Mollie's spirit stumbled. Fell. It was hard to even breathe as the grief descended and covered her.

"Dear Lord, help us all," she whispered before collapsing into tears.

14

No one was sure what had happened to Declan after the attack. Mollie remembered seeing him lunge at one of the men, but after that, he had vanished.

"I'm worried about him," Mollie told the police officer who came to inspect the scene the afternoon following the crime. "Declan is a good man, but a fragile one. Can you help us find him? I fear he may come to harm."

Officer O'Malley shook his head. "Ma'am, we've got our hands full trying to get this city back in order. An able-bodied man is not someone we can afford to spend time tracking down."

It was another blow to her reeling mind. The logical portion of her brain told her it was right for the police to focus on hunting down the ruffians who had killed Frank. She could accept that, but every instinct in her body feared for Declan. Frank had passed over to a better place, but Declan had sunk backwards into his mind-shattering torment.

And he wasn't the only one to go missing after the raid. Ralph Coulter, the lumber merchant, was nowhere to be found. Mollie told the officer she thought she'd heard Mr. Coulter's voice during the attack. "I think he said, 'Jesse, don't be an idiot.'

I can't be certain it was Mr. Coulter's voice. It was dark and everything was so confused."

"Did anyone else hear it?" the officer asked.

Gunner agreed with Mollie and thought Mr. Coulter said it, but one of the other men said it sounded like Declan. Whoever the intruders were, they had known about the watches.

Mollie's shoulders sagged as she sat on the steps. The police had been there for two hours, interviewing everyone and making Mollie relive those horrible minutes over and over. Had Zack gotten her telegram yet?

It was wrong of her to be so focused on Zack, but this morning she had been on the verge of cracking into a thousand pieces, and it was going to be at least two weeks until Zack came back from New York. She didn't think she could wait even two more hours to fling herself into his arms and sob out her heart onto his shoulder.

Alice had walked with her to the telegraph station that morning. Her message to Zack was brief and to the point. *Frank killed. Need you. Please come.*

That had been four hours ago. It was possible that even now Zack had received her message and was on his way back home. Knowing that Zack's strong presence would soon be there was the slender thread of strength to which she clung as her world collapsed around her.

They held Frank's funeral at a church north of the burned district. The barren sycamore tree limbs looked black against the leaden skies, and Mollie's heart was so heavy it hurt to even draw a full breath of air. Frank had been a second father to her. Papa's death had been terrible, but it was a normal and natural part of life. There was nothing natural about what had happened to Frank. During his last desperate moments he had tried so valiantly to hang on to their watches, the product of a company that had given him work and dignity. Those ignorant jackals had escaped with the watches, leaving a man of immense pride beaten to death in their wake.

It was three days before Mollie returned to the rented attic space above the brewery. The intellectual challenge of assembling a watch was a perfect task to occupy her frazzled mind.

Except that her new landlord was blocking her access to the staircase. "Your rent is late."

Mollie blanched. He was right, but she didn't have so much as a dime to her name. In addition to the watches that had been stolen, the thieves had made off with the five dollars Mollie had earned from collecting bricks.

"I'm sorry," Mollie said. "There was a death in my family, and I have been occupied elsewhere." Frank Spencer was no blood relation, but he was family, and Mollie would refer to him as no less.

The landlord pursed his lips. "I heard about your troubles, and I'm sorry. But I need rent, and if you can't pay, I will lease the space to someone who can. I get people asking every day for space, and it was only out of respect I've been holding it for you. I'll need full payment by the end of the week, Miss Knox."

He wouldn't even let her into the attic until she'd paid. She returned to the church and asked members of the 57th if they could help. Ulysses had nine dollars, and Dr. Buchanan offered thirty, but it wasn't enough.

"What about Mr. and Mrs. Kazmarek?" the dentist asked. "They know Zack would loan you the money in a heartbeat."

She wouldn't feel right going to the Kazmareks. Zack had not responded to her telegram, and she couldn't even be sure he had received it. His parents looked as poor as church mice, and it would be awkward asking them for money.

Besides, Mollie knew exactly where she could turn for a favor. Sophie's father was one of the most powerful architects in the city. Given the amount of work that was flooding his way, he ought to be flush with cash, and he had already told her to let him know if she ever needed anything.

Never in her life did she think she would stoop to begging, but when the fate of the 57th was on the line, Mollie wasn't too proud to ask Mr. Durant for a loan.

~

As Mollie walked down Prairie Avenue, she could hardly believe she was still in Chicago. The homes were monumental in scale, but so different in style. Some looked like castles made of ivory granite with turrets, spires, and balconies. Others were sober red sandstone with mansard roofs and iron gates. All of them were tucked beneath the spreading branches of cottonwood and sycamore trees filling the air with a mossy scent. Mollie had always known there were spectacularly wealthy people in Chicago. After all, they were the people who had bought her gold and gem-encrusted watches, but she had never actually seen the palaces where they lived.

With her donated clothing and the heels of her shoes worn to a nub, Mollie felt like a crow among swans as she approached an impressive Romanesque home built of native granite with rough-hewn arches marching across its front. A flagstone path led to a grand entryway and massive mahogany doors. After pulling the bell, she wondered if there was a different entrance she should have used. Didn't houses like this have a servants' entry? But it didn't matter, because when she gave the butler her name, it wasn't long before Mr. Durant came striding

ELIZABETH CAMDEN

through the hall to clasp her hands as though she were a long-lost friend.

"Miss Knox!" he said. "Won't Sophie be glad to see you. Not an hour goes by that she does not regale us with stories from the church."

Mollie dropped her gaze. She was embarrassed to admit that coming to visit Sophie had not entered her thoughts. She cleared her throat. "I'd be happy to visit with Sophie, but I actually came to speak with you about a bit of business."

His brows shot up in surprise, and he stroked his neatly trimmed beard. "Of course. Let us take some tea in the parlor and we can chat there."

While they were waiting for the tea, Mr. Durant offered his sympathies over Frank. "I saw it reported in the *Tribune*," he said. "Sophie was upset when I told her, but she needed to know. She had been pestering us to take her to the church for a visit ever since she returned. Everyone else is in good health, I take it?"

"As well as can be expected, I suppose." She did not want to discuss the continuing absence of Declan. No one believed he had been physically injured, but it had been five days, and he had failed to return to the church. Mollie had made inquiries at the brewery, and no one had seen him there either.

"The men who came to the church stole some valuable watches," Mollie said. "I had intended to use those watches to restart my business. I expect to collect payment soon for a plot of land I just sold, but the cash will not be available until early November and I am in need of rent money this week. I was hoping you might extend a short-term loan. I can pay you back by the middle of November."

Mr. Durant waved his hand. "Nonsense. I would be honored to help after all you did for Sophie. How much do you need?"

Mollie named the figure, which did not cause Mr. Durant to

171

even blink. She followed him down a hallway into a library that had been set up as a temporary office for his use while he was a guest. Even rich people had to be tucked into spare rooms, but this one had a diamond-pane window overlooking a Tudor garden that would have made Alice weep at its beauty. As Mr. Durant wrote out a check, Mollie tried to persuade him to consider it a loan.

"The land I sold is on Columbus Street," she said. "I will have no trouble paying you back as soon as the bank releases the funds."

Mr. Durant whistled. "I should think not. I hope you sold it for a pretty penny."

"I did," she confirmed, remembering the day she'd signed the agreement of sale with Zack. They had both been so foolishly excited that day, flirting and daydreaming about the future. "I got two thousand dollars for half an acre, which is a handsome sum, considering the street is utterly destroyed."

Mr. Durant's hand froze as he was writing out the check. "Two thousand dollars?" He stood and fixed her with a serious look. "The value of land on Columbus Street has soared since the fire. The street was too narrow to become the grand type of avenue people wanted it to be. Now that it is a blank slate, it is some of the most valuable land in the city. I would not have settled for less than fifteen thousand."

Mollie stared at him in drop-jawed amazement. She felt dizzy, then hot. Mr. Durant caught her elbow just as she began to sway. "Let me help you to a seat," he said, guiding her into a chair. "Poor thing, you look as white as a ghost. Now, what scoundrel got that land off you so cheaply?"

Zack! Zack did this to her.

Although he didn't actually buy the land for himself, he was acting for Hartman's, wasn't he? "Louis Hartman," she said faintly. "It is where he intends to build his new store."

Mr. Durant's face darkened even more. "That man is a wiz-
ard, no doubt about that. He and that lawyer of his have managed to win their entire insurance claim, worth eight hundred
thousand dollars, the rumors say. Can you imagine? More than
three-quarters of a million dollars for a building that burned
down. I gather they had their insurance spread out amongst a
number of carriers on the East Coast, which is why they were
able to score a full settlement. *Kazmarek*, that's the man's name.
Rumor has it he's the toughest lawyer in Chicago. A real street
thug Hartman found on the docks and dusted off to become
his lawyer."

Mollie couldn't say anything as she curled over in the chair.
Mr. Durant leaned over to pat her hand. "You haven't been paid
for the land yet?"

"No."

He rubbed his jaw. "I'm no lawyer, but it seems to me you
should be entitled to a slice of that eight hundred thousand in
addition to the value of the land. No wonder the lawyer wanted
to close the deal so quickly."

Mollie felt sick. She had never wanted a piece of that store
or the insurance money; she simply didn't want to be swindled.
Frank had mistrusted Zack from the moment they'd met, and
she should have listened to his advice.

She was such a naïve fool. For three years, she had triple-
checked her accounting, researched suppliers, and overseen every
aspect of production. The first move she'd made without relying
on Frank had been a disaster, all because Zack Kazmarek had
flattered her.

The pity in Mr. Durant's eyes was unbearable. She had to
get out of there.

"Excuse me," she mumbled. She made a dash for the door
and down the hallway. There had to be some room where she

could collapse in private. At the end of the hall was a room with a double-wide opening, with tubs and heating kettles within. The laundry room. Blessedly, it was empty.

Breathe, just breathe. She bent over the sink and clasped her hands over her face. She had survived worse than this and could do so again. She just felt so *stupid.* Stupid for being taken in by a pair of flashing black eyes. For believing a dance by the firelight of the braziers meant anything. Tears leaked between her fingers as she tried to steady her breath.

"I'm mad about what happened to Frank too."

Mollie whirled around. Sophie stood in the doorway, staring at her with a somber expression. She wore a velvet dress dripping with layers of lace. A porcelain doll dangled limply from her hand.

Mollie swiped her tears aside, ashamed to be caught sniveling over a street-thug lawyer when even Sophie knew who the real victim was. She wiped her face. She had just shed her last tear over Zachariasz Kazmarek. She had allowed herself the indulgence of a pathetic cry, but that was over. "Sophie." Mollie painted a pleasant expression on her face. "How pretty you look in your new dress."

"It's wrong to beat up a blind man."

What could one say to that? "Yes. Yes it is." Mollie straightened and adjusted the collar of her blouse. "Do you like living in your uncle's house? It certainly is splendid."

"I hate it," she said. "It's boring here. I want to go back to the church."

"My goodness. I thought you hated living at the church too."

Sophie's sullen expression did not waver; she merely shrugged. "So? I hate it here too. My uncle and my little brothers are stupid."

What is wrong with this girl? "Sophie, you are far too young to hate everything and everybody."

"I didn't hate Frank." With that, Sophie turned her back and walked away, dragging the porcelain doll on the floor behind her. The doll's head bounced along each seam in the tile floor.

Mollie felt like that doll. Dragged along and buffeted by the whims of fate. Every muscle in her battered body was exhausted from struggling against the wind.

That ended today. She had a check for a month's rent at the brewery and the ability to make the world's most beautiful watches. She had been betrayed by the man she loved, but wallowing in pity was a luxury she could not afford.

Mollie was ready to take her life back, and it would happen without Zack Kazmarek by her side.

15

It was time to leave the church and find shelter somewhere else. Mollie folded her few belongings and set them in a crate. By noon today she would leave this church behind forever, just as most of the others had already done.

The ruined church had once been a place of comfort to Mollie. It did not matter that it was dirty and uncomfortable and she nearly froze in the mornings. The people who had found shelter here had lingered for a good reason. Some of Mollie's best memories had happened right here. Sitting on the steps in the evening to share memories and dreams with other refugees who had been wiped out by the fire. Listening to the Germans in the nearby post office sing in the evening. There was something about a shared crisis that brought out the best in people. The warmth of the camaraderie she had found within these crumbling walls would be engraved on her soul until her dying day.

But it hurt too much to stay. The temporary barracks built by the city had just opened their doors. The hastily put-up buildings were like giant boxes, made of unfinished pinewood boards and stocked with bunk beds and a small coal-fueled heater. She and Alice would begin living in the women's barracks tonight.

It would be crowded to the rafters with strangers, but Mollie was eager to get there.

After paying her rent at the brewery, the owner had loaned Mollie a few crates to help her move out of the church. All of her belongings fit into a single crate. One spare skirt, a shirt, a blanket, and a scorched green paisley scarf. As Mollie folded the scarf, her fingers touched each of the burn holes. How terrified she had been the night of the fire, when it had seemed like the whole world was burning around her, but Zack had been so brave. No matter how badly he'd deceived her, he had been a hero that night. Zack had risked his life when he could have stayed in the safety of his townhouse. How could she look at this scarf and not be reminded of him?

She dropped the scarf to the ground. She would leave it there with the other memories that were too hard to endure.

Alice's voice interrupted her dreary thoughts. "Will you help me with this tent, Mollie?"

All the tents needed to be folded and returned to the relief society. There were surely other homeless people who would need them. "Let's gather them up and fold them outside," Mollie said.

Ulysses and Gunner were sharing a pipe on the steps of the church. "Need any help, Alice my love, light o' my life?"

"Mollie and I will do it," Alice said. "I am wise enough not to stand between a man and his pipe."

Mollie glanced around the street. It was hard to believe how attached she had become to this ruined landscape. If she ever came back to this place, it would look entirely different. The contorted lampposts would be removed and replaced with straight ones. The church would be torn down, and it was anyone's guess what would stand in its place. Who would remember the infant that had been born in the chancel? Or the wonderful stories they'd told one another, huddled around the brazier?

A movement caught her eye at the end of the street. A group of men were headed this way. Strange, it seemed as though they were marching in a square, like a platoon of soldiers. Mollie shielded her eyes from the sun and squinted to be sure she was seeing correctly.

"Declan?" Sure enough, Declan McNabb was at the head of the group of men heading toward the church, and he was smiling. She'd never seen Declan smile before, but there was another man beside him who looked familiar. She couldn't put her finger on where she'd seen that handsome blond man before. . . .

Ulysses shot upright, bracing himself against Alice's shoulder. "I don't believe my eyes," he said in a shattered voice. "I don't believe my eyes!" he repeated, shouting this time as he reached for his crutch. He tucked it under his shoulder and launched toward the group of men as fast as he could hobble. "Colonel Lowe!" Ulysses shouted. Old Gunner went racing to join the crowd of men as well.

The men in the distance broke ranks and started running toward Ulysses, who sent up a hearty round of laughter. Mollie glanced at Alice, who looked as bewildered as Mollie felt.

By now, the group of men had circled around Ulysses, laughing and pounding one another on the back. Mollie wended her way through the rubble on the street toward the group. As she drew closer, she noticed some of the men were wearing sack coats and caps from the Civil War.

The blond man moved away from the group to stand before Mollie. With faultless posture and high cheekbones beneath clear blue eyes, he was certainly a handsome man. There was a cleft in his chin, and he was smiling at her. "Miss Knox?" he asked.

At her nod, he saluted her. "Colonel Richard Lowe, commander of the 57th Illinois Regiment. At your service."

Her eyes widened. Her father had praised Colonel Lowe

so highly she thought he probably walked three inches off the ground. Colonel Lowe was one of the youngest colonels in the Union Army and had led the 57th through one fierce battle after another.

"I'm pleased to finally meet you," she said, her gaze tracking to the other men who were still clustered around Ulysses and Gunner. "But what? Why?"

Before the colonel could reply, Declan stepped forward. He looked flushed with good health, but the laughter faded from his eyes as he approached. "After Frank died, I figured we needed help," he said. "I knew the men of the 57th wouldn't let us down. Not after what happened to Frank. I took the train to Waukegan to get Colonel Lowe, and we've been rounding up the others ever since."

Mollie looked in amazement at the group of healthy able-bodied men. Her father had extended work to the crippled soldiers of the 57th, but throughout the state there were plenty of able-bodied veterans who had survived the final three-day clash at the Battle of Winston Cliff. And they had just come to her rescue.

As one man after another stepped forward to introduce himself, Mollie lost the ability to speak. There was Ernest Jones, a dairy farmer from Belvidere, Josiah Coleman, a shoemaker, and Grady O'Manion, a bricklayer. There was a man who insisted on being called merely "Moose" who ran cattle in the western part of the state. Eighteen men in all.

Mollie was dizzy by the time they all introduced themselves. "Declan tells us you've got land to build on, but no money and no labor," Colonel Lowe said. "We have come to fix that. O'Manion is a bricklayer, and he'll get the land ready to lay a foundation. Bridgerton has connections in the building trade and can get us mortar. Billy Thompson will be in charge of getting hardware and plumbing. Moose will do the hauling."

Mollie's mind was awhirl. *Oh my goodness, eighteen mouths to feed.* And shelter. "You must be hungry," she said, scrambling for a solution. "I know of a butcher who can supply us with—"

Colonel Lowe cut her off. "We've made arrangements for provisions," he said. "And I've secured housing from General Sheridan for my men in one of the barracks. The only thing I need from you is to tell us what kind of building you want for a watch factory. We will take it from there."

It was an answer to prayer. All throughout the city, workmen were worth their weight in gold, and eighteen had just walked up to her front step. Mollie was breathing so fast she was getting light-headed. "I can't thank you enough," she said. "I will be sure that you are all well compensated for—"

This time when Colonel Lowe cut her off, there was a thread of steel in his voice. "Miss Knox, we are here because wild horses could not keep us away. Your father did for my wounded brothers what I was unable to do. Every man I have brought with me owes your father a debt we can never repay. We are honored to rebuild his company. *Honored.*"

Was this a dream? As the colonel spoke, layers of anxiety peeled away from her spirit. It was as if an army of angels had descended to earth to ease her burdens.

She must not cry in front of all these men. They would think her a useless watering pot unworthy of her father's inheritance. Everything went blurry as she turned away, trying to hide the tears.

Colonel Lowe bent down to peek beneath her lowered head, a trace of humor on his strong face. "Tears? We've come all the way across the state to meet the famous Miss Mollie Knox, and all she has for us are tears?"

She swiped them away. "It is just that I have felt so overwhelmed. It has been a difficult few weeks."

"Then those are the last tears you will shed from being overwhelmed," he said. Colonel Lowe's face was a blend of kindness and humor as he smiled at her. "We will not leave this city until your factory is rebuilt and you are once again producing the world's most magnificent watches." Then the softness evaporated and his voice lowered. "And we will find the men who killed Frank Spencer. This I vow to you."

There was a rumble of agreement from the men who stood in a half circle around her. What had she ever done to deserve such a blessing? Declan was watching her, his face firm in determination. And that was when Mollie figured out why he looked so different. Standing tall and confident, his demons were nowhere to be seen. He had accomplished a mighty deed, and she would be forever in his debt.

She stepped forward to embrace him. "Declan McNabb, you have saved the day."

16

Zack's lungs were bursting and the muscles in his legs ached from the two miles he'd sprinted from the train depot. After almost forty-eight hours of constant travel, he had finally arrived in Chicago and wasted no time sprinting to the church. He vaulted up the steps and into the ruined nave. It was empty inside except for an old man picking through the rubble.

"Where is she?" he demanded.

The man stood. *"Ich spreche kein Englisch,"* he said.

Zack didn't speak German, and apparently this man didn't speak English. He took a few steps farther into the crumbling church. The tents were gone. There was no sign of the water barrel or the braziers. Mollie's scorched paisley scarf, lying tattered and abandoned on the ground, was the only sign she had ever been there.

The last two days had been the most frustrating of his life. Legal wrangling in Philadelphia had taken longer than expected, delaying his arrival in New York. By the time he got Mollie's telegram, it had been sitting at that New York hotel counter for five days. *Frank killed*, it said. If it had been an accident or natural causes, Mollie would not have used the word *killed*. Throughout the eight-hundred-mile journey, those two words had haunted him. What happened? Had she been hurt too? Even as he stood in the church like a helpless idiot, Mollie could be in a hospital or out on the street.

Zack dragged a hand through his hair, scanning the church. He poked through the rubble, looking for any sign of where she might have gone. That was when he saw the dark stain on the floor. A cold fist of anxiety gripped his stomach.

He tried the German man again. "What happened?" he asked. He pointed to the bloodstain on the floor. "Frank Spencer? What happened?"

The German pointed to a trio of people across the street sitting beside the burned-out post office. Zack bounded toward them. This group of Germans spoke English, and Zack listened in horror as they told him of the raid and the beating of a blind man until he was dead. As the details poured forth, Zack's mind reeled. He should never have allowed Mollie to stay there. He should have thrown her over his shoulder and carried her home that first day after the fire. Zack had never gotten on well with Frank, but he was the closest thing to a family Mollie had left, and Zack cursed himself for his failure to be there when she'd needed him.

The brewery was the next logical place to look. He was halfway down the street before he remembered something. Sprinting back to the church, he scooped up Mollie's discarded scarf and shoved it into his pocket.

It took him thirty minutes to get across town to the brewery district. He vaulted up the stairs and through the narrow opening into the brewery attic. Relief washed through him at the sight of two dozen people filling the space. Mollie was sitting before one of the tall worktables with a large piece of drafting paper before her. A blond man he had never seen before was sitting beside her.

She was alive. She was healthy. The wave of relief crashing through him was so powerful he swayed and leaned against the frame of the doorway. Exhaustion settled over him like a heavy wool blanket, but his eyes dilated as he drank in the sight of her. "Mollie."

When she glanced up, her face tightened. "Hello, Zack." Her voice was calm. Cold. Then, unbelievably, she sidled closer to the blond man and turned her attention back to the document spread out before her.

He pushed away from the doorway and stepped farther into the workshop. "I came as soon as I got your telegram. Are you okay?"

Her shoulders sagged and she turned away from him, bracing an elbow on the worktable and sinking her head into her hand. His heart turned over and he moved to her side. "Let's go outside, and you can tell me how you are doing."

She still hadn't moved. Everyone in the workshop had frozen, staring at him like he was a bomb about to explode. He glanced around. Most of the faces were familiar, but there were several men he'd never seen before. He could understand Mollie being upset by his delay getting there, but there was no need for her and everyone else in the room to treat him like a leper.

"Mollie?" He placed his hand on her shoulder, willing her to look at him. "Mollie, let's go someplace where we can talk," he said gently.

Her entire body stiffened. "I've got work to do," she mumbled. Was it his imagination or did she inch a little closer to the blond man beside her?

Zack grasped her elbow and leaned down to whisper in her ear. "Mollie, get your backside off that stool and come outside with me. I'll buy you a pretzel, and you can tan my hide for being late."

Mollie sprang down from the stool and marched to the door, still refusing to look at him. At least she was acknowledging he had a pulse. She snatched a cloak off a coat-tree and left the room, her trim little form hustling down the stairs. The cloak looked new, which was a good thing . . . he was sick of seeing her dressed in rags. The sound of his boots echoed on the narrow wooden stairway as he followed her downstairs and out the door.

"Is that a new cloak?" he asked as the cool November air surrounded him.

She turned to face him. "Do you have my money?"

He was taken aback. The bank in Philadelphia had released the funds to Hartman, so Zack was now able to pay Mollie for the deed, but he was certain there was more to her anger than a delayed payment. If any of his business associates had spoken to him in that tone, he'd have suggested taking it into the back alley and settling things the old-fashioned way. Instead, he drew a calming breath. Whatever had happened to Mollie in the past week had been horrible. Her dearest friend had been killed, and she was bound to be staggering under the weight of grief. He set his hands on her shoulders.

"Mollie, tell me what happened. I haven't slept in two days."

"Guilty conscience?"

"Yes!" he bellowed. "I never should have let you stay in that church so long! I wish I'd thrown you over my shoulder and dragged you to my house that first night." He tried to wrap his arms around her, but a stiff arm kept him at bay. The expression in her eyes was even worse. "For pity's sake, talk to me. Scream at me, hit me . . . just quit glaring like that."

There was no softening of her attitude, only a voice dripping with disdain. "Do you have my money? That is really the only thing I want from you."

He was so tired he could barely stand upright, but he still

wrestled with the temptation to shake her until that stony expression vanished. He shoved his hands into his pockets and forced his voice to be calm. "I just walked away from the most urgent business of my entire career because I got a telegram from you begging me to come home. I've been traveling nonstop for eight hundred miles to see you."

"Eight hundred? Funny you should mention that number. I have eight hundred reasons to be angry at you."

He locked glares with her. She couldn't be referring to what he thought. The details of Hartman's insurance policy were private information, but that didn't mean it wasn't well known to certain people in the city. Why would Mollie have even known anything about it? Against all odds, Zack succeeded in getting the East Coast insurance companies to pay exactly what they owed, and now Mollie was tossing that number around like it was something he was supposed to be ashamed of?

"The bank has your funds," he said in the businesslike voice he knew she despised. "Meet me at the First Continental Bank tomorrow at noon, and I'll get the funds signed over to you." There was no softening of her glare, no acknowledgment that he had just put his entire career in jeopardy on her behalf.

He stepped forward, blocking her retreat by grasping her arm and leaning close to growl quietly, "And try to act nicer than an angry troll with fleas." He straightened and left the brewery without a backward glance.

Colonel Richard Lowe was a civil engineer and operated one of the most successful railroad development companies in America. Could she have asked for a more qualified man to rebuild her factory on East Street? He was unfailingly polite and efficient. After the blowup with Zack yesterday, Colonel Lowe was a balm to her spirit. Good manners, a pleasant demeanor, and no bombs that would detonate on a street corner while he shouted insults at her.

Colonel Lowe's wife had died three years earlier, and they'd had no children. Mollie was selfishly grateful he had no family obligations to pull him away from Chicago. The plans he'd sketched for the factory would require a skilled engineer to steer them through to completion.

As they stood on the ruined acre on East Street, Colonel Lowe's competent eyes surveyed the land, noting the uneven tilt of the ground beneath the crumbled bricks that still littered the plot. "Did you have drainage problems in the past?" he asked.

Mollie nodded. "My father knew about the problem when he built. That was why we could not risk adding a basement. The builder said it would flood."

"I gather your builder knew nothing about modern drainage. It is a simple enough matter to install a French drain that will funnel the water toward the southern edge of the property, where it will do no damage. You will have a fine basement in your new building."

Mollie sucked in a hopeful breath. With more storage, she'd be able to free up valuable floor space for expanded operations. "Can you really do that? Build a drain on top of everything else you hope to accomplish?"

Colonel Lowe braced a boot atop the rubble of the foundation. "Miss Knox, I was first in my class at West Point. I built railroads in the Dakota territories and bridges for the state of Illinois. During the war, I supervised detonations and built fortifications using only army surplus. I was shot in the arm at the Battle of Winston Cliff but still led the defenses for three days." He winked at her. "I think I can manage a French drain."

From a man with less charm, it would have sounded like a

boast, but this was Colonel Lowe, and everything he said made Mollie feel marvelous. From the moment he'd arrived in Chicago, he had been slaying one dragon after another for her. His small platoon of soldiers had already carted three wagonloads of rubble from her land. He'd stationed other men at the train depot to purchase bricks the moment they were offloaded from the railcar. In the hours she sat beside him at the worktable in the brewery attic, he sketched endless designs for her new building. It would be bigger than before and would have room for Dr. Buchanan's dental office and at least one other rental property tucked onto the back.

Colonel Lowe rose when she walked into the room and spoke in soothing, cultured tones. When Zack got angry, his voice took on the rough ethnic edge of the docks. Everything about Colonel Lowe was a relief after the tumult of Zack Kazmarek.

She fiddled with her father's watch, seeking reassurance by pressing her thumb into the dented cover. She would have to meet with Zack in an hour to finalize the sale of her land on Columbus Street. She would rather grasp a snake by the neck and pry the two thousand dollars out of its jaws, but that wasn't an option.

The lobby of the bank was lined with alder wood and topped with coffered ceilings. Zack hadn't known rich people decorated their ceilings until he had started consorting with Louis Hartman, but now he rarely walked into a bank where the ceilings weren't as lavishly decorated as the floors. Thick oriental rugs beneath his boots absorbed all sound, making the lobby of the bank seem as cloistered as a library. Bank clerks spoke in hushed tones, sitting behind desks illuminated with glass-shaded lamps. The atmosphere of dignified competence saturated every square inch of the bank.

Unlike the indignation roiling through Zack, which was as raw and primitive as his marauding Eastern European ancestors. What had gotten into that woman? Had there ever been a more mercenary, mistrustful woman than Mollie Knox? He wasn't sure what had sent her into a royal sulk yesterday, but he had a hunch. She hadn't pulled the number eight hundred out of thin air, which meant someone in this city had been filling her suspicious little brain with claptrap.

The Louis XIV chair he sat in was designed for appearance, not comfort. He stretched his legs and shifted on the hard seat. A glance at the oversized clock hanging on the wall indicated Mollie was ten minutes late. The fire had wreaked chaos on the public transportation system, so there could be a perfectly logical explanation for her delay, but it ratcheted his annoyance up even higher. Did she have any idea what it had cost him to abandon Louis Hartman in New York? Although Zack had succeeded in forcing the insurance company to make good on the eight-hundred-thousand-dollar policy for the loss of the building, well over half a million dollars in merchandise had been lost. He and Louis were in a pitched battle to make good on those policies, and in the middle of the high-wire act he was managing, Zack had gone racing home to Chicago on a personal matter. All to comfort Mollie.

Louis still hadn't forgiven him, if the barrage of angry telegrams streaming in from New York was any indicator. Josephine Hartman had descended on his townhouse last night in a rage, suggesting he surrender his Yale diploma to her since Zack seemed to have lost interest in the pursuit of a legal career. He practically had to promise her his first-born child in order to soothe her ruffled feathers.

He inserted a finger beneath his starched collar, shifting it to sit a little higher. Mollie had better not be prowling up and down Columbus Street, nosing into land prices. Two thousand dollars for a half acre was practically highway robbery, and he supposed she might have a legitimate bone of contention with him about that, but it was better than a protracted court battle. He had her signature on the deed, and Hartman was ready to rebuild. This deal was going to close today or he would turn the city upside-down until he found her.

The tinkling of a bell sounded as the door opened and Mollie walked inside. She glanced around the lobby until she saw him, her face as stony as it had been yesterday. Zack remained seated. If she intended to heap another pile of bad attitude on him, he wasn't going to stand while she did it.

She stood frozen in the doorway, glaring at him across the expansive lobby. He glared back. If she wanted her two thousand dollars, she could cross the room and come get it.

At last she started moving, her stiff figure twitching in disdain. When she was standing alongside his chair, he forced a smile to his face. "Back to wearing braids? Pity."

"Do you have my money?"

He flicked a glance to one of the clerks sitting at a desk on the far side of the lobby. "Mr. Tobbin will arrange the transfer. You are twenty minutes late."

She glanced at the clock on the wall. "That must be the ugliest clock I've ever seen."

"Spare me your professional musings, Miss Knox. The subject of clocks and watches is of zero interest to me. What I'd *really* like to know is what turned a beautiful, intelligent woman into such a foul-mannered brat. You give Sophie a run for her money."

She leaned over until her face was inches from his. "Frank was right about you," she said in a whisper that vibrated with rage. "Exactly when did you intend to tell me you won an eight-hundred-thousand-dollar insurance settlement?"

His gaze did not waver. "Never. It is none of your business."

"Considering I own a quarter of the land that building sat on, I think it was a relevant detail, Mr. Kazmarek."

He wished she would shut up. The woman he had idolized for three years was ruled by logic and rules and order. He wanted no part of the avaricious harpy standing before him. Still, he didn't intend to spill confidential details to anyone who cared to wander through the lobby of a public bank. He leaned a little closer to her and kept his voice low. "Your name wasn't on that insurance policy, Mollie. You never paid a dime for it, and you aren't entitled to a dime of it. End of story."

That seemed to take her aback. She had a legitimate claim to the land, but not a dime of the insurance policy Louis had been paying on all these years. She quickly regained her steam. "I trusted you when I signed that proposed bill of sale," she spat. "You misled me about how much the land is worth. Fifteen thousand dollars is what I've heard, although some say as high as twenty. Not two."

She had him there. The value of land on Columbus Street was soaring by the day, but a cloud hung over her deed. He stood and looked down at her. "Don't fool yourself, Miss Knox. Two thousand dollars is the best you'll get for that plot of land. No one in this city will touch it, because the title is questionable and it will be mired in the courts for years."

She crossed her arms over her chest. "Is that what you tell your conscience so you can sleep at night?"

"Ahem."

Zack swiveled to see Mr. Tobbin had joined them. Behind his spectacles, the bank clerk looked as uneasy as a fawn caught on the field of battle.

"Pardon the interruption," Mr. Tobbin said, "but I have an appointment with the Board of Commissioners in twenty minutes.

If we wish to conclude the land transaction today, we need to begin."

Zack gestured to Mr. Tobbin's desk on the far side of the lobby. Mollie hesitated.

Zack decided to have no mercy. "Well, Miss Knox? What is it to be? You can have two thousand dollars in cash today or you can hire a lawyer, get in line at the state courthouse, and prepare to wait years for an uncertain outcome while your energy and resources dwindle away on the small chance you might score a few more dollars. Oh, and on the slim chance that you win in court, you will immediately owe Louis Hartman four thousand dollars in back taxes. Your choice."

She looked angry enough to spit nails. "I'm selling," she ground out. A hint of relief lightened Mr. Tobbin's face and he gestured toward his desk. Mollie followed, but Zack snagged her elbow and pulled her to a halt. He needed to kill the parasite festering inside the woman he loved.

"As you sign those papers," he whispered into her ear, "understand that this is *over*. You are making a good deal. A court case would suck your energy and finances dry, and you know it. This is the last argument we will have over that blasted deed."

She jerked her arm away and followed Mr. Tobbin in the same manner she used to flit about Hartman's store. Quick, brisk, and efficient. He had to admire that about her. Even while she wore mismatched clothing that had been pulled out of a donation bin, she carried herself with the dignity of a warrior queen. He grinned as he followed her. Life with Mollie would be an adventure, but one he had been anticipating for years. When two hurricanes came together, what could one expect? After this deal concluded, he'd take her out to lunch at the fanciest restaurant in the city.

Mr. Tobbin pushed a form across the desk toward Mollie.

"Here is the account I have set up to accept the transfer of funds," he said in one of those soft voices all bankers seemed to have perfected. Mollie read the entire form before affixing her name to the line at the bottom. The scratching of the pen was the only sound in the silent bank.

And with a few scrawled signatures, the deal was complete. The funds were deposited into her account and she withdrew a few dollars for immediate expenses.

"Come on, Mollie. Let me take you out to lunch."

She ignored him as she marched out the door. A blast of cold air smacked him in the face as he followed her. He pulled his coat tighter and flipped up its collar against the chilly wind, shouldering through pedestrians on the sidewalk to catch up to her. "What exactly are you mad about?" he demanded. "Did you think you could get a better deal by rolling the dice in court? Is that it? I never thought you were the sort of woman who would walk away from a magnificent relationship over a few dollars."

The glare she shot him would have incinerated a lesser man. "Funny, I thought the same thing about you."

Mollie skirted around a boy pushing a wheelbarrow of mattress ticking and hustled down the street, but Zack was blocked by a group of nuns crossing the path. He clenched his teeth until he could get around them and pulled up alongside Mollie. He enjoyed a healthy, air-clearing argument, and Mollie seemed game. She reeled around to face him and jabbed a finger at his chest. "You knew," Mollie accused him. "You knew about that deed, and that was why you tried to buy my company and all its assets before the fire."

Zack sucked in his breath. So, she had finally figured it out. He turned away, unable to meet her eyes. He'd hoped to carry that tidbit of damning information to his grave, but the game was up. "Fine, I knew about the deed," he ground out. "I owe Louis

Hartman my loyalty, and knowledge of the deed was confidential information. I couldn't tell you about it without breaking the law." Besides, she got her blasted two thousand dollars, which was probably more than she would have won had she gone to court.

"Don't hide behind fancy ethics. You would do anything to haul yourself out of the docks, and it didn't matter who you needed to squash on your way up."

He took a step closer to glare down at her. "I didn't do it for the money."

"I thought you were so straightforward," she spat out. "Fish dumped on the desk, cutting deals with rowdy Irish gangs. I thought you were an honest man of business, but you're only a jumped-up longshoreman. Look at you! Such fancy clothes and that ridiculous little blue finch you carry everywhere. You can pretend all you want, but you've got filth beneath your nails that will never wash away because you are still wallowing in the gutter."

He flinched before he could mask his feelings. He'd spent a fortune on these blasted clothes and wasn't going to apologize for working his way off the docks. She turned and darted between pedestrians to escape him, but he wouldn't let her. Following in her path, he reached out to grab an elbow. "You can't hurl that load of garbage and then scurry away."

"Watch me."

He pulled up alongside her. "I never took you for a coward, Mollie. Stay here and fight it out."

Her mouth compressed into a hard little line, and every muscle in her face was tense. When they came to the corner where the streetcar picked up passengers, she was forced to stand and wait. A couple of women loaded down with sacks of vegetables and a newsboy also waited for the streetcar, but Zack didn't care about the audience.

He leaned down to whisper in her ear. "Your eyes turn an even darker shade of blue when you are angry."

She refused to engage, staring straight ahead. He kept pressing, determined to crack through her shell.

"I've heard that when black widow spiders are angry, they bite the heads off their mates. You look like you'd enjoy doing that now."

Even that didn't cause a flicker in her stony expression. The clopping of hooves signaled the arrival of the horse-drawn streetcar. Mollie waited for the shoppers and the newsboy to board, then she stepped up to the driver.

"The gentleman wearing the maroon vest is pestering me. Will you see to it he does not board the car?"

The driver tugged on a lever and shut the door in Zack's face.

17

M ollie withdrew enough money from the bank to pay
her debt to Mr. Durant. Although Sophie's father had
insisted the money was a gift, Mollie wanted the debt paid and
went directly to Prairie Avenue after leaving Zack on the street
corner. The loan would nag at her until it was repaid, and she
wanted her memories of the church and everything associated
with it scrubbed from her mind.

Mr. Durant was with Sophie when Mollie was shown into
the lavish parlor of the Prairie Avenue mansion. Poised on the
end of a brocade-covered settee, Mr. Durant held a tiny teacup
in his large hand while Sophie served him from a silver teapot.
Two porcelain dolls, with identical teacups before them, were
propped on either side of him.

"Miss Knox, you are just in time to join us for tea."

Mollie would rather drink a cup of lye, but it would be churl-
ish to refuse. She lowered herself onto the settee. She could
endure precisely ten minutes of Sophie's company before spon-
taneous combustion was likely to strike her. There were only
four place settings, so Sophie took a cup from a doll wearing an
embroidered dress so elaborate it had probably taken a seam-
stress a month to stitch.

"You have to set your cup down after each sip," Sophie ordered. "Otherwise it is tacky."

Mr. Durant laughed a little nervously. "Now, Sophie, Miss Knox may have her own style of drinking tea." He took a little sip of the tepid tea. "Tell us how the watch business is progressing," he asked kindly.

Mollie related a few details of how the work was commencing. Alice and Ulysses had finished their designs for engraved cases commemorating the fire and had constructed the templates. Her metalworkers were once again making the tiny screws and springs that were needed in the body of the watches. They still lacked a few supplies for making the casements, and there wasn't enough work for Declan and Old Gunner, who had been moved to help at the new construction site on East Street.

"I don't like Old Gunner," Sophie said. "He smells bad, like dirty cigars."

Mr. Durant cleared his throat. "That isn't polite, Sophie. If we can't say something complimentary about someone, it is best not to mention anything at all. We discussed this last week and need to make improvements in our manners if we are going to be invited to the Johnstons' again, right, pumpkin?"

Sophie kicked the leg of the table. "I don't care if we don't get invited again. I hate the Johnstons' house. I want to go back and live at the church."

Mollie would have preferred a bout of indigestion over another hour of Sophie's company, but she forced a polite tone to her voice. "We aren't living at the church anymore. The temporary barracks built by the city are now open. Alice and I are in the women's barracks, and it is very crowded. I don't think you would like it."

Sophie's face darkened. She bunched her legs close to her chest, planted her feet on the rim of the table, and with one mighty heave, pushed the entire table over. The silver tea set crashed to the floor, spewing dark liquid across the silk rug. "I don't care. Playing with dolls is stupid. This house is stupid."

Mr. Durant shot to his feet. "Your behavior is disgraceful! You have everything a little girl could ever wish for, and all you do is spit on it. Now, stand up and apologize to Miss Knox."

Sophie wore the mutinous expression Mollie had seen hundreds of times. The girl kicked the sugar bowl to the side, spraying a fan of white sugar into the sodden rug before standing up. "I'm sorry, Miss Knox," she said, her voice dripping with disdain. "I'm sick of dolls, and I'm sick of tea parties. *I want to do something hard.*"

Hard? Mollie remembered Sophie stooping over to haul bricks from the rubble. The girl had done so only because she would get nothing to eat otherwise, but once Sophie got moving, she rarely complained. In fact, the only time Sophie had gotten angry was one evening when she'd filled a whole wheelbarrow with salvaged bricks and Ulysses had refused to come look when Sophie ordered him to. Mollie had taken pity on the girl and gone outside to see the wheelbarrow, filled to the rim with useable bricks stacked in perfect order. "Well done, Sophie!" Mollie had said, genuinely impressed. Sophie had beamed as though she had just put the final touches on the ceiling of the Sistine Chapel.

Mollie looked at the girl, who was staring at the carpet beneath her feet. A glance around the room showed Mollie that the girl had been showered with toys and dolls and new clothes. All splendid, but Mollie would have been bored too. When she was Sophie's age, her father had entrusted her with enameling the watch dials. It was gritty, exacting work. It took hours of baking before the beauty of the dials would finally emerge, but the sense of satisfaction Mollie earned from accomplishing something hard was more fulfilling than playing with any gorgeously embellished doll.

"Sophie, how would you like to come and help at the new factory?" she asked, stunning even herself. "There is plenty of hard work to be done preparing the foundation. Hauling gravel. Leveling the ground." She glanced up at Mr. Durant. Mollie realized she had overstepped her boundaries, but he did not appear taken aback. Rather, he was intrigued. Sophie simply looked stunned.

"You would need your father's permission, of course," Mollie said. "This is a real construction site, and there is no room for temper tantrums or little girls who do not follow instructions. Perhaps we can find something for you to do for a few hours to see if it suits you."

After her initial surprise, Sophie resumed her nonchalant air. "I don't care," she said.

But Mr. Durant did. Pulling Mollie aside, he shared his years of frustration in trying to mold Sophie into a decent child. Sophie's mother had nearly died during childbirth and was unable to care for the infant in the following months. When Charlotte Durant was finally able to rise from her sickbed, she'd showered the baby with every conceivable luxury, bringing musicians to play for the infant and seamstresses from Ireland to stitch delicate garments. And when Sophie grew older and expressed dissatisfaction, her parents funneled more and more her way to appease the child's voracious need for attention. She was a smart girl and knew exactly how to play her parents off each other in order to win ever more extravagant shows of affection.

"But ever since she got back from the church," Mr. Durant said, "she can't stop talking about it. She rambled on about the blind man that she read to. The bricks she salvaged. She claimed to have hated every minute of it, and who wouldn't have? I saw the blisters on her hands and the scrapes on her arms, but why can't she stop talking about it? I think . . ." He paused as he rubbed his chin, his face drawn in thought. "I think the girl had a sense of purpose at that church. Maybe that was what appealed to her."

Mollie supposed it was possible. How long could a child gorge on an endless stream of amusement without becoming bored? Hard work was not easy to become accustomed to, but it provided a sense of satisfaction beyond compare. Silas Knox had taught her that. It was why he had been so determined to find work for the wounded veterans. Without a sense of purpose, the spirit withered and died. Even humble work like cleaning the workshop floor or hauling bricks provided the seeds of dignity the human spirit craved.

She bit her lip. "I am serious about no temper tantrums. The men on the worksite are all volunteers, and I can't have Sophie making their jobs any more difficult than they already are."

Mr. Durant's answer was swift. "If she misbehaves, send her back. But I think this may be what she needs. Sophie is an intelligent girl, but we have never asked much of her."

"Will your wife object?"

"Almost certainly. Charlotte will think I am trying to punish the girl, but I think perhaps this will be the greatest gift Sophie has ever been given."

~

"Mollie, stop it."

Someone shook her shoulder, but she threw the hand off. She needed to get Frank out of the building before the roof collapsed and burned them both alive. She pressed forward harder.

"Mollie, *stop it*, love."

She jerked awake. Alice was beside her, dressed in her nightclothes and bracing her arms on the straw mattress of the top bunk bed. Something still felt terribly wrong as Mollie clutched the blankets to her chest and glanced around the barracks. She was safe. It was dark and other women were snoring, the smell of new pine boards thick in the air. It was only a nightmare. Mollie took a deep breath, hoping she hadn't made too much of a ruckus. Alice slept on the bunk directly below Mollie, so she had probably felt Mollie tossing about.

"Another nightmare?" Alice asked.

Mollie didn't even need to answer. Ever since the fire, they both had suffered from horrible dreams, and they weren't the only ones. It was rare for a night to go by when Mollie didn't hear at least one of the sixty women or girls who lived in this barracks whimpering at night. "It was something about Frank," Mollie said. "He was trapped in a building, but I couldn't get to him. Or maybe it was the new factory, but that doesn't make any sense." Mollie twisted the corner of the scratchy wool blanket between her fingers. "Do you ever dream about Frank? Or only about the fire?"

Alice shook her head. "I can never remember after I wake up. I just remember the panic, so bad I can hardly breathe."

"Frank is always in mine," Mollie said. "He is always just out of reach. He is trying to shout something to me, but I can't hear because of the roar of the fire." She rolled over onto her back, staring at the bare plank ceiling a few feet above her nose. "I feel so guilty for what happened. If I hadn't been so full of pride, we would have been living in Zack's house on that night and Frank would still be alive."

Alice's answer was swift. "Don't you go talking like that," she said in a fierce whisper. "The only people responsible for what happened to Frank are those thugs. If not for you, Frank would have died on the night of the fire."

Mollie rolled back onto her side so she could look at Alice. "If we find out who killed him, I wonder if it will make these awful dreams go away."

"All I know is those thugs had better pray to be caught by the Chicago Police Department," Alice said darkly. "If anyone from the 57th gets ahold of them, there won't be enough left to identify for burial."

Alice was probably right, but the police had lost interest in the case. With so much to be done keeping order in the city and no quick leads rising to the surface, they'd moved back to more pressing issues. Frank's case was filed away and would grow old unless Mollie or someone from the 57th kept it alive. With no blood family, the mark Frank Spencer had left on this world was already growing dim. He had once been a powerful lawyer, helping shape the legal landscape that transformed Chicago into a city bursting with industry, lumber mills, stockyards, and shipping. All that had come to a crashing end after the war. Unable to practice law in a regular sense, he withdrew behind the sheltered walls of the 57th Illinois Watch Company, and there he had been the linchpin around which they all relied. For wisdom, for a steady head. Sometimes simply for spinning tales in the long afternoon while they worked.

Now, in the rush to rebuild, her waking hours were filled with so many concerns, memories of Frank were being crowded out. Only guilt remained.

She had to find out who'd killed Frank. She pushed up on her elbow to meet Alice's eyes. "None of the watches with your twining rose vines were ever sold, were they?"

"None of them," Alice confirmed.

The watches that had been stolen that night featured the distinctive pattern of rose vines curling around the rim of the watchcases. If any of those watches surfaced, it would be easy to identify them as the watches stolen that night. That ought to provide the police with a white-hot lead that could be traced back to the killers.

In the morning, she would ask Colonel Lowe to take some men off the construction project and start haunting the pawn-shops in search of those watches.

18

A lice quickly sketched from memory the distinctive rose vine pattern that graced the covers of the stolen watches, then distributed the drawings to Colonel Lowe's men.

"I don't know much about fencing stolen goods," Mollie said to Colonel Lowe, "but there are plenty of pawnbrokers on the south side of town."

With three of Colonel Lowe's men searching the city for the stolen watches, Mollie could funnel all of her energy into the creation of her watches. She had missed her first deadline to supply a jeweler in New York with a shipment of watches. For a woman who had never once been late to class, work, or Sunday services, missing that deadline for her only remaining contract was a humiliating blow.

The New York jeweler had been understanding. It was only a month after the fire, and he knew the 57th had been among the destroyed businesses. By now, the stark photographs of the barren landscape were circulating all over the country. To Mollie's surprise, the New York store had generously doubled their order, but only if the watches were delivered before Christmas. *We are pleased to help our brothers in Chicago*, the telegram had read.

"Christmas!" Ulysses had said. "Does that New York jeweler know what sort of wizardry goes into building a watch? Would he ask Michelangelo to deliver the *Pieta* by Christmas? Would he ask Milton to write *Paradise Lost* by Christmas?"

"Ulysses, all I ask is that you deliver engraved cases by December. I'll take care of the rest." Although, as Mollie scanned the attic workroom, she knew time was not her only challenge. The attic was less than a third of the size of her old factory on East Street and too cramped for all of the employees to work at once.

"We will operate around the clock," she said. "The brewery never shuts down, and neither shall we." If the watch technicians arrived at six o'clock in the morning, they could assemble the internal mechanisms, finishing their day's labor by two o'clock. Then the artisans would come in, clear the worktables, and begin pressing the engraved cover designs, finishing up by ten o'clock at night. The last shift would be the enamelers. Enameling required a lot of space and time in order to fire the ovens. It would make for a grueling schedule, but it was the only way they could meet that Christmas deadline.

The only task in which Mollie was unskilled was the artwork. She could build watch mechanisms, as well as lay and fire enamel. Because she was the one who ordered the around-the-clock schedule, Mollie felt obliged to share in the miserable shifts. She would be working from three in the morning until the early afternoon, but if it meant she could deliver those watches to New York in time for Christmas, it would be vindication. It would be proof that she had survived the fire and had salvaged her company from the ashes.

It was eight o'clock one morning when a message arrived. She would recognize that bold scrawl on the envelope from across the room. Her breath caught in her throat. She didn't want to read Zack's apologies or excuses for what he had done. Zack was a master at undermining her defenses and playing with words to ease her into a false sense of security. He was likely to try to sweet-talk her into compliance, minimize what he had done by covering it over with a layer of frosting until she was intoxicated by the sugar.

She ought to return the note unopened, just to demonstrate how immune she was to his flattery.

She ripped open the flap and grabbed the note.

Mollie. I hope you are over your sulk. If so, please join me this evening for a walk by the river. Wear your hair down.

Zack

Unbelievable.

She crammed the note back inside the envelope. The coals in the enameling oven were still warm. Before she could think twice, she shuffled across the workroom floor, grabbed a pair of tongs to twist the metal door handle of the oven open, and tossed the note inside. If Zack was looking for a fight, she wasn't coming out to play.

At least three days per week Mollie went to the property on East Street to monitor the progress. The process of clearing the land had gone quickly, but it took two weeks to excavate the basement, frame the walls, and lay the French drain. To her surprise, Colonel Lowe had rolled up his sleeves and participated in the manual labor. "Jesus was a carpenter, and I am not too proud to do the work," he cheerfully said. "Besides, the more hands the better, if we are going to get this built before it gets too late in the season."

Winter was coming on fast, and it was her enemy. Mortar could not be laid in the frigid months when the temperature dropped below freezing. Normally, all construction in Chicago stopped by November, but this year was different. Desperate to get the city rebuilt, builders were stretching the season by keeping braziers burning alongside the vats of mortar as it was mixed and laid. Torches were set up along newly laid walls so the mortar could properly cure without cooling too quickly. Those additional few degrees were enough to keep the mortar and her building rising.

Every night, she prayed for the weather to hold.

~

Mollie did not know what to expect from Sophie Durant on her first day of work, but true to form, the girl arrived at the East Street site in a closed town carriage and escorted by a liveried footman.

"Do you have anything more suitable to wear?" Mollie asked. "Play clothes or something not so costly?" Sophie's tartan plaid dress looked new, as did her matching plaid beret and dark velvet overcoat with ivory buttons. Only her large canvas work gloves gave any indication Sophie or her parents understood what she was going to do.

"These are the only kinds of clothes I have," Sophie said. Her gaze flitted over the worksite and her mouth worked nervously. Even beneath the tailored coat, Mollie could see the girl was cringing. Perhaps she thought she would be working alongside the people she had known from the church. Most of the wounded veterans of the 57th were making watches at the brewery, and the men slinging mortar and hauling gravel were strangers to Sophie.

The poor girl was afraid. Dressed like one of her porcelain dolls, Sophie looked ridiculous on a worksite swarming with brawny, sweating men whose faces were streaked with grime and sweat. A train came roaring down the nearby tracks, tons of metal and coal-fueled steam barreling past them in a barrage of noise and clattering vibration. Sophie covered her ears and squeezed her eyes shut. She was completely out of her element, and she clearly knew it. After the train passed, Mollie squatted down to meet Sophie's eyes. "Are you sure you want to do this? It will be messy work, and no one will think less of you if it isn't what you expected."

Sophie opened her eyes, glanced back at the uniformed servant waiting at the carriage, then at the two men shoveling gravel into a wheelbarrow. She swallowed hard and met Mollie's gaze. "I want to do it," she said. "I want to do something hard. Even if it is scary."

"All right, then. Let me see if I can find Declan, and he can show you how to help with the mortar."

"Declan is here?" The prospect of a familiar face brought a slight easing to Sophie's shoulders.

Declan arrived with the bricklayer, who showed Sophie how to get started. With the temperature getting colder by the day, they mixed only small batches of mortar so it would be easier to keep warm. Declan showed Sophie how to fill sacks with the right amount of lime and sand, then haul it to the mixing vats. The sight of the little girl clad in velvet laboring alongside the brawny workers was so strange that people on the neighboring construction sites stopped to stare.

Declan planted a mixing stick in Sophie's hands, then glanced up to see Mollie watching from behind Sophie's carriage. "You can go on back to the brewery," he said. "I'll look after Miss Sophie."

Mollie didn't leave until Declan shooed her away.

~

When Mollie arrived at the brewery attic worksite, there was another note from Zack awaiting her.

Apparently you misunderstood the meeting time and place for our walk by the river. Please join my family for dinner tonight and we can discuss it.

Would he never give up? Mollie had never been blind to the tough, bare-knuckled world that ruled Chicago politics and business, but Zack had been so charming when he'd strong-armed her she'd never even known he was doing it until she had signed, sealed, and delivered to him exactly what he'd wanted.

How long would it be before she could think of Zack without this weight on her chest? Throwing herself into work ought to have solved the problem, but it seemed everywhere she looked brought a fresh round of memories. The coverage in the newspapers of the White Stockings made Mollie wonder what Zack would think of his favorite team's flagging record as they struggled against East Coast rivals on the road. The scent of fresh pierogis in the deli made her remember evenings around the brazier with him. Heaven help her, when she watched construction workers hauling granite stone to building sites, it reminded her of Zack's powerful build. She went back to her table and tried to assemble watches but was unsuccessful in banishing Zack from her thoughts.

A full-bodied horn from the stockyard train signaled it was time for Mollie to go check on Sophie. Was two hours enough to make the girl want to flee back to her world of porcelain dolls and handmade lace?

The first thing Mollie saw as she approached the East Street property was the grand maroon carriage, so Sophie must still be there. Mollie sidled up alongside the carriage to watch Sophie's progress from a distance. The girl's dark coat was smeared with lime dust, but she was still working, lugging a canvas sack of sand to the mixing area. The sack was heavy, and Sophie had to set it down every few steps while she panted from exertion, but she eventually delivered it to Declan at the mixing station. Declan gave her an approving nod, and Sophie beamed.

Mollie paused. It was the first time she had ever seen a smile on Sophie's face, and it had come after two hours of gritty manual labor most girls her age would have run from. Other than Declan, Sophie still appeared intimidated by the men who were working at the site, but the girl watched in fascination as Grady O'Manion wielded his trowel like a maestro conducting an orchestra, slathering on mortar and setting a row of bricks with precision.

"She's something else, isn't she?"

Mollie startled. "Colonel Lowe." How long had he been standing there? He had one booted foot braced on a workbench and a framing square dangling from his hands, but it was his tender, curious smile that made her heart skip a beat.

"I wonder if I could persuade you to call me Richard," he said. "We have only been acquainted a few weeks, but I feel I have known you far longer. Your father used to brag about his clever daughter, how she could attach a winding stem to a watch with her eyes closed."

Her gaze skittered away. She had not missed the way he had been watching her whenever she came to the worksite, but she had not seriously entertained the notion that Colonel Lowe could be interested in her. After all, he had a legendary reputation among the veterans of the 57th. With his blond hair ruffling in the breeze and face flushed with the chill of the autumn day, Colonel Lowe looked even younger than his thirty-five years. Her father would be walking on air at the prospect of a romance between her and the colonel.

She cleared her throat. "Colonel Lowe—"

"Richard. At the very least, you should stop calling me a

colonel. The war has been over almost seven years, and I am simply Mr. Richard Lowe now."

There was nothing simple about a man who could race across the state, round up eighteen able-bodied men, get her land cleared, a basement dug and framed, a foundation laid, and bricklaying underway in less than three weeks. At this rate, she'd have a workshop by Thanksgiving. She grinned. "Richard, then."

She joined him on the bench and listened to him speak of his life in Waukegan, a small town north of Chicago, where he designed bridges and helped renovate the aging railroad beds. How easy it was to talk to this man! Even though her business was very different from his, they used precisely the same variable costing system for tracking operations. They liked the same novels and drank the same blend of oolong tea. Mollie was surprised when the uniformed footman interrupted them.

"It is time to deliver Miss Sophie home," the footman said.

"Of course," she said. Mollie fetched Sophie from where she was helping stir the mortar to keep it pliable in the chilly air. Sophie looked a mess with lime dust smeared down the front of that beautiful velvet coat. Mollie tried to swipe away the white dust, but it was hopeless.

"How do you feel after your first day on a construction site?" Richard asked Sophie.

The girl shrugged, reluctant to meet Richard's gaze. "Okay, I guess."

"Okay?" Richard said with mock indignation. He grasped the girl's shoulders and turned her around. "Look at that wall! It was less than a foot high when you arrived this morning, and now it is taller than you. Someday you can bring your children to this site, point to that wall, and tell them that you built it."

"All I did was help make the mortar." Sophie looked a little wounded, as though Colonel Lowe was making fun of her.

"Don't fool yourself, Miss Durant," Richard said. "Very few things in this world are done in isolation. It takes an entire crew of people to make a building rise, and you were part of that crew today. We could not have laid those bricks if the mortar was not properly mixed and kept at the correct temperature. That wall will forever be something you can be proud of. When you and I are both old and gray, that wall will still be standing there."

Sophie's eyebrows rose. "Really?"

"Really," Richard affirmed. "Are you coming back tomorrow to help finish out the corners?"

Sophie looked to Mollie for permission. "Can I?"

What a transformation had come over this girl. It confirmed everything Frank had ever said about the value of work and having a purpose in life. "Yes, Sophie. I hope you will."

19

There was a fine ladies' store on Jefferson Street just across the river, and Mollie longed to wear something that had not been pulled from the donation bin. Six weeks of mismatched, ill-fitting, and threadbare clothing was enough to test even her tolerance. After paying her debts and setting enough aside for three months of operating expenses, she still had enough money to fund a shopping excursion for Alice and herself.

The shop was fronted with two large glass display cases filled with ready-made dresses, dainty hats, and bolts of fabric spilling forth in a lavish display of silk, brocade, taffeta, and velvet. A little bell tinkled as she pulled open the door and stepped inside the lavender-scented shop. Glass cases displayed kid leather gloves, hand-painted buttons, and silk scarves in saffron, peach, and indigo. Spools of ribbons were lined up atop the display cases like a colorful waterfall, but most tempting were the gowns.

"Look at all those dresses." Mollie gawked at the display of a dozen choices of gowns. She needed a sturdy calico that would be comfortable enough to wear at the workshop, but was tempted by a stunning gown of peacock blue with a skirt that pulled away to reveal an ivory satin underskirt. It would be impossible to think of ashes and smoke stains while wearing a gown like that. She wanted silk against her skin! Drawers and knickers and petticoats made of superfine cotton and scented with lavender.

Never had Mollie been so excited to purchase new clothing as at this very moment. She reached out to finger a fancy overskirt of blue silk supported by tiers of interior bustling to lend it a delightfully feminine silhouette.

She leaned over to whisper in Alice's ear. "I'll take one of everything," she teased.

"Such restraint! I want the whole shop!"

The feel of silk and velvet triggered memories of what life was like before the fire, and she craved it. Mollie stepped behind a screen and tried on a ready-made skirt of bronze taffeta.

Alice's look of approval made Mollie certain she needed to own this skirt. "Help me pick a few blouses to pair with it," she said. With her flair for color and style, Alice could dress a potato and make it look presentable. Mollie leaned over to examine the hem and determine how much it would need to be raised to fit her stature.

"I don't suppose this sudden urge to make yourself look fetching has anything to do with a certain Colonel Lowe, now, would it?"

Heat rushed to her cheeks. This was *entirely* about Colonel Lowe, and she'd be a fool to try to deny it in front of her oldest friend. "He helps me get my mind off Zack," she confessed.

"Is that all?" Alice asked with a pointed look.

Was that all? Given that Zack Kazmarek had been in and out of her brain every three minutes like a mosquito she could not bat away, Richard Lowe's distraction was a blessing.

"Can you imagine what my father's reaction would have been if he knew Colonel Lowe had an interest in me?"

Alice crossed her arms across her front. "Silas Knox would

rise from the grave and walk across town to give you away at the wedding. But I hope you aren't buying new dresses to please your father's ghost."

She wanted new dresses so she could feel normal again. So she could pretend, even if only for a few minutes, that her life had resumed its ordered, clean, tidy routine. And so she could appeal to Richard Lowe and extinguish the inconvenient memory of Zack once and for all.

Which was hard to do when he kept having those notes delivered to the workshop. Sometimes they rudely implied she was to blame for the falling-out between them; others tried to cajole her into forgiving him and rushing back to fling herself into his arms. He even had the gall to suggest they elope. Mollie had carefully disposed of each of the notes in the company kiln and set them on fire.

Did he feel as bad as she about the way it all had ended? Never in her life had Mollie been as deliberately cruel as she had been that afternoon on the sidewalk outside the bank. "Jumped-up longshoreman," she had called him. Zack was covered with a shell as rugged as battle armor, but that barb had slipped through where it could do the most damage. The way he'd flinched, a flash of hurt mingled with embarrassment, had been real. How quickly he had masked it, but she knew her arrow had found its mark and he remembered it.

She knew because his last note had suggested they get dinner at the fanciest restaurant in town where she could "savor the way the jumped-up rich people ate." When she told Alice what she had said, her friend had been reproving. "Aren't we all a little jumped-up?" she'd asked. For a girl who'd grown up pulling blackened lumps of potatoes from the Irish soil, Alice Adair had come a long way. Even Mollie and her father had pandered to the new rich of Chicago, hadn't they?

Standing before the mirror in the shop, Mollie adjusted the soft cambric of the embroidered blouse into the waistband of the bronze skirt. Aside from the overlong hem, the outfit would need no tailoring to fit perfectly to her frame. How badly she wanted to be polished, poised, and in control of her world once again.

And for that to happen, there was no room for Zack. He was a wild force of uncertainty, mistrust, and emotions that would snap and flail like a wire that had been pulled too tight. Colonel Richard Lowe was a much safer choice.

Zack strode down Waubansia Avenue, whistling a perfect imitation of Lizzie's morning chirp. The cold air made whistling easy, and he was in a good mood. For the first time, Mollie had responded to one of his notes. True, it had been only two lines in which she'd ordered him to quit pestering her, but he wasn't discouraged. Mollie's preferred style of argument was retreating behind her fortress of ice, so this note was exactly what he'd expected. He also knew that her logical, business-oriented brain would eventually come around to understand the situation about the land deed correctly. Her feelings had been hurt, but it was a business transaction.

Besides, he had the perfect gift in his pocket. Dr. Buchanan had let him know of the one thing Mollie lacked to get her operation back in full working order, and Zack intended to supply it.

Dr. Buchanan's fascination with his mother's cooking meant that Zack had a constant source of information on exactly what Mollie was up to. It was a rare evening when the dentist did not stop at their house for dinner. At first it was because Dr. Buchanan craved a decent meal and his mother would never turn a hungry man away. Then the relationship had deepened. When Dr. Buchanan noticed Zack's father working a piece of leather in preparation for making a hand-sewn wallet in the style of his Polish ancestors, the dentist had been intrigued. Jozef Kazmarek gladly showed Dr. Buchanan how to use a glover's needle to bend and fashion the leather into shape. Zack had never had much interest in Polish handicrafts, but Dr. Buchanan had lapped up Jozef's instructions like a calf seeking mother's milk. Now every night after dinner, Dr. Buchanan and his father sat by the light of the fire as they each worked a piece of leather. After a little practice, Dr. Buchanan began making a leather pouch for his dental instruments.

Dr. Buchanan's regular visits meant Zack knew exactly what was happening with the 57th. "She's got that attic workshop in full operation," the dentist said. "All except the metal polishing. There is no diamond powder to be had in the city. Her supplier got burned out and is nowhere to be found. If she can't get more diamond powder, that means no polished metal, and pretty soon all the other operations are going to come to a grinding halt."

Dr. Buchanan went on to tell of Mollie's need to meet the Christmas order for a store in New York. Zack was pleased she'd landed such an impressive contract. Not that he'd doubted for a second she would. Her bold, outlandish idea to sell watches commemorating the Chicago fire was just the sort of daring plan that was going to keep her company afloat through this disaster.

Zack grinned as he hopped over the railroad tracks leading to the industrial mills. He was good at solving problems, and Mollie's need for diamond powder was tailor-made for him to slide in and start making himself indispensable to her. A more conventional man would try softening her up with flowers or jewelry, but Zack knew what made Mollie's practical little heart beat faster, and that was having her supply pantry fully stocked. Zack had visited three jewelers to buy scrap diamond chips. They were knocking against his leg where they were stored in one of his father's handmade leather pouches.

Magruder's Industrial Mill on the northwest side of town specialized in producing the kind of high-end industrial equipment that was fueling the growth of the city. Master machinist Caleb Magruder built the hydraulic lifts for the elevator that had graced Hartman's, and Zack had already contracted with him to build another elevator in their new building.

Dark clouds pumped from the smokestacks and a wave of hot air enveloped him as he stepped inside the mill. A wall of noise from the Bessemer furnace and huge grinding wheels was an assault on the ears, but it was the heat that caught Zack by surprise. He winced at the lungful of hot air but pushed the unwelcome sensation away. Memories of the fire still reared up at the most inconvenient times. He'd probably hate the feeling of hot air in his lungs for the rest of his life, but that didn't mean he couldn't walk across the floor of a mill and get what he needed for Mollie.

Every square foot of the floor was in operation. The mill had been operating around the clock to replace the metalwork destroyed in the fire, but luckily he only needed Caleb Magruder's equipment for less than an hour. He found the master mechanic standing beside a huge ring of metal at least eight feet wide and three inches thick. Wearing a leather apron and holding tongs to steady the metal ring, Caleb was in the process of installing a series of petal-shaped blades along the ring's perimeter.

"A new water turbine," Caleb shouted over the noise of the forge. "Installing them all over the city. Better control of water pressure."

"I've got a quick job for you," Zack shouted. Caleb nodded to a sweaty-faced worker to take over and motioned for Zack to follow him to an office in the rear of the mill. When the door closed and the racket dimmed to a dull roar, Zack tossed the sack of diamond chips to the mill owner.

Caleb snatched it out of the air. "What's this?"

"You can grind diamond powder, can't you?"

Caleb peeked inside the pouch. "Nothing to it, but get in line. I've got work stacked up into the next decade." He pulled the strings of the pouch tight and tossed it back to Zack.

It was the answer Zack had expected. There wasn't a factory or forge in the city that was not swamped with work. The temporary swell of goodwill following the fire had encouraged merchants to keep their prices fair, but as exhaustion set in, people were raising their prices to what the market would bear.

Zack was ready to play ball. "One hour at the wheel of your grinding station, and I'll make arrangements for you to share shipping space with Hartman's on our next train."

"Not good enough," the master mechanic said. "My grinder is making silica for glass. I'll need to clean the grinder before and after the diamonds. If you want that diamond powder today, I'll need a shot at your shipping space, plus a 5 percent price hike on the elevator I'm building for the new Hartman's store."

"No deal," Zack said. He could bend the rules at Hartman's, but he wouldn't break them. One of the advantages of growing up on the south-side docks was that Zack had connections with every union leader, alderman, and politician in the city. Caleb Magruder could use those connections, and when Zack offered to invite the mechanic to the December rally for the mayor, it was a tempting offer. Caleb rubbed his jaw, pretending great reluctance before caving to the deal, as Zack knew he would.

"I'll do it this one time," he growled as he snatched the pouch from Zack, "but don't expect any other favors. I've got a business to run."

Two hours later, Zack had ten ounces of diamond powder. By this time tomorrow, Mollie would be eating out of his hand.

~

Zack was exhausted when he finally stepped off the streetcar to walk the final three blocks home. The afternoon's diversion to get the diamond powder had made for a late night. A delivery of hardware from Cincinnati was short five casks of metal door hinges, and contracts with the city for jacking up the foundations on Columbus Street had hit a snarl. By the time he untangled the mess the sun had long since set, it was after eight o'clock, the air was freezing, and it had begun to sleet. Last week the gas lines had finally been repaired, so a glow from the streetlamps made it easy to see the sleet coming down sideways. He pulled the collar of his jacket up higher and darted toward home.

Inside, the house smelled delicious. His parents were sitting with Dr. Buchanan by the light of the fire. "Zachariasz!" his mother exclaimed as she shot to her feet. "We were about to give up on you. It is Andrew's patron saint day, and we are celebrating."

Zack grinned, knowing exactly what was coming. In Poland, the celebration of a saint's day was far more important than birthdays, and his mother always loved a good celebration. Ever since she had taken Dr. Buchanan under her wing, she had been foisting these little traditions on him. On saints' days his mother always made *makowiec*, a loaf of sweetbread with layers of minced almonds and poppy seeds, and drizzled with a honey glaze. It was Zack's favorite dessert, and his mouth watered at the scent that permeated the house.

Dr. Buchanan stood, his face flushed but pleased. "I didn't realize celebrating a saint's day was a Polish custom. My birthday is in June, but I am game for a celebration in November."

When Zack went back to the kitchen to help his mother set tiny candles into the makowiec loaf, she murmured to him, "No one has celebrated a saint's day or a birthday for that man since he was ten years old and lost his parents. That ends today."

Zack had seen the signs coming. His parents had always wanted more than one child, and when they recognized a lost soul like Dr. Andrew Buchanan, they embraced him with both arms. Dr. Buchanan had been invited to spend Christmas with them, and he had already become a permanent fixture in their house for dinner.

His mother's face was illuminated by the candles as she carried the cake into the parlor. She sliced the cake and distributed plates, and his father raised his glass in a toast. "Good luck, good cheer; may you live a hundred years!"

Dr. Buchanan looked pleased enough to levitate. "As soon as my dental practice is back in business, no Kazmarek will ever pay for tooth work as long as they live."

Zack stretched his legs out. "And how is the rebuilding going?" He had heard about the influx of volunteers from the able-bodied survivors of the 57th. Once or twice he had even passed by the construction site, glad to see Mollie's new building taking shape so quickly. Large windows were on each of the walls, as Mollie had told him how important light was in the watchmaker's craft. Last week, roofing materials had been delivered to the site.

"It all depends on if the weather holds," Dr. Buchanan said. "Colonel Lowe wants the building finished by Thanksgiving, but certain things can't be done when it gets below freezing. Of course, I think Colonel Lowe will be happy to become a permanent fixture in Chicago if it means he can stay around Mollie. I've never seen a man so awestruck."

His head shot up. "Has he been pestering Mollie?" Zack demanded.

Dr. Buchanan had just shoveled a huge bite of makowiec loaf into his mouth, and Zack's blood began pounding through his system. Why had he been so blind to overlook what would happen when eighteen able-bodied men showed up on Mollie's doorstep? He'd been letting Mollie lick her wounds in private, but what kind of idiot abandoned her when there were plenty of strapping young men there to take her mind off things?

Dr. Buchanan finished eating and wiped his mouth. "I don't think *pester* is the right word, although not an hour goes by that he isn't paying her compliments. Yesterday, Colonel Lowe brought her a basket of oranges, although where he got oranges at this time of year is anyone's guess."

Zack narrowed his eyes. "Why would Mollie be interested in some old man?"

"Colonel Lowe isn't an old man. I'd guess he's about your age. Thirty-four, maybe thirty-six. And he's a handsome fellow, no doubt about that. Miss Mollie seems quite taken by him."

The memory of a blond man sitting beside Mollie in her workshop with drafting paper before them smacked Zack in the face. He shot to his feet. "I'm going over there."

His mother tried to talk sense into him. "Zachariasz, it is cold outside. Sleet! You will catch your death."

He had lived through worse, and he wasn't about to sit home eating makowiec loaf while the woman he loved was falling prey to some predator out to seduce her. As if diamond powder would impress her when Colonel Lowe was building her a whole new factory!

He yanked his coat from the rack in the hall, still wet from his trip home. He'd put up with a lot from Mollie in the past few weeks, but this was the limit. While he was selling his soul to cut a deal for diamond powder this afternoon, she had been eating oranges with Colonel Lowe.

"Zack, that girl lives in the women's barracks," his father said. "They aren't going to let you in."

His hand paused. Mollie was going to be skittish, and he needed to handle this carefully. He removed his jacket, hanging it up silently before turning around to look at Dr. Buchanan standing in the corner of the parlor. He rejoined the group.

"Tell me everything you know," he said. If he was going into battle with a colonel, Zack was going to launch his campaign fully prepared.

It was late in the afternoon the next day when Zack approached the brewery. Old Gunner was standing outside, shivering in the chilly air to smoke a cigar, and was happy to tell Zack that Mollie had gone down to Lake Park.

It took him thirty minutes to walk to Lake Park. It was a strange place for Mollie to go, as the park had been destroyed by the fire. What had once been a grassy shoreline was now a blackened wasteland that served as the dumpsite for rubble from the burned district. There were rows of horse-drawn wagons leading up to the lake, all overflowing with debris ready to dump into the lake. Already, two new acres had been added to the city, and it was estimated the park would gain an additional five to ten acres of land after all the rubble was dumped and covered over with top soil.

Mollie sat on one of the workbenches that lined the shore of the lake, and as Zack walked closer, he saw a hopeful expression on her face. Mollie loved this city for the same reason he did.

There was a buzz of invention and industry that never stopped. Even here, in the plot of land that epitomized the devastation of what they had endured, the signs of rebirth were everywhere. They were actually *making* new land out of this devastation. Someday this promontory would be a beautiful addition to the city.

Mollie hugged the edges of her cloak tighter around her throat as a chill wind rolled off the lake. He knew to the bottom of his soul that this was the woman he wanted walking by his side as he went through the decades of his life, but it wouldn't happen if Colonel Lowe was invading her heart. He needed to put a stop to it. Mollie was the woman he had been gazing at like a lovesick fool for the better part of three years, and admiring her from afar was no way to win her.

At least she wasn't wearing rags any longer. She once again looked like the woman who had visited Hartman's . . . prim, ladylike, but with the heart and soul of an idealist throbbing beneath an exterior like a carefully wrapped package. She didn't notice him until he was standing a few feet behind her.

"You look beautiful, Mollie."

She whirled around, so startled she shot to her feet and held up her hands. "Zack! You scared the daylights out of me." She adjusted her cloak and glanced nervously around. "You shouldn't be here."

"In a public park? Granted, it looks a little worse for wear, but it is a park, Mollie. Even jumped-up longshoremen sometimes go to a park."

Color stained her cheeks, and she dropped her gaze. "I never should have said that. I'm sorry." She plopped back down on the bench, the wistful expression that had lit her face just moments ago gone. Now she just looked sad and tired.

Was she really feeling that guilty over what she had said on the street outside the bank? He moved closer and propped a booted foot on the bench so he could lean down to her. The only way to clear the air was to lay it all out. Mollie usually fled from this kind of confrontation, but he would help her see that two people could lock horns and still wake up to a new day. "I suppose I am, you know. Jumped-up."

She swallowed a little nervously and looked even more heartsick. "I still should not have said it. Most people want to improve their station in life, and there's nothing wrong with that. You were just better at making it happen."

He waved his hand impatiently. "Forget about that," he said. "You were snapping mad and had a right to be. I was glad to see you blowing off a little steam, for once in your life, instead of keeping it bottled up inside. Here. I've brought you something."

He tossed the leather bag of diamond powder onto her lap. It was no bigger than an egg, but still curiously heavy, and Mollie weighed it in her hand. But she didn't open it, she just handed it back to him.

"Zack, I don't want anything from you."

"I expect you will change your mind once you know what it is." He kept his arms folded across his chest, refusing to take the sack back.

She sighed and dropped the bag into her lap, still unopened. "I'm glad you came," she said. "I've been feeling bad about that day at the bank, and I wanted to apologize. I know you weren't at liberty to disclose anything about the deed to me, but I was angry at the world that day, and you happened to be the easiest target." Her brow furrowed, and it seemed for a moment as if she was about to cry. "I keep fearing I might die. I know it sounds strange, but I keep worrying that if I die, the last words you will have heard from me would be something so hateful. So

I am glad I saw you today and can tell you that I didn't mean those things I said."

The wind tugged at her hair, and her face was sculpted with sorrow. She seemed to have aged so much in these past few months. Holding his breath, he lowered himself to the bench beside her, relieved she made no move to flee.

"Why do you keep thinking you are going to die?" he asked softly.

"It is pathetic," she said dismissively. "I'll get over it." But her gaze was troubled as she looked out at the lake, tracking the slow progress of a trawler on the horizon.

He took her hand. She was wearing new kid leather gloves, but he could feel her slim hand trembling within. "Mollie, tell me. You don't have to carry this by yourself."

She squeezed his hand. "I have nightmares," she said in a shattered whisper. "I don't remember the details, just that I am in a fire and there is no way to get out. I keep trying to find Frank, but he is somewhere in the flames and I can't get to him." She turned to face him, and in her eyes he could see the shadows of fear lurking. "Do you ever have that kind of dream?"

He stiffened. He wasn't tormented by nightmares, but he understood what she was going through. "It isn't nightmares so much as the sound of bells that gets to me." The first time it had happened, Zack had been writing contracts to raise the foundation for the store on Columbus Street. The church on the corner had concluded a memorial service, and the pealing of bells ricocheted through the streets for over a minute. By the time it was over, a sheen of perspiration had covered his body, and he'd had a headache so bad he could hardly see straight. It must have been his imagination, but it had seemed he could smell smoke and feel pinpricks of cinders landing on his skin. The echo of those bells had hammered in his brain for over an hour, destroying his concentration. He shook off the memory. "The ringing of church bells catches me unawares sometimes," he said. "They set my nerves on edge."

Mollie nodded. "I thought we had all made it through the fire, and I was just starting to feel like things were returning to normal again, but I don't think I'll ever feel entirely safe. Not without Frank. How can it be that one moment we are happily rebuilding our lives, and the next moment he lies beaten to death on the floor of a church? And whoever did that to him is still out there." She squeezed his hand tighter. "Frank Spencer was a second father to me. I think about him every day, and my heart breaks to think that some . . . some ignorant brutes took his life in exchange for a little bit of gold."

"Do you think it would help your nightmares go away if those men were caught?"

"I don't know." Then she tipped her head up to look at him with curiosity brimming in those clear blue eyes. "Why did the two of you fight so much?"

"We fought plenty, but I always respected him."

"But why all the arguing? The nitpicking? It always seemed strange to me."

It would. He smiled and turned his face to the sky. For all her practical, level-headed business sense, Mollie didn't understand much about men. "Sometimes men just like to argue," he said simply. "We like the competition. We sniff out the opposition, measure it up, challenge it. Frank never backed down. Even though he was blind, Frank was still a man, and when I came on the scene, I think he immediately sensed my interest in you. Long before *you* ever did."

A flush deepened on her cheeks. It looked like she didn't know if she wanted to fling herself into his arms or get up and bolt. It was time to start circling in.

"I like seeing you in decent clothes again," he said. "You look like the Mollie Knox who used to scurry across the floor at Hartman's. The only thing that would make you look more perfect would be getting rid of those braids."

She smoothed back a strand of hair that had broken free and was blowing in the wind. "My hair gets in my face when I wear it down," she said in a weary voice.

"When you wear your hair down, you look like a medieval princess in one of those pre-Raphaelite portraits that are all the rage in Europe."

She withdrew her hands. He wasn't sure what had happened, but an invisible barrier had just been erected. "Zack, I really hate wearing my hair down, all right? For a few insane, delirious weeks in October, I thought I was in love with you, and I wore my hair down to please you. But I am not one of those portraits in the museum, and I'm not the girl in the garden in the painting on your dining room wall."

She twisted on the bench so she could face him better, taking his hand between her soft leather gloves. His chest expanded with hope blazing inside, and he opened his arms, waiting for her to move into them, but he froze when she pressed the little sack of diamond powder against his chest.

"Zack, I will be forever grateful for what you did for me the night of the fire. You were like a hero out of the storybooks." She grabbed one of his hands and curled his fingers around the leather sack, but was unable to look him in the eyes. She couldn't reject him, not now.

"I'm not sure why you care for me, but I don't think we are a good match. I like a safe and orderly world, while you want to ride the whirlwind. I'm not the girl in your painting—the girl in the garden—and you can't change me into her. I tried to be that carefree girl, wear my hair down and stroll under the sun. It isn't who I am. I want to go back to my orderly business charts and make my watches."

He couldn't believe his ears. She was rambling on about nonsense, and he needed to put a stop to it. "I don't want to *change* you—"

She cut him off. "From the day you came to the workshop, you told me I should sell the company and go to the south of France to celebrate. That I should wear my hair down and quit being a howling mass of anxiety. Zack, I don't want to go to the south of France. I want to turn the clock back and reconstruct my life exactly as it was before the fire. I want my workshop back. I want to make watches and know what is on the schedule for the next day, next month, next year. I need order and stability."

His fist clenched around the leather sack. She was trying to cut him out of her life, and he wouldn't let her. "And what about Colonel Lowe?" he demanded. "Is Colonel Lowe among the things you want?"

She stiffened and couldn't meet his eyes. "Richard means a lot to me," she said softly.

Richard. So he wasn't even Colonel Lowe to her. A wave of heat crashed through his body, and he wanted to break something. He stood and stalked a few feet closer to the lake. He couldn't bear to sit beside Mollie while she talked about another man, but she hadn't stopped speaking.

"Richard and I are very much alike," she said. "I feel . . . safe with him. I don't need to change to suit him."

"*I don't want to change you,*" he said through clenched teeth. Where did she get these insane ideas? He could feel her slipping away from him, like water dribbling out of his cupped hands, and there was nothing he could do to stop it from draining away.

"Please let me go," she said. "I need to move on with the rest of my life, and I can't do that with you in it. The notes need to stop. And the visits. I will be forever grateful for what you did for me on the night of the fire, but, Zack . . . that's all there is. It was gratitude and the temporary rush of insanity because I was glad to be alive. You and I will never work."

The wind gusted in from the lake, blowing long strands of her hair that escaped like a cloud of smoke whirling around her head. How could he have lost her so completely? "And you think Richard will make you happy?"

The tension on her face eased. "I do." When the lines eased around her eyes, her face was transformed. A faint smile graced her mouth, and she looked peaceful. Happy.

It stunned him to realize he had never really seen Mollie look peaceful. He'd seen the business side of her, the logical, competent aspect that first drew his admiration. He'd seen her valiant courage the night of the fire. In the following weeks, he had seen how she'd borne up under stress, battling challenge after challenge without breaking her stride. He had seen her hopeful and triumphant. But he hadn't really seen her at peace.

He needed to be smart about this. If Mollie thought Colonel Lowe would make her happy, she would resent any attempt to interfere with that. He would wait for Mollie into the next century if need be, but for now, he needed to get out of her way.

"All right, then." He couldn't believe he was speaking the words, but to the core of his soul he wanted Mollie to be happy. If that meant giving her the breathing space she needed to explore this curiosity with Colonel Lowe, he would do it. It was like letting someone carve a piece of his soul from his chest. Stepping aside to let Mollie's rich, handsome golden boy slide into place beside her went against every impulse in his body. Once again, he was the grubby wharf rat laboring on the docks while the white knight trampled over him.

"If Colonel Lowe doesn't treat you like a goddess, he'll have me to answer to," he said gruffly.

She mustered a little laugh. "Please, no basket of fish on his desk."

"Trust me, I'll be far more creative if he hurts you." The diamond powder weighed in his hands. "You will want this," he said as he extended the sack to her.

"Zack, I don't want any gifts."

He picked up her hand and pressed it into her palm. "It's diamond powder. I heard you were in short supply, and Caleb Magruder has a mill that can produce it."

Her eyes widened in surprise, and she peeked inside. It looked as if she was about to cry as she pulled the drawstrings closed. "Zack, I can't accept this. It wouldn't be right."

"Take it. What would I do with diamond powder?" He tried to sound light-hearted, as if this glorious woman had not just trampled on the dreams he had been building for three years.

She still looked hesitant, which was insane because he knew she craved that diamond powder like a drowning man craved a life raft. He sighed impatiently. "If you don't take it, I'll throw it in the lake. You know I will."

She must have believed him, because she relented and accepted the gift. "Thank you," she said quietly. "Thank you for everything, Zack."

"You deserve it," he said bluntly. "I've never seen anyone work as hard as you."

"Don't be nice to me," she said. "I'll start bawling like a watering pot if you do."

His hand looked big and clumsy against her delicate cheek. He was such a sap where this woman was concerned. Had been from the first time he ever clapped eyes on her. "Don't shed any tears over me. I'm not worth it."

He had to get out of there before he made a complete fool of himself. Before he fell to his knees and begged her not to fling herself at a man who would never feel a fraction of the soaring love he had for her. Stepping aside and letting Richard Lowe court his woman made his gut tie itself into knots, but it had to be done.

20

How long would it be before she could quit crying? The naked pain on Zack's face would probably haunt her for the rest of her life, but she had done the right thing. She couldn't ride the streetcar while she was blubbering, so Mollie walked the three miles back to the brewery. Why did it feel like she had just torn her heart out? Her chest ached, and it hurt to even draw a full breath of air. In a couple of weeks, Zack would realize she was right—that this insane rush of madness that had flared up between them would never last—but that didn't ease the gnawing pain in her heart and mind.

She dreaded seeing anyone. For once in her life, the prospect of making watches held no appeal. She just wanted to go home and bury her head underneath a pillow and escape, but this diamond powder needed to be delivered.

Pulling the gloves from her hands, she pressed her cold fingers against her cheekbones, hoping they would ease her swollen eyes and mask the fact that she had been crying. People at the 57th would want to know why, and she couldn't speak of this yet. Not without starting the water spigot again.

The yeasty scent of beer comforted her as she mounted the steps to the attic. Getting her factory back in business had been one of the most exhilarating experiences of her life. Difficult and scary, but necessary.

She pushed open the rickety attic door. "Sophie," she said in surprise. There was no longer any suitable work for the girl at the construction site, so she had been helping Declan at the workshop. Usually the girl was gone by now, but she sprang down from a stool and darted across the room to Mollie.

"Gunner said that Zack brought you diamond powder! I wanted to wait and see it. That means we will be able to start making parts again, right?"

The lump in her throat grew larger. A glance around the room showed everyone watching her. The technicians should have gone home by now, but Oliver and the others were still here, watching her with hopeful expectation.

"Yes, I've got the diamond powder."

Sophie jumped up and down, begging to get a peek. There was a collective sigh of relief throughout the workshop, and Mollie's shoulders sagged. She did not realize that everyone was aware of how close they'd been to having to cease operations for want of polished metal parts.

Declan got out the almond oil and began making paste, showing Sophie how to judge the correct viscosity and blend it properly. Mollie pulled out some paper work. Now that she knew they would have more parts, she could begin filling in a production schedule. As she charted her operations, sliding the familiar tasks into the calendar and projecting due dates, her tension began to ease.

It made her want to begin crying again, but Zack's gift of diamond powder meant she could meet the Christmas deadline for sending her watches to New York.

"I don't trust you," Dr. Buchanan said.

Zack leaned against the wall of his parlor and glared at the dentist. They had spent the afternoon boxing up the multitude of his parents' towering stacks of paper that had once again overwhelmed the front room, spilling into the hallway and creating a fire hazard of towering Polish memories. Whenever his mother's hoards of junk got out of control, he systematically boxed whatever spilled into the hallway and transported it to the third-floor attic. There was so much dust in the air he'd had to move Lizzie's cage into the kitchen so his poor finch wouldn't choke to death.

"You can trust me," Zack said. "I'm not going to do anything foolish where Mollie is concerned."

"But why do you have to get involved? Colonel Lowe has the situation well in hand, and given your feelings for Miss Mollie, I don't think it's a good idea. Not prudent."

Zack shoved a newly filled crate of papers to the side and plopped another down in its place. "Colonel Lowe doesn't know this city like I do, and he is heading down the wrong track if he hopes to catch the men who killed Frank by watching pawnshops."

Pawnshops, he thought contemptuously as he tossed another sheaf of papers into a crate. Scanning the pawnshops wasn't completely foolhardy, but if those watches hadn't surfaced by now, they weren't going to, and Colonel Lowe didn't have an alternate plan of attack. Mollie needed to be able to sleep at night, and that would never happen as long as those thugs were still roaming the streets. Zack could find them. For years, he had been rubbing elbows with people from the top of the city government all the way down to the street sweepers. He knew how to get things done in this city.

Besides, he wanted to get a good look at Colonel Lowe.

Richard. Not that he intended to interfere with Mollie's stellar new relationship. She'd made it brutally clear she had carefully considered her two suitors and made her choice. Not that Zack intended to accept her decision, but if he tried to interfere, she would build Colonel Lowe up in her imagination as the perfect alternative to Zack and his brash courtship. He needed to step aside for the time being.

Provided that Richard Lowe was not a complete and unabashed scoundrel. Given the praises Dr. Buchanan, everyone from the 57th, and even Sophie Durant had for Colonel Lowe, that appeared to be unlikely.

"Just tell me where the man lives," Zack prodded. "I can't go near the construction site because I promised Mollie I would stay clear of her, so finding him at home is the only way I can meet him."

Dr. Buchanan leafed through a couple of photographs that were slipped among the towering pages. "Look at the clothing this woman is wearing. Do they really dress like that in Poland?"

Zack batted the picture away. "Don't change the subject. Where does Colonel Lowe live?"

"I hear he has been staying with General Sheridan."

Zack dropped the sheaf of papers he was holding. Brilliant. Mollie's fair-haired soldier had connections to the most famous war hero in the city.

"I know you don't want to hear it," Dr. Buchanan said as he nervously fiddled with the corner of his mustache, "but everyone in the 57th is placing bets on when the wedding will be. Most are going for summer, but some think late next autumn. No one is betting any longer than that."

The words came tumbling down on him like acid, but he forced his voice to remain neutral. "And when did you place your bet?"

"I put my money on May first. They both seem very taken with each other."

His shoulders sagged. This was worse than he had anticipated. His gaze tracked to the painting of the girl in the garden. She looked so much like Mollie it was as if he had his very own portrait of her. It hurt him to look at it, but if he lost her, that portrait would be the closest he would ever come to having Mollie Knox.

He would find the men who'd killed Frank. Right now, that was the only thing he could do for Mollie.

Colonel Richard Lowe was exactly as he was rumored to be. Handsome, competent, and a gentleman to the marrow of his bones. Educated at West Point, he had an understanding of battlefield tactics and strategy to rival Napoleon. He was a warrior young boys wanted to grow up to become like. He was a son any mother would be proud to have. He was Lancelot without the pesky adultery problem.

Zack loathed him on sight. Standing on the porch of General Sheridan's elegant townhouse, Colonel Lowe refused to see reason, no matter how clearly Zack explained.

"Just give me the names of three of your men who can read and write," Zack said to Colonel Lowe. "I'll need them to hunt down the *Marianne*. You won't need to be involved at all." Ralph Coulter, the redheaded lumber dealer, had disappeared from the church immediately following the attack. His ship had been called the *Marianne*, and if Zack could find that ship, it wouldn't be long before he could hunt down Coulter himself. Coulter knew something about the men who had raided the church or he wouldn't have made himself scarce after Frank was killed.

Colonel Lowe wouldn't budge. "Now that the construction

work on Mollie's new factory is almost complete, most of my men will be leaving soon. I have vowed to stay until the hoodlums have been apprehended."

What kind of real man used a word like *hoodlum*? For all of Colonel Lowe's vaunted accomplishments, he didn't know the city of Chicago and was floundering at catching Frank's killers. Zack didn't need or want Colonel Lowe on the hunt. It was hard for him to even be in this man's presence without seething in resentment. Colonel Lowe had had his path smoothed for him from the moment he had hauled himself upright in his cradle. With a railroad baron for a father and an education at West Point, who wouldn't be successful? Richard Lowe was born with every natural and man-made advantage in this world, and Zack wanted him to use those advantages in finishing Mollie's factory, not glued to Zack's side as he tried to hunt down the *Marianne*. All Zack needed was a couple of Colonel Lowe's men to do some grunt work, but Colonel Lowe was being an overbearing prig.

"I promised Miss Knox I would help apprehend the men responsible for Frank Spencer's death."

"Fine," Zack bit out. "You can help by loaning me three men who can read and write."

Colonel Lowe's smile was artificially bright. "I volunteer my own services. Let's go."

Annoyance simmered through Zack as he strode toward the customhouse, Colonel Lowe matching him stride for stride. Zack's plan was to pull the bills of lading for the past several months, making a list of every 106-foot lumber schooner doing business in Chicago. He had already confirmed that the *Marianne* had not been seen in Chicago since Frank's death. If Ralph Coulter had an ounce of intelligence, he would have renamed and repainted the *Marianne* to alter its appearance, but Coulter

ELIZABETH CAMDEN

couldn't change the basic structure of the ship. Zack was looking for any 106-foot lumber schooner that had no record of
conducting business in the ports of Chicago prior to Frank's
death. If he could find such a schooner, the odds were good he
would have found the *Marianne* and its absentee owner.

Colonel Lowe was annoyingly cheerful as he strode alongside
Zack. As they neared the intersection of Randolph and Clark,
the street was jammed with wagons and horses jostling for space
with pedestrians. A train was stalled on the tracks ahead, back-
ing traffic up for blocks. Zack shouldered his way through the
crowd, pushing past a woman with an overflowing basket of
bread on her shoulder and a newspaper boy anxious to get out
of the snarl of traffic.

"What is going on?" Zack asked the newsboy.

"Something on the tracks ahead," the boy said. "The trains
are backed up for a mile. We'll be here forever."

Zack glanced down the tracks. Sure enough, trains were
stalled as far as the eye could see.

"Let's go see what the trouble is," Colonel Lowe said as he
set off to the north end of the tracks.

It was clear to see. A wagonload of cement had overturned
on the tracks, mixing with the melted snow puddled between
the railroad ties. Enough of the mix had been shoved up onto
the iron railings, solidifying almost immediately and making it
impossible for the trains to pass. A single railroad repairman
was chipping at the mass helplessly, a wagonload of tools beside
him, but no labor to help.

"What's going on here?" Colonel Lowe asked.

The man stopped to swipe the sweat on his brow. "I've sent
to the north side for more workers, but no one has showed up
yet. There was a fire on the tracks at Taylor Street, so that's
where all the repair workers are."

Colonel Lowe stripped off his jacket. "I can lend a hand," he said amiably. "Kazmarek, are you up for it?"

Zack was thrown. "I thought your family owned railroads. Not built them."

Colonel Lowe grabbed a large-handled wrench from the supply wagon and expertly attacked a bolt on the metal plate that fastened two sections of the rail together. "Same thing," he said as he began twisting the head of a bolt loose. "My father didn't believe in traditional schooling. He said if the railroads were going to pay for the roof over my head, I was going to learn how to make them." The end of his sentence trailed off as he strained to force the bolt loose. "Instead of sitting in a schoolroom, I got my education on the Dakota plains, alongside the railroad workers. I slept in their tents. Ate their food. This seems like old times!"

Another bolt popped free. Zack grabbed a wrench and began working on the bolt plate on the opposite rail. He tugged at the wrench but made no progress. He tugged again, harder, and the bolt twisted a fraction of an inch.

Colonel Lowe kept working at a brisk pace. "We should be able to get these rails disengaged in about ten minutes," he said without even looking up from his task. "I see everything we need in the repair wagon to install two good rails." He glanced up at the exhausted railroad worker who was leaning on his shovel to catch his breath. "If you can get the rest of that concrete cleared, we can have this track operational within the hour."

Zack tried to match Colonel Lowe bolt for bolt. It was getting hard to keep his resentment burning. Hauling concrete off the docks of Chicago was no one's idea of an easy childhood, but neither was laying track in the Dakotas.

It took a little longer than Colonel Lowe had originally suggested. Some of the railroad ties were too heavily coated in concrete to be salvaged, and they would have to be pried up and replaced, but after three additional repairmen showed up, the work progressed quickly. Colonel Lowe supervised the removal of the damaged rails, the insertion of six new railway ties, and then the fitting of clean rails.

By all that was holy, it hurt to work alongside the man who had captured Mollie's heart. A man who had waltzed into her life less than a month ago and swept her so thoroughly off her feet she was ready to dash down the aisle with him. Zack hauled the oversized wrenches back to the supply wagon. Why had he let Louis Hartman's rules keep him away from Mollie? During those first few years, it was enough to simply enjoy the sight of her as she flitted through the store, visiting his office every few months. It wasn't until he saw her face by the light of the fire that he saw her true glory, and then he was hopelessly in love with her. He knew Mollie on a level Colonel Richard Lowe could never imagine.

"About Mollie Knox," he said.

Colonel Lowe straightened immediately. "Yes?"

"It is probably best not to mention my involvement in getting justice for Frank. She . . . we . . . well, it's best not to mention my name."

"What exactly is your interest in Frank's case?"

Zack met the Colonel's gaze squarely. "Hartman's did business with the 57th," he said. "Of course I want to see justice done."

"I'm sure your company did business with plenty of suppliers. Although I bet none of them were run by a woman as fetching as Mollie Knox."

Zack did not bother to respond as he hoisted the last of the tools in place. He merely set off for the customhouse and began telling Colonel Lowe his plan. "I remember Coulter talking about his ship," he said. "He named it the *Marianne* after his sister who died when she was a baby. If we find that ship, Ralph Coulter won't be far away."

Finding the *Marianne* would be a challenge. Chicago was the world's largest lumber market, with close to two hundred ships arriving daily at the dozens of ports along the shores of Lake Michigan. The forest products from Wisconsin and Michigan were shipped into Chicago, where they were transferred to the train depots and funneled throughout the burgeoning western settlements of the United States.

"Can the police help monitor the ports?" Colonel Lowe asked.

Zack shook his head. "The police are overwhelmed with keeping order and relief work. Half of them lost everything in the fire, and they are exhausted from double shifts just getting the city running again. They won't waste manpower on something like this."

They spent the rest of the afternoon at the customhouse, where they set up an indexing system to alphabetize the name and description of every flat-bottomed lumber schooner measuring 106 feet that had done business in Chicago. Colonel Lowe was indefatigable. Even after the sun went down, he kept plowing through records until they had sorted and indexed the entire file. Working by the light of a kerosene lantern, Zack matched him record for record until they were both bleary-eyed and exhausted, but they finally had their list.

It would take several more hours of scrutiny to track the records and determine which could be the *Marianne*, but this was Zack's best chance of tracking down the wayward Ralph Coulter.

It irked him down to the bottom of his soul to admit, but Mollie's new man wasn't so bad.

21

"Keep your eyes closed, Mollie."

Richard's voice was warm against the side of her face. With her hands covering her face and her eyes squeezed tight, she was blind and helpless, but Richard's hands were firm on her shoulders as he guided her toward the new workshop. Each step scared her, but she trusted Richard to guide her safely. A gust of cold wind tugged at her cloak, but nothing mattered now that she was about to see her new workshop for the first time. Three days ago Richard had banished her from the worksite as the finishing touches were added to the building, but today the suspense would be over.

"Turn to your left just a bit, and then you are inside," Richard murmured in her ear. Instead of the crunch of gravel beneath her boots, she was now walking on smooth plank flooring. The shuffling of feet and murmuring of voices indicated the workshop was filled with people. All the employees and the able-bodied members of the 57th were on hand to celebrate the opening of the new space.

"Open your eyes, Mollie-girl!" Ulysses shouted from somewhere to her right. She held her breath and dropped her hands.

It was a miracle! Light streamed in from the windows, and

rust-colored bricks gave a warm tone to the oversized room. One wall was entirely covered in shelving for storage, and a dozen shoulder-height worktables were in tidy rows, but it was the smiling faces of over a hundred people packed into the space that most moved her.

"Welcome back, Mollie!" A cheer went up from the crowd, and she covered her mouth lest she burst out into tears. Not that she would be the only one crying. The employees of the 57th had brought their wives and children, and plenty of them were wiping away tears of gratitude and relief. Sophie and her father stood in the front. She recognized Charlie Frisch from the piano factory next door and the Kauffman brothers who were rebuilding their vinegar distillery across the street. Any building that reopened so quickly was cause for celebration for the entire neighborhood.

Colonel Lowe stood beside her, smiling down. She didn't know what to say. How did she thank a man for saving her business? For saving the livelihood of forty people and their families? The workshop was larger and more spacious than the old one, with even more light flooding through the oversized windows.

"I don't know how to thank you," she said breathlessly.

Richard nodded to Moose, a towering presence in the front row. "They are the ones who did most of the heavy lifting," he said graciously. She recognized the bricklayers and other volunteers from the 57th who had done the manual labor necessary for getting this building up in record time.

The scent of warm cinnamon rolls filled the air. A few of the children were standing by the shelves piled with cookies, cinnamon rolls, and a huge cake. She needed to say something, acknowledge her gratitude, but speaking before a crowd ranked somewhere near a public stoning as something Mollie enjoyed.

Still, on a day like today, she found it easy to simply open her mouth and speak from her heart. "Two months ago, it seemed like the end of the world," she said. The crowd settled down, and the faces sobered. The fire had only lasted thirty-six hours, but it would burn brightly in everyone's memory for years. "I remember the night when I staggered into the ruins of a church. The fire was still burning, and I thought I had lost everything. I wanted to lie down and go to sleep and never wake up."

A handful of people nodded. Only people who had lived through the horror of those thirty-six hours could really know what it was like. "I didn't know how I was going to survive, and I was struggling along all right, but I know it would have taken me at least a year to rebuild if it hadn't been for . . ."

The clog in her throat grew. Alice's arm tightened around her shoulders, and Mollie drew a breath to begin again.

"My father used to tell me about a band of brothers he once knew. These men came from all over the state and had nothing in common except for serving in the same regiment and fighting for a common cause. He said that in normal life he probably wouldn't even have *liked* some of them—"

"She's talking about you, Moose!" someone hollered, and laughter bubbled up from the 57th.

She waited for the laughter to subside. "My father said he had nothing in common with most of those men, but by the end of the war, he would have given his life for any one of them. They were a band of brothers whose bonds were forged more strongly than they could have been by blood or money. And now I know that even after death, my father's brothers felt the same way. You would not have come if it were otherwise." A rumble of approval and the stamping of feet cut off her words.

She'd forgotten to bring a handkerchief and tears streamed down her face, but the cuff of her blouse worked just as well. "All of us have gone through a terrible experience. I finally understand what my father was speaking of." She glanced at Charlie Frisch, the piano maker. "To my brothers in the piano factory and the vinegar distillery, please come to us as you need help with your new building. There is no reason watchmakers can't do a little heavy lifting in the weeks ahead. And to the 57th . . . you are my heroes. And if I don't quit talking, those children at the dessert table are going to have my head."

Alice hustled her across the room, where a cake glowing with fifty-seven candles was waiting to be cut. Mollie did the honors, while Alice began filling mugs with warmed cider. With so many people to be served, Alice had cut small squares of the sturdy shipping boxes to serve as plates.

Sophie was first in line for a piece of cake. When Mollie handed her a slice, she looked at it skeptically. "I don't like to eat off pasteboard."

"Oh, Sophie, I'll bet you've never tried it," Mollie said as she pushed the piece of cake toward her. The girl had come a long way since the fire, when she'd demanded to be carried like a princess through the flames, but there was bound to be a little backsliding on occasion. As expected, Sophie took the cake and started happily gorging herself on it.

It took them a while to serve everyone, but the wave of exhilaration made her feel like she could do this for weeks and never get tired. She looked up to survey her wonderful new workshop, filled with friends and laughter and hope. Richard Lowe, standing beside the newly installed kiln, gazed at her with warm approval. Heat flushed her cheeks as she smiled at him.

She knew that today was the beginning of something wonderful.

A week after Frank Spencer's death, a flat-bottomed schooner named the *City of the Century* had made its first appearance in Chicago. Its arrival coincided with the disappearance of the *Marianne*, a schooner of the same size, grade, and ports of call.

It didn't take Zack long to track down Ralph Coulter after he discovered this. Zack watched the *City of the Century* pull into the narrow slip that had been excavated into the bank of the lake, leading to miles of docking space in the timber yards. The timber yards swarmed with dozens of lumber shovers who scrambled to offload the logs into the waterway and prod them along the current and into the slips where the logs would be counted, sorted, and stacked. Zack spotted Ralph Coulter leaning over the railing of a walkway suspended over the rushing waters. The noise of the river and the bumping of the logs made it easy for him to approach without Ralph's notice.

"Mr. Coulter!" Zack shouted in an artificially cheerful tone. The man whirled around. When he saw Zack at the end of the bridge, his face blanched white and he looked ready to bolt, but Zack blocked the only way off the suspended bridge. Zack didn't want to trap the man, he just wanted to pump him for information. He strolled a little closer, holding his hands open in an easy manner. "Relax. I just want to chat."

Coulter shot a nervous glance at the rushing waters below. With no avenue of escape, Coulter's shoulders sagged and he directed Zack to the loading house. Zack trailed closely behind as he followed Coulter across the timber yard. It was cold enough to see their breath in the air inside the empty loading house, and Coulter was breathing heavily.

He was also adamant in asserting his innocence. "Look, I cleared out of the church because I didn't want any trouble. I didn't have anything to do with what happened to that man. I liked Frank Spencer."

The bellow of a foghorn sounded from off the lake, startling Coulter, who mopped at the perspiration beading on his brow.

Zack didn't mind applying a little pressure, which was why he didn't want the golden presence of Richard Lowe with him today. He doubted Mollie's fair-haired hero was quite as skilled in the delicate art of arm twisting.

"So you don't know anything about three dozen gold watches? Strange, because they disappeared the same day you did."

"I never saw any watches, I never *touched* any watches. I've been working in the lumber business since I was twelve years old. I wouldn't even know what to do with a passel of fancy watches."

Zack kept his face carefully neutral. "And how about Jesse? Has he been in the lumber business as long as you?"

Coulter's eyes widened. "How do you know about Jesse?"

In the confusion of that night, both Mollie and Ulysses reported hearing Ralph Coulter shout out the name Jesse, but he obviously did not remember doing so. Zack saw no reason to enlighten him. Zack angled his chair so he could prop his booted feet up on a sawhorse, fiddling with the buttons on his vest. "My guess is that Jesse was never the sort to get up before sunrise to meet lumber schooners coming in from the north woods. Not the sort to begin saving for his first schooner at age twelve the way you did. People who filch things to earn a quick buck seldom are. What a shame if you were the only person left holding the bag on this one."

"*I didn't steal any watches,*" Coulter ground out from behind clenched teeth.

"Have you talked to a lawyer about this?" Zack asked casually. "Because I don't think it matters if you stole the watches or not. Jesse knew there were watches in the church, and that means someone told him about it. Maybe it was just in casual conversation, maybe it was more calculating. Either way, if you were the one who told Jesse the people of the 57th were guarding something valuable, and a man was killed as a result of that, that makes you an accomplice to the crime. You could hang for it."

Ralph Coulter fixed him with a steady glare, the angry heat in his face so strong it looked as if it could ignite, but he made no move to offer any information. If this man was willing to take the blame rather than roll over on Jesse, it was likely Jesse was a family member, probably a brother. Zack rolled the dice. Whipping his feet off the sawhorse, Zack planted them on the floor and leaned closer to Coulter.

"The thing is, your mother was always proudest of you," Zack asserted. "You were the one who worked hard to earn an honest dollar. Who made sure the family never went hungry and paid the bill when the doctor needed to be called. How would she feel if you were locked up in prison trying to save Jesse's hide? Jesse will come to a bad end sooner or later, and what a shame that your family will be left with no one to make sure they have heating oil in the winter." He glanced out the window, crusted over with a layer of frost. "And it looks like we're in store for a cold one this year."

Coulter swiped his brow again and then twisted the handkerchief in his hands so tightly his knuckles went white. Zack didn't move a muscle as he watched Coulter wrestle with his conscience. Outside, the steady splashes and thumps from logs tumbling into the slips carried on while Zack held his breath.

Finally Coulter looked up to meet his eyes. "Jesse is long gone, but I might know where he is. I *might*. But here is the thing. My brother has two boys, and they mean the world to me. I'm not going to see them wind up homeless orphans."

"How old are the boys?"

"One is nine, the other six." Coulter folded his arms across his chest, leaned back in his chair, and glared at Zack as he continued talking. "I am not a rich man, but I can provide a home for the boys." He gave a bitter laugh. "They live with me more often than not anyway. But I can't give them the best of everything."

"Neither can I," Zack said. "Don't get carried away here, Coulter. Give me a reasonable request, and I'll see what I can do."

"I've heard about you," Coulter said. "I know you came out of nowhere and then pulled strings to get into Yale. I want the same for the boys. Both of them."

Zack's eyes narrowed. He didn't have those kinds of connections, and even if he did, he wouldn't squander them on a man he already had over a barrel.

Mollie's face rose in his mind, her eyes two blue pools of grief. *Frank Spencer was a second father to me,* she had said in an aching voice. There was a wide swath of pain Mollie kept hidden, and it was tormenting her with nightmares that put shadows under her eyes. He could solve it for her. He could give her the peace of knowing Frank's murderers had paid for their deed. He stared at the sawdust on the floor, his brain sifting through his options, connections, and favors still to be called in.

"I can't get those boys into Yale, but I have connections at Notre Dame. Will that work?"

There was a minuscule easing of the lines on Coulter's forehead. "That will work. I want it in writing. And I want immunity from what happened in the church that night. Signed by a judge."

Zack gave a hollow laugh. "It sounds like you've already been to a lawyer," he said cynically.

"I'm no fool," Coulter said.

~

It took Zack two days to get the necessary documents in order. Coulter's attorney relayed the entire story. After the fire, Coulter paid regular visits to his mother and brother's family where they had taken shelter in the basement of a woolen mill with dozens of other burned-out refugees. When Coulter's mother asked if they would be better off moving to the church, Coulter said they wouldn't, telling her there was no roof, few provisions, and a spoiled little girl who made everyone miserable. He said most of them would probably leave soon, because they had recently come into possession of a bag of gold watches and would surely use them to purchase better accommodations for themselves soon. It was an innocent comment, but enough to set Jesse Coulter and a gang of thugs on the hunt.

The meeting took place in the book-lined office of Coulter's lawyer. In addition to the paper work signed by a judge, Zack brought Colonel Lowe to attend the meeting. It was likely they were going to need the manpower of the 57th in order to round up the entire load of criminals who had descended on the church that night, and as much as he hated it, he still needed Colonel Lowe's help.

Colonel Lowe looked like he smelled rotting fish as he glared at Coulter across the smooth surface of the walnut table. "Why are we rewarding this man?" he demanded. "His foolish talk led to the death of Frank Spencer."

Zack wanted to lunge across the table and shove a sock down Colonel Lowe's throat. Ralph Coulter already looked nervous enough to bolt from the room, and this sort of antagonism could scuttle the deal before Coulter talked. Zack forced his voice to be neutral. "I'm sending two boys to college. I hope you don't have a problem with that."

"I have a problem with anything that turns a blind eye to justice," Colonel Lowe said.

Which was why Colonel Lowe was probably a better match for Mollie, after all. Mollie liked safety and security. Her fair-haired hero could give it to her without ever having to stray from his comfortable world of black and white ethics. Neither Zack nor Ralph Coulter had ever had such a luxury.

When the papers were signed and notarized, all eyes turned to Ralph Coulter, who looked ready to weep. He knew his next words might condemn his brother to death by a hangman's noose, but it would be a greater evil to allow Jesse Coulter's rampant crime spree to continue unabated. Or to allow Jesse to influence the lives of his two young boys, who might be set on the proper path if raised by a decent man.

Coulter buried his face in his hands, his voice so soft it could barely be heard. "You should look in Milwaukee," he said. And over the next twenty minutes, as a man turned his own brother over to the law, Zack thanked God he had never been painted into such a stark corner.

After the meeting, Zack stood in the doorway and watched Ralph Coulter walk down the street, beaten and defeated.

"There walks away a sorry excuse for a man," Colonel Lowe said.

That night, Zack stepped inside a church. Normally he lit a candle for the safety of his father hauling grain off the docks, or for his mother's insane quest to single-handedly rescue the nation of Poland. This evening, after he tipped a coin into the donation box and sank to his knees, Zack lit a candle and said a prayer for Ralph Coulter.

22

Mollie couldn't believe her ears, but Moose confirmed it with his usual blunt efficiency as he stood in the doorway of the new workshop. "Colonel Lowe says Declan McNabb is to come with us to Milwaukee," he growled. "We need every able-bodied man we can get."

But Declan wasn't able-bodied! He jumped at the sound of a slamming door and descended into quaking anxiety the moment he was under stress. Mollie glanced around her brand-new workshop. It was after dinner, and most of the employees, including Declan, had left more than an hour earlier. Gunner was mopping the floor and waiting for the kiln to cool so he could retrieve the last of today's enameled dials. This wasn't the kind of conversation she wanted anyone to overhear, so she snatched her coat from its hook and gestured to the door.

"Can we discuss this outside, please?"

Frigid wind pierced her clothing as they stepped into the darkness and she wrapped her arms around her middle. "What in heaven's name is Richard thinking, dragging Declan into a war zone!"

"It's Milwaukee, lady. Not a war zone."

She lifted her chin a notch. "I was in the church that night.

253

There were at least five men, and it felt like a war zone to me. I doubt they will gladly follow you back to Chicago to face the hangman."

Moose grunted, although it may have been a laugh. She couldn't tell the difference with Moose. "I suppose you'd better take that up with Colonel Lowe, then."

Which was what she intended to do. She knew exactly where he would be at this time of day, and it was going to be a fair distance. Her lace-up shoes were not the best for walking, and she wobbled a little on the delicate heels as she scurried toward Randolph Street.

The pharmacy on the corner of Jefferson and Randolph Street had escaped the flames by less than four city blocks. Within days of the fire, Western Union had set up a temporary telegraph station at the rear of the pharmacy. Ever since the fire, so many telegrams had been sent in and out of Chicago that Mollie was surprised the wires had not burst into flame. Most telegraph stations were operating around the clock, and even so, the line at the Randolph Street Pharmacy stretched out the door.

Mollie scanned the crowd, grateful for the glow of a nearby gaslight. When she didn't see Richard, she pushed inside the warmth of the snug pharmacy. Sure enough, he was getting near the front, the next in line to send a telegram. He came here at the close of every day to check on the progress of a new train interchange his company was overseeing, picking up the day's telegram and then sending back instructions.

Mollie shouldered her way past the counter of medicinal syrups and herbs, her skirts brushing against the wet wool of others waiting in line. Richard was stooped over a notepad, making calculations with a stubby pencil, oblivious to her presence.

"Richard."

He looked startled to see her. "Mollie, aren't you a fetching surprise!"

Her feet ached, and the crowded pharmacy smelled unpleasantly of wet wool and menthol paste. "Is it true?" She clenched her teeth, praying to hold on to the edges of her frayed nerves.

"I certainly hope not, given your ferocious expression. Is what true?" Richard folded the notepad closed and put on a pleasant face.

"Are you taking Declan with you to confront those murderers?"

Richard glanced around the pharmacy, a look of confusion on his face. Other people in the line cocked their heads to listen, and Richard angled his body in a vain attempt to provide a little privacy. "Yes, we could use another pair of hands. You object?"

"Object!" she blurted out. More heads were turning their way, and she lowered her voice to a fierce whisper. "I will lie down in front of Declan to prevent him from leaving! He isn't ready for that sort of confrontation."

"He seemed perfectly willing to go when I put the idea to him this afternoon."

That was because Richard had no idea of the hold he had over Declan. From the moment Declan had joined the 57th, he had idolized Colonel Lowe, and now he continually berated himself for failing to live up to Colonel Lowe's expectations of what a man should be and do. She drew a steadying breath. "Declan worships you. He would follow you over a cliff if you asked him to."

Richard's mouth compressed into a hard line, but the man in front of them completed sending his message, and Richard turned away from her to set a few coins on the table. Mollie stepped back so he could send his message. "Commence laying track to old Cheney Pass," he dictated. "Send diagram of bridge for approval."

How confident he sounded. And how grateful she was that he had taken more than a month out of his life to come to her rescue, yet here she was, confronting him in a public pharmacy like a harpy.

The staccato click of the telegraph machine tapped Richard's message while she waited. Richard would never be deliberately cruel to any of his men, but did he understand how frail Declan was? How little resilience remained beneath that strong exterior? Mollie had never fully understood Declan's uncontrollable terrors until the fire, but now she had personal experience with the irrational anxiety that could descend upon an otherwise healthy person. Her nightmares had worsened after Frank's death, and she knew what it felt like to constantly be on edge, waiting for the ground to crumble beneath her.

Richard had endured the awful three days at Winston Cliff. He had first-hand experience of staring down death and emerging from the trauma. Perhaps he understood more than she gave him credit for.

How did one ask a man if he had ever snapped awake in the middle of the night, shaking and drenched with sweat, so frightened it was difficult to draw a breath? Half the time, Mollie could not even remember the specifics of her dream, but the terror lingered, holding her in its grip for hours and leaving her restless and exhausted the next day.

If Richard was the man she was destined to marry, he had a right to know she suffered from such a thing. And given Richard's extraordinary past, he might even know how to cope with it.

Richard paid the telegraph operator and stepped away from the table. He gestured toward the front of the shop, where the wall was lined with shelves of medicinal bottles and cans of liniment. "I need to wait for a reply," he said. "It can take any-where from twenty minutes to an hour. Now, what was it you were so concerned about?"

He remembered very well, but the pleasant tone of his voice made it clear he was giving her the opportunity to start over with a clean slate. She swallowed hard and met his eyes. "Do you ever suffer from nightmares?" she asked.

"What do you mean?" He looked curious, but not insulted.

"I understand it is not uncommon for people who have en-dured great terror to be haunted by it. Sometimes I am troubled by dreams of the fire. The feeling of being trapped with no way to escape. I think this sort of thing torments Declan. In the years since the war, he breaks down over the smallest things. I never know what is going to trigger his demons, but they are real, and they won't go away. I merely wondered if you . . . if you have ever battled such an enemy."

For the first time since she had met him, Richard looked ill at ease. He inched back a tiny bit and braced his elbow against the hickory countertop, looking somewhere over her left shoulder. The clattering of the telegraph machine clicked away in the background and an awkward silence stretched between them, but finally Richard took a breath and met her gaze. "Mollie, if I had such . . . torments, you must under-stand . . . this is not the sort of thing a man would ever choose to revisit. With anyone."

Zack did. She didn't think less of him for sharing his anxiety over the ringing of bells. Actually, it had drawn her closer to him, allowing her to share her own shortcomings without feeling any judgment from him. But Richard was a different man, perhaps even a better man. He would not foist these burdens on her.

"Forgive me," she said. "I didn't mean to pry. I just need to know if you can understand what Declan is up against. If you can help him. I fear he may go to Milwaukee and break into pieces at the first sign of real danger."

Richard kept scrutinizing her with that perplexing stare. Finally, he spoke. "Declan is a man. He will rise to the occasion. It is hard for him to do that if you keep hovering over him."

"I don't *hover* over Declan." But even as she spoke the words, the skepticism on Richard's face deepened. She knew Declan felt like a failure, and perhaps he would never be able to rise above that harsh self-assessment in the safety of her watch factory. It was wrong of her to try to stand in his way if he wished to follow Richard to Milwaukee.

She tugged on her gloves, dreading the long walk home when she was already exhausted. "If Declan wishes to accompany you, of course I can spare him," she said stiffly. "But I think you are being shortsighted and, frankly, a little bit cruel to play on his hero worship of you like this, but it is Declan's decision. I need to get back home."

Richard glanced to the back of the pharmacy. "I should hear back from Waukegan soon. Wait a few minutes, and I'll walk you back to the women's barracks."

She just wanted to be alone. She wanted to fall into bed and pray for a decent night's sleep, however unlikely that was. She tied the strings of her cloak, unable to meet his gaze. "I'll be fine."

"Mollie . . ."

"It's nothing. I am a foolish woman. . . . I'm sure you know best."

She angled her body to negotiate her way through the crowded shop. Richard made no effort to follow, for which she was grateful. On some level, she knew he was right, but it still bothered her that Richard had sought out Declan without asking her.

The cold air hit her in the face. Why should he ask her permission? Declan was a grown man who was free to make his own decisions. She had been hovering over him like a mother hen for years, shielding him from any hint of distress. Was she part of the reason he still had a crippled mind?

By the time Mollie arrived at the women's barracks, her feet ached and her spirit dragged. The snow was a slushy mess on the plank walkways, and the air carried tiny flecks of sleet on the wind. Mercifully, the braziers were lit and the oversized room was warm. Mollie shook her cloak, flinging off the ice crystals.

"I hear there was quite a ruckus at the workshop this evening." Alice had rolled into a sitting position from where she lounged on the bottom bunk.

"How did you hear that?"

"Word travels, Mollie. We will be lucky if it doesn't get back to Declan."

The strength drained from her limbs and she sank down onto the straw mattress beside Alice. "Maybe I am just terrified at the thought of them all going to confront those terrible men. I can't endure another loss." She didn't want to dwell on her troubles. So many of the women crammed into this crude barracks did nothing other than enumerate their losses, and she did not want to become like them. Sometimes it was disheartening to even be in the same room with all the complaining.

Alice produced a checkerboard, and Mollie did her best to concentrate on the game. A few other women gathered to watch, but as it grew colder, Mollie longed for the nights the refugees had gathered around the brazier at the church, where people shared stories and laughed at their troubles. Everyone at the 57th accepted that they would be in for a long, difficult slog toward rebuilding their lives, and that attitude made Mollie grateful for their triumphs, rather than dwelling on her losses. She needed to work harder on recapturing that attitude.

There was a pounding on the door. "Mollie!"

Her heart leapt to her throat. It was Richard's voice.

"You can't have any men in here," the barrack's matron growled from the front of the room. Mollie sprang off the mattress. He must be freezing outside!

She unlatched the metal hook and cracked the door open. Richard stood outside, a smile on his face and a handful of licorice sticks in his hands. "I came to say I am sorry."

Her brows rose. "You did?"

"Close the door!" a woman hollered behind them.

Richard reached through the opening and grabbed her hand, his strong and warm despite the chill outside. His cheeks had bright red flags of color on them, but his eyes were brimming with excitement. "I'm sorry I implied you are anything less than the most caring, generous woman I have ever encountered. I am sorry I gave you one moment of needless anxiety."

She couldn't believe he was apologizing to her. Apologizing! Zack would have marched across town to rip into her, to continue their argument out on a public street. Mollie was pretty sure she was in the wrong about what had happened in the pharmacy and didn't know how to respond now that Richard was offering her complete and total surrender.

"Lady, if you don't shut that door, I'm going to set your mattress on fire!"

Alice rushed to her side, pressing her cloak and gloves into her hands. "Take it outside, Mollie, or these women will be gearing up for a public execution!"

Mollie wrapped the cloak around her. Her boots clattered on the plank steps and it was freezing outside, but at least the sleet had turned into gentle snowflakes, and she could be alone with Richard.

While she tugged on her gloves, Richard reached behind her to pull her hood up over her head. He was smiling as he tied the strings loosely beneath her chin.

"We need to find you someplace a little more hospitable to stay," he said warmly.

Mollie gazed up at him. "It's not so bad. I have everything I really need."

"Mollie, I want to give you the world."

Her breath stopped. This man was everything any woman could hope for and more, but she wasn't ready for this. Richard hadn't stopped talking and he clasped her hands within his. "It cannot have escaped your notice that I think very highly of you, and before I leave . . . I need to know if there is anyone else who might be standing in my way for your affections."

It was hard to breathe. She pulled her hands away, a sudden rush of anxiety flooding her nerves. Wasn't this what she had been hoping for? A more permanent alliance with a man who seemed tailor-made for her?

She did not want to repeat the same mistakes she had made with Zack Kazmarek. It was in her nature to proceed slowly and with caution. Allowing herself to act impulsively had only caused her and Zack heartache.

She turned and walked farther away from the barracks. Snow crunched beneath her feet and a chill penetrated her cloak. She drew it a little tighter. "There is no one else," she said softly. Although, was that really true? If Richard Lowe was the man she was going to marry, she wanted to be completely honest and open with him. She didn't want to be the sort of woman who had corners of her heart she needed to hide. She walked toward an iron lamppost, the gaslight casting a glow in the darkness. She leaned her back against the post and turned to look up at Richard.

"There was someone I cared for once," she said. Richard froze and his gaze darted to her. "He was a rather . . . overwhelming person. Everything went very fast. I felt like I was on a runaway train careering down the tracks. It was wild and exhilarating . . . but I couldn't control what was happening, and it ended badly."

She risked a glance at Richard. He was watching her with caution, but no judgment. "I don't want to make that same mistake with you," she said earnestly. "You came riding into town at the lowest moment of my life with a platoon of soldiers at your command! What sort of woman wouldn't be dazzled? You seem so perfect, and I fear becoming overwhelmed in the same manner as I did once before."

"What is it you are asking of me, Mollie?"

She glanced away, staring at the snow whirling softly on the air. Richard would need to leave soon, and she was nowhere close to being ready for a life-altering decision. In just over two months, she had endured the loss of her home, her business, and Frank. She had indulged in a wild, exhilarating fling with a most inappropriate man who still made her heart pound when she thought of him. She would not race headlong into another alliance until she had both feet firmly on the ground, and that would take time.

Besides, Waukegan was only an hour away by train. After Richard returned home, she could visit him and see his town and be back home by dusk.

"I need time. I am not a reckless person who can make decisions quickly. I think very highly of you, but I fear repeating the mistakes of the past."

Richard picked up her hand, confidence brimming in his clear blue eyes. "Good things are worth waiting for." He kissed the back of her hand. "I am happy to give you all the time you need."

How pleasant he was. No quibbling or impassioned arguments. When Richard leaned down to press a kiss to her forehead, he made no demands on her. She stepped into his arms and felt like she was coming home.

23

As the weeks rolled past, Mollie settled into her new life as though putting on a favorite pair of shoes, comfortable from years of predictable wear. She rose every morning and arrived at the workshop by nine o'clock. She helped Gunner get the kiln started and updated her business charts with the daily chores. The shipment of watches was delivered to New York three days ahead of deadline, and a telegram from the shop said that two of the watches sold on the first morning they were put on display. Mollie had received an order for another dozen watches, and her workshop was fully operational.

Which meant she had time to make good on her promise to her neighbors on East Street and assist with the rebuilding of their shops. The Kauffman brothers were making progress on rebuilding their vinegar distillery, and Mollie volunteered to help them build the wooden racks where they stored barrels of vinegar while they aged. Wearing her sturdy canvas work gloves and the old mismatched clothing she had pulled from the donation bin, she sat amidst the sawdust on the floor to hold freshly cut pine boards while Archie Kauffman nailed them into place.

"Promise me you will make apple cider vinegar," Mollie said.

"I can tell from half a mile away what you are brewing, and apple cider vinegar always smells the best."

Mr. Kauffman grinned, holding two nails clamped between his teeth as he pounded another into the beams Mollie held flush against the frame. "I think malt vinegar will be our first batch. Quicker to produce."

Mollie groaned. "Malt stinks up the whole neighborhood, and I just escaped from the brewery attic too! If this keeps up, I'll go to my grave smelling like I've been marinating in a cask of beer."

Mr. Kauffman finished securing the beam in place, and Mollie lowered her hands, rolling her shoulders to ease the ache in her muscles from holding her hands aloft so long. "Not to worry, I won't be brewing any time soon," Mr. Kauffman said. "I've found a metalsmith who can make three oversized brewing vats for us, but I can't start making vinegar until I've got a decent turbine. The metalworker says it is beyond what he can supply."

Mollie nodded, well aware of the problem. Caleb Magruder's mill was the only high-quality mill left in the city, and he had more work than his men could handle. The Kauffmans would either need to wait in line at Magruder's or travel to a neighboring city to get the kinds of turbines they needed.

"Three more beams, Miss Mollie, then we are done for the day."

Mollie braced the board against the top rack of the barrel frame, the muscles in her shoulders resuming their familiar ache. Not that she minded. These few hours were a pittance compared to what the volunteers of the 57th had done for her, and she was glad to be able to pass along the favor.

There was a commotion near the front of the shop. A wave of cold air rushed in from the open door and she heard a familiar voice.

"Mollie! Hustle on back to the workshop. You are needed." She craned her head to see Ulysses, who was grinning like it was Christmas morning.

Trapped with her arms overhead as she held the pine beam in place, she smiled back. "Give me ten more minutes," she said. "Mr. Kauffman vows I am the best construction assistant in the city and can't be spared."

"You can say that again!" Mr. Kauffman agreed as he commenced the banging of his hammer.

"You need to come now, Mollie. Someone else can hold that board."

There was no mistaking the urgency in Ulysses's tone. He would not be insisting like this if it were a trivial matter, and a niggling of concern took root inside her mind. She glanced up at Mr. Kauffman, who summoned another man to take Mollie's place.

Mollie brushed the sawdust from her skirt. "What has you so excited?" she asked Ulysses. She couldn't place his mood. Was it possible to be agitated and happy at the same time? Given the way he was smiling but gripping the handle of his crutch like it was a lifeline, something had Ulysses wound up pretty tight. He propelled himself on his single leg and crutch with impressive speed, crossing the street and leading her into the workshop.

Colonel Lowe was inside, standing with Declan and three other members of the 57th who had gone to Milwaukee. There were men in police uniforms as well. She caught her breath.

"Miss Knox," Richard said formally. "I am pleased to report that Jesse Coulter and the other five men who invaded the church have been apprehended and are on a train back to Chicago to face justice."

The room tilted, and she swayed. Richard reached out, securing her against his side. She pressed her hand against the thudding of her heart, a whirlwind of emotion swirling inside. The wave of exhaustion that settled on her was so strong she would have sunk to the floor had Richard not been holding her up. "I don't know if I am supposed to laugh or cry," she said a little helplessly.

It wouldn't be right to rejoice. Celebrating wouldn't bring Frank back, nor change the terrible way his life had ended. She merely leaned into Richard and closed her eyes, grateful to God for sending her such a hero to lean on when she had no more strength left.

It seemed right to visit the cemetery where Frank was buried to tell him the news. With every stonemason in the city deployed in the rebuilding efforts, Mollie had not been able to commission a gravestone to mark Frank's final resting spot, but Declan had carved a simple wooden cross that would serve until the day they could arrange something more permanent.

The cemetery was deserted, barren limbs silhouetted against the gray sky. Mollie knelt on the snowy ground, hardly noticing the cold on her knees. "They got him, Frank," she whispered, her breath turning into wisps on the cold air. "Colonel Lowe came through for us, and you don't have to worry those men will go unpunished."

She knew Frank was no longer here in this bleak cemetery, nor was his spirit troubled because of the foolish deeds of a passel of criminals. Frank Spencer had passed on to a place where earthly concerns no longer mattered, but she knew he would be pleased that Richard Lowe had come to rescue the 57th during their darkest hour. "He has been such a hero," she whispered, feeling a little foolish talking into the air, but desperately needing to talk to *someone* who would simply listen and not tell her to sprint down the aisle of matrimony into Colonel Lowe's waiting arms. Even Alice was no longer a neutral party. She thought Mollie had been an idiot for asking Richard to be patient. Mollie knew to the marrow of her bones that Frank would have approved of her marriage to Richard. As would her father. So did everyone else working for the 57th. Why was she still hesitating?

Marriage to Richard would solve so many of her problems. Who didn't want to slide into the comfort of being a good man's wife? He was wealthy and handsome, a Christian with excellent values and a pleasant demeanor. He came from a family whose blood was bluer than a summer's sky, and she could surely learn the proper manners and decorum to fit into such a privileged group of people. She had analyzed the situation forward, backward, and sideways, and each time, the final analysis told her she'd be a fool to turn him down. To her mortification, one night she had even made a list of Colonel Lowe's qualities in one column and those of Zack Kazmarek in the opposite column. She considered each man's comportment, temperament, and ability to be a provider, a father, and a husband. After weighing the qualities and calculating the percentages, the calculations told her that Richard was the clear winner.

Ashamed she would attempt to use a mathematical calculation to guide herself, Mollie tore the paper into tiny bits and tossed them into the brazier. She didn't need a piece of paper to tell her Richard was the logical choice. And she was certain that if given enough time, she would come to love him.

But the proper opportunity would never come as long as she kept indulging in memories of Zack Kazmarek. Like a child who kept poking and prodding a loose tooth despite the pain, the temptation to relive her memories of Zack was irresistible.

It had been a month since that morning at Lake Park when she told him she no longer wanted to see him, and yet, the day she shipped the commemorative watches to New York, it had been Zack with whom she'd wanted to share her triumph.

She pushed to her feet and brushed the clumps of snow from her skirt. She would *will* the memories of Zack away. The next time Richard asked her to Waukegan to meet his parents, she would go. It was time to consign Zack to her past and meet the future with a brave face. Her resolve firm, she turned and headed toward the cemetery's stone-arch gate to catch the last streetcar home.

Zack Kazmarek was leaning against the entrance, watching her with gentle affection in his eyes.

She blanched. Had her attempt to exorcise him from her mind conjured him up? She had forgotten how darkly handsome he was, the wind blowing his hair like Heathcliff on the moors. "What are you doing here?" she asked.

He pushed away from the gate and walked toward her. "I heard about what happened in Milwaukee, and I guessed this is where you would come."

Her eyes narrowed. "That's a lie. I told everyone at the workshop I was coming here, and you pumped someone for information. Who?"

His black brows lifted. "I thought we had moved beyond your bad habit of calling me a liar, Mollie. It doesn't reflect very well on you."

She folded her arms across her chest. She wasn't going to let Zack draw her into an argument, not when all she wanted was to purge him from her heart, soul, and memory. "I'll step aside and let you pay your final respects to Frank. I know how highly the two of you regarded each other."

She tried to move past him through the gate, but he blocked

her exit. "I *did* think highly of Frank. And I adore you, which is why I am not going to let you waltz out of my life so easily. I've given you a month, Mollie."

"I didn't ask for a month, I asked for a lifetime. Zack, it is over. I don't want to see you again. I don't know how to make it any more plain to you than that."

"Why can't you look me in the eye when you say that?"

She forced herself to meet his gaze. Against the snowy backdrop and dull gray sky, he was a smoldering dark force. His face was flushed with good health, his dark gypsy eyes beaming at her. Looking at him was unbearable. Her heart swelled and ached. She wanted to fling herself into his arms and tell him everything that had happened with Sophie and her triumph with the commemorative watches and her alliance with Dr. Buchanan. Most of all, she wanted to listen to his laughter and let him tease her about her braids.

She raised her chin and held her gaze steady. "It is over, Zack. If not for the fire, there would never have been anything between us at all." She turned, and this time when she pushed past him, he turned to walk beside her.

"A little bird tells me there are no wedding bells on the horizon. I wonder why that is."

"Maybe because Colonel Lowe is a decent man who doesn't toss out marriage proposals to a woman he barely knows. His self-restraint is one of the things I admire about him."

She could hear him snickering. "Then you ought to adore me. I knew you for three years before I tossed a marriage proposal your way."

He was doing it again, drawing her into an argument against her better judgment. She picked up her pace as she turned the corner and headed toward the streetcar stop. *Don't engage with him.* Anything she said would just give him ammunition to keep the argument going, and how many times had Zack told her he loved a good air-clearing argument?

"So am I getting the cold shoulder?" he asked, striding alongside her. "Just as well. Look, you told me you wanted a chance to get to know the sterling Colonel Lowe a little better, and I gave it to you. But I'm not going to surrender without a fight." He wrapped a firm hand around her arm and spun her toward him, smiling down at her with lethal charm. "I'm getting back in the battle. Fair warning."

She jerked her arm away and kept marching toward the street corner. "Would you just stop?" she said between clenched teeth. "You may think this is fun, but I don't."

"Fun? Actually, that's not a word I'd use to describe you, Mollie." He returned her glare with a roguish smile. "You are fascinating, admirable, exhilarating . . . but fun? Sorry, Mollie, that's never been you."

Hadn't Frank often said the same thing? That she should learn how to seize the day? Unwind the braids she had twisted tighter than a Gordian knot? On the previous New Year's Eve, a group of people from the 57th had made plans to watch the fireworks, but Mollie had been working on a deadline and insisted she needed to get to bed by nine o'clock. "*Mollie Knox, you could steal the light from a sunrise*," Frank had laughingly said. He had hugged her when he'd said it, and they had all shared a glass of champagne, but Mollie had gone to bed that night at nine o'clock while the others went to celebrate.

Frank was allowed to tease her; Zack hadn't earned that right. Her heart squeezed. She should have gone with Frank that night. She couldn't even remember what she had been working on so hard, but she had lost her last opportunity to ring in the New Year with a man whose wisdom and kindness had been a lifelong gift.

They arrived at the intersection, where half a dozen factory workers and two nuns were waiting for the streetcar. The nuns occupied the lone bench, and Mollie loitered nervously. Was Zack really going to continue this conversation while they were surrounded by a bunch of strangers? She couldn't leave. This was the last streetcar of the day, and being stranded five miles from home after dark was not an option.

Zack drew alongside her, leaning down to murmur in her ear. "Mollie, I'm not leaving you again. If the city burns to the ground for a second time. If an earthquake splits the land in two or a plague saps us dry . . . I am not leaving. I'll show up at your doorstep every morning and every evening for the rest of the year if that's what it takes."

She needed Zack to get out of her life. Forever. How could she let a good man like Colonel Lowe into her life if Zack wouldn't give her any breathing room?

"Don't you have any pride?" she snapped. He blanched, but she was too angry to stop. "You're like a stray dog I can't get rid of. I want *nothing* to do with you. Not with your business, not with you. Just go away. Please, just go and stay away."

A burly factory worker snickered, and another man started making barking sounds.

Zack looked like she had punched him in the gut. He reeled back, and his face lost color. If he heard the factory workers making dog sounds, he made no sign.

"So it's Colonel Lowe, then."

She forced herself to look him directly in the eyes. "It has *always* been Colonel Lowe."

The little color left on Zack's face faded away. His dark eyes aching with pain, he touched her on the shoulder and opened his mouth to say something. Then thought better of it. Finally, he nodded and turned away.

She wanted to call him back. Her hateful words tasted sour, and she wanted to wipe the wounded look from his eyes. She clenched her fists so tightly her nails cut into her palms. Calling him back was the wrong thing to do. He needed to understand she was never going back to him, and saying it nicely had not worked.

But she knew the sight of his tall, dark figure striding alone down the street would haunt her for years.

24

What kind of insane man went to New York City in December? Zack pulled the collar of his coat higher in a useless attempt to block icy wind from seeping through every seam of his clothing. The meeting with the insurance adjusters had ended on time, but the streetcar running from downtown was out of service, meaning Zack was darting through piles of slush to be on time for his meeting with the imperious Josephine Hartman.

Zack was still making amends for dashing home from New York when he had gotten Mollie's panicked telegram. Neither of the Hartmans had forgiven him for that dereliction of duty, but he would make it up to them. He had just spent a solid week negotiating mind-numbing insurance claims for the merchandise lost in the fire. When the store burned, it had liquefied jewelry, melted silver, and destroyed precious furs. All store records of the inventory had burned, and Zack's attempt to document the merchandise had resulted in days snarled with litigation and short tempers.

He sighed with relief as he darted inside the Charen Hotel, where the lobby was decked out in a lavish display for Christmas. A towering pine tree dripped with ornaments and garlands. The mantel over the crackling fireplace was covered in boughs of greenery, with tall candles behind glass lanterns. Even the air smelled of evergreens and warm cider.

Louis Hartman and his wife stood beside the fireplace, waiting for him. Josephine tapped her satin-clad foot in annoyance. "You're late."

Zack pulled off his scarf, shaking away the ice crystals. "The streetcar on Fifth is out of service, but we've still got time to make it to Bloomingdale's before they close."

"That little store in Brooklyn?" Josephine tilted her chin up a notch. "They are no competition for us."

With fingers still numb from the cold, Zack bit the tip of his gloves to yank them off. He sighed in relief as he rubbed his hands together before the heat of the fire. "That's not what I heard," he said. "Rumor has it they've broken ground on a new flagship store on Third Street. We will want to keep our eyes on them."

Josephine narrowed her eyes. "We will build Hartman's bigger and grander than before. I don't need to be scouting the competition like an oily spy. Besides, I intend to use this trip to seek out the very best artisans and jewelers. I want you to negotiate exclusive contracts with them."

Zack glanced at Louis, sending him an infinitesimal shake of his head. Exclusive deals were costly and would serve little benefit at a store halfway across the continent. Louis understood and nodded.

"My poppet," Louis murmured. "Let Zack work his negotiating wonders. I need you to find us the most exalted merchandise this side of Paris. Tomorrow we shall go to the Ladies' Mile and see what goodies we can find for our new store. I also want to get a look at Macy's. That fellow has some innovative ideas. I hear he even hires an actor to impersonate Santa Claus. Quite clever, that."

The next day the trio walked the Ladies' Mile, which stretched along Fifth Avenue all the way to Madison Square. The streets were dense with carriages, but it was the people on the walkways that Zack found so fascinating. Despite the sea of black wool overcoats, Zack could see the money in the exquisitely crafted ladies' bonnets and the men's walking sticks topped with shiny brass knobs. The street was lined with specialty shops featuring goods imported from the Orient, silks in every imaginable shade, and more jewelry than Zack had ever seen in one location.

Josephine insisted on getting out of the carriage so she could inspect each of the display windows, carefully designed to mimic the finest European shops. Her eye for detail was astounding. She could glance at a row of thirty pairs of shoes that looked identical to Zack's working-class eyes and hone in on the one pair that cost three times as much as the others because of the quality of the workmanship. She moved through store after store like a shark trolling through fishing grounds. She sampled perfumes, fingered silks, tried on jewelry. It generally took her less than ten seconds to render a verdict on each item. She took careful notes of who supplied the goods so she could arrange private meetings.

Toward the end of the street was a larger store that spanned double the length of the other shops. Zack was surprised Josephine was even willing to set foot inside, as it was an older store with racks of merchandise displayed with no more care than loaves of bread stacked on shelves. Bolts of cloth from a midrange silk down to homespun calico were propped against the wall.

Zack's attention was snagged by a display of watches on top of a counter. He moved past a display of ready-made hats to get to the watch counter. He didn't want to think about it, but Hartman's would need to find another supplier of watches for the new store. After the contested land deed, Louis Hartman would never do business with Mollie again.

A shaft of pain cut through him. How long would it take him to get over that woman? Whenever he glanced at his watch, he thought of her. Although that was to be expected, he supposed. Odder still was his longing to feed her properly. Whenever he sat down to a piping hot meal, he wondered what they were serving in the women's barracks. When he saw a display of raspberry chocolates in Macy's, he wanted to buy the whole case and ship it to her. And whenever the sky was that clear, shocking shade of brilliant blue, he thought of Mollie's eyes as she gazed up at him.

Maybe this time next year he would be over her, but he doubted it. He had been on this planet for thirty-six years, long enough to know that Mollie Knox was one of a kind. Without thinking, he reached out to finger one of the watches displayed on the counter.

"Don't bother," Josephine said from behind him. "Too cheap and ugly."

Zack hefted the watch in his hand. She was right, the watch was big and not particularly attractive. Cheap metal too. He rolled it in his palm, examining it from every angle. It wasn't a bad watch. In fact . . .

He glanced up at the clerk who was folding handkerchiefs several yards down the length of the counter. "Why do you keep these watches outside of a case?" Zack asked. "Surely they are too valuable to display so carelessly."

"We've got the pricey watches down here under glass," the clerk said. He set the handkerchiefs down and walked to stand before Zack. "The watches on top of the case are the new ones, made by a factory over in Newburgh. Can't beat the price. You can get a good solid watch for only three dollars."

Zack almost dropped the watch. *"Three dollars?"* Even the Hartmans seemed stunned.

The clerk nodded. "You should see the operation they've got going over there. Hundreds of workers, feeding the pieces through a machine. That is how they make them so cheaply. Those watches sell so fast we can't keep them in stock, even though we buy them by the caseload."

Zack stared at the watch. True, it did not have gold or diamonds on the cover . . . but three dollars!

"Do they make any other versions?" he asked. "Other styles?"

"Oh yes," the clerk said with a nod. "They've got a five-dollar model and one for ten dollars. They are a little nicer, but we find most folks prefer the one you are holding in your hand." The clerk leaned a little closer and lowered his voice. "Although just between you and me, in a year or so that company is going to be turning out ones that are much nicer. They'll look as fancy as the watches that Bloomingdale fellow is selling. I've got a sample in the back room if you want to see it."

Zack did. He followed the clerk to the rear of the store, where the man unlocked a drawer, withdrew a box, and set the sample watch into Zack's palm. The watch was smaller than the clunky watches on the counter, and it had more delicate artistry on the dial. Still not beautiful, but surely it was only a matter of time before these new factory-made watches would overtake the industry.

Zack's fingers closed around the cold metal of the watch. In his palm he held the seeds of the destruction of the 57th Illinois Watch Company.

And Mollie didn't even know it was coming.

25

The best part about Mollie's new apartment was her view of the bright green tips of the lilies pushing through the layer of mulch in the narrow garden beds that lined the front of the building. She always enjoyed watching bulbs flower into bloom, but this year they carried a special poignancy. Those bulbs had been planted before the fire. As the bulbs hibernated safely beneath the soil, the city of Chicago had burned to the ground. The fire had wiped miles of the city from the map, but now buildings were rising from the ashes, just as the bulbs were renewing themselves.

Shortly after Christmas, Mollie had moved into this modest rooming house. It was smaller than her old apartment—just a single room—but every square inch of it belonged to her. There was a bed, a dresser with three drawers, and a window overlooking a vibrant street of mercantile shops in a section of town that had escaped the blaze. After months of living packed in alongside dozens of people, it felt strange to sleep alone. Isolated. Still, she was grateful her life had finally settled into some semblance of normalcy. The barracks had been closed,

279

and the burned-out residents of the city had all found new homes or left the city.

Rebuilding in the burned district proceeded at a breathtaking pace. Skeletal outlines of buildings had taken shape several stories taller than Chicago had ever seen. Mollie could scarcely believe her eyes as the structures rose higher each month. Workers used pulleys and steel-wire ropes to raise huge girders; scaffolding was everywhere as the new buildings rose higher and higher. Mr. Durant explained to her how modern steel construction made it possible to construct buildings higher than ever before. "Someday our buildings will scrape the skies!" he laughingly told her. The air was electric with the hum of energy as the people of Chicago rebuilt the city. Within a year or two, they would have the most modern business district anywhere in the world.

A rainstorm the previous evening had cleared construction dust from the air, and it was a beautiful June day. The sky was shockingly blue, and birds chattered as they rummaged through the dampened soil in search of earthworms. Mollie's favorite birdcall was the whistling twitter of the tree swallow as it flitted about. The gentle calling was soothing to her.

Which she sorely needed this afternoon as she hastened her step to catch the streetcar that would carry her across town to the Durants' hotel, where she shared a meal with the family on the first Tuesday of every month. Sophie still came to the workshop twice a week to help Declan polish metal, and the girl seemed to think Mollie walked on water. So did her parents, who were amazed at the gradual transformation of a spoiled princess into a young girl who had finally found her calling in "doing something hard."

The Durants leased the top floor of the Michigan Avenue Hotel. It was not as grand as the house on Prairie Avenue, but it was closer to the buildings Mr. Durant was designing. Mollie enjoyed her dinners with the Durants, where she reported how Sophie was doing at the factory and shared tales of the reconstruction efforts. It might have seemed strange for a woman like her to be socializing with a millionaire architect, but as Mr. Durant had so often said, he would be eternally grateful to Mollie not only for saving his daughter on the night of the fire, but for taking the girl in hand and giving her life some structure.

Mollie was hoping that gratitude would pay off one more time. As she walked down Michigan Avenue, she clasped a small watch in the palm of her hand.

Dr. Buchanan now leased a small room off the side of her new workshop, and his dental business had finally found momentum. At Christmas, he had given her an inexpensive watch from the Newburgh Watch Company, along with a postcard with a picture of the company's workers. The photograph depicted the elaborate machinery of the company with rows of pulleys and conveyor belts and somber-faced workers standing before each station.

The watch was an odd gift. He refused to say how he had come across it, but it terrified Mollie. Homely, basic, and made of cheap metal, it still kept perfect time. And it sold for only three dollars.

Ever since he'd given it to her, Mollie had been researching the Newburgh Watch Company. Not that she could learn much through scrutinizing the newspaper advertisements, but she gathered the company was now supplying watches all the way to Topeka. Their homely watches were no match for the 57th, but they would be soon if Mollie could not figure out a way to become more competitive.

And that was why she needed to strike a deal with Mr. Durant. She waited until after dinner, when the family traditionally retreated to the parlor and Mr. Durant showed her the progress on the nine buildings he was supervising. Mr. Durant's wife, Charlotte, lounged beautifully on a chaise while Sophie sat at her feet and sketched pictures. "I like to listen to grown-ups talk," Sophie said. "My little brothers are too stupid to have anything interesting to say."

Sophie was still not the most gracious child, but at least the girl no longer seemed to hate everyone and everything. And she certainly seemed attentive as she sketched pictures in the corner and quietly listened to her parents talk. The parlor contained a settee and two armchairs, but two oversized drafting tables were pressed against the room's only window. Mr. Durant's architectural drawings were tacked up on the expensive flocked wallpaper.

All of his designs were for commercial buildings. Two banks, three hotels, a new theater, and three office buildings. Each building was several stories tall with large glass windows lined up in a grid style. They had little ornamentation and looked shockingly modern to Mollie's eye. The prettiest of the buildings, a new bank that was going to be on State Street, was five stories tall, with clean lines and a gambrel roof. The only real decoration was a clock tower that rose from the center of the building. Two of the other buildings Mr. Durant had designed also featured prominent clocks on the outside. In all likelihood, the others would have large public clocks inside the lobbies.

"How is the bank progressing?" Mollie asked, proud of the casual tone she managed to achieve.

"Coming along well, except we can't get the type of limestone I want. We'll have to settle for Indiana limestone, as I can't afford any more delays on the project."

Mollie's finger traced the outline of the clock tower. "And who will be building the clock?"

"I'm not sure," he said. "That sort of thing is usually handled by my chief design engineer. The clock is a finishing detail we haven't contracted yet."

Mollie swallowed hard and drew a steadying breath. "The mechanics for designing a watch and a clock are the same," she said. "It appears to me that your buildings are very bold. Modern. You will want to be sure the people who build your clock understand that vision and can produce a clock to enhance it. Not compete with it."

"And I suppose you know of such a clock designer?" Mr. Durant's intelligent eyes were fastened on her as he pulled a long draw on his pipe.

This was it. This was her chance to vault the 57th into an entirely new realm of prominence. "I have the best designers in the world working for the 57th," she stated boldly. "We have designed watch faces to reflect everything from Medieval Gothic to Baroque to Neoclassical."

"I know what Baroque is!" Sophie chimed in from where she was drawing in the corner. "Ulysses showed me. He thinks it is gaudy, but he designs it because it sells so well."

Mr. Durant turned his curious gaze to Mollie. "You think I should put a Baroque clock on the outside of my bank?"

"Absolutely not!" she said. "Your buildings are very distinctive, and you will need a style that is equally modern, but still harkens back to an earlier era to lend a sense of continuity with the past. I have a team of artisans who can work up several options for your design engineer."

Charlotte Durant waved a lavender-scented fan before her face. "I can't imagine why you would want to," she said. "The thought of all that work makes me want to sit down. If I wasn't already sitting," she amended.

That was because Charlotte Durant did not need to fear for

the continued livelihood of forty employees and their families. The cheap watch heavy in Mollie's pocket was a constant reminder of how important it was for her to stay ahead of the competition. She could never compete directly with the Newburgh Watch Factory or any of the other factory-made watch companies that were on the horizon. It would cost a fortune to mechanize the 57th. Even if she did, such a move would put most of her employees out of work, and that was unthinkable.

"We have never been afraid of hard work," Mollie asserted. "The clock tower is the only significant embellishment on the outside of that bank. It is your best chance to make a statement, and our artisans will handle that design with more care than any ordinary clockmaker in this city. The 57th has made a name for itself based on our unique designs."

Mr. Durant set his pipe on a small dish at his side. Leaning back in his chair, he laced his fingers over his satin vest. It was obvious he was not pleased by her suggestion.

"These contracts tend to be awarded along very clannish lines," he said. "Chicago is a tough city, and I am certain to offend somebody if I break with tradition and hire an entirely new company. Especially one headed by a woman. Now, don't take offense," he rushed to add. "You know I have the highest regard for you and the 57th. I even bought my wife one of your watches for Christmas."

"I picked it out," Sophie said proudly.

Mollie needed to play this hand of cards carefully. Mr. Durant was a powerful ally, but she couldn't risk offending him by reminding him of his debt to her. She smiled at Sophie. "I know you did, Sophie. It has been such a treat to have you with us these past few months. Everyone in the workshop comments on how helpful you have been."

Which was a stunning about-face from the spoiled child Mollie had met on the night of the fire.

"Poor dear," Charlotte said. "I worry you'll stunt your growth with all that bending and stooping in a workshop. Like those pitiful Irish laboring down at the factories."

Charlotte Durant might have been oblivious to Mollie's subtle reminder of the debt they owed her, but her husband was not. He narrowed his eyes at Mollie while he twiddled his thumbs. Only the clattering of dishes as the servants cleared the dinner table in the adjoining room filled the silence that stretched between them. Mollie's nerves were clenched tight enough to snap. At last, Mr. Durant looked over at Sophie.

"What do you say, pumpkin? Should we give the 57th a chance to make the clocks in our new buildings?"

Sophie had only a touch of vinegar in her reply. "I think clocks are stupid, but I'll bet Alice can make a pretty one."

Mr. Durant picked his pipe up and drew a long puff before speaking. "I am willing to take a chance on you, Miss Knox. Are you certain you have the skill to produce clocks on a massive scale? It will be very different from making a pocket watch."

She could not afford to show any weakness. Mollie had been researching the clockmaking industry for months. Aside from the gigantic size, the only additional challenge of a public clock was protecting it from the elements. Other than that, it was easier to build than a watch. It did not need to be designed with the precision to keep ticking accurately as it was shaken, held upside-down, and constantly handled.

"Clocks are much easier," she asserted. "And I have the best technicians in the business. Clockmaking will be a cakewalk in comparison to watchmaking."

Mr. Durant stood and crossed the room to where she stood beside the sketch of the bank. He extended his hand to her.

"Then we have a deal. My lawyer will draw up the contracts and communicate a timeline." His hand tightened and the warmth left his eyes, replaced by the hard steel of a businessman. "Don't let me down, Miss Knox."

It was unusually warm for June, and, as was their custom, workers from the 57th gathered at the Krause Biergarten to relax at the end of the work week. Mollie had invited Colonel Lowe to join them, but he had politely declined. This sort of gathering really wasn't to his taste. At the far end of the table, Declan was throwing dice with Oliver, and Ulysses was showing off by cracking walnuts with only the mighty force of his thumb and forefingers. Platters of spicy German sausages were passed around the table, and wind rustled in the leaves of the chestnut trees above.

It was a perfect summer evening, up until the moment Mollie broached her new plan for making clocks. She knew it would be a surprise to the watchmakers but had not expected the resistance that came at her from every angle. Ulysses proclaimed his talent would be wasted confined to the face of a clock, when his real talents lay in cover design. Oliver insisted that working with oversized clock mechanisms was an insult to his technical abilities. Even Gunner disapproved, claiming there was not enough space in the workshop to accommodate the massive size of a public clock.

Mollie's fingers curled around her cool glass of cider. "It is our best chance at staying competitive," she asserted. "We can't compete with the Newburgh Watch Company on price, and the market for high-end watches is going to dwindle as soon as they figure out how to get those machines to make smaller, more elegant watches."

"So how is building clocks going to help us?" Alice asked, confusion in her voice.

"*Public* clocks," Mollie asserted. "There is a difference between a public clock and the ordinary clocks sitting on everyone's bedside table. As this city rebuilds, every new railway station will need a clock. Every theater. Every schoolhouse. *And we can build beautiful ones*," she said earnestly. "Have you seen the crude clocks in most public buildings? With the 57th's reputation for quality and beauty, we can move in and dominate this market. If we can deliver on Mr. Durant's nine buildings, it will catapult this company's reputation like nothing else. The extra profit will subsidize our custom watchmaking business. We can still keep making the kinds of watches we love, but it will be the clock business that pays the bills."

Oliver looked like he'd just eaten a sour apple. "Clocks," he sniffed. "We are watchmakers. Artisans. Any ham-fisted drudge can assemble a clock."

"That sounds pretty arrogant," Declan said, still fiddling with a pair of dice in his hands.

"You're just a metal polisher," Oliver said. "What would you know of fine craftsmanship?"

Mollie shot to her feet. "You apologize to Declan right now!"

Before she finished speaking, Declan had shoved away from the table, jostling the mugs and sloshing cider all over the table. With his hands clenched into fists, Declan stormed from the table, bumping into serving girls as he made for the exit.

"You should be ashamed of yourself," Mollie snapped at Oliver before she darted after Declan. He was moving quickly and ignored her appeals to slow down. He was halfway down Cohasset Street before she caught up to him, reaching out to grab his arm. "He didn't mean it, Declan. Don't be upset at Oliver."

He whirled around. His muscles were quivering and anger flared on his face. "I'm not mad at Oliver; I'm mad at you!"

"What have I done to make you mad?"

He dragged a hand through his hair, then looked up at the sky, as though the answer to a prayer were written in the clouds. "Mollie, you've got to quit hovering over me like I am a child. I am a man."

She stiffened. "I know that, Declan."

"Then why did you beg Colonel Lowe to leave me home when he went to Milwaukee?" At her indrawn breath, an aggravated look came over Declan's face. "Oh yes, I heard about that. Do you know what it does to a man's pride to have a woman hovering over him as if he is too fragile to stand up to a good stiff wind? I've had it, Mollie. I quit."

The words were like a door slamming in her face. Before she could respond, he stalked away from her, his back rigid with tension. She pulled up her skirts to run after him. "You don't mean that," she said as she pulled alongside him. "What will you do without the 57th?"

He stopped, and the anger faded from his eyes. "That's what I need to find out. As long as I keep hiding beneath your wing, I'll never be anything more than a failure. A metal polisher who needs your pity to keep a job."

"You're not a failure! Are you suggesting Ulysses is a failure? Or that Frank was?"

Declan flinched. His hands trembled, and he looked like he was about to spiral into one of his mind-numbing attacks of panic, but he swallowed hard and met her gaze. "It doesn't matter how they feel about working here. It isn't right for *me* anymore. When I rounded up Colonel Lowe and the others after Frank was killed, it was the first time I felt like a man since the war." His trembling eased, and a look of such stark longing covered his face that it made Mollie's heart ache. "I had that feeling again in Milwaukee. I need to go find what I was meant to be before I got sidetracked by the war."

"I see," she said softly. But she didn't. She had been fighting so hard for the veterans, and now Declan told her she was crippling him? Smothering him? All she had been doing was fulfilling her father's wishes in making sure his brothers-in-arms would always be provided for.

Exhaustion pulled at her, and she hugged her arms around her middle. "You can always come back," she said. "If things don't work out, I want you to know—"

"I won't be back." Fear lurked in his eyes, but so did a thread of determination. "I'm not sure what I am going to do, but I was never meant to be a metal polisher."

She stood on the footpath, watching as Declan disappeared into the crowd. As hard as she had been fighting to restore her company to its previous glory, it felt like the 57th was beginning to slip away from her.

26

Thank heavens Richard had built the new workshop with a surplus of space, for they needed every square inch of it. Watch technicians worked at shoulder-high tables only a yard wide, but the clock for the bank was going to be twelve feet in diameter, requiring a table big enough to feed a whole platoon of soldiers. The containers they used to store watch parts were the size of a cigar box; the bins for clock hardware were three yards wide.

The workshop smelled of pine resin as Ulysses cut timber and began assembling the new bins. Oliver Wilkes looked at the massive tables and bins, wrinkling his nose in distaste. "Large enough to assemble plowshares," he sniffed.

The value of a watch technician was measured by a steady hand, an eye for detail, and the ability to crouch over tiny specks of metal until they had been assembled into a whirring, ticking piece of machinery. The wheel pinions in a watch were usually the size of Mollie's pinkie fingernail. The pinions of the bank clock were going to be two yards wide.

It was anathema to a master technician like Oliver Wilkes, but Alice and Ulysses were slowly coming around to Mollie's point of view. "Our company will either perish or we will rise from the ashes stronger than before," Ulysses said with his typical flair. "This gargantuan clock will be our great test. Our Thermopylae. Our Waterloo. Our Agincourt."

He finished pounding the last nail into the bottom of a bin. "Where do you want this, Mollie?"

"It will have to go down in the basement." Ulysses could build a bin, but with only one leg, he couldn't carry it down a flight of stairs. "Oliver, will you take the new bin downstairs? I can help if you need."

Oliver set his jeweler's loupe down and scowled at the bin, refusing to get up off his stool.

"Or you can find a job somewhere else, if you like," she snapped out. Her voice was louder than she'd intended, but it was getting so hard to keep fighting for people like Oliver. Didn't he understand what the cheap watch in her pocket meant? Every employee in the company had seen that watch, but most seemed to think it was no competition for the quality and artistry that made the 57th famous.

In the past, Mollie had feared the wounded veterans would have trouble finding another job if her company went under. Now she feared for every single watchmaker in this workshop. Unless they wanted to become unskilled workers on a production line cranking out mass-produced watches, they had to do *something* to ensure their survival.

Oliver's angry footfalls echoed in the silent workshop as he carried the bin downstairs, and Mollie felt the scrutiny of every employee as they watched her warily.

She tossed a watchcase down and darted after Oliver, the clatter of her feet echoing off the brick walls as she scrambled down the staircase. Narrow windows at the top of the basement wall let in dim light, illuminating the cavernous space filled with mostly empty bins.

Oliver was the best watch technician she employed, having been with the 57th since its earliest days. Her father relied on him to train the junior technicians in the exacting craft. On the night of the fire, Oliver had come here to pack up the equipment and get it safely out of the city, even as his own house was in the path of the flames. Oliver Wilkes was a bedrock in the company, but she couldn't let him poison the atmosphere.

Her feet crunched across the gravel of the unfinished basement floor as she crossed the space to where he positioned the crate alongside the other empty bins. "I need to know if you will help make clocks," Mollie said, her voice vibrating with urgency. "You are the best person in this company to help me make the transition. I know you *can* do it, but I need to know if you *will*."

He braced his hands against an empty crate, the weak light making the lines and planes of his narrow face look haggard. "This is the most harebrained scheme I've ever heard of," he said. "Your father made a name for this company with quality and beauty. Not monstrous clocks twelve feet across. He would rather see us make plumbing fixtures."

Mollie winced, knowing Oliver was right about her father's opinion, but her father never knew about the Newburgh Watch Factory. The photograph would be forever seared into Mollie's mind. The picture showed a room crammed with machinery, with wheels and pulleys hanging from the ceiling as a handful of workers assembled the watches. Her father had belonged to a different era of watchmaking. It was her job to keep this company afloat in a world none of them had seen coming.

"We can't compete with the Newburgh Watch Factory," she said. "I don't have the money for that kind of equipment, and I am afraid of what those machines can do. We need to keep one step ahead of them, and if burnishing our reputation by making public clocks will help, then that is what I will do. The market for gold and diamond-encrusted watches will always be tricky. Not many people can afford them, and when times turn bad, we need to be able to earn a living. Even if it is through something as clunky and pedestrian as a clock."

Oliver maintained his stance, braced against the bin, but Mollie sensed, for the first time, that her words had penetrated his thick, leathery hide. "I'll help you," he finally said. "But I'll be looking over your shoulder at every move you make, because I owe that to your father. I still think this decision will be the end of us."

Disapproval weighed every one of his words, but she would accept his reluctant help. At this point, she did not have much choice.

~

Mollie's eyes widened as the soprano's voice climbed and wavered on an impossibly high pitch. Sitting in the straight-backed chair of Mrs. Matilda Lowe Horner's parlor alongside fifty-five of Chicago's most elite citizens, Mollie was coming to accept how little she knew of music if this operatic singer represented the finest in vocal performance. Beside her, Colonel Lowe wore his perpetually agreeable expression even as the soprano's voice took on great strident tones as she labored through the final notes of a Wagner aria. No one else in the room seemed to be uncomfortable, so Mollie kept her hand resting inside Richard's warm palm rather than clapping both hands over her ears, which were beginning to hurt.

This type of gathering was standard fare for Richard's sister, who enjoyed hosting her brother whenever he was in Chicago. Matilda had grabbed on to Richard's coattails as he had risen to fame after the Civil War, but Richard had never minded. He had told Mollie of his profound affection for his older sister, nurtured during the freezing winters he had endured as a young boy in the Dakota territories while building railroads. The constant stream of letters and packages filled with warm socks and homemade treats from Matilda had been his salvation during those lonely years. His sister had wanted to become an actress, but when her father forbade it, Matilda dutifully married Archibald Horner, millionaire shoe manufacturer, and nurtured her artistic impulses by hosting evenings such as these.

The soprano's aria came to a triumphant conclusion, and the assembled guests graciously applauded. Mollie leaned over to whisper in Richard's ear, "Is it over?"

The polite expression on his face did not waver. "Three more arias." He flashed her a wink. "Be brave."

Her heart sank. Only a few feet away, a pair of French doors opened onto a lovely terraced garden, allowing the evening air to cool the overheated parlor. How she longed to escape into that garden and seek the seclusion behind the rhododendrons, where she could pour out her fears to Richard. No matter the problem, Richard seemed to know a solution.

And Mollie needed help with the business. She had been slow in finding the proper equipment to make the clocks, but that wasn't her biggest fear. It was the continuing reluctance of her workers to follow her lead. Richard Lowe was a born leader, whether the task was to direct an infantry charge or build a railroad across the state. He knew how to get men on board and working toward a common goal.

The residual loyalty most of her employees felt for Silas Knox's daughter was fading. Every day she could sense the dwindling respect as the technicians looked to Oliver for guidance. Each time she entered the workshop, she could hear murmurs of disapproval as she moved more and more technicians away from the watch tables and into the cavernous space downstairs to begin assembling the massive clock components. Alice and Ulysses were still faultlessly loyal, but they were artists whose opinions carried no credibility with the technicians.

The soprano bellowed through the next aria, and Mollie wondered if her eardrums could tolerate the abuse of two more songs.

Zack would cringe at this sort of music too.

She sat a little straighter. Where had *that* thought sprung from? Zack loved music, but not like this. He liked a good polka band or some rousing folk tunes. It seemed no matter how hard she tried to forget, memories of Zack still arose to haunt her at the oddest times. She had effectively burned that bridge last December. Zack wanted nothing to do with her, and she couldn't blame him.

She had seen him only once since that terrible day by Frank's grave. It had been at an outdoor concert in Claxton Park. She had been walking into the park with Alice and Ulysses to hear a polka band when she looked across the pathway and saw Zack with a pretty blond woman on his arm. Mollie could tell the moment he saw her. For an instant he looked surprised, then his face iced over and he turned away, cutting her dead. Later that evening, she saw him sitting on a blanket with the young lady, their heads bent close together as they studied a small book. They had been laughing.

She dragged her attention back to the present, reaching out for Richard's hand. He gave her fingers a gentle squeeze. He had been openly courting her since last winter, coming down to Chicago weekly to escort her to soirees such as tonight's gathering. He had introduced her to his sister and brother-in-law, who had been generous in welcoming her into their home. Mollie had hoped that with time, her affection for Richard would grow to overtake the lingering memories of a man who frightened, challenged, and annoyed her.

For the most part, her plan was working, but sometimes she simply wanted to escape. The temptation to run away from Chicago and the 57th clawed at her. The 57th wasn't a joy anymore, it was becoming a burden. One that woke her in the middle of the night with her mind twisted into knots. She was trying to swim, but there was an anchor tied around her leg dragging her down. And that anchor was the 57th Illinois Watch Company.

If the fire hadn't happened, she could have sold her company to Hartman's. With sixty thousand dollars she could have run away to the south of France, just as Zack had suggested. Now she was stuck with people who mistrusted her, debts that were growing by the day, and a contract for clocks she was not certain she could fulfill.

Another excruciating aria came to an end, followed by polite applause. Without conscious thought, Mollie rose to her feet and fled out the door.

Mollie couldn't imagine what Richard's sister must think of her abrupt departure, but she didn't care. These were Richard's people, not hers.

The cool evening air was scented with moss, and instead of the wailing of a soprano, the soothing chorus of crickets filled the air. Her slippers cut through the carpet of soft grass beneath her feet as she walked toward the wrought-iron gate that sheltered the Prairie Avenue estate. The muffled sound of the opera singer momentarily became louder as a door opened. Richard's tall form was silhouetted in the doorway as he scanned the grounds, looking for her. She could tell when he spotted her, as he closed the door and cut across the lawn in long, confident strides.

"Feeling all right?" he asked as he drew closer.

She mustered a smile. "Better. I've never heard an opera singer at such close range. She is rather awe inspiring, isn't she?"

"That is one term for it," he said congenially as he scanned her face. "But you've been distracted all evening, even before the operatic assault. Tell me what is bothering you."

Scanning the sky as stars began to emerge, she wondered if this was the right time to lay another round of burdens on Richard's shoulders, but she needed his advice. She needed to unload her problems and have someone older and wiser tell her what to do.

She explained the troubles that had begun when Hartman's burned to the ground. After scrambling, she had found two stores to carry her watches in New York and Philadelphia, but no one had heard of the 57th Illinois Watch Company in those cities, and establishing a reputation there was taking time. The watches commemorating the Chicago fire had sold well, but after the initial wave of orders, business had slowed, and she couldn't ride that wave of sympathy forever. And in the long run, the competition from mechanized watches was going to make earning a reliable income even trickier. Household clocks had long been made by factory workers, but she had never imagined they would figure out a way to make machines handle the tiny components used in watches. Building public clocks was different. The massive size of a public clock made mechanization almost impossible. There would always be a need for skilled technicians to make monumental clocks, and the 57th had something to offer that other clockmakers did not. They had style and artistry. If she could make her mark in Chicago, she might even earn commissions in neighboring cities.

Unfortunately, Richard agreed with Oliver Wilkes. "I don't understand how clocks are going to improve your cash flow." He swooped down and plucked a strand of grass to twirl between his fingers. "It strikes me that your problem is lack of mechanization. You can't solve it by skirting the issue. If you need to compete with the East Coast watchmakers, then do it. Mechanize."

Those words were like a stab in the chest. "I can't *mechanize*," she said. "I would have to let go of half my workers. And it would cost a fortune."

"I've got a fortune."

She drew a quick breath and looked away. Every time he suggested anything like this, it made her feel light-headed, and not in a good way. A firm hand on her arm turned her to face him.

"Mollie, perhaps it is time you funneled more responsibility to Oliver. Or Ulysses. If running the 57th brings you no joy, then leave. You have plenty of other options."

"Oliver is too hidebound to understand how the industry is changing," Mollie said. "And Ulysses has no head for business. I'm the only one there who can see what is ahead of us."

Richard's voice rose a notch. "Did you hear what I just said? If the company is bringing you no joy, then leave. Don't tell me reasons you can't. I can bring an infusion of cash to mechanize the company and hire an experienced man to run the operation. I'll make certain every wounded veteran of the 57th has a job for as long as he wants it. Just say the word."

Her stomach clenched. She couldn't accept an infusion of cash like that without forever putting herself in his debt. Richard had made it clear in the past few months that he would welcome a marriage between them, but the prospect only brought Mollie anxiety.

How long had she been waiting for a rush of infatuation for this handsome man to overtake her? Last week, she had even dragged out a piece of paper and re-created her list of Richard's sterling qualities as measured against Zack. Richard still won, but why couldn't her heart accept that?

Zack wasn't even an option for her anymore. He seemed quite taken with the lovely blond woman in the park, but the fact that Mollie was still trying to browbeat her heart into accepting Richard did not engender confidence in her.

"I think we should rejoin the others," she said, unable to meet his gaze. She'd rather have a tooth pulled than return to the opera singer, but she would do it for Richard. He and his sister had been so good to her, and they didn't deserve to have her sulking through their party. She just wished she felt like she belonged there.

"Mother, no," Zack said. "Absolutely not."

Joanna Kazmarek was skilled at ignoring him when she wished. Pushing the bottle of vodka into his hands, she tried to shoo him out the door. "Go on with you," she said with a sunny smile. "Give that bottle to Mr. Jablonski with our compliments."

Zack eyed the bottle of vodka, suspicion crawling through every vein in his body. "What does the red ribbon mean?" Polish people were some of the most superstitious, tradition-laden people on the face of the earth. Every color, flower, food, or name had some hidden meaning veiled in centuries of tradition, and he knew his mother was up to something.

"Why should a ribbon mean anything?" his mother asked, her voice steeped in innocence.

He knew his mother well and could take an educated guess what a bottle of vodka tied with a red ribbon meant. "It's a token a man gives when he wants to court someone's daughter, isn't it?"

His mother didn't even have the grace to look embarrassed. She pinched his cheek and smiled up at him. "So clever, my son! And where is the harm in that? Anka Jablonski is a lovely girl."

She certainly was, and he had enjoyed every moment he'd spent in Anka's presence. With long blond hair and intelligent blue eyes, she looked like an alpine goddess. She was also bright, had a laugh that sounded like music, and baked Polish makowiec bread better than any he had ever tasted. She also didn't speak a word of English, which had made his courtship somewhat problematic.

Not that it had discouraged his parents. The Jablonskis were regular visitors to his house ever since they had emigrated from Poland five months ago, and his parents had happily provided translation services. Besides, Anka was working on her English. Every word that came out of her mouth was charming. Her accent was usually too thick for him to make much sense of whatever she was trying to say, but he didn't care. He was spellbound. He could listen to Anka mangle the English language for hours and not grow bored.

That didn't mean he was going to give her father a bottle of vodka tied with a red ribbon. Anka was certain to know what it meant, and he had too much respect for her to set up false expectations. He liked Anka but was nowhere near to being ready to offer for her.

He handed the bottle back to his mother. "I am running late for a meeting and won't have time to stop by the Jablonskis."

"More of that insurance business?" his mother asked, disapproval obvious in her voice. Zack said nothing, just grabbed his overcoat, as it would be dark and possibly chilly by the time the meeting ended. Lately, these meetings had run well past midnight.

"It's important, Mama. Maybe the most important work I've ever done."

As far as his parents were concerned, Louis Hartman walked on water and could do no wrong, and whatever time Zack devoted to getting Hartman's rebuilt and running was time well spent. They thought the exact opposite of anything that linked Zack closer to the mayor, the city council, or the burgeoning insurance reform movement.

Chicago was a big, unwieldy city, ruled by aldermen and a municipal ward system, which made reform difficult, but if this city had a prayer of surviving another catastrophe like the fire, the laws governing insurance needed to be changed. No one had ever imagined a fire could wipe out so much of a city's expensive business district. Because most of those businesses were insured by local companies, it was impossible for the fire's victims to collect. To date, less than one-third of the money owed by insurance companies had been paid, and it was unlikely any more funding would emerge. There were heroic stories of insurance agents who'd sold off their own property in an attempt to make good on the money they owed, but company after company had failed.

The only way to stop a repetition of the catastrophe was to change the way the insurance laws worked. It was going to be a tough balancing act to push these reforms through, but it was the sort of hard-hitting, high-stakes game that ignited Zack's blood. He thrived on tackling big problems and finding solutions to solve them.

His stride was brisk as he walked through the neighborhood, scanning the shop fronts and the apartments on the upper floors. The city was more crowded than ever, with people flooding in from the East Coast in search of work. Anyone with a trade, a skill, or a strong back could get work in Chicago, although finding decent shelter was more difficult. At least the tents that had sprouted up throughout the city were mostly gone. And Mollie Knox had finally found a decent home.

Not that he let himself think about Mollie much anymore,

but he was always eager to hear news of her when Dr. Buchanan came for dinner. It seemed she was now building clocks, which was a good thing, since Hartman's would no longer carry her watches.

A large stone building loomed on the corner of Hubbard and Wabash Avenue. Ever since the fire, the mayor and city council had been meeting here until they could find more permanent quarters. A long night awaited him, the air thick with the smoke of cigars and the weight of rampant mistrust. There would be more than a few frayed tempers as they worked toward a new way of regulating business, entirely unknown in the United States. Or anywhere in the world. They were figuring things out as they went, but if they succeeded, no city that endured a massive catastrophe would be faced with the collapse of the local insurance industry again. It took brains, brawn, and a will of steel to shove this sort of reform through the system.

Zack had all three.

Zack nodded to a pair of aldermen as they filed into the building. This was an unusual coalition of insurance agents, elected officials, lawyers, and union leaders. It was going to be a long night, but this was the kind of work he loved best. He followed the others inside and closed the door.

27

Mollie cupped her hands tightly over her ears, but the roaring noise of the metal grinders leaked through. She had thought last evening's soprano was bad, but it could not compare to the shrieks of an industrial mill in full operation.

Glancing down at her smartly tailored navy suit, Mollie wished she hadn't dressed like she was coming to see a banker. Caleb Magruder ran the best industrial mill in the city, but his office looked like a pigsty. She had been waiting there for thirty minutes and was about to give up hope when the mill operator finally arrived. He was grimy and sweat-streaked, but Mollie sprang to her feet and gamely extended her hand. "Mr. Magruder, I'm pleased you could make time to see me."

Caleb Magruder wiped his hands on a canvas apron but made no move to shake her hand. "What can I do for you, ma'am?" His words were polite, but his tone reeked of annoyance. He kept glancing out the office window toward the immense forge where two boys were feeding coal into the furnace.

"I understand you can produce precision metalwork, suitable for a large-scale public clock." She tried to keep the tremble from her voice. Caleb Magruder owned the *only* industrial mill left in the city that could produce this sort of work.

He leaned against the wall of his office, crossed his arms across his beefy chest, and scrutinized her through narrow eyes. It reminded her of the way a police officer would glare at a truant child. "Might," he said. "What do you need?"

She described the specifications for a nine-foot center post, upon which all the internal wheels and gears of the clock would be mounted. It needed to be strong and faultlessly smooth lest the friction throw off the mechanisms.

"That sort of clock was always done by the Potter Clockworks in the past," Mr. Magruder said. "Why didn't they get the contract?"

Mollie refused to let the brusque question rattle her. "I gather nothing is quite the same after the fire, but I have the contract here in hand. My money is good, and the deal will go through. How much will such a center post cost?"

"If I can do it, and I stress *if* . . . it will cost six hundred dollars."

She gasped. "That's robbery!"

"That's what a nine-foot center post costs. Take it or leave it."

She calculated the figure. It would result in a cost overrun, but perhaps it would be worth it for the first clock. The costs for her subsequent clocks would be able to ride on the steep development costs for this first clock. And the longer she delayed, the more the costs were mounting.

"When can you have the work completed for me?" she asked.

"Lady, I don't know if I can do it at all. I need to check my production schedule."

Mollie glanced at the blackboard directly behind him, the production schedule apparent for all to see. "Can't you check right now?"

Mr. Magruder did not break eye contact with her, nor did

his expression change as he folded his arms across his chest and glared at her. "Nope." He pushed away from the wall. "Come back in two days, and I'll be able to tell you if I can do the work."

Mollie's hands began to shake. He was more than capable of handling her request, but there was a reason he was stalling. "Would it help if I sent a man to negotiate on my behalf?"

His gaze did not flicker. "It would help if you weren't a woman. It would help if you weren't a stranger. Frankly, it would help if doing business with you wasn't likely to annoy people I've worked with for the past two decades. Come back in two days, lady."

It was exasperating to walk away, but what choice did she have? As she returned to the workshop on East Street, the comforting sound of watch engravers tapping away at work greeted her.

Over the past few weeks, Alice had drawn more than a dozen designs for the bank clock to coordinate with the bold new lines of the building, and when Mollie walked in the workshop door, still tense with anger over Mr. Magruder's treatment, Alice presented her with a new design. It was brilliant. The roman numerals were drawn in the neoclassical tradition, but with a slight Gothic twist in the lengthening of the letters.

"*That's it,*" Mollie whispered. Those classic numerals represented stability and tradition, but the Gothic tone injected a hint of energy and style. It was simple enough to read from a distance and captured the beauty that had made the 57th famous.

Two days later, she returned to Magruder's Industrial Mill to finalize the center post, but the man wouldn't even let her set foot in the building.

"You've managed to annoy half the builders in the city with

that deal you cut with Raymond Durant. Forget it, lady. Find someone else to make your center post."

～～

Mollie reclined in the dental chair at Dr. Buchanan's office. She wasn't there as a patient or a landlord, but merely as a friend. It felt a little odd to be tilted slightly backward, with her feet propped on a small stool, but there wasn't enough room in the cramped office for a second chair. Dr. Buchanan had a steady stream of business at this compact office built alongside her watch factory. At the time she'd asked Richard to include it in the plans, she had considered it a favor to a man she pitied. Now she was grateful for the monthly revenue.

Dr. Buchanan sat at his desk with the chair swiveled to face her, concern on his face as Mollie poured out her frustrations. "If you could have seen the look on Mr. Magruder's face—so smug, so . . ." She searched for the word. "I think he knew all along he wouldn't do business with me, and that two-day delay was just to annoy me."

"Or set you backwards," Dr. Buchanan said. "If he has a long-standing relationship with the other clockmaker, he probably never had any intention of taking your job."

Mollie vaulted upright. "That's what is so frustrating! Potter Clockworks went out of business after the fire. They don't even *want* those contracts." There might be industrial mills in neighboring cities that could handle her job, but she didn't know how to find such people. And time was growing short. Mr. Durant was coming at the end of the week to assess her progress, and she had nothing to show him. He had warned her of the old-boy network she was up against, but she had underestimated it. This sort of nastiness was simply alien to her.

Dr. Buchanan twirled a small hand drill between his fingers. "I hate to say it, but I think Magruder may want his palm greased. Or some other favor."

Mollie let out a huff and flopped back down into the dentist chair, staring at the ceiling. "I can't afford to pay any more than his highway robbery price, and I don't have pull with anyone who can grant him favors."

"What about Zack Kazmarek?" Dr. Buchanan asked. "That man has ties all over the city. I expect he might be able to get things moving over at Magruder's."

At Zack's name, Mollie stiffened. Even after the fire, Zack's reputation for plowing through obstacles continued unabated. Rumor had it that when the city had slowed down reconstruction efforts in the Polish neighborhoods, Zack retaliated by encouraging a slowdown among the longshoremen unloading imported building materials at the docks. Within the week, the city ordered reconstruction work to begin again in the ethnic enclaves.

Mollie laced her fingers across her waist and tapped the toes of her boots together to relieve the nervous tension. Even thinking about putting herself back into Zack's orbit sent a charge of nervous energy through her. "I'd rather not," she said. She doubted he would even speak with her after the terrible things she had said to him that day in the cemetery.

Dr. Buchanan shifted in his chair, the skin on his cheeks going beet red behind his handlebar mustache. "Forgive me if this is a delicate topic, but I don't think you need to fear Zack's lingering attentions toward you. There is another young lady who has caught his fancy."

Mollie's feet stopped tapping, and her mouth went dry. "Yes?"

"Her name is Anka Jablonski. She and her family go to the Kazmareks' almost every night for supper, as they don't have a proper kitchen in their apartment. Miss Anka is quite the cook, and I've noticed that Zack makes a special point of showing up for supper. Much more than he ever did in the past."

Mollie stared at the ceiling. Miss Anka must be the blond girl she had seen him with that evening in the park. Why should this hurt so much? Wasn't this what she wanted for him?

"Mollie, Zack sold the Monet painting of the girl in the garden," Dr. Buchanan said softly. "The one of the girl holding the watch."

She sat bolt upright. "He did?" It shouldn't surprise her, but it did. It hurt too.

"Hartman's is going to reopen within the month, and Zack has put the painting on the floor for sale. It will be one of the first things customers see when they walk through the doors."

She felt a little light-headed, probably from sitting up so quickly, but Dr. Buchanan had not stopped speaking. "I'm telling you this because you've been a good friend to me. I want to make sure the 57th survives, and I think you might need Zack's help. You need to know he isn't harboring any irrational feelings for you. He's not the sort to hold a grudge, and he might be able to help."

Her fingers curled around the edge of the seat. On the other side of this brick wall, her factory was in danger of going under unless she could deliver on this clock contract. She would do whatever was necessary in order to make it happen.

Even if that meant reestablishing contact with Zack Kazmarek.

Mollie wore her smartest outfit, a coral rose suit with a cinched-in waist complemented by a little beret of the same fabric atop her head, for the meeting. She also wore the white cotton gloves Richard had given her for Christmas. It seemed silly to wear gloves at this time of year, but Richard told her a lady ought to keep her hands covered whenever outdoors, and she had been trying to remember to do so. In any event, she thought the entire outfit looked very smart and lent her a much-needed confident air as she walked toward the new store Hartman was building.

Columbus Street was a hive of activity, with thousands of construction workers scrambling over five- and six-story buildings rising out of the newly elevated street. Chicago had always had a problem with mud in the past, but now, with the slate burned clean, they were rebuilding the city properly. The streets had been raised several inches, and mud would be a thing of the past. Most of the buildings were still mere shells, lacking window glass and with scaffolding outlining where the top floors would someday be, but Hartman's was ahead of the rest. From the outside, the store looked complete. The palatial building was clad in white limestone, new window glass sparkled in the sunshine, and a glossy front door had already been set in place. It wasn't until Mollie mounted the freshly poured concrete steps that she noticed the first startling change.

Instead of a doorman ready to hold the door for visitors, an armed guard blocked her passage. She drew up short, stunned by the stern expression on the guard's implacable face.

"I would like to speak with Zack Kazmarek," she said, glancing nervously at the rifle the man held loosely in his hands. Then she had to wait on the front stoop for twenty minutes while he sent a message upstairs.

Would Zack even see her? From her spot on the front stoop, she could hear the racket from hammers and workmen calling orders to one another. Surely Zack had better things to do than rush to her rescue, but what choice did she have? The 57th would fall into bankruptcy if she could not deliver these clocks.

The door opened and the guard emerged. "He'll give you five minutes."

The surge of relief made her dizzy as she scrambled to her feet. He couldn't hate her too much if he was willing to see her.

It was dim inside, the vast space illuminated only by daylight as workers hung immense chandeliers that looked like they belonged at Versailles. Everything smelled of fresh plaster and varnish, but one end of the unfinished showroom was already stacked to the ceiling with crates of merchandise, handwoven rugs, and bolts of satin and silk. Two men were working to hang cables in a towering compartment that surely was going to be an elevator.

She was breathless by the time she climbed the five flights of stairs, but that couldn't account for the shakiness of her legs. The shakiness was from the prospect of facing a man she had once loved and walked away from.

Zack's office was at the end of the long corridor. After she knocked on the freshly painted door, Zack's firm voice bid her to enter. She took a deep breath, twisted the knob, and stepped inside.

Zack sat behind a desk, reviewing stacks of papers, his handsome face carved into stern lines. He did not rise when she entered.

It was too hard to look at him. Instead, she glanced around the office, noting its stark walls yet to be adorned with any decoration. The room was empty except for a desk, a filing cabinet, the chair he was sitting in, and another empty chair. The floors were bare, and her heels made loud echoing sounds as she crossed the room.

"Hello, Zack," she said, her breathless voice echoing in the stark office. It still smelled like sawdust. She pressed a trembling hand against her chest. "Forgive me, I'm a little winded from the stairs."

He tossed a piece of paper on the desk. "I have four hours of

310

paper work and only three more hours of daylight, so I hope you can make this quick."

So . . . no thaw in his chilly disdain. Zack still hadn't bid her to sit down, and she swept the cap from her head to give her hands something to do. "The store is coming along splendidly. You must be very proud."

He kept glowering at her. He'd probably been practicing that glower since he first learned to order rowdy longshoremen into line, but she needed to find something to set a cordial tone.

"And your parents?" she asked pleasantly. "They are doing well?"

"Miss Knox, I assure you, there is no need to go through these little pleasantries. I would prefer it if you got to the point and stopped wasting both our time."

She stepped forward and lowered herself into the chair opposite him, feeling a little starch go out of her spine. Zack was a blunt, direct man and appreciated her sense of business. She licked her lips and swallowed hard. "You once procured diamond powder for me," she said, still unable to meet his eyes. "I suspect it came from Caleb Magruder's mill. Did it?"

There was an infinitesimal quirk of one brow. "You suspect correctly."

She drew a ragged breath. "The 57th has recently expanded our business to include clocks. We've got the contract for the clock tower at a bank on State Street, and I need the work of a skilled industrial metalworker. Mr. Magruder is my only option, and he has proven . . . difficult."

"Caleb Magruder is always difficult. Get used to it."

She went back to fiddling with the beret in her hands. "He won't do business with me because I am a woman. And because he had some kind of alliance with Potter Clockworks, even though they've gone out of business. In fact, he had a whole slew of reasons for not making a center post for me, none of which make much sense." She looked up to meet his gaze. "Do you have any pull on Caleb Magruder? Anything you can say to smooth my way?"

Zack's face remained blank, but his eyes glittered. "What makes you think a stray dog would have any pull with Caleb Magruder?"

She flinched, and the memory of his wounded face flashed in her mind. Shooting to her feet, she paced in the open floor space, her heels echoing in the room. "You have cause to resent me," she said, sounding a little breathless again. She owed him some sort of explanation for the harsh words. Something to soften the anger still simmering beneath his stony exterior. She lifted her chin and looked directly at him. Her mind went blank. The only thing she could think to say was the truth. "I was clumsy that day. I had no experience with romantic entanglements, and I didn't know how to handle it. I was stupid and scared. I'm sorry."

There was no change in his hard face. "So, what exactly do you want me to do for you?"

"Can you help persuade Caleb Magruder to accept my commission? You know how this city operates, and I don't."

"Miss Knox, are you suggesting I use my sweaty strong-arm tactics on your behalf? What would the fair-haired Colonel Lowe think?"

She glanced away and began pacing again. She didn't want to discuss Richard with Zack. "Colonel Lowe has been a tremendous help to me, but he doesn't know this city like you. He hasn't been able to help."

"Hasn't, or won't?"

Last night, she had spent an hour with Richard in the workshop, showing him the progress they were making on the clocks, the two thousand dollars they had already spent on parts, the beauty of Alice's new clock design. The faceplate had already been built and layered with two hundred dollars' worth of enameling. None of it had made an impact on Richard. "This is a foolhardy plan," he had said. "If I help you, it will be throwing good money after bad."

She turned back to face Zack. "Richard doesn't have any pull on the industrial mills of this city. He is a stranger in Chicago."

Zack shot to his feet, bracing his hands on the desk, and scrutinized her like she was a bug pinned to a card. "Richard Lowe is one of the biggest railroad engineers in the state. He designs bridges and tunnels. You think he doesn't know his way around a few industrial mills?"

Her shoulders sagged. If she wanted Zack's help, she couldn't keep skirting the issue. "You are correct," she said simply. "He could help if he wished to. He won't."

The hint of the smile that curved Zack's mouth reminded her of a wolf. "So the golden Colonel Lowe has finally started playing tough, and you don't like it. What is it that he wants, Mollie? For you to quit the company? Marry him and move back to Waukegan and have you scrap all these audacious plans?"

She winced. That was exactly what Richard wanted, and it was bothersome how clearly Zack read the situation. She didn't know how to respond, so she walked to the window, staring down at the dozens of workmen below.

"Does he know you are here?" Zack asked from behind her. "No."

A fresh bolt of anger laced through his words. "Then you shouldn't have come. Get out of here, Mollie."

She whirled around, feeling her last hope slipping away. "Zack, I wouldn't be here if this wasn't important." She scrambled for the words, knowing her company—her father's company—hung in the balance. "The 57th will go under unless I can figure out a way to earn more revenue. That's where the clocks—"

He cut her off. "Dr. Buchanan told me all about your venture into clockmaking. Good luck with it, but I can't help you." He strode to the office door and held it open. With every moment, she felt the foundation crumbling beneath her feet.

"And Mollie, don't come here again."

The door closed behind her with a smack.

28

By all that was holy, that woman had a lot of nerve.

Zack stalked down the street, anger roiling through him. He had spent his morning digging out from the financial avalanche that was pouring down on the company's head. Bill collectors were threatening to repossess merchandise if he couldn't pay them, a new lawsuit about city zoning had landed on his desk, and another insurance company had just defaulted on their payments. A crate from Paris had arrived with a gilt-covered chandelier Josephine had purchased for the outrageous sum of thirty thousand dollars, and the sellers wanted payment immediately. A construction crew across the street had broken a water line, so the plasterers could not get back to work for another two days. Which meant another delay in reopening the store and finally generating some revenue.

In the middle of this, Mollie Knox had strutted back into his life.

He had been burned by that woman. Scalded. Even now, months after he ought to have consigned her to his past, all she had to do was waltz into his office like a damsel in distress, and he was putty in her soft little hands. Instead of a meeting at the bank to restructure Hartman's loan, he was dashing across town to go make nice with Caleb Magruder.

Who was vastly amused by Zack's request. Magruder grinned as he wrestled with replacing a belt sander on a polishing machine. "Yeah, I remember her. She was gonna let me gouge her on the price of a center post. Too bad I don't do business with women."

Zack leaned against the grainy wall of the equipment repair room, casually folding his arms across his chest. "You were going to *gouge* someone on a price? I'm so disillusioned."

"Just earning an honest dollar." Magruder grabbed a wrench as big as his forearm and began twisting the bolts into place.

"How about if you made an honest dollar building a center post for the 57th? You served in the Civil War, didn't you?"

"Battery D, First Light Artillery," Magruder said, a glint of pride in his eye.

"Then build the lady her post. She employs a bunch of crippled veterans."

Zack thought it might spark a note of sympathy in Caleb Magruder, but he needed to quit overestimating the man. Magruder picked up a rag and began cleaning his grimy hands. "Hey, didn't I make some diamond powder for you last year? The kind watchmakers use?"

Zack knew better than to answer, and Magruder pounced. "Yup, it is all starting to make sense to me now. Of course, last year I didn't know the watchmaker had such pretty blue eyes, or I'd have charged you double. This one is going to cost you, my friend."

Zack pushed away from the wall. "I'm not your friend, and I already *know* it's going to cost me. The question is how much?"

～

The thundering bang on the front door caused Mollie to rear up in alarm, the jeweler's loupe dropping from her eye. Everyone else in the factory also stopped work, but the pounding on the door continued. Five loud, hard blows that sounded like someone was assaulting them with a battering ram.

Mollie rushed across the floor and up the short flight of steps. Whoever was pounding so obnoxiously was probably leaving gouges in their brand-new door. "For heaven's sake, can't you knock properly?" she shouted as she tugged the door open.

Caleb Magruder stood on the other side, a nine-foot steel center post balanced across his beefy shoulders. He had been beating on her door with it.

"Here's your center post. If you want more, there are conditions. And I need a down payment."

She went light-headed. This had to be Zack's doing. The beautiful center post glinted in the sunlight, made to the exact specifications she needed. Even as Zack had fumed and glowered at her, he had still cared enough to make this happen.

"Lady, this thing is heavy!"

She stepped back. "There is room along the back wall. Oliver! Alice! Come help me clear some space." It was going to be a tight fit. They'd need to move things down into the basement, but heavens, that center post was dazzling! Breathtaking! A watch center post was the length of a grain of rice, while this was taller than she was!

Everyone in the factory stopped working to stare in open-mouthed wonder at the monster center post, and for the first time in months, Mollie felt the bud of creative energy inside her stir awake. She could start assembling the bank clock today. *Today!* The moment Caleb Magruder set the huge column down against the wall, she couldn't resist. She grabbed his shoulders and hugged the most disagreeable man in all of Chicago. "Thank you! Oh, thank you!" she babbled.

"Don't thank me until you hear the terms. Kazmarek has conditions."

Her breath froze. Pushing away from him, she looked up in trepidation. "He does?"

"Yeah, lady, he does. I made this center post as a goodwill gesture. If you want the other eight for your contract, you need to meet Kazmarek's conditions."

Her hand trembled as she gestured to the office at the back of the workshop. She knew it wasn't money Zack wanted. The disdain in his face that day in his half-finished office was scathing, and he wasn't going to make this easy.

When Mr. Magruder told her what Zack wanted, she was struck dumb. "He wants *what*?"

Mr. Magruder shrugged his massive shoulders. "I told him it was insane too, but he insisted. He wants you to make three dozen of those Copernicus watches, or the deal is off."

The strength left her knees as she sank against the surface of her desk. Mollie had forgotten about that autumn evening beneath the chestnut trees in the Krause Biergarten when Ulysses had proposed a watch celebrating the accomplishments of the great Polish astronomer by using gemstones to portray the solar system. The plans had never advanced beyond the talking stage because of the fire. It seemed like more than a decade had passed since that magical evening, even though it was less than a year ago. She'd mentioned them to Zack later, but he had never shown much interest in the Copernicus design in the past. Why would he feel so passionate about it now?

"I have no idea," Mr. Magruder growled. "All I know is that he is willing to strike a deal with me over the center posts, provided you come through with those watches. Otherwise, the deal is off."

Mr. Magruder had no additional information. When did Zack

want the watches delivered, and most importantly, who was going to buy them? Never had Mollie made so many watches of one design, especially one as unusual as the Copernicus watch.

She would rather cozy up to Ghengis Khan than deal with Zack, but there was no way she could get her center posts without getting more details about this outrageous demand.

~

There was no softening in Zack's attitude toward her as he outlined his demands to keep Magruder's mill producing for her. He sat behind the desk of his half-finished office on Columbus Street as he tossed his requirements out.

"I want sketches of the Copernicus design within one week," Zack said. "And I want you to go into production by the end of the month."

It was a ridiculous and unreasonable demand. For one thing, she needed a down payment from him if she was going to undertake an expensive watch design. The Copernicus watch, as Alice had envisioned it last autumn, featured a large ruby in the center with other gemstones to represent the planets, including a tiny diamond to represent the moon. This watch was going to cost a fortune, and she didn't want to bankrupt herself because Zack Kazmarek had figured out a way to gain leverage over her.

"Don't you know how risky this design is?" Mollie asked. "Nicolaus Copernicus is not someone the world is clamoring to celebrate, and it will be a hard sell."

"Last autumn, you believed people remembered the crazy Polish astronomer who dared to believe the earth actually moved."

"I don't think there are enough wealthy Poles who want to spend a fortune on such a watch."

Zack stiffened. "So you think we are all a bunch of dock workers and drones who labor in the stockyards?"

Zack often joked about his Polish heritage, but this was the first time she had seen this smoldering defensive side of him. She stood and began pacing in the blank space before the window. "We've made specialty watches before, but never more than five or six. That limits our risk and drives up the value of the watches. I am not confident I can sell this kind of watch."

Zack steepled his fingers and eyed her. "There are rich Poles in Europe. Zurich. Florence. I don't care what it takes, I *will* sell those watches."

"In Europe?" she scoffed. "Thank you for pointing out there might be a market in Europe, but I don't have any connections there and can't afford to develop them."

"I can."

She looked at him quizzically. "Why would you help me like that?"

"I'm doing this for my mother, not you," he said pointedly. "She wants to exalt the reputation of Poland, and she likes the idea of these watches. I want them sold at Harrods. On the Ponte Vecchio. I want them in the glittering cities where the merchants and intellectuals of Europe mingle with kings and generals. I want each watch to come with a card outlining the contributions of Nicolaus Copernicus to history and science. Galileo rode on Copernicus's shoulders. *Polish* shoulders. I want the world to know that."

The glint of determination in Zack's eyes was unlike anything she had ever seen before. He might deny it, but he wasn't doing this for his mother. This was something deeply personal to him, but she couldn't afford to bankrupt her company so he could help glorify the memory of Poland's most famous scientist.

"Are you serious?" Mollie asked. "The fate of Polish cultural pride rests in the hands of Alice Adair and the 57th Illinois Watch Company?"

Zack didn't move a muscle. "Strange, isn't it?"

He wasn't going to let this go. He had latched on to this insane idea at which even Silas Knox would have balked and wasn't going to let it go. He was doing this so he could flex his muscles and assert his power over her, and it was unsettling. Dr. Buchanan swore Zack was over his fascination with her, but there was a predatory gleam in his eye.

She folded her hands and drew a steadying breath. "Zack, I didn't mean it when I called you a stray dog."

Zack's smile was tight as he stood and leaned over to whisper in her ear. "Don't worry, I've got a nine-foot center post in my jaws to keep me happy. Now, get out of here and go make me those watches."

It was maddening, but she didn't have much choice.

Colonel Lowe simmered with aggravation when he heard about Zack's demand, but as always, he was too well bred to let it rattle his calm demeanor. His voice maintained an even tone, but there was an edge of steel beneath the words.

"This has the stink of unseemly manipulation all over it," he said as they navigated through the crowded street market on a quest for summer fruit. After months of dried, salted, and canned food, Mollie always savored the arrival of fresh fruit in the markets. It was unseasonably hot for June, and Mollie waved a fan before her face as they perused a bin mounded with colorful produce. She reached for an apricot, holding it to her nose and breathing in the sweet fragrance. "Do you prefer apricots or peaches? Some people are very particular."

"Get them both," Richard said as he tapped his foot impatiently. "So when did you meet Kazmarek about this? It isn't proper for you to be alone with a man like that."

Mollie set a few more apricots in her basket. "He holds the keys to the kingdom," she said. "I can't get Magruder's help unless I make the Copernicus watches for Zack. If that's what it takes to get my center posts, that is what I'll do."

The crate of peaches sat awfully high, so she angled around the stall to reach it. She pretended great fascination as she fingered a piece of the velvety fruit. Anything rather than look at the annoyance on Richard's face.

"It is a foolhardy move," Richard said. "Those clock parts may have bought you a temporary reprieve, but Mollie . . . the whole idea of building public clocks is an ill-advised plan. All Kazmarek is doing is providing you with enough rope to hang yourself."

Richard meant well. Hadn't he offered her an infusion of funds to finance the mechanization of the factory so she could produce sensible inexpensive watches to compete with the East Coast watchmakers? "The business for public clocks is going to soar, and it is going to be our salvation," she said. "Chicago is building hundreds of new railway depots and banks and public squares. They will all need clocks."

She was reaching for another peach when Richard grabbed the basket from her. "I think you are wrong about the business, but what I really care about is why you were running to Zack Kazmarek for help."

She had never heard that level of annoyance in Richard's voice, and it set her on edge. Rather than answer him, she moved toward a stall selling parsnips. She had always hated this kind of conflict. "There is no affinity between myself and Mr. Kazmarek, if that is what you are implying."

Richard held her gaze so long she could feel a trickle of perspiration snake down her back. A fruit fly buzzed nearby, and she used the distraction to swipe it away with her fan. A woman setting out tomatoes stared openly, but glanced away when Mollie glared at her.

"*No* affinity, Mollie?" Richard pressed. "As in, Kazmarek means no more to you than the anonymous lad who delivers your milk, or is he the man you once loved so passionately that you've kept me at arm's length for the past six months? Forgive my persistence, but I'm a little curious."

The tomato lady was still listening to every word, so Mollie slid a little farther away. "It's only a business arrangement," she said in a harsh whisper. "In the last six months, I've spoken no more than a few dozen words with him."

Richard didn't care who overheard them and planted his hands on his hips. "They must have been powerful words to put that kind of flush on your face."

She moved on to the next vegetable stand to avoid the nosy tomato vendor. She scanned the bins, looking for something to distract her from the tension that was crackling in the air. "Cherries!" she burst out.

"Forget the blasted cherries." Richard dropped the fruit basket onto the street, kicking up a cloud of dust as he turned her shoulders to face him. "Is Kazmarek the man you once cared for? I need to know."

The crowd was dense in front of the fresh vegetable bins. People were knocking into them as they reached around to make their selections, but Mollie couldn't move anywhere as Richard kept his hands locked in place. "Do we need to have this conversation right here?" she asked tightly. She glared at the tomato vendor, who had waddled forward to continue eavesdropping. "I think the lady behind your left shoulder can't hear very well, so perhaps we should move closer to her tomato stand so she can listen to every word."

Richard did not break eye contact. "Don't change the subject.

I care for you and won't allow you to be manipulated by a man who overwhelmed you with his attentions. I won't stand for it."

Mollie reached down and picked up the basket of apricots, getting warmer by the moment. It was hot, and she was angry he would be questioning her like this, but when she looked into Richard's eyes, she remembered that long-ago day when he had walked through the rubble of the burned-out streets of Chicago, leading a band of men to come to her rescue. After months of tireless work on her behalf, how could she begrudge him this piece of her soul?

"Yes, Richard. Zack is the man I once cared for, but it is *over*. Any association I have with him now is solely about business."

Richard locked eyes with her. Although she'd never seen him in uniform or in charge of a battle, it was easy to recognize the glint of command. "Then I will be at your side for any future meetings with Mr. Kazmarek. I think this is fitting, Mollie."

A trickle of relief eased the tension in her shoulders. She'd be safer with Richard at her side as she negotiated with Zack, and the smile she sent him was genuine. "Fair enough."

Annoyance rippled through Zack when Mollie arrived at his office to present her Copernicus designs with Colonel Lowe beside her. Wearing one of her prim dark suits, she had a frothy little scarf knotted up beneath her chin. With her hair swept into an elegant twist at the crown of her head, she looked like an aristocrat. A perfect companion for Richard Lowe's classical perfection.

Zack rose as the pair crossed his office and stood before his desk. He glared at Colonel Lowe. "Ah, the living legend."

Colonel Lowe flicked a nonexistent speck of lint from his sleeve. "A burden, but I carry it proudly."

Zack resumed his seat, clearing the latest lawsuit papers from the top of his desk and gesturing for the pair to sit. At least his office now had a decent set of chairs. There was no money for carpets or other amenities in the offices, although the store downstairs was resuming its formal splendor. With luck, they would open in three weeks. He had been working twelve-hour days to juggle incoming merchandise, stave off bill collectors, and insure the construction work was completed on time.

Which was why it was insane for him to be getting distracted by Mollie and her blasted watches. Why was he subjecting himself to this? If he wanted to indulge in self-torture, it would be more efficient to find the nearest vise and stick his head in it.

"What have you to show me?" he asked pleasantly.

Mollie set four proposed designs on the desk, sliding them toward him for assessment. A surge of wistful memories seized him. In the past three years, how many times had Mollie come to his office to present watch designs? Twenty-five? Thirty? And each of those times, he had sat in his chair like an emotionless drone, pretending she was not the most spectacular, intelligent woman he'd ever been privileged to know.

Today was no different. Even after holding this woman in his arms, after kissing her as a firestorm raged around them, after comforting her in the ash-filled days that followed, it was as though that magical time had never happened. Colonel Lowe sat beside her like a mastiff guarding a princess, and Zack kept his face neutral as he looked at the designs.

The drawings showed a stunning concept featuring the solar system depicted with gemstones from front, back, and profile view. They were bold, audacious, and spectacular designs. Those were the only words that came to his mind, and an irrational surge of pride flooded him. He had nothing to do with Mollie's success in leading this company, and yet he was still so proud of a woman who could inspire a team of artisans and technicians to produce these remarkable miniature machines.

"Alice has certainly outdone herself this time," he said, the words completely inadequate to express the awe the designs engendered.

"They are ridiculous," Richard said. "A frivolous waste of money only rich people can afford."

It was exactly what Zack had thought of Mollie's watches when he had first come to work at Hartman's, but he was surprised Colonel Lowe shared his opinion so openly in front of Mollie. She must be used to hearing such criticisms of her watches, as she remained sitting proudly in her chair, awaiting his assessment.

Colonel Lowe was wrong. These watches might not appeal to the average man on the street, but that didn't mean they were a frivolous waste. Zack pulled a design closer, holding it up to study the delicate tracery of lines indicating movement as the celestial planets circled the sun.

"There is something magical about these designs," he said. He raised his gaze and looked directly into Mollie's bottomless blue eyes. "I don't understand how the solar system works, but I can accept on faith that Copernicus knew what he was talking about. I don't understand how God could have made the universe and everything in creation, and then set it all into motion, but I believe He did. Sometimes I don't need to understand something, but I just *know*. These watches capture the glory of God's universe, and they make me want to rejoice in it. They are a hymn to God's creation. A celebration in gold and rubies." He slid the design back at her.

"Build them," he said confidently. "Don't worry about how they'll sell. I will find a way. If I have to carry them to Europe and hawk them on the street corners myself, I will find a way to sell these watches."

Mollie's eyes kept widening as he spoke. He'd never been so passionate about her watches in the past. Before, she would present her designs, he'd sign the necessary paper work, and they'd set an appointment for the following quarter. Maybe Colonel Lowe couldn't understand what made these watches so spectacular, but Zack did, and he was holding the most original design he'd ever seen from the 57th's workshop. He smiled at Mollie, who had caught his enthusiasm and beamed back at him.

Colonel Lowe's voice was a dash of cold water. "While Mollie is occupied with producing the watches, I will handle all future business transactions for the Copernicus watches. Miss Knox need not distract herself with these tedious business meetings."

Zack hid his smile. Another tactical error on Colonel Lowe's part. Mollie *loved* business. Put an accounting book and a production schedule in front of her, and she was like a Viking on the warpath.

His gaze flicked to Mollie. A flash of annoyance crossed her face, but she hid it quickly and gave him a tight nod. "Very well," Zack said. "I will make arrangements to discuss a vendor with you at a later date."

It was going to be interesting to monitor how this played out. Colonel Lowe might have the glory of the nation riding on his shoulders, but he didn't understand Mollie Knox.

29

Zack battled waves of exhaustion as he stepped off the streetcar and headed toward home. Eight months and three weeks after the fire that had wiped out four miles of his city and burned Hartman's to the ground, the palatial store had reopened.

In Josephine's classic style, she'd greeted customers wearing a ball gown, with footmen distributing roses to the ladies as they streamed through the doors. Servers handed out glasses of chilled champagne, violin music wafted through the air, and people weary of reconstruction flooded the store for a few hours to forget the grime and soot of the past nine months. The governor of the state cut the ribbon. Aldermen and millionaires mingled with opera singers and artisans. A photographer was on hand to memorialize the day, and the cash registers began ringing as money once again started flowing into the store's parched coffers.

Louis Hartman was flushed with pleasure, bankers clapped Zack on the back, and reporters wanted to interview him. It should have been one of the happiest days of his life, but when Zack wandered to the counter selling watches, his energy dimmed.

Displayed on a bed of royal blue velvet, the elegant gold watches looked excessively ordinary in comparison to the watches produced by the 57th. Mollie shouldn't be his concern anymore. He probably should not even have intervened to get Magruder's cooperation or those Copernicus watches underway, but he couldn't help it. Mollie had such passion, such a hard-nosed logical approach to getting her exuberant company back in action, he found it impossible not to cheer her on.

It had been after eight o'clock before he could escape from the store. As he turned the corner onto his block, all Zack wanted to do was sink into his bed and sleep for the next month. Instead, he knew his mother had prepared a celebration for him, inviting half of the Polish population of Chicago to his home. Her son, the Pole who had climbed off the docks and into a plush office wearing a starched collar, was back working for the most prestigious store in Chicago. It was biologically impossible for her to restrain herself from throwing a party.

A tight group of people were clustered on his front porch. One separated herself and came flitting toward him, her blond hair streaming behind her. Anka bounced as she sprang up to kiss him on the cheek. "Congratulations," she said, mangling the tricky word in her awkward English, but her eyes were brimming with genuine happiness. Inside, the house smelled of pierogis and roasted duck.

"How did it go?" his mother asked. "I heard traffic on Columbus Street was backed up for a mile. Did they sell the Monet?"

Zack nodded, remembering the bidding war that had broken out in front of his painting of the girl in the garden. It was hard to watch, but it would have been odd for him to excuse himself from the grand event.

"It sold within the first hour," he confirmed. "Thirty percent more than I paid for it in Paris."

Anka's father clapped him on the back. "You are rich!" he said.

Not quite. Like half of the people supplying goods to Hartman's, Zack could not expect payment on the Monet for months. Hartman's was hanging on by the skin of its teeth, and they would need today's revenue simply to pay the store clerks. It would be a while before Zack would see a return on that painting, but he could hardly begrudge Louis that. He would be hauling crates off the docks were it not for Louis Hartman, and Zack would mortgage the shirt off his back if it meant getting the store back in business.

He was so tired, he just wanted to close his eyes and forget about the fire and Mollie and the mounds of bills that would greet him on his desk tomorrow morning. Escaping into the corner of the kitchen, he saw Dr. Buchanan sitting alone on the hearth of the fireplace, a plate of beef stew balanced on his knees.

Zack sat on the empty space beside the dentist. "I think you and I are the only people here who don't speak Polish."

The dentist nodded. "I like listening to everyone talk, even if I can't understand them. It feels good to be part of a family like this." He used a piece of rye bread to soak up a little of the beef juice.

Zack eyed the people clustered around the dining table as they laughed and talked. In the months since the fire, Zack had found a new appreciation for his heritage, watching in pride as the Polish community bonded together to rebuild their burned-out neighborhoods. All across the city, it had been the same. They would not have survived the fire without the bonds of family and community to pull them all through this nightmare. The people who sought shelter in that church had been a family, as were the people who worked at the 57th.

Dr. Buchanan set his plate aside. "Say, you didn't really sell that Monet, did you?" he asked.

"I really did," he said. After all, it wasn't actually a painting of Mollie. The girl in that garden was the embodiment of serene grace, and that wasn't Mollie. Mollie was ferocity and strength and indefatigable logic that would plow through any obstacle. She was far more impressive than the bland girl in the painting.

Dr. Buchanan slowly nodded. "Probably just as well," he said. "Colonel Lowe seems to be a permanent fixture in Chicago now."

He stiffened. It was inevitable that one day soon he'd hear Mollie was finally engaged to be married, and then she would be as lost to him as that Monet painting.

Dr. Buchanan nodded to the coat tree in the corner of the hallway. "As long as you got rid of the painting, don't you think it's time to get rid of that green scarf?"

Zack's gaze trailed to the coat tree in the corner. Amidst the family's coats and jackets, the tattered green scarf looked a little odd, but that scarf meant far more to him than any painting. After all, he had been right there beside Mollie as every cinder burned its tracery pattern on the fabric. That scarf was precious to him, representing the fierce beauty of a woman who would never surrender. "It doesn't mean anything," he said.

Doctor Buchanan didn't buy the nonchalant tone. "It's unhealthy. Wrong. Toss it in the lake and move on. Mollie certainly has."

Zack glared at the scarf. It triggered fresh waves of pain as he saw it every morning, and again when he walked through the front door at the end of every day. But throw it away? He'd as soon carve out a piece of his soul.

Anka drifted over to them, carrying a platter of gingerbread. "Eat. Work hard," she said.

Dr. Buchanan reached up and helped himself to a slice of gingerbread. "I can see that you did!" he said. "Everything you made is excellent. Very good," he said.

Anka shook her head. "No! Work hard. Work hard eat."

Dr. Buchanan scratched his head. "I think we have a translation problem." Setting down the gingerbread, he took a little Polish-English dictionary from his coat pocket and offered it to Anka. She flipped through it. After a few tries, she managed to land on the correct words, which amounted to telling them both that they worked far too hard and should have some dessert.

Dr. Buchanan nodded enthusiastically. "So long as you bake it, I'll eat anything!"

Anka joined them at the hearth, and it felt good to have her there. She was such an easy person to be with. Kind, hard-working, and relentlessly cheerful.

He looked at the green scarf again. Then at Anka.

Maybe Dr. Buchanan was right and it was time to put the scarf behind him.

~

"This sounds like the most bizarre Fourth of July celebration in the history of mankind," Ulysses said, not looking up from the piece of metal he was engraving.

Mollie agreed, but there wasn't much she could do about it. Colonel Lowe's sister took great pride in her annual celebration to raise money for the orphaned children of the war. Each year, Matilda Horner asked her closest friends to pick a state representing one of the original thirteen colonies. They were to bring an item that represented the cultural contributions of the state, while other guests would place monetary donations beneath the most original or clever cultural artifact. This year, given Richard's courtship, Mrs. Horner had included Mollie among the women selected to represent an original colony. It was considered a great honor, but Mollie merely thought it one more obligation to squeeze in between building three dozen Copernicus watches and completing the bank clock.

"I picked Georgia," Mollie said. "Apparently, the rebellious states are always last to be chosen, so I thought I might buy Mrs. Horner's goodwill by taking it off her hands. I'm not sure what I'll bring. Maybe peaches?"

"Bring a bucket of shrapnel," Gunner said from across the room. "Georgia spewed plenty of it during the war." He shook the stump of his left arm in the air.

Mollie swiped a tendril of hair away from her face. "I'll be lucky to make it to the celebration at all. It comes two days after we install the bank clock, and five days before I need to have the mechanisms on the Copernicus watches completed." To her amazement, Zack had succeeded in getting the Copernicus watches placed with a jeweler in Florence, Italy. Richard had grudgingly shared the news, announcing that Zack's contacts with the jewelers of the Ponte Vecchio had paid off, and Mollie's watches would begin selling throughout the major cities of Europe.

The Fourth of July celebration came at an inconvenient time. Exhaustion pulled on Mollie as she struggled to complete the watches by the contract's deadline at the same time she was trying to complete the oversized clock for the bank. Mollie twisted her spine and rubbed the weary muscles of her back. "I'll be lucky if I'll be able to get even a can of peaches, let alone a bounty of fresh ones."

"Not to worry," Ulysses said. "You can extol the miracle of

the modern canning process. During the war we would have perished from scurvy without canned fruit." At Mollie's skeptical look, he amended his statement. "Oh, hang it, Mollie, we'd have perished from culinary boredom without canned fruit. There is only so much rice and beans a man can eat before turning into a legume."

She smothered her laughter in her sleeve as she got back to work, still completely at a loss for what to take to represent the state of Georgia.

On the corner of West and Harrison Street, a four-story office building was nearing completion. Far from the glamour of Columbus Street, this was in a working-class section of town, not far from the lumber mills and the stockyards. Zack's boots echoed through the partially finished suite of rooms on the first floor.

"Are you sure this is the right place?" Dr. Buchanan asked, looking at the stark rooms. None of the interior rooms had any windows. Two window holes had been cut into the front room, but no frames or glass had been installed yet.

"It doesn't need to be pretty," Zack said. "It just needs to be big."

Big enough to hold the boundless storehouse of memories his parents had been collecting from the waves of Polish immigrants. He would order shelving to be built in the back rooms, where hundreds of bundled Polish-American newspapers could be housed. Those newspapers recorded the struggles and triumphs of people who had risked everything to make their way to Chicago, giving men like Zack a chance to become something more than conscripted foot soldiers in the czar's army. The other rooms would store the diaries, photographs, and books about Poland. The front room had two large windows that let in decent light from the street. Anyone who wished to come pore though his parents' clearinghouse of Polish memorabilia could do so here in a clean, well-lit room.

"My parents believe their Polish treasures are something the world is dying to see. I don't know if they are or not, but those 'treasures' have overtaken my house, filled my attic to capacity, and are now spilling into the hallways. They will be better off here, where others can appreciate them."

It would be a place where his mother could complete her book about Polish immigrants in Chicago. He did not know if the book would ever see completion, but it mattered to his mother, and these rented rooms would give her the space she needed to make progress.

Dr. Buchanan fidgeted as he eyed the space. "Will your mother agree? She seems very passionate about those papers."

Zack sent him a pointed look. "I'm not giving her a choice."

"Good, good," Dr. Buchanan muttered, wiping his hands on the front of his pants. Zack raised his brows. Dr. Buchanan was usually so fiercely protective of Joanna that the distracted answer surprised him.

Little beads of perspiration formed on the man's brow. "Actually, I'm glad I have a chance to speak with you," Dr. Buchanan said as he paced the empty room. "I wanted to talk with you last night, but there were too many people around."

Zack tensed. Was Mollie finally ready to announce a pending marriage to Colonel Lowe? It would be like Dr. Buchanan to tell him personally rather than let him read about it in the newspaper.

He clenched his hands into fists and wished he hadn't sold the Monet portrait. If Mollie really was lost to him, he wanted it back. Which was insane. He'd gotten rid of it precisely so he wouldn't need to keep thinking about her every blasted day of his life.

Dr. Buchanan took a deep breath and looked him in the eye. "I want to ask you about Anka," he said. "Everyone seems to think the two of you are destined for each other, but it's been seven months and, well, not much is happening. I talked with her last night. I mean, I *tried* to talk with her, and she—" Dr. Buchanan stopped talking and his face flushed cranberry red. "It is astounding, but she seems to care for me. I went over and over it to make sure she had her English straight. Finally she dragged her brother over to translate, and there was no mistake. She, uh . . ." He cleared his throat and tugged at his collar. "She said she would welcome my courtship."

Zack leaned against a wall, a little stunned. "I see."

"I don't want to intrude if you have your eye on Anka," Dr. Buchanan rushed to say.

Zack gave a short laugh. He liked being around Anka because she was dazzling to look at, but she had never touched his soul or made him ache for things that could never be. "So long as I can still partake of Anka's almond cake, I would be very happy for you."

Dr. Buchanan looked ready to faint. He doubled over and drew a breath as though he'd just finished running a mile. "Thank heaven," he breathed. "Your parents have been very good to me, and I can't risk losing another family. Not over a woman." Dr. Buchanan straightened and smoothed the hair back from where it had fallen over his forehead. "You can't imagine what it is like to be alone, year after year. This year was the first time I didn't spend Christmas alone since my parents died, and I owe your family for that."

Zack had always been surrounded by family, one that sometimes encompassed the entire community of exiled Poles. That simple fellowship was something he had always taken for granted, but Dr. Buchanan had had no experience with it until he'd stumbled upon a group of people seeking shelter in a burned-out church.

He reached out to clasp Dr. Buchanan's shoulder. "We are glad to have you," he said with genuine warmth. "And I hope Anka will be as well."

Zack rubbed his eyes, then fed a little more kerosene to the wick of the lamp. Why did they print law books with such minuscule type? If he kept poring through these manuals, he would be blind soon, but he didn't mind. Nothing in his professional career had ever been as satisfying as working toward the total overhaul of the insurance industry. An unconventional coalition of insurance brokers, lawyers, and politicians was hammering it out. It made for a rough-and-tumble atmosphere, but he relished every moment of it, especially since it was important work.

If they did their job right, small-business owners like Mollie and Dr. Buchanan would never again be wiped out because their insurance defaulted in the wake of a city-wide catastrophe.

Before she went to bed, his mother had set a slice of Anka's homemade makowiec beside him, but Zack had not stopped to eat. He had three more legal briefs to read before tomorrow's meeting.

A pounding on the front door broke the silence of the night. Who would come banging on his door at ten o'clock on a Friday night? Zack put on his jacket and approached the front door with caution.

It was Louis Hartman, looking as annoyed as a wet dog with

fleas. Whatever sent Louis here in the dead of night couldn't be good. Zack opened the door wide and gestured toward the dining room, where he pulled out a chair for Louis. "What can I help you with?"

Louis looked exhausted as he pinched the bridge of his nose, then held out a small notecard to Zack. The message was brief and to the point.

The thirty-thousand-dollar chandeliers Josephine had bought were going to be repossessed on Monday if Louis could not pay for them. Zack's breath left him in a rush. Traffic at the store had been brisk, and they were hauling in profits beyond their expectations, but it would be months before they'd earned enough to start paying their major creditors. The illusion of grandeur would come to a skidding halt if they suffered the humiliation of creditors repossessing chunks of the store.

"I told the agent we would meet with him tomorrow to hammer out some kind of deal," Louis said. "We'll meet him at the bank, and I'll try to shake a few more loans through."

The meeting to finalize the insurance proposal was tomorrow. It was bound to last all day and into the night, and Zack had spent months preparing for it. "I can't be there," Zack said. "I'll be at an insurance meeting. It will be the linchpin meeting of the entire reform effort."

"And on Monday I'm going to have a dark store with gas lines dangling from the ceiling if we can't get this judgment reversed."

Zack blew out a breath in frustration. "What possessed your wife to spend thirty thousand dollars on light fixtures?"

Louis's smile was tight. "Josephine likes the finest, and so far, her taste has served this company very well."

"Then get Josephine to explain it to the bill collectors. The insurance meeting tomorrow is too important for me to miss."

Louis said nothing as he stared at Zack, but he twirled a

pencil between his fingers with the intensity of a madman. Louis Hartman had not crawled to the top of the mercantile world by playing nice, and Zack could see the steel emerging behind Hartman's slate gray eyes. "I never thought I would need to remind you how your college education was paid for," Louis said. "Or where you would be today if I had not gambled on a brash-talking longshoreman. I think a little loyalty would be in the offing."

Zack leaned forward, his voice vibrating with months of suppressed anger. "I was *loyal* when I crammed that deal through with Mollie Knox when I knew her deed was legitimate."

"That was perfectly legal," Louis said. "You would have been in breach of confidentiality if you had told her."

"It was legal, but it cost me the woman I love," Zack lashed out. "A woman I've loved for three years. I can't keep summoning up that kind of loyalty over a *store*. Not when there is important work that will protect every small business and homeowner in this city." Zack tossed the note back to Louis. "You need to find another attorney to handle this."

Louis shot to his feet. "You owe me a debt you can never repay. Never."

Zack stood as well. "Keep the money from the Monet painting. That ought to make a dent in the Yale bill. Other than that, I'm done, Louis. I quit."

Louis swallowed hard, his Adam's apple bobbing in his thin neck. The man had lost weight over the past few months, and the fit of his collar was not quite correct. Zack let out a heavy sigh. "The agent wants his money, not some secondhand chandeliers. Tell the judge they will be more likely to get their money if the store is allowed to keep operating under normal conditions. They've been bending the law ever since the fire. I don't expect this to be any different."

He noticed a trembling in Louis's hands as he tucked the note into his breast pocket. Divided loyalty ripped through Zack. This man was almost a father to him. A clever, imperfect father who had gambled on him and lost.

"I'm sorry it has to end this way," Louis said stiffly.

There was no hesitation in Zack's reply. "So am I."

30

Mollie had been banished to stand on the street to watch the installation of the clock for the State Street Bank. She winced with each crank of the pulley as her magnificent oversized clock was hoisted ten, twenty, then fifty and sixty feet off the ground. The monumental clock began looking smaller as it was raised higher into the sky. Four burly workmen stood on the top layer of scaffolding, waiting to grab the clock as it rose higher.

"Breathe, Mollie," Ulysses instructed.

"I can't," she gasped. "My precious child is dangling eighty feet off the ground, held only by a rickety pulley that looks like it sailed over on the *Mayflower*."

She craned her neck to see properly. Blocking the glare of the sun with her hand, she nearly fainted as she saw the clock sway like a pendulum as the construction workers leaned over the scaffolding to haul it into place. Beside her, all forty employees from the 57th were assembled to witness their first clock being raised into place. At least two hundred other bystanders and construction workers had also gathered on the street to watch.

Until this very moment she hadn't been certain it would succeed, but as the workers slipped the clock into its moorings, a smattering of applause rose up from the street. Gunner clapped her on the back. "It looks good, Mollie," he said.

She stared at the clock. Pillars had been carved into the entablature surrounding the clock that made it appear even larger. Inside the building, Oliver Wilkes stood ready to hook the final gears in place and set the hands into motion.

"It was really hard, and I helped make it," Sophie said from where she stood next to Alice. Mollie turned to smile down at the girl, who was telling no lie when she claimed partial credit. For six hours per week, Sophie helped fetch and carry with more enthusiasm than many of the other skeptical employees at the 57th. What the girl lacked in experience, she made up for with enthusiasm. Energy and enthusiasm were valuable commodities in any business, but never more so than in the grueling months after the fire.

From the corner of her eye, a dark-haired man turned and shuffled deeper into the crowd.

He was familiar. Mollie took a few steps, craning her neck to see around the hundreds of bystanders collecting on the street. Declan?

She was certain it was Declan. The same shoulders, the same build. Leaving Sophie and Ulysses behind, Mollie darted into the crowd. "Declan!" she shouted.

His steps accelerated. Why should he flee from her? She grabbed a handful of her skirts so she could hop over a stack of construction joists that were piled on the sidewalk. As the crowd thinned, it became easier to catch up to Declan as he strode away.

"You don't have to run from me," she shouted. "Declan, there are no hard feelings!"

He stopped, turning to look at her with caution in his eyes. "You sure about that?"

She was breathless when she caught up to him. She cuffed him on the arm. "Don't be an idiot. I'm glad to see you."

"You didn't seem too happy about it when I left the company."

She blanched. It wasn't that she wasn't happy, she was merely terrified he would shatter into a million pieces if she wasn't there to protect him. Not that she could say such a thing. "I only wanted what was best for you. Although, my goodness, you look so fine. . . ." He looked healthy, with clean clothes and the beginnings of a new beard that was neatly groomed and clipped close to his face. There was a lump in her throat, but why was she getting weepy over Declan McNabb? Apparently he was doing much better without her hovering over him, but that was how it should be, shouldn't it?

"The clock looks grand, Mollie. Really grand."

"It was Alice's doing. She must have drawn twenty different designs. We presented four of them to the bankers, and they were very impressed."

Declan nodded. "It was good to see you all again. I didn't feel right barging in, since I didn't have anything to do with that clock. But will you tell everyone how fine I think the clock is?"

"Of course!"

He shifted awkwardly on his feet. "I wanted to let you know that I took your advice. About going back to church. I can handle crowds better these days, and I've learned a lot from being there. I don't know if I'll ever be whole again . . . but you were right about there being worse things than death. Living in fear all the time . . . that was worse. Learning about Jesus and hope has helped with that."

"Move it, people," a voice growled. Behind her, a line of men were angling wheelbarrows full of mortar down the street. Declan grabbed her arm and guided her farther down the sidewalk.

"There is a pretzel vendor a few blocks down, if you'll let me buy you one?"

He still seemed so tentative, and she smiled broadly as she followed him. They found a bench and Mollie began pulling apart the warm, salty dough. Richard did not approve of eating food with bare hands, so it had been months since Mollie had indulged in the salty treat. She quickly devoured one, then purchased another. Alternately nibbling and throwing tidbits to the pigeons, Declan said he had taken a job as a clerk in a bank, reconciling accounts at the end of the day. If all continued to go well, he planned on enrolling in an accounting program in September.

"It was what I wanted to do before the war," he said. "That single year when I studied accounting was the best time of my life. Zack Kazmarek said he would write a letter of recommendation when the time is right."

Just the mention of Zack's name was enough to make her catch her breath. "I didn't realize you were in contact with Zack."

Declan tossed a few more hunks of pretzel to the pigeons. "When we were in Milwaukee, we struck up a friendship. He seems like a good man."

She cocked her head. "Milwaukee?"

"It wasn't all about business," Declan said. "There was plenty of time when we were stuck on the train and we got to talking. And then again on the way—"

"*Milwaukee?*" Mollie pressed. "Are you talking about the time when you went to catch Jesse Coulter? That Milwaukee?"

Declan looked confused. "Yes, that Milwaukee."

"I didn't realize Zack went with you." She felt confused and disoriented, but Declan was matter-of-fact.

"Zack planned everything. He had a contact at the Milwaukee police who helped us track down the Coulter gang."

"I thought Colonel Lowe did all that."

Declan shook his head. "Colonel Lowe was there, but Zack led the operation."

She felt light-headed as she turned her attention back to the pigeons. Declan kept talking, outlining the details of how the mission had been organized and executed. She had never asked for details of the raid; she'd just assumed it was something Colonel Lowe had organized. It was the kind of thing at which he excelled. He had never lied to her or exaggerated his role in Milwaukee, she had simply never asked for any details.

And Zack—immediately after Richard had told her of Jesse Coulter's capture, she had gone to Frank's grave, and Zack had followed her. Instead of thanking him, she had called him a stray dog.

She shot to her feet. "I need to go see someone," she muttered, scurrying down the street and leaving Declan on the street bench with the pigeons.

She was breathless by the time she arrived on Zack's street. It was insane for her to go running back to Zack when she had to shop for Matilda's fancy Fourth of July celebration, but this was something that couldn't be put off. She could buy the peaches later, but if she didn't see Zack today, she would shrivel up from shame and become useless to the world.

Hopping off the streetcar, she picked up her skirts and scurried down the tidy avenues. Would he even see her? It would be impossible for her to sleep until she removed this horrible weight of guilt that had settled over her chest. Zack went to Milwaukee and hunted down a band of murderers on her behalf, and she hadn't even thanked him! No, in her generosity, she had banished him from her sight, but not before she had made it clear to him where he ranked compared to Colonel Lowe.

She skidded to a stop across the street from his townhome. Three horse-drawn wagons were lined up before his house, where the front door was wide open. Laborers were carrying boxes and crates to the overflowing wagons.

Was he moving? The volume of material mounded in those wagons looked like enough to supply an entire wagon train heading west.

Butterflies warred in her stomach as she crossed the street and was about to mount the steps when an impossibly beautiful blond woman scampered down. Mollie's lips pressed together. The woman's smooth hair swung freely down her back, bouncing as she descended the stairs with a stack of books in her arms. Mollie touched the pile of hair she had twisted into a tight bun at the nape of her neck. Zack probably loved that woman's hair.

Anna? Anka? She was the girl Mollie had seen Zack with that day in the park. Whatever her name, Mollie hoped she was as pretty on the inside as she was on the outside. Zack deserved a fine woman.

"What are you doing here?"

She startled. Zack was standing at the top of the stairs, a crate in his arms. The collar of his white shirt was open, and his skin was tanned by the summer sun. Her mouth went dry.

Zack carried the crate down the stairs, handing it to a laborer who loaded it into a wagon. He brushed his hands as he turned back to her, curiosity, but no anger, in his eyes. "Mollie? What do you need?"

After a struggle, she found her tongue. "I just . . ." She wanted to weep at his feet because of what he'd done for Frank. For sacrificing on her behalf and never asking for a word of thanks. A man jostled her out of the way as he came down the steps with another oversized crate, and she felt dizzy. It was hot, and her skin felt prickly, and Zack looked much bigger and more imposing than she'd remembered.

He grabbed her arm. "Come inside," he said gruffly. "You look about ready to pass out from the heat."

What in the name of all that was holy was Mollie doing here? It had been almost a month since he'd seen her. Ever since the great and glorious Colonel Lowe had accompanied her to present her Copernicus designs to him, Zack had not set eyes on Mollie.

He led her toward the dining room, which still doubled as his office. Lifting a stack of insurance paper work from a chair, he gestured for her to sit, then grabbed another chair and sat opposite her. He wished to the bottom of his soul that she would simply stay away so he wouldn't have to shrivel into a helpless sap the moment she showed up.

Mollie's fingers were long and delicate as she fiddled with them in her lap. Those fingers could coax pieces of metal wire and screws into a magnificent timepiece, but today they made her look as nervous as a hummingbird. Whatever had sent her flying across town to him didn't look like good news. His hands clenched. Heaven help him, she was going to tell him she was marrying Colonel Lowe. The golden boy who walked on water. She was finally going to marry him, and then the tortured fantasies he'd nurtured over her would have to be snuffed out once and for all. He picked up a pencil to roll in his hands, anything to stop him from breaking something in half.

"What's going on, Mollie? Whatever it is, just say it—I won't bite your head off."

He held his breath, dreading her next words. Finally, she met his eyes. "I came to thank you for what you did in Milwaukee."

That took him by surprise. It looked like she wanted to say more, but tears pooled in the bottom of those magnificent blue eyes, turning them into a shade of violet. He wanted to lunge across the table and sweep her into his arms, rock her like a baby over whatever it was that had her so rattled.

Instead, he forced himself to stay calm. "Forget about it, Mollie. It was nothing."

"Zack, I didn't know it was you! I didn't know you had anything to do with catching those men, but Declan tells me it was all your doing. I never knew. I thought Richard did it all."

He stopped fiddling with the pencil. "Did he say that?"

"No! I never asked, I just assumed it was his doing."

He bit back a bitter laugh. "The fair-haired colonel can do many things, but navigating back alleys isn't one of them."

She dropped her chin. "I'm so sorry about that day at the graveyard," she whispered. "So ashamed—"

"Forget about it," he said again. "It's ancient history." His chest squeezed, and this conversation was giving him a headache. She was here because of a guilty conscience, and there was only so much he could take. "Look, today isn't the best day to talk. I've found a space where my mother can store Poland's national treasures. It's going to take the better part of the day to load it all up, so unless you've got something else to say . . ."

She swiped her nose. "No, there is nothing. But I still feel—"

"Zachariasz?" Anka popped her head inside the door. "Mother say eat. Pierogi. Pierogi on kitchen."

"Not now, Anka. Later."

She looked confused. Anka could speak English better than she could understand it, which wasn't saying much. He stood and held up both hands, fingers splayed. "Ten minutes. Tell my mother ten minutes."

She mimicked the motion back. "Ten minutes," she said with

a broad smile and mangled English. Before leaving, Anka drew the pocket doors closed.

Mollie cleared her throat. "She is very lovely. I think she is the lady I saw you with in the park last spring?"

"Yes. That's Anka."

"She seems perfect for you. Very Polish. Very pretty." She rose to her feet. "Well, I wish you and Anka all the best." She paused, staring over his shoulder.

Zack froze. He didn't even need to turn around to know what she was looking at.

"Is that my . . ." She drifted forward, reaching out for the green paisley scarf draped over the coatrack. If he had known she was coming, he would have hidden the blasted thing in the attic.

She laid her hand against the scorched, stained scarf, curiosity brimming in her eyes. "Why do you have this?"

He looked away, unable to lie about that scarf. He could pretend her visits didn't rattle him, he could let her jump to inaccurate conclusions about Anka, but he could never lie about that scarf. That scarf was precious to him, and he'd never let it go.

"I kept the scarf because when I look at it, I remember that night," he said simply. "Mollie, you were amazing during the fire. A warrior. A valkyrie. If I live a thousand years, the memory of you dashing through the blazing streets, that scarf wrapped around you . . . I don't ever want to forget it."

Her eyes widened, but as she turned away there was a droop in her shoulders. "I'm not that woman you just described. I was petrified down to my toes. I've spent the past nine months trying to get back to my orderly life with no exploding buildings or walls crashing down around me. I want the comfort of my timelines and schedules. I want to turn the clock back to October seventh of 1871 and have the entire Chicago Fire Department standing guard outside Mrs. O'Leary's barn so none of it would have happened. I just wish things could go back to the way they were before."

Zack let his gaze trail to the green scarf. If the fire had never happened, he'd still be working at Hartman's, looking forward to every one of Mollie's visits, but never doing more than signing off on her quarterly invoices. Decades would pass, and he never would have seen the true strength and glory of this woman rise to the surface.

"I'm not sorry it happened," he said truthfully. "Nothing will ever be the same again, for either of us. And I think that's a good thing."

Mollie's spine sagged, and she looked old. There were shadows beneath her eyes, and there was tension in every line of her face. Nine months of anxiety and struggle weighed down each of her words. "I don't. I want my old world back. I don't think I'll ever really feel safe again."

"Do you still have nightmares?" he asked softly.

She nodded. "Not so much about Frank anymore, but I have nightmares about the clocks I've built falling down. Last night, I dreamt I was climbing the clock tower to reach it, but no matter how high I climbed, it kept getting farther away. I felt like I was about to fall the whole time." She glanced at him from the corner of her eye, her voice cautious. "Does the sound of church bells still get you rattled?"

"Yeah, it does."

For some reason, that seemed to please her. "Well then! The fire wasn't all sweetness and light for you."

He bit back a grin. "I never said it was a jolly time, Mollie. But sometimes it is the hardest things that make us great."

She looked old again. She bent her head and stared at the floor. "I'm tired of hard times. So very *tired*. I just want to feel safe again." Her voice trembled with exhaustion, and he wished he could do something to make life easier for her. He would give up the shirt off his back if it would just buy her a decent night of sleep.

Zack dropped his head. He couldn't give Mollie the sense of security she needed. He didn't even have a *job*, but Colonel Lowe could give Mollie the protection he never could. Colonel Lowe was a safe and orderly gentleman, while Zack would never be happy unless he could roll up his sleeves and tackle some new challenge. Even if it meant walking away from a perfectly good job so he could work on an unpaid crusade to clean up the insurance industry.

Mollie's instincts were right when she chose Colonel Lowe last autumn, and Zack loved her too much to drag her down into the tumult of his life.

"Go back to Colonel Lowe," he said softly. "Leave the scarf."

31

In the elegantly appointed drawing room of Mrs. Matilda Lowe Horner, surrounded by one hundred of Chicago's finest citizens, Mollie wanted to sink through the floor and never be seen again.

Apparently, she had misunderstood the magnitude of what went into representing a colony for Mrs. Horner's gala celebration. Charlotte Durant, Sophie's mother, had been the first to present her offering earlier in the evening. She represented Delaware, called "the first state" because it was the first to ratify the constitution. Mrs. Durant provided each guest with a copy of the Constitution in an embossed leather volume, beautifully illustrated with engravings of the founding fathers on handmade paper. The volume rested heavy in Mollie's lap as she worried her lip.

It seemed that each contribution became more spectacular as the evening progressed. The woman representing Maryland brought oysters. Mollie thought it a rather charming and appropriately simple gift, until she realized that each oyster contained a genuine pearl. At the front of the room, an actress portraying Pocahontas expounded upon the settling of the nation. She was there to represent the colony of Virginia and had passed out expensive cigars in hand-carved humidors to all the gentlemen earlier.

Mollie had brought a can of peaches.

Richard had been mortified when he arrived by carriage to escort her to the gathering, his face blanching white when he saw the two-gallon can of peaches in her hands. Mrs. Horner had been more gracious, hustling Mollie back to the kitchen and pouring the peaches out into a spectacular crystal bowl. But the glistening lumps of fruit still looked exactly like what they were: canned peaches.

After Pocahontas stepped down, the lady representing New Jersey glided to the podium, wearing a gown of glittering yellow silk. She carried a large flat rectangle covered in a matching swath of silk. Apparently, the state bird of New Jersey was the goldfinch, and the woman made a great show of unveiling an original watercolor painting by the renowned John James Audubon, depicting the goldfinch in its natural habitat.

"I present this painting to you, Mrs. Horner, to be auctioned off to benefit the poor orphans of the war, whom you have so generously helped through the years."

The applause was hearty and well deserved, but the lump of anxiety was expanding in Mollie's stomach. Her turn at the podium was next, and how precisely did one compete with an original Audubon?

The crystal bowl filled with glistening blobs of canned peaches rested on the sideboard. Feeling like a prisoner on the way to an execution, Mollie made herself rise and walk to the sideboard. The bowl was heavy as she carried it to the podium, and the room settled into an uncomfortable silence as a hundred faces turned to her in expectation.

How pleasant they all looked, and how foolish she felt standing in front of them with a bowl of canned peaches.

She cleared her throat. "The best peaches in the country are grown in Georgia," she said. And what was there left to say after that? As the pause lengthened, Ulysses's words suddenly sprang to mind, and Mollie latched on to them like a drowning victim to a lifeline. "The canned peach is very nutritious," she asserted. "It helped prevent scurvy during the war."

Richard sat in the front row, and his scowl could slay a man at a hundred paces. Other ladies looked embarrassed on Mollie's behalf, and Pocahontas giggled in the back row. Mr. Horner leaned over to his wife, his whisper growing louder as he tried to smother a surge of laughter. "Who knows how many more orphans we'd have if not for the canned peach." His whisper was loud enough to be heard by everyone. He lost control and had to cover his mouth to choke off the laughter.

Mollie pasted on her brightest smile. "Well said, sir!" This time the laughter was hearty and unrestrained. As she returned to her seat, a number of the gentlemen rose to shake her hand. One leaned over to whisper in her ear, "Thanks for lightening up the evening."

She resumed her seat and leaned over to Richard. "That wasn't such a disaster, was it?"

He stared stonily ahead as Miss New York made her way to the podium.

~

By the end of the evening, Mollie had quit berating herself over the peaches. The president of the State Street Bank was in attendance and had enthusiastically praised the clock that had been installed just two days earlier. "I wouldn't trust you in my kitchen, but you can build a clock for any building I ever commission."

Mollie chatted with the Durants and was soon the most

popular woman in attendance as one man after another stepped forward to share a joke or a war story. But it was the clock that seemed to hold everyone fascinated. The bank wasn't even open for business yet, but plenty of people had seen that clock. "It will be so nice to get back to normal," the kindly lady representing Maryland said. "When I rode down State Street and saw all those buildings rising higher and higher, I could finally see how it will look in a few years' time. It brought tears to my eyes."

Richard was not so amused. Sitting opposite her in the carriage, he waited until a servant closed the carriage door before finally meeting her eyes. "Scurvy?"

Exhausted from weeks of relentless anxiety as she struggled to get the clock completed on time, Mollie was in no mood to be repentant. "Yes, scurvy. Apparently the invention of canned fruit has made it a thing of the past. Ulysses said so himself."

"I can just imagine," Richard muttered. He grasped his walking stick tightly in his hand, staring moodily out the window.

The carriage rocked and bumped over the cobblestone streets, and Mollie wondered if she had been wrong to be so dismissive of his annoyance. She did her best to soften her tone. "I'm sorry if I embarrassed you in front of your sister. I should have prepared a little more carefully, and I vow I will never bring canned peaches to any event again."

"You didn't embarrass me, you embarrassed yourself." He didn't even look at her as he spoke.

The words hung in the silence of the night. While it was true she had initially been mortified when she had seen what the other ladies had brought, her embarrassment soon faded. As if she had time to waste getting embarrassed over such a silly incident! For months, she had been struggling to resurrect her company by learning how to make gigantic clocks, while all Richard had done was send one wave of disapproval after another toward her.

She hadn't been able to share any of her anxiety with him because the moment she tried to open her heart about her hopes for the 57th, he would relentlessly discourage her. She didn't need more disapproval, she needed support! She'd gotten more support and camaraderie from five minutes of sitting in Zack's dining room than she'd gotten from Richard in the months since she began making clocks.

Richard was too mannerly to continue the argument, but she could tell he was angry by the way he squeezed the top of his walking stick.

It was a hurtful sight. Her gaze drifted out the window, each of the homes lovely in the moonlight. Richard Lowe was a lion of a man. He'd come riding to her rescue at the lowest point of her life, and if she married Richard, she would never need fear financial insecurity again. She could walk away from the 57th and all the headaches associated with trying to reinvent a company.

But money could not solve all her problems. For all his sterling qualities, Richard did not understand her heart. She would never truly be at ease with him or with trying to fit into his world.

Mollie took a deep breath and looked across the seat to Richard. "I'm not sure I can marry a man who goes white at the knuckles over canned peaches."

"What?"

At least he was looking at her now, but that made what she was about to say even harder. "I'm sorry I disappointed you tonight. You are a wonderful man, and I should have tried harder, but I am not perfect, and I don't really want to be. You would have learned that about me pretty quickly if we had gotten married, but I don't think we ever will. We aren't right for each other."

"I can't believe you are rejecting me over a can of peaches."
He looked dumbfounded.

Her smile was sad. "I'm not." She was rejecting him because
she would never be comfortable trying to live up to the legendary
glory of Colonel Richard Lowe. She just wanted to make her
clocks and watches and have a man who loved her, imperfections
and all. A man who clung to a stained, scorched scarf because
he thought it perfect.

She had probably lost Zack Kazmarek forever, but that didn't
mean she should flee into the arms of a man she could never love.
She had been trying for months to develop a deep and lasting
affection for Colonel Lowe, but all she really felt was gratitude.

She would be forever grateful for what Colonel Lowe had
done for the 57th Illinois Watch Company, but that was as far
as her heart would be engaged.

32

Mollie positioned the mainspring into place. Assembling this piece of the watch was always the trickiest part of the process, and she'd already botched it twice this morning. After Richard had dropped her off last night, Mollie had lain awake until almost four o'clock in the morning, and she was exhausted.

Had she just committed the biggest blunder of her life? Would she be stuck in this workshop assembling watches when she was a toothless old spinster? Marrying Richard would be the sensible thing to do, but honestly, how safe could a man make her feel if canned peaches upset his world?

The mainspring slipped from her tweezers, clinking as it bounced to the table, then onto the floor. She sighed. It would need to be steamed to be sure it was free of grit before she could try again.

She was bone-tired as she stooped over to pick it up. All around her, the technicians were moving at full speed on the Copernicus watches, while Oliver and Gunner were in the first stages of assembling their next monumental clock, this one for a hotel. It wouldn't be right to crawl home and pull the covers over her head, but she was so exhausted. And heartsick. And lonely. How could a person be in a roomful of people and still feel alone?

She glanced over at Alice. "I've got a toothache. I'm going next door."

"Really? What's the problem?"

Mollie shrugged a little helplessly. "Nothing. I just need to talk to Dr. Buchanan."

She didn't even feel guilty as she slipped out of the workshop in the middle of the morning. If she couldn't unburden her heart to someone she was going to sink into a nervous collapse, and Dr. Buchanan was always such a good listener.

She rapped on his door and did not wait for a response before pushing inside. There was a woman at his desk, and she scrambled to hide something before turning around.

It was the blond woman Zack was so fond of. There was no sign of Dr. Buchanan, and the woman had a flushed and guilty look on her face as she slid a piece of paper beneath a book. "What are you doing?" Mollie asked, her gaze tracking across Dr. Buchanan's desk, looking for any sign of tampering or missing items.

Anka picked up the black book and held it out. "I learn English," she said. The lettering on the spine of the book indicated it was a Polish-English dictionary, but Mollie was curious about the paper Anka seemed to be hiding. She stepped a little closer.

"What are you doing?" she asked again. "Where is Dr. Buchanan?"

"Andrew," she began, then made a scraping motion across her face.

Mollie tried to understand. "Shave? He has gone for a shave?"

Anka nodded. "Yes. Shave."

It still did not explain the woman's presence here. Mollie glanced pointedly at the piece of paper on the desk, and Anka followed her gaze. Picking up the page, Anka looked like she was struggling to find words. "My English . . ." She made a waffling motion with her hand. "I write English for Andrew. Bad English. Help?" She held the page out to Mollie.

"You are asking me to help with your writing?" Anka nodded vigorously. It seemed a little odd, but she certainly wanted to know what Anka seemed so embarrassed about. Mollie glanced at the page, her eyes widening with astonishment as she read:

> *Dear Andrew. We are same people. I am alone, like you. I have big hope, like you. Please wait for me to find English. You make my heart fly.*

Mollie plopped down onto the dentist chair, staring in astonishment at the letter. Did Zack know the girl he was courting was dallying with another man? With his best friend, no less? She looked up at Anka, and the girl covered her heart with her hand and pounded. "Andrew." The way she said the word was heavy with a combination of yearning and hope. "I need Andrew. I hope Andrew."

"Does Zack know how you feel?"

"Zack?" The women looked confused, and Mollie repeated herself several times, but it did no good. Anka did not understand.

The door opened, and Dr. Buchanan strode inside, freshly shaven and flushed with good health. "Hello, Miss Mollie," he said jovially. "I hope you've only come for a visit and are not suffering in dental misery."

"I just stopped by for a visit," Mollie said. "I was surprised to see Anka here."

The dentist's grin broadened. "I'm teaching her how to help in the office. She has the makings of a fine dental assistant."

Anka nodded vigorously, picked up a tooth puller, and gave it a hearty twist as she made a grisly cracking sound. Both Dr. Buchanan and Anka roared with laughter. Mollie made a mental note never to allow Anka near her with that wicked-looking piece of equipment.

"Dr. Buchanan, may I speak with you outside for a moment?"

"You can speak freely in front of Anka. I intend to marry her, so there should be no secrets."

Mollie was dumbfounded as she looked between Anka and Dr. Buchanan. They were out in the open with their scandalous liaison? "But, Zack led me to believe . . ." How precisely could she say this? While she scrambled for words, Dr. Buchanan spared her the embarrassment.

"Zack never had any serious intentions toward Anka, nor she to him. If he allowed you to believe otherwise . . . well, it would not be the first time a man tried to salvage a little pride by escorting a pretty woman about town."

Her breath left her in a rush, and she sank back down onto the dental chair. What an idiot she had been! He had pretended to hide it, but Zack had more pride than all the kings of Poland rolled together, and she had kicked him in the teeth repeatedly over the past nine months. Her heart picked up tempo, and she felt light-headed. There was *nothing* between Anka and Zack!

But there was a green paisley scarf hanging from Zack's coatrack, and she had been a fool to accept his blithe dismissal of it.

Mollie sprang to her feet. "Thank you for your time!" she tossed over her shoulder as she hurried through the open doorway.

After making two streetcar connections and crossing three bridges, Mollie raced toward Hartman's as fast as her legs could carry her. She was breathless as she hurried up the steps and recognized the same doorman who had held the door for her throughout all the years she had done business with Hartman's.

"Mr. Kern, I'm glad to see you have survived the fire! Can I go up and see Zack Kazmarek?"

"He isn't here anymore."

Her spirit dimmed just a fraction. "Has he gone to lunch? When is he expected back?"

The doorman looked distinctly uncomfortable as he shifted his weight and glanced around the landing to the store. "I heard a rumor that he quit, but some say he was fired. Either way, he isn't here anymore. His office was cleaned out last week."

Her skin started tingling all over, and she clutched Mr. Kern's arm. "What happened?" she asked in a trembling whisper. Zack would follow Louis Hartman to the ends of the earth! Whatever had caused a rift must have been terrible and completely unexpected.

"No one is saying anything," the doorman said. "I don't think anyone except Mr. Hartman even knows."

Mollie turned and left the store, wandering toward the streetcar stop. Not until she walked smack into a construction worker did she realize she wasn't even seeing what was directly in front of her face. All her thoughts were consumed with Zack and whatever had caused him to quit so abruptly.

She clenched the handrail on the streetcar as it delivered her to the west-side neighborhood where she disembarked. Her footsteps picked up pace. She'd seen all the moving men outside his home a few days ago and had not questioned him when he'd asserted it was merely about relocating his parents' Polish collection.

Why had she accepted that so easily? On that day he was no longer working at Hartman's, but he hadn't mentioned a word to her. Could he no longer afford the home and was forced to move? Anxiety gripped her as she quickened her steps.

If Zack was in financial trouble, she would figure out a way to help. If the fire had taught her nothing else, she knew the value of pulling together in times of crisis. But she'd have to be careful. Men had such pride.

Hoisting her skirts to her ankles, she dashed up the steps of the landing and pounded on the door of his townhouse. "Zack? Are you here?"

She leaned toward the door but could hear no one moving inside. She set both palms against the door, the blue paint cool in the summer heat as she pressed her ear to the door, listening for any sounds inside.

Which was why she nearly jumped from her skin when the door was yanked open. "Zack!" she said, a surge of relief rushing through her. "I was so worried."

He wore a look of mild amusement. "What were you doing to my door? Licking it?"

She caught her breath and adjusted her shirt. When he held the door wide, she looked into the house with dismay. It was nearly empty!

"Are you moving?"

He tugged her inside and closed the door behind her. "I told you. I leased a space for my parents to store their treasures. They are over there unloading it as we speak. I don't expect I'll see much of them in the coming months. My mother is happier than a pig in mud." He held his arms wide, spanning the huge open space. "I've got no idea what to do with all this liberated square footage, but my first step will be to build a legitimate parlor. Have a seat, Mollie."

There was only a single settee and a footstool in the front room. She lowered herself onto the settee, and he pulled the footstool a few feet out, splaying his legs and looking ridiculously large as he sat on the tiny piece of furniture. "And to what do I owe this unexpected visit?"

There was no point in quibbling or trying to find delicate words. "I went looking for you at Hartman's, but the doorman said you don't work there anymore."

"That's right."

"What happened?"

Zack didn't appear upset or embarrassed as he peered at her with assessing eyes. "Louis and I had a falling out. It was time to press ahead."

"But . . . but . . . you don't seem upset. Louis was like a father to you; you told me so yourself! Why are you so calm about this?"

He sobered, lacing his fingers together and staring at the floor. "I owe Louis a debt I can never fully repay. Ever. But that loyalty sometimes led me to places I shouldn't have gone. There were other people in my life who deserved my loyalty, and I couldn't serve them as long as I was with Louis." He put his hand on her knee. "I should have figured out a better way to handle your land deed. I'm sorry about that, Mollie."

"I see," she whispered. "What are you going to do now?"

"If you are worried about the Copernicus watches, don't be. My quitting Hartman's will have no effect on the Ponte Vecchio deal."

She hadn't even considered the watches, but she had a fortune tied up in those spectacular, impractical watches. Zack grabbed her hand and tugged her upright. "Let's go back to the dining room and I'll show you the paper work."

～

Heaven help him, but seeing Mollie again was torture. Dealing with her would be unavoidable until those Copernicus watches were sold, but if he had known she was coming he could have braced himself. As it was, all he could do was pretend it didn't hurt to have his heart taken out and stomped beneath her dainty-soled boots one more time.

Behind him, those boots clicked on the hardwood floors, and the sound echoed off the bare walls as she trailed after him into the dining room. He picked up a sheaf of papers from the table. "Have a seat, and we can go through these together." The last thing he wanted to discuss was business, but he cleared his throat and looked around for a pencil.

Mollie remained standing at the entrance of the dining room, staring as though caught in a trance. He followed her gaze to her cinder-pocked silk scarf still draped over the coatrack. A flush heated his face. Why hadn't he stashed the blasted thing out of sight? Now she was going to start jumping to conclusions and realize what a milksop he still was over her.

There was no help for it. He kept his tone steady and professional as he held the stack of documents toward her. "The contracts will need to be amended to remove my name as the intermediary. As soon as you find another attorney to represent you, we can transfer all responsibility into his name."

"Zack, I walked in on Anka writing a love letter to Dr. Buchanan this morning."

Great, now he could no longer hide behind Anka either. He stood a little awkwardly and fiddled with the pages in his hand. He could not be happier for Dr. Buchanan's good fortune, but squiring Anka around had let him salvage a teaspoon of pride.

"I take it you found that surprising?" he asked.

He remained motionless as she walked across the nearly empty dining room to stand before him. She didn't look surprised, she looked . . . hopeful? He didn't move a muscle as she laid her palm against his chest. What was she doing?

"Yes, I found it surprising. I also found it surprising that you still have my green scarf, although I'm glad you do."

"I'm not giving it back, if that is what you are after."

"I don't want it back, I want you to have it."

His eyes widened as she stepped even closer, his chest tingling where her hand lay softly against him. Why was she staring up at him with her heart brimming in her eyes? It was the way she had gazed at him last autumn. He wanted to swoop down and haul her into his embrace like a marauding Viking and forget Colonel Lowe had ever existed. Instead, he stayed carefully still. "And why is that?" he asked softly.

"Because you don't scare me anymore." She placed her other hand on his chest. "You used to intimidate me down to my toes, but since the fire, everything is different. I can be myself around you. Flaws and all."

"You don't have any flaws." None that mattered anyway. Sometimes he wanted to drag her to the lake and throw her in, but she was still perfect in his eyes and he would flatten any man who said otherwise.

"Neither one of us is perfect, but I love you, Zack."

His heart threatened to stop beating. He clenched his fists to stop himself from scooping her up into a bear hug and shouting to the world. She had let him down so many times before, but she hadn't finished speaking. Her voice was soft and a little breathless.

"I'm sorry it has taken me so long to realize it, but I've never been good with squishy things like emotions. It took me a while to put a name to what I was feeling."

"What about Colonel Lowe?"

She shook her head. "Richard is a wonderful man, but I grew exhausted trying to live up to his expectations. He went back to Waukegan last night. He won't be back."

"I see." His tone was indifferent and his stance was relaxed, but the sun was starting to blaze inside him. When Mollie slid her arms around his neck, he pulled her into a hug so hard it probably drove the breath from her lungs. He couldn't help it. He breathed deeply of her scent and pressed a trail of kisses along her forehead.

"I feel safe with you," she said against his cheek. "Even that night as we were racing through the fire, I felt safe with you beside me."

He froze. Disappointment came crashing down and his arms fell away. He should have known this was too good to be true. It was impossible to even look at her as he tugged her arms down from around his neck. It took every bit of strength he had to walk away from her, his back stiff as he stared out the front window.

"Mollie, I've never been a safe choice for you. I don't even have a job. Do you understand what that means?"

"You just arranged the sale of thirty-six watches to a jeweler on the Ponte Vecchio."

He whirled to face her. "That was a one-time deal, and it was *your* deal. Mollie, I don't have a job. I can't promise to keep you safe and protected like Colonel L—"

She cut him off. "*I am safe with you.* I can be myself and make mistakes, and I know you'll forgive me. You've already done so time and again." She walked to him, and when he tried to turn away, she grabbed his shoulders and forced him to look at her. "I remember when you came to visit me at the church. I was hungry and dirty and didn't even have a roof over my head, but when you were with me the world was perfect. And I was happy. I had a sense of purpose and belonging with you by my side. There isn't anywhere else I'd rather be."

He was embarrassed that his hands trembled as he cupped them around her face. "I can't go through you walking out on me again," he said. "I've got skin tougher than a rhinoceros hide, but I've always been a big weakling when it comes to you. If you want back into my life, it has to be for good this time."

"For better or for worse, for richer or poorer . . . is that what you mean?"

"Till death do us part. Yeah, that's what I'm getting at."

Her face was beautiful and shining and confident. "That's what I want too."

The breath left his body in a rush. The way she gazed up at him with hope sparkling in her fabulous blue eyes . . . he was hot and dizzy and was about to make a real fool of himself. He needed air. Fast. Stumbling toward the window, he jerked up the sash and braced his hands on the windowsill, dragging in huge gulps of oxygen. Cool air blew in from the window, but he was still swamped with heat and could not stop trembling. He would be lucky if he didn't pass out right here.

"Are you all right?" Mollie asked in a panicky voice. She dashed to hover beside him, kneeling down to look up into his face. "Do I need to get you something? Water? A chair?"

Maybe a spine. Curled over the windowsill, he doubted he had the ability to stand upright on his own. His insane gamble of granting Mollie breathing room with Colonel Lowe had finally paid off. Mollie had had the chance to know both men, and she had made her choice. She'd come back to him, and she wasn't leaving again.

A slow grin curled his mouth as he looked out the window. "I'm okay, Mollie. Everything is okay now."

And he knew it would be. They lived in a vibrant city, one that was impossible to hold down. The smoke and the clouds had cleared, and sunlight was shining again. He couldn't know exactly what the future held, but was that so bad? The Lord had never promised them an easy life, nor did they have one.

Faith and hope had already powered them through a terrible, wonderful time.

When his head stopped spinning, he was finally able to stand upright again, even though he kept both hands braced on the window frame just to be sure. Mollie stood behind him, her arms sliding around his waist as she hugged him from behind. He reached down to squeeze her hands as they looked out the window. The woman he loved was standing with him, ready to walk beside him into a city where he would forever be challenging, testing, and pushing the limits. They had forged a bond that would glimmer through the darkest nights and survive the worst firestorms, and now they would ride the whirlwind together.

Epilogue

"I want to test the bell one more time," Mollie said, peering up inside the clock tower.

Oliver swiveled to look at her. "We've already checked it twice. Do we really need another test?" Slats of sunlight filtered in beneath the bleachers, which would soon be filled with thousands of people as they poured in to the brand-new baseball stadium, ready to see the White Stockings make their triumphal return to the city. It was two years, seven months, and five days since the city of Chicago had burned to the ground. In a few hours, the new stadium would host Chicago's first professional baseball game since the fire.

"The mayor is going to be at this game," Mollie said. "As is the governor and every alderman in the city. If my bell doesn't ring precisely on the stroke of five o'clock, it will be a humiliation I will carry into my grave."

Oliver shook his head, but he was smiling as he climbed up the ladder inside the clock tower to reset the dial. Over the past two years, the 57th had built and installed dozens of public clocks, but this was the first one to feature a bell that would ring on the hour. The centerpiece of the new stadium was the grand white clapboard façade that stretched across the back row of bleachers. It featured a scoreboard and a row of box seats flaring out from each side, but what gave the stadium distinction was the cupola in the center, featuring a clock tower rising above the scoreboard. The bell was to ring at the top of every hour, and this afternoon it would herald the return of baseball to the city.

Mollie stood on the gravel beneath the bleachers and listened to the grind of the suspension chains as Oliver reset the clock's hands to one minute before the hour. "All right, one more time," Oliver hollered from inside the bell tower.

The minute hand clicked into place, and Mollie covered her ears. A second later the reassuring gong echoed through the narrow chamber with five strong, steady tones.

Oliver climbed down, looking pleased with himself. As much as he'd grumbled about moving into clockmaking, he seemed ten years younger since he had undertaken the new challenge.

"Satisfied?" he asked.

She brushed her damp palms against her skirt. "As much as I'll ever be, I suppose."

She'd feel better once Zack got there. Change was still something Mollie struggled with, but she was learning to let life unfold without smothering every day with new insecurities. If the past two years had taught her nothing else, she now accepted there were no guarantees in life, but she'd still be able to survive whatever traumas came her way. Plan, prepare, and pray . . . but eventually she had to let go and allow the world to unfold as it was intended. Zack had been a tremendous help in teaching her these things.

Which, given his chosen profession, was a good thing. Really, she must have been insane to marry a politician.

An hour later, she was sitting beside Zack in the bleachers. They could have joined the mayor and the governor in the reserved seats near the front of the stadium, but Zack never missed an opportunity to rub shoulders with the people from his ward. Shortly after the new insurance laws had been finalized, Zack had run for alderman, representing one of the Polish wards on the city's northwest side. He was a born politician, creating an unusual alliance between the Polish and Irish workers and pushing reforms not only in insurance, but also in building regulations and fire safety. On the day baseball finally returned to Chicago, Zack wanted to be sitting alongside the people who'd voted him into office.

The weather was clear, the food smelled wonderful, and Mollie grinned as she joined Zack in the bleachers. She had never even *liked* baseball, but today she was the White Stockings's biggest fan. They were a symbol of hope and a return to normal. Five thousand people filled the new stadium, and the air was electric with anticipation, especially once the players appeared in the bullpens and began stretching their muscles and swinging bats.

The players jogged into place on the field, and an umpire took position behind home plate, tossing a ball between his hands. Mollie eyed the clock, the huge minute hand just a fraction shy of five o'clock.

A flash of tension raced through her. Had Oliver remembered to reset the hour train line? They'd tested the clock several times, but if he hadn't remembered to pull that train line back into position after that final test . . .

"Relax, Mollie," Zack said. "I'm sure Oliver reset everything correctly."

Before he even stopped speaking, the minute hand clicked into place and a clear, echoing gong rang forth. It worked! The resonance of the gong was magnified by the stadium. It echoed throughout the stadium, bouncing off the bleachers before being carried off by the wind. How many times had Mollie imagined this precise moment?

What she had not foreseen was the hush that descended on the crowd. Everyone stilled. People held their breath. When the second gong sounded, spectators began to rise to their feet, the new bleachers creaking and groaning as thousands began to rise. A third gong, and then a fourth.

The White Stockings's pitcher began jogging to the center of the field. Tears blurred her vision as a buzz of excitement raced through the crowd. The final bell sounded, and the umpire stepped forward, his voice firm and confident.

"Play ball!"

The crowd roared with a cheer that could be heard across the entire city.

Historical Note

The Great Chicago Fire of 1871 began in a barn owned by Catherine and Patrick O'Leary on DeKoven Street. Legend says the fire began when a cow being milked by Mrs. O'Leary kicked over a lantern, but years later a newspaper reporter admitted he made the tale up. The details of how the fire started will never be known, but it did indeed begin in the O'Leary barn. Catherine O'Leary became a recluse and rarely left the safety of her home until her death in 1895.

Driven by gale-force winds, the fire devoured the city, which had been parched of rain all year. In the month before the fire, only .11 inches of rain had fallen. The wall of flame was estimated to be a hundred feet high, and the winds whipping down the alleys created columns of fire that resembled tornadoes. The force of the wind picked up wooden boards and shingles, flinging them through the air and spreading the fire north and east toward Lake Michigan.

In the following thirty-six hours, the mayor of Chicago wired other cities to send fire brigades, many of which arrived while the flames were still burning. Fire companies as far away as

Milwaukee, Detroit, and Cincinnati arrived and did their best to contain the fire, but at three o'clock on the morning of October 9, the roof of the city's waterworks became engulfed in flames. When it collapsed onto the pumping station below, all hope of saving the city was lost. Evacuation was the only recourse, and it is estimated that over 330,000 people flooded the streets in an effort to escape the flames.

By the morning of October 10, the fire had burned itself out, aided by the miraculous arrival of a rainstorm. Over 73 miles of streets, 18,000 buildings, and 2,000 lampposts were destroyed. Although the death toll will never be known, it is estimated that only around three hundred people died.

In the days following the fire, some references spoke of the strange euphoria among the survivors. It did not last long. In the coming weeks and months, crime rose and despair took root as the magnitude of the loss sank in. At the time of the fire, about two hundred insurance companies did business in Chicago, and the fire bankrupted sixty-eight of them. Policyholders in Chicago only succeeded in collecting about 40 percent of what was owed to them, although many who were insured through local companies received nothing at all. The catastrophe in Chicago revealed the inadequacy of existing insurance laws, and local boards were established and regulations governing geographic diversification for insurance companies were put into place.

The town crier who wandered the streets shouting words of comfort in the dark morning hours is fictional, but I took many of the lines my character spoke directly from signs people propped outside their ruined homes, proclaiming hope and belief in their city. That faith was not misplaced. Although the central business district was destroyed, Chicago was rebuilt with amazing speed. Most of the railroads survived intact, allowing them to be used to haul away rubble and send in massive amounts of building supplies.

The fire encouraged iron and steel construction in the new buildings. As the price of land rose and steel-frame construction became viable, Chicago was the perfect location to test the construction of skyscrapers. Some of the most famous architects of the era congregated in Chicago to build these dynamic new skyscrapers, featuring bold designs of steel-frame construction, fireproof cladding, and clean lines. The trend caught on around the world, but no matter where it appears, this style of architecture is still known as the Chicago School.

Discussion Questions

1. Near the end of the book when Mollie still longs for life before the fire, Zack says "sometimes it is the hardest things that make us great." What are the really hard things in your life? Do they have hidden blessings, or would you wish them away if you could?

2. Before the fire, Sophie had an endless supply of entertainment but had never been required to work. Although entertainment is fun, can it ever provide a sense of satisfaction? In our modern era, when children have limitless sources of entertainment, how can we teach them the value that comes from doing something hard?

3. Mollie has two attractive suitors. Did she make the right choice?

4. Colonel Lowe has a strong moral code, while Zack often bends the rules. Do you agree with the deal Zack cut with Ralph Coulter to get his nephews into college in exchange for details about who killed Frank? Does this mean Zack doesn't have a moral code?

5. The dentist, Andrew Buchanan, had no family and craved the sense of belonging he finds at the church and with Zack's family. Do you know anyone in your neighborhood

or workplace who seems rootless? What would it cost (or benefit) you to bring that person into the fold?

6. During the fire, Mollie notices the best and worst of people as they struggle to escape the flames. What made some people become drunken revelers while others allowed their own homes to burn in order to help others? Is it possible to predict who will be a hero during a crisis and who will act selfishly?

7. Zack has immense loyalty and respect for Louis Hartman, who pulled him off the docks and launched him in the business world. Yet, at a crucial point, Zack turns his back on Louis in order to finalize insurance reform in the city. Was he right to do so? What happens when personal gratitude is at war with loyalty to a larger cause?

8. Mollie was never able to warm up to Colonel Lowe, even though she wanted to. Why was this? What would your advice to Mollie have been? Have you ever experienced this type of situation?

9. Near the end of the book, Mollie grabs a can of peaches to bring to a fancy party. Did you agree more with her response or with Colonel Lowe's? Have you ever felt pushed into a social obligation when more pressing concerns from work or family were already stretching you too thin? Is there a better way to handle it than turning in a substandard performance?

10. Zack's attitude toward his Polish heritage strengthens throughout the book. Why is this? Do you have an ethnic, religious, or cultural heritage that has evolved over the years?

Elizabeth Camden is the award-winning author of five novels, including *Against the Tide*, winner of a RITA Award, Christy Award, and Daphne du Maurier Award. With master's degrees in History and Library Science from the University of Virginia and Indiana University respectively, she is a research librarian by day and a writer by night. Elizabeth lives with her husband in Florida. Learn more at ElizabethCamden.com.

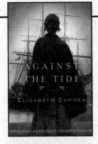

If you enjoyed *Into the Whirlwind*, check out...

Eoghan Hamilton longs to rejoin the Fenians, a shadowy organization pushing for change back in Ireland. But gaining their trust requires favors—all of which lead to Ana Kavanagh. Who is this woman and why are they so interested in her? When the truth about Ana's past comes to light, Eoghan will have to choose where to place his trust.

Dark Road Home by Elizabeth Ludwig
EDGE OF FREEDOM #2
elizabethludwig.com

Arabella Beckett is in the business of helping other women, but she's not in the habit of accepting help herself—especially not from some arrogant knight in shining armor sent by her brother. But private investigator Theodore Wilder is just as stubborn as she is. Could this feisty suffragette have finally met her match?

A Most Peculiar Circumstance by Jen Turano
jenturano.com

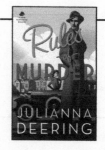

Drew Farthering loves a good mystery, but he expects to find it in the pages of a novel, not on the grounds of his country estate. When a party at Farthering Place takes a deadly turn, can Drew and Madeline, a beautiful and whip-smart debutante guest, catch the killer before he claims another victim?

Rules of Murder by Julianna Deering
A DREW FARTHERING MYSTERY
juliannadeering.com